I0671976

Human Adulthood

A Spiritual Romance

by William Frank Diedrich

Transformative Press

© copyright 2014

Human Adulthood: A Spiritual Romance
by William Frank Diedrich
© Copyright 2014 William Frank Diedrich and
Transformative Press

This book is a work of fiction. All characters and situations are purely from the imagination of the author. Any resemblance to real people, living or dead, is coincidental.

ISBN 978-0-9710568-5-5

Fiction
Printed in the USA
Cover photo by Karel Moonen
Cover design by Melanie Diedrich

Non-fiction by William Frank Diedrich:
• 30 Days to Prosperity: A Workbook for Well-Being
• Beyond Blaming: Unleashing Power and Passion in People and Organizations
• Adults at Work: How Individuals and Organizations Grow Up
• The Road Home: The Journey Beyond the Spiritual Quick Fix

Transformative Press
East Lansing, Michigan USA
http://humanadulthood.com
http://noblaming.com

To: You, the Reader,
who is not satisfied
with the status quo.

Human Adulthood

Chapter One

A man had two sons.

Chapter Two

One cold Friday evening in January, Coach Kevin Neill drove home from his high school basketball game. His team had won. Game highlights replayed in his mind, and he ran his mental fingers over each play as if he were still courtside.

Outside the warmth of his new, blue Ford Escape he was besieged by a wintry Michigan night. Snow blasted sideways, drifted, and formed wind-sculpted dunes along the streets. The world was black and white, as his headlights bleached the roadsigns and parked vehicles. The steady beat of the windshield wipers reverberated like the dribbling of basketballs, adding audio to his mental movies.

Kevin turned his vehicle into the driveway, just clearing several inches of powdered landscape. It was the kind of night that made him wonder why he didn't live in Arizona, but he dismissed the thought. Still under the spell of the warm glow of victory, he was convinced nothing could change his good mood. Prolonging the moment, and the comfort of his Escape, he closed his eyes.

As he entered the house, Dana called out: "How was the game, Honey?"

"It was great. We won! The guys really played their best. I was so proud!"

"Wonderful. Come sit by me and tell me all about it." She snuggled under a cotton blanket on the soft leather couch. A fire burned in the fireplace.

He sat with her, and she kissed him on the lips, lingering several long seconds like they used to. They talked and she enjoyed his success with him. Then she cuddled close, rubbing her hand in slow circles on his chest, letting him know that she wanted him. They slipped off to bed. It was just like they were in college again. He kissed her. Thunk!

Kevin jolted awake; a pile of snow sat on his hood, fallen from an over-laden tree branch above his driveway. "A guy can always dream." Kevin sighed, turned off the ignition and again pictured the scene at the game. "If I can win on the court there is no reason why I can't win at home, too." He smiled and again imagined holding his wife. The thought encouraged him.

"Okay, here goes." He jumped out of the vehicle and trudged through the drifting snow, icy moisture seeping into his shoes. Despite the wind and the frozen feet, he arrived safely inside his front door. A chill cut through his body, and he quickly shed his coat, wet shoes and socks. Rubbing his palms together, he stepped onto the throw rug.

The house was dark, except for the glow of the fireplace reflecting off the walls and into the foyer. "Ah! Perfect!" He purred softly to himself. Kevin strode into the living room eager to see his wife and tell her about tonight's victory. His bare feet cushioned by the padded Persian rug, he shuffled sideways around the wooden coffee table that he had built for her ten years ago. He smiled, and looked down at Dana who was now sitting across from him. "Hey. We won tonight!"

His enthusiasm dissolved into the semi-darkness as he saw her more clearly now, still, staring at the fire. It was as if a sculptor had carved her from ice. Her dark hair was pulled back tightly, seemingly sprayed on the sides of her head. The play of the shadows made her nose and chin appear more pointed than normal. Trepidation clenched his solar plexus.

She threw him a glance. "We need to talk."

Her monotone deflated the last of his fantasies. Inhaling deeply and then exhaling, he attempted to release his tension. Ignoring his deep breath, his abdominal muscles seized. Fear turned to dread. *Now what?* It was never a good thing when Dana wanted to talk. "O--kay." Kevin's voice climbed a few notes at the end of the word. "What are we talking about?" He sat down on the microfiber couch, the coffee table still between them, pretending that he wanted to know what she had to say.

Normally a perfect place for conversation, tonight, the cozy sitting room was illuminated with an eerie glow. Dana's wing-backed chair gave the illusion of huge, dark wings protruding from her back. Kevin shivered in spite of the fire just three feet away. He was a little boy waiting to hear what his punishment would be for some misdeed he didn't know he'd committed.

Half of Dana's face was visible--the right half--the left being shrouded in shadows. The right side of her face was her strong side. Her left side offered a softer, more gentle countenance. It would be the right side doing the talking tonight. Definitely the right half did not love him. *When was the last time she was actually affectionate toward me? Has it been months? Years?*

Dana looked at him, as if reading his face, then looked down at the floor. She took a deep breath and exhaled slowly. She again made eye contact, and this time it was a hard look. "I don't love you anymore, Kevin. I haven't been happy for several years now, but you should know that." She paused, as if waiting for him to confirm her discontent. When he didn't respond she took a breath. The words burst forth from her mouth. "I want you to move out, and I want a divorce."

Her words exploded in his mind, and the emotional shrapnel peppered his heart. The room blurred as he slumped back against the sofa cushions. As if coming to after being knocked unconscious, his mind struggled to make sense of the moment. *Did she say what I think she said? She doesn't want to be married to me? This is a dream, isn't it?* "Uh, what did you say?"

"You heard me, Kevin." Her voice became louder. "Don't make this harder than it has to be." She paused and softened her tone. "I don't want to pretend anymore. The girls are both out of high school now, and it's time. I need to move on. You haven't been happy either."

Kevin sat up straight and found his voice. "Bullshit! I'm happy. I've been *very* happy. Sure we've had problems, but who doesn't? All in all, I think we have a good marriage." He nodded his head and arched his right eyebrow, silently begging for reassurance.

Dana rolled her eyes and shook her head. "Are you kidding? There hasn't been any spark in years. You're not happy; you're asleep! Life didn't just change tonight. It's been changing for a long time. I can't do this anymore." She looked away into the darkness.

"Shouldn't we be going to counseling or something? I mean, can't we at least try?"

"Time for talk and time for trying is done." She faced him again. "It's over." The words marched out of her mouth like little soldiers she had drilled and practiced a hundred times. "You usually do what you want until I raise an issue, then you give in. You always try to preserve the status quo. I need more than that. I have never been more sure of something in my whole life."

"Maybe we should do a trial separation. I'll move out for a few months, and we can see each other a couple of times a week. We could try to work this out." He nodded his head again and raised both his eyebrows.

Her eyes widened, and her voice hardened. "As usual, you're not hearing me, Kevin." She wielded the next two words as if they were sabers. "It's over! Nothing you say will change that."

Kevin took a deep breath. He felt the certainty in her voice and the lack of certainty in himself. He looked at her, suddenly curious. "What do you plan on doing?"

"With my life? I don't know yet," Dana shrugged, "but I'll figure it out. I--"

He leaped off the sofa, moving between her and the fire, arms springing out from his sides, palms facing her, yelling, "You'll figure it out! What aren't you telling me, Dana? Are you seeing someone?"

She looked at him without a word.

"Well, are you?" He could see both sides of her face now, his eyes having adjusted.

Her voice was razor-like. "Am I what?"

"Are you seeing someone? Are you leaving me for some other guy?"

She waited, as if considering what to say. "No."

Fueled by his indignation, he stood over her, folded his arms and scowled, expecting a conciliatory gesture on her part. "Then why? You don't even *know* what you want!"

She glared at him, the two sides of her face joining in anger. "I already explained why. I may not know what I want, but I know what I *don't* want. I don't want to be married to you! Is that clear enough? What I decide to do with my life from here on is none of your business. In the meantime, you can use one of the girls' rooms to sleep in until you find a place." With that, she stood up, careful not to touch him, and marched toward the master bedroom. She turned. "Your pillow and pajamas are on Jessica's bed."

She vanished into the room, closed and locked the door. The sound of the lock echoed in his head, a final punctuation point.

Kevin sat down, deflated and defeated, and the house became still again. The distant sound of weeping drifted from behind the bedroom door. He listened to the faint crying of his soon-to-be ex-wife, and then turned off the fireplace. Light and warmth both fled the room at once. As he rose up, his head struck the overhang of the wooden mantle, and pain flashed in front of his eyes. "God damn it!" He slapped it, but the thick wooden shelf stood unmoved by the impact. Hand pressed against the sore spot on his head, he stumbled toward Jessica's room.

He sat on her bed and pulled the chain on the lamp. His pajamas and slippers were neatly stacked on the lavender duvet. His feet were still numb with cold, so he put on his slippers. It felt strange to be doing something so common, so normal, on this night. A picture of Dana and him and the girls taken last year came into view. Grasping it in his hands, the throbbing of his head lightened as he stroked the glass with his finger. *Twenty-one years of marriage down the tubes. Just like that! What did I do wrong? I've always been a good father, provider, and husband. Haven't I?* He squinted at Dana's smiling face. *She doesn't look unhappy. What am I going to do?* Elbows on his knees, he hung his head, the picture still in his hand. His life dissolved into tears.

All the reasons why they shouldn't separate rushed through his mind. Hopeful thoughts of resolving their issues floated across the monitor of his imagination. He plotted and planned, envisioned the hoops he would jump through, and then reprimanded himself for holding on. It was futile! *Obviously Dana has planned this for some time!*

That thought set fire to his anger. On the screen inside his mind he saw himself confronting Dana, and then telling his parents what a bitch she was. He imagined the low opinion his family and friends would have of her once they learned that she was leaving him. *How could she leave me? People will be on my side. I'll make sure everyone knows. She'll pay for this.*

The drama in his head came to a halt as he thought about his daughters. Any attack on their mother would also hurt them. Protective instincts took over, and he riffled through all the things he shouldn't do and shouldn't say.

As he stared at the photo of his girls, tears streamed down his face. *I can't remember the last time I cried.* He wiped his face on the sleeve of his shirt. There would be no more family Thanksgivings or Christmases. No more family vacations. No more family. Emptiness sucked at his being, as if his chest had been hollowed out. Dana had surgically removed his family life, and he was powerless.

The thought that she could disenfranchise him with a few brief sentences was unacceptable. Rage flooded the empty pit in his chest. Within seconds he found himself at the master bedroom door yelling. "Dana! Dana!" He grasped the knob, but it wouldn't budge--banged on the wood until his hands hurt--no answer. He was locked out--locked out of his bedroom; locked out of Dana's heart; locked out of his familiar life.

"I can't believe you're doing this, Dana. Let me in! God damn it! This is my house, too. Let me in!" His fury stirred up a hunger for something to destroy. Dana's favorite Waterford Crystal basket vase was waiting for him on its table. He lunged toward the table, grabbed the vase and flung it at the door. The sound of glass smashing against the wood satisfied his craving for violence. He listened for her response. There was none. Carefully sweeping the broken glass to the side with his foot, he approached the door and kicked it. It was solid. He had built and installed it himself. Kevin walked away, leaving the broken glass on the floor.

His mind and body were exhausted, but his thoughts wouldn't let up. Trying to think about what he should do, he couldn't focus. Thoughts of the past took charge and competed for the chance to torture him. His future was inconceivable. Finally he curled up on the bed, hugging a pillow. "I'll think about it tomorrow." It was after two in the morning before he fell asleep.

Chapter Three

He awoke around 8:00 a.m. and again walked the infinite distance to the master bedroom. The broken glass had disappeared. Turning the knob, he entered. The bed was neatly made. Back in the living room, the winged-back chair appeared more welcoming in the daylight. Sitting in the chair, he stared at the couch where he had cowered last night. To his left was a side table with a ceramic lamp bridging to an identical wingback on the other side. His mind skipped back twenty-four years.

It was a memorable summer day between his freshman and sophomore years in college. His father had asked his brother, Bryce, and himself to meet at the office. Kevin had plans to take the day off and go to Lake Michigan, but agreed to meet his father first. "What's this about?" Bryce had asked him. Kevin shrugged.

Bryce was two years older and ready to begin his senior year at Michigan State, while Kevin had chosen Western Michigan, mainly to get away from home. Their father ran a successful plumbing, HVAC and remodeling company, and they had worked summers learning the trades and earning money for college.

Their father, Jim, walked in and sat down behind the massive oak desk. In his usual get-down-to-business manner, he addressed his sons. "Boys, I started my business and made it the best company in the area. Of course, I didn't do it all myself; I had help. People invested in me, and I made good on their investments. I'm offering you the same chance. If you want to start your own business, I'll put up $50,000 to get you started. Of course, I'll want to see a business plan.

"If you don't want to start your own company, you can go to work in my business, and one day you can run it. Consider it your inheritance. I don't plan on leaving you boys a fortune when I die. I expect you to make it on your own efforts. The money, plus the interest it earns, will be set aside for you in case you change your mind or as an inheritance for you after I'm gone."

Bryce spoke. "That's generous, Dad, but I don't think you'll be checking out anytime soon. You're only fifty years old! I'd like to keep working for you. I'll have a Business Degree in a year, and I want to be a manager."

Jim nodded his head, thoughtfully. "Your management training begins today, Bryce. I'll be proud to have you take on more responsibility in the company."

He turned toward Kevin. "What about you, Kevin? Start your own business? Or, there's room for you here."

"I'll pass." Kevin met his father's gaze. "It's been great for a summer job, but it's not what I want." He paused and took a deep breath. "Dad, I have other plans. I'm switching to Education. I want to teach."

"Not much money in that, Son. You'll end up working summers just to make ends meet."

"It's not just about money. It's about doing something I like."

"Well, I'd always hoped you would join the company, or at least do a start-up locally that could work with us. You're good with people, so I can't pretend I'm not disappointed. But, it's your life."

"Yes, it is." Kevin nodded. "Sorry to ruin your plans."

Jim shrugged, shook his head, then grabbed some papers to study. The meeting was over.

Kevin left the office feeling richer even though he had yet to receive any money. *It's there when I need it.* A few hours later he met his friend and college roommate, Al Stewart, at the beach in Grand Haven. Hopeful about picking up dates, that led him to meeting Dana. She had worn a bright yellow, two-piece that set off her tan.

She had smiled when they met, and that had given him the confidence to talk to her.

He hadn't dated much in high school, and had just begun to find success in that realm in college. His brother had been the popular one with girls always calling. However, Bryce had met Brenda in his freshman year at State, and was crazy about her-- because he was with her every weekend.

Fortunately Al had paired up with Dana's friend, and they stayed well past sunset. He remembered the physical attraction and the many kisses they had shared on a blanket in the sand. Dana was also a student at Western. They dated for a couple of years before moving in together in their senior year. They were married the summer after graduation, and Kevin began his teaching career a month later.

"Twenty-one years down the tubes." He repeated aloud to himself, stared at the floor, and shook his head.

It had seemed to be his lucky day, meeting Dana and having fifty-thousand dollars in the bank. Now, his bank account was still full, but his account with Dana was apparently empty. Grabbing the classifieds, which had been strategically placed on the coffee table, Kevin began searching for a place to live.

Chapter Four

Kevin moved out a few days later, and Dana told him he could take whatever he wanted. Since the new apartment was furnished, he took very little. She handed him divorce papers as his going-away present.

"Thanks a lot, Dana." His tone ripped the space between them, much like the way he wanted to tear the papers in his hand.

"Would you rather I had you served in your classroom?"

When he didn't answer she added, "I didn't want you served at basketball practice or at your new apartment. It's not about *getting* you, Kevin. I *just* need to move on."

She emphasized the word *just* such that Kevin felt like a mosquito being flicked away. He stifled his sense of outrage, in the same way he had kept most of his true feelings from her. It lay trapped beneath his ribs, unable to escape. Instead, he quietly fled Dana's presence.

* * *

The house was put on the market, the split handled with civility and fairness, and Kevin continued to contain his anger. During that time Bryce had his own marital crisis.

It was in April, and they sat in a cafe. Kevin sipped on mint tea, and Bryce slurped his dark roast coffee. A few college students were scattered around the room, working on their laptops. Two young women sat at a nearby table in animated conversation about somebody's boyfriend. Amidst the sounds of frothing milk, clanging metal and tinkling ceramic, Bryce stared uneasily out the window. Kevin sensed his brother's anxiety. "What's going on?"

16

"Brenda says she'll leave me unless I go to counseling with her." He lifted his mug to his lips, clutching it in both hands.

"What are you going to do?" *Bryce, too?*

"I'll go!" Bryce set his coffee down and massaged his temples. "I still love her, and I'll do whatever it takes to keep her."

"Who are you going to see?" *Mom will think she failed both of us!*

"The minister at our church, Reverend Turner. Brenda likes him and thinks he can help. I don't go to church every Sunday, but I still believe."

"Believe what?"

"You know, in God and in Jesus and in the Holy Ghost. I know that Jesus died for my sins, and that he's my savior."

"Yeah? What did he save you from?"

"Hell. Damnation."

"Well, if you believe in all that stuff maybe this Turner guy is the person you should be talking to." Kevin tipped his mug, hot liquid mint tingling his tongue.

"So you don't believe?"

"There is definitely something greater than me, and I guess you can call it God. But, it's not a big person in the sky. And Jesus is cool, but he didn't save me from Hell, because I don't think there is a hell. Unless you consider divorce to be hell, and no one can save me from that." Kevin raised his eyebrows and shook his head.

"Do you have to be so negative? You shouldn't be disrespectful of Jesus." Bryce raised his voice, and quickly swiveled his head to see if he had been heard.

No one seemed to notice. "I'm not disrespectful. I just don't agree with your belief. I hope that you and Brenda can work it out. I wouldn't wish divorce on anyone, especially not my own brother."

"Thanks for that." Bryce set down his cup and looked at his cell phone. "I need to go. I'll let you know what happens. Maybe you should go see the Reverend, too."

"I'll pass. Thanks. I'm carving out my own path, and I don't need a minister to tell me what to do. I wish you and Brenda luck in working things out, however you do it."

* * *

Bryce and his wife went to counseling and then to church every Sunday. Bryce found what he needed to do to keep her happy: offer compliments, really listen when she talked, and spend more quality time. Previously, he had thought that being affectionate was enough. They remained together.

Bryce's new found success in marriage and his renewed Christian belief quickly made him a self-proclaimed expert in both marriage and religion. He bought Kevin a Bible.

"All the answers you need are in here, Kevin. Brenda and I read it together every day. I'm sure this will help you."

Kevin promised to read it, but he soon began to avoid his brother. Every conversation included the Bible and Jesus. Bryce ignored his protests. His goal was always Kevin's conversion.

In spite of Bryce's efforts to save him, Kevin felt lost. Teaching high school no longer satisfied him, and he felt out of place wherever he went. He looked at his male friends and colleagues who had been divorced. A few had moved on, dating and remarrying. Others had given up on relationships, taking refuge in sports, drinking beer, or playing video games. None seemed happy. Some, who were teachers, were holding on, waiting to get their thirty years in. *Then what?*

* * *

It was June, and the semester had ended. Kevin sat at his desk finishing his record keeping.

"Hey, Kevin. How's it going?" Derek, the I.T. manager, had slipped into the room unnoticed.

"I'm just about done and ready for school to be out."

"So what are you and your wife doing this summer?"

"Getting divorced."

Derek sat in a nearby desk. "I'm sorry."

"Thanks. How about you?" Kevin finished entering his data, and hit the return button.

"I may be doing the same."

Kevin pulled his attention from the laptop and studied Derek for a few moments. "I'm sorry to hear that."

"Thanks, but it's okay. I've been attending this evening class on forgiveness."

"Probably something I should do." Kevin folded his arms.

"Yeah, well, I met this woman in class, and we started talking. We made a connection. I'm so impressed with her spiritual growth, and she has great insights. Every week we talk, and we've gotten really close. I'm thinking about being with her."

Somewhere in Kevin's brain, a fuse was lit. "And your wife?"

"Well, if I do this, I'll need to leave her."

"And your kids--how many do you have?"

"Three. I wouldn't be leaving my kids. They would still be in my life."

A bomb burst in Kevin's head. "Yeah right. Don't bullshit me, Derek. You said it's *okay*. It's *not* okay. For you maybe. You're running off with this spiritual chick to have some kind of enlightening experience, but your wife and kids--they'll be hurting."

"It's *my* life." Derek expressed quietly between clenched teeth.

"No, it's *their* lives, too. My wife left me. It's been almost five months, and I'm still hurt and pissed off. Fortunately my girls are grown and in college. But, your kids are young. Is your wife a terrible person or something?"

Derek folded his arms across his chest. "No. She's really nice. We just don't have much spark anymore. I spend most nights sleeping in the basement."

"Because she kicked you out?"

"No. I needed my own space."

"Do you ever talk to your wife about how you feel?"

"We don't talk that much." Derek dropped his elbows to his knees and stared at the floor.

"Forgive me if I'm not too sympathetic toward your new adventure. I don't know how your wife, who's been married to you for how many years..?"

"Fifteen."

"--fifteen years and had three kids and between raising them and paying bills and cleaning house, and probably working a job, too--I don't know how she can compete with *Miss Wonderful Spiritual Woman* who probably has no responsibilities beyond herself, looks great, and has all these insights into the nature of the universe. So maybe you'll have this great romantic experience, but it'll come at a price--and your wife and kids will pay it. Eventually, you will, too."

"Gee, thanks for your advice, Kevin. Glad I stopped in." Derek's words shredded the space between them, and he bolted from the desk. At the door he turned, his eyes meeting Kevin's, and he left.

"Have a nice summer." Kevin mumbled to himself. He returned to his screen, energized with anger, as if he had somehow put the world in order. *I shouldn't have been so hard on him. Aw, screw it! He needs to know how much it's going to hurt them. Why doesn't he just talk to his wife and work it out? Why didn't I?*

For the next two weeks basketball camp consumed his time and energy, but once the camp ended, he found himself with nothing to do. He and Dana usually took a trip the first two weeks in July. This year they had talked about Glacier National Park. As much as he

20

loved being in the mountains, vacationing alone sounded empty, depressing. One more reason to be angry at Dana.

With nothing to keep him busy, loneliness closed in, like a predator cornering him--its sharp teeth threatening to devour its prey, forcing him to face himself. He paced the apartment, needing to escape, but didn't know where to go. He had no close friends. His social life had been connected to school and outside of school, friendships with other couples had been arranged by Dana. Those friends were really hers.

What am I going to do with my life? That question hadn't been asked since college. The future seemed like a deep dark hole, and he was teetering on the edge, afraid of losing his footing, being pulled into a years-long free-fall that would someday end with his death. There *was* no future, at least not as things were.

Throughout the summer, between restless pacing and unnecessary trips to the grocery store, he read self-improvement books, took online classes, and studied parts of the Bible. He hoped for something to point him in a direction--any direction. Bryce followed with other religious literature, and Kevin threw it in the recycle bin. He wasn't looking for a religion that had all the answers. He needed to find his own answers.

Since that terrible night in January, everything had been Dana's fault. In July he tried to tell himself it was nobody's fault, or that it could be his fault. In August he admitted that maybe it was his own damn fault for not paying attention. He called it his "Margaritaville Progression," and thanked Jimmy Buffet in his thoughts. That worked for his brain, but not for his emotions. Despite the self-help books and scripture, he was an angry man trapped in an unwanted life.

Autumn approached. Both daughters, who were staying with their mom, would go back to college, one a senior and the other a sophomore. The divorce was finalized, and the house sold. Dana had moved on and seemed to be doing well, feeding his anger which continued to boil.

Then he heard about Mike. They agreed to meet at the same cafe where Bryce and he met a few months ago. Mike, a yoga and meditation teacher, was highly recommended by a fellow staff member at Kevin's school.

"I don't know much about yoga or meditation, except that, maybe they could help." Kevin sipped on his tea. He told his story about the divorce. Mike listened calmly. There was a depth in his eyes that made Kevin think this was a man of wisdom. His shaved head added to his sort of eastern mystique. Kevin dismissed that notion when he learned that Mike had a successful business career.

"I'm just a regular person, like you or anyone else." Mike's quiet laugh reminded Kevin of a bubbling brook he used to visit. "What is it that you want, Kevin?"

Regular person? Mike exuded a calm confidence, something Kevin had never felt. "I want to feel better--to be calm like you. I'm angry most of the time."

"Meditation and yoga can help, but so much of what we experience in life isn't about what happens to us. It's how we respond to it."

"I know. That's what all the books I've been reading say."

"So, who's responsible for your life, Kevin? Is it Dana?"

"I guess it's not Dana."

"You guess?"

"Okay, I know she can't fix my life, but I'm still mad at her."

"No matter how angry you get, you're still going to wake up tomorrow morning without your wife. So, do you want to spend the rest of your life being angry, or do you want to take responsibility and find a way to be happy?"

Kevin felt a shockwave from that, but sensed it was the truth. He swallowed that truth even though he didn't like the taste.

"Take the time you need to grieve and to be angry, and then decide what you want." Mike reached for his cup of coffee and sipped, holding Kevin in his gaze. "Once you have an idea about what you want, you need to act."

"Yeah, I think I need to move forward. Will you teach me to meditate?"

"I will. I'm teaching a class on Wednesday night. Are you free?"

"Yes, I'll--"

"Hey, Kevin." Bryce grabbed a nearby empty chair.

"Hi, Bryce." Kevin covered his disappointment toward his brother's interruption with a smile and a friendly tone. "Have a seat. This is Mike. He's going to teach me how to meditate."

Bryce sat down as they shook hands.

"Good to meet you, Bryce." Mike extended his hand and shook with Bryce. He slowly withdrew it, and reached again for his cup.

Bryce studied Mike's face in silence for a few moments. "Are you a believer?"

Mike's eyes narrowed, and then he returned to his calm state. "That's a strange question to ask someone you've just met, Bryce. What I believe is meaningless, unless I live it. You won't know that until you get to know me."

"Yeah, I--I guess." Bryce stammered a bit, and seemed confused by Mike's response.

"Class is this Wednesday night, Bryce. You could learn to meditate, too." Kevin smiled inside knowing Bryce would refuse.

Bryce shifted his eyes between Mike and Kevin. "I don't believe in that crap. I'm a Christian, and I pray. Meditation is for New Age types."

Mike laughed. "Bryce. I have Christians, and people of other faiths, and some who don't have *any* religion in my classes. I adapt to whatever a person's spiritual path might be. If they don't have a path, they just use it to relax, to de-stress."

"Well, my minister says that meditation is a cult practice, and it's dangerous."

"How is it dangerous?" Mike sat back in his chair.

Bryce furrowed his brow. "He says that an empty mind is the devil's playground. We shouldn't look inside for understanding, We should look to God." He turned to Kevin. "Don't do this. It's not good for you."

"Bryce, why don't you come to my class and see for yourself-- and bring your minister with you. I've taught several ministers to meditate. They often meditate on scripture." Mike leaned in, his arms on the table.

Bryce twisted his face into a frown. He planted his elbows on the table, as if facing off with Mike. "No way. Maybe you should come to my church instead."

Mike paused and nodded. "I'd love to. Why don't you write down the name of the church and the service time. You can introduce me to your minister, and we'll talk about meditation."

Bryce jerked backward. "I doubt he would do that. I gotta go." Bryce stood up quickly, and knocked the chair over backward. He quickly picked it up. Ignoring Mike, he looked at Kevin. "See you later."

Kevin shook his head inwardly, grateful that Mike could deal with his brother. "So would you really have gone to his church?"

"Of course. Every path has truth in it. We can focus on the differences, or we can focus on what we have in common. I prefer the latter."

"Makes sense. Thanks, Mike."

"For what?"

"For helping me see that it's up to me to find my own happiness, and that maybe I should let this anger go."

"You're welcome."

"I have to figure out what I want." Kevin stared into his mug.

"Then you need to act. Dreams are important, but they don't mean anything unless you act."

Kevin nodded. On Wednesday, he attended the meditation class.

Chapter Five

Two weeks before the fall semester began, Kevin drove to the high school. He had intended to enter his classroom and plan his year, but sitting in his car in the parking lot, he couldn't move. He restarted his vehicle and returned to his apartment.

Other than loving his two daughters and his parents, there was nothing else in life to care about. He trudged up the steps, located the door with the number two, and put his key into the lock. At the site of his sparsely finished living room he plummeted into his own personal darkness. *This doesn't feel like home.* He turned on the local Classic Rock station and cranked it up.

In an attempt to shake his mood, he sang along. He took the *Stairway to Heaven* with Robert Plant and played air guitar with Jimmy Page. Alone and free of inhibitions, he acted out his rock-star fantasies.

There's a feeling I get when I look to the West,
And my spirit is crying for leaving.

Bob Seger's *Old Time Rock and Roll* blasted into the room and he remembered Tom Cruise's performance in the movie, *Risky Business*, in his briefs. Kevin laughed for the first time in several months, and stripped down to do his own boxer-shorts version. He leaped around the room, avoiding the triangle of a small couch, recliner, and a television. Singing, playing, and bounding about until out of breath, he rolled onto the floor and lay on his back, laughing. The release gave him strength and a new perspective. He yelled at the ceiling. "I'm tired of being the victim, and I need a change!" Rising to his feet, the fantasy rockstar waited to hear the next song.

As Eric Burden and he finished up on *We Gotta Get Outta This Place*, the thought of escape took hold. Energized by the music, and motivated by the idea of casting aside his unsatisfying life, he envisioned being free, and he could think of nothing else. "I stay here, and I go crazy." He spoke out loud. "I have to do something." A decision crystalized in his mind. Not sure if it was smart, it at least afforded him a sense of confidence.

For the first time since that dark winter's eve in January, he slept through the night. As he awoke in the morning, the memory of his new commitment triggered a flood of anxiety. He bounded out of bed and paced the apartment in an attempt to walk off his nerves. *I don't know about this!* Stopping in front of a full-length mirror in the hallway, his six-feet-one-inch, naked reflection stared back at him.

His body was fit with only a little tummy sticking out. *I could flatten that in a few weeks.* His dark brown hair was still thick, with no sign of gray, yet. *Ha! Bryce's hair is literally running away from his eyebrows!* He combed his hair back with his fingers. *I'm still an attractive guy. The only reason I haven't had any dates is because I haven't asked anyone.* He flexed his biceps and assumed a bodybuilder pose. *Hey, it's all about confidence.* He nodded to himself.

He stepped closer to the mirror and looked into his own eyes. They were hazel. Some days they were gray. *Who are you, man? What do you want? To find a new life? You can do this!* He breathed deeply and exhaled, leaving a hazy, silver-gray circle on the glass.

That morning he visited his classroom. The school environment that had always been familiar and comforting felt odd and ill-fitting. Thoughts of escape permeated his mind. He sat, and began typing his letter of resignation.

"Kevin. How are you?" Derek stood in his doorway.

"Derek. Come on in. Have a seat."

Derek grabbed a chair and slid it toward the desk. He offered his hand to Kevin.

Kevin grasped his hand. "I'm sorry I was so hard on you back in June. That was my anger toward my ex. Nothing to do with you."

"It's okay. You helped me." Derek sat down.

Kevin closed his laptop as Derek took his seat. "I did. How?"

"Both you and the *I Ching* gave good advice, but I didn't want to listen."

"Is that the thing where you toss some sticks or coins to get an answer to a question?" Kevin made a tossing motion with his hand.

"I use coins."

"Is it like fortune telling?"

"Some people have used it that way. It's a tool for guidance. The guidance is general. No magic involved. Bottom line is that each time I used it, the message was to follow principle. And it said if I didn't, there would be disaster."

"So what happened?"

"Nearly a disaster. I thought about what you said, how much hurt I would cause my family and the unfair comparison I was making between my wife and this other woman. To live according to principle requires honesty, so I told my wife everything."

"You told her you were leaving?"

"No. I told her what had been going on, and that I'd been wrong, and that I hoped we could work things out--because when I really looked inside myself--" Derek faced his palms upward. "--I still loved her. Then I went to the other woman and told her I was staying with my wife. So they were both hurt and angry."

"That took courage. You could've ended up with no one."

Derek nodded. "My wife and I are talking a lot more. It's not easy, but I think we'll be all right."

"I'm happy for you."

"Thanks. What about you?" Derek gestured with his hand toward Kevin.

"I'm quitting teaching." Kevin folded his arms and leaned back.

"Wow. Where are you going?"

"I don't know yet." Kevin shrugged.

"You definitely have courage." Derek offered an approving nod.

"Either that or I'm a fool. You're the only person I've told. So please, don't say anything."

"I won't. I just stopped in to say thanks." They shook hands again.

"You're welcome."

As Derek walked toward the door, he turned back. "Kevin, trust yourself. Listen to the Inner Voice. You'll do fine."

Kevin nodded. "Thanks."

Derek left. Kevin felt pleased, that somehow, although he couldn't save his own family, he had, in a small way, helped another man save his. He hoped that it was the Inner Voice encouraging him to leave his secure job, and not some foolish urge.

Kevin re-opened his laptop, printed, and held onto the letter in case he changed his mind. It was one thing to think about leaving and another to do it. Where would he go? He posted on Facebook that he was considering resigning his teaching position, and he was looking for new opportunities. Friends responded.

> Gary James: Cool. What are you going to do?
> Jeanette Harris: Hey, Kevin, why not hang in nine more years and get the retirement?
> John Feldkamp: Go for it, man!
> Sherri Rathburn: Don't leave, Mr. Neill. You were the best teacher I had.
> Brett Thomas: Hey, Coach. The basketball team needs you. Don't quit now!

What about my salary and benefits? What about my retirement? The questions seemed unimportant. After all, being security-minded for over twenty years had done nothing to prevent upheaval in his life.

Reminding himself there were no guarantees, he threw down the gauntlet: he would *live* rather than just hang on. He heard Mike in his head. *Who's responsible for your life? You need to act.* He decided to turn in the letter with or without a definite plan. *But, don't I need a destination first?* Next he heard Derek. *Trust your Inner Voice.* Checking the Facebook account again, he noticed a private message from Al Stewart. *It's been years since I talked to him!*

> Al Stewart: Kevin, how are you? This is perfect timing. I'm starting a restaurant in Tucson, and I need a partner, both as an investor and as a manager for the staff. Message me if you're interested.

Could I manage people at a restaurant? How different can that be from running a high school class or an athletic team? Kevin wrote back; messages were exchanged; and a plan began to form. It was time to talk to his father.

The next day Kevin gave his notice at work. The superintendent of schools and his principal wanted to know why he was leaving. All he could say was: "It's time." They thanked him for his years of service and expressed that he would be difficult to replace. Although Kevin appreciated the sentiment, he knew there would be young teachers standing in line to get his job. The hardest part was contacting his returning basketball players.

Kevin listed his possessions for sale, except for what could fit into his Escape. Whatever couldn't be sold quickly, would be given away. As he closed out his old life he focused on his new life, the one he would build out west. He researched the Tucson area and had several phone conversations with Al and his wife, Jenny. Al sent him a business plan, and walked Kevin through it on Skype. Jenny talked to him about Tucson and all of it's opportunities. Her warmth and friendliness welcomed him.

Kevin invited his daughters, Jessica and Melissa, to dinner at his apartment.

"So, Dad, what's this about? Mom already told us the divorce is final." Jessica spooned mashed potatoes on to her plate. She quickly put a forkful into her mouth. "Mmm, Dad. I love your garlic mashed. So good! It's cool that you and mom put aside money for our college. Thanks for that. So, what else is there?" She tilted her head slightly sideways and arched her left eyebrow. "Well?"

Melissa finished filling her plate, careful not to let the salmon, potatoes, and asparagus with Hollandaise touch each other. She gave her plate a satisfied look then faced her father. "Yeah, Dad, what's going on?"

"I quit my job, and I'm moving to Arizona."

"Cool!" Jessica reached over and patted his shoulder. "You're stepping out. What're you going to do?"

"I'm starting a restaurant with an old friend of mine."

Melissa stopped with her fork halfway to her mouth and set it on her plate. "If you quit your job and move to Arizona, what are you going to live on? Since you put your equity money into our college funds, how can you start a business?"

"Good questions." He told them the story about their grandfather offering him his inheritance over twenty years ago.

"Then I think you should do this." Melissa nodded, separating a small piece of salmon from the rest.

"He doesn't need your permission, Lissy." Jessica reprimanded her older sister.

"I know, but I thought I'd give it anyway." Melissa smiled.

Jessica rolled her eyes.

"He doesn't need our permission, but I think he wants our blessing." Melissa pointed her fork at Jessica. They both looked at their dad.

"Well, yeah. I feel a little like I'm abandoning you two."

"Don't be ridiculous, Dad. We're both going off to college tomorrow. It's not like we'd be seeing you that often, anyway. You're still a phone call away." Jessica reached for more mashed potatoes. "I expect you'll fly back and visit, right?"

Kevin nodded. "Definitely."

"I'll still miss you." Melissa wiped her hands on her napkin. "Even though I'm not in town, I'll know you aren't here. I want you to go, and I'm sure you don't want to stay and work for Grandpa."

Kevin shifted his eyes between his two daughters. "Thanks, you two. I appreciate your support."

Later that evening as he hugged and kissed his daughters, he felt sad, knowing it would probably be awhile until he saw them again.

The next day Kevin walked into his father's office and sat down. "Hey, Dad. How's it going?" He remembered the day his dad had offered the money. Success had tripled the size of the company since then. The office was larger, the desk smaller, and his father was a little more approachable. At seventy-four, his dad was different--warmer, a better listener, and more relaxed than the father Kevin had grown up with. His coarse edges had softened, and Kevin felt less compelled to rebel. *When did he change? Or, did I?*

Except for a single pile of neatly stacked papers, the desktop was clear. The only other item was a nameplate that read: Jim Neill, CEO. To his left, a large oak bookcase stood from floor to ceiling against the white wall. All the shelves were filled with books except for the one at eye level, which was dedicated to family pictures. There were five-by-seven's of his parents, of Bryce and Brenda, one for each granddaughter, and a picture of Kevin and Dana. That stopped him, as if he were suddenly transported to another reality. *I need to have him get rid of that picture.*

His father stood behind the desk, sorting papers into the one pile, disposing of some. He looked at his son. "Good morning, Kevin. This is a surprise! It's been awhile since you've visited."

Kevin refocused. "I need to talk to you about something."

"Sure. Looks like you've made a decision. What's going on?"

He hesitated a few moments, surprised that his father read him so well. *Get on with it!* "Dad, I--er--I want my inheritance."

"Your what?" His father sat down and put his elbows on the desk, leaning toward Kevin, his brow furrowed in confusion.

Kevin made himself sound more confident than he felt. "My inheritance. I'm ready for the money you promised me twenty-four years ago. You said that if I wanted to start my own business that you'd put up fifty-thousand dollars plus whatever interest that's been earned since then. I'm here to take you up on your offer."

"Oh!" He relaxed his brow and pursed his lips. "What business are you starting?"

"I'm going out west. An old friend and I are opening a restaurant. You remember my roommate, Al, from college? He already has a building, and we've put together a business plan. In a month or so we'll be ready to go. First, I'm going to take a little vacation in Vegas." He set a copy of the plan on the desk. "This is a draft. We're still working out a few details."

Jim picked up the papers. "You sure about this?"

"Never been more sure about anything." Kevin lied. At least having the money and a plan made him feel he had some control over his destiny.

Jim scanned the pages quickly and put on his authority voice. "How well do you know Al? I'll need to study this plan."

Kevin matched his father's tone. "No, Dad. I have to do this myself. Just like you did."

"What do *you* know about the restaurant business, Kevin?"

Kevin thought a moment, recognizing his father's need to play the discerning businessman. "I'm learning. I won't be doing the cooking, but I'll manage the staff and our customer service. You've said that I'm good with people. I've been managing high school students for years. Only difference is the kids will be older."

"Kevin, I don't feel comfortable with this." Jim paused. "It's your life; and I did promise you the money; but this seems kind of sudden!" His father raised his grey eyebrows and set the plan down.

"It's been building up for the past several months, Dad. I'm not happy with my life, so I need to create a new one. I don't want to be stuck in a job that no longer excites me, and I don't want to be a prisoner in a life that has become meaningless. Dana is gone. The girls are at college. It's time for me to do something different."

His father listened and nodded. "I'll have a cashier's check for you in three days. Let me know if I can help in any other way."

"Thanks. I appreciate it."

"Be careful, Kevin. Hire an attorney to go over whatever agreement you make with Al."

"I will, Dad. Thanks again." He stood and reached to shake his father's hand. His dad stared into his eyes. Kevin could feel his doubts. "It'll be okay, Dad. You'll see."

"A little bit of doubt is healthy. It makes you search for everything that could go wrong, and then you can work out solutions. I'm glad you want to go into business. Just make sure you keep your eyes open."

"I will, Dad. Thanks"

They shook again. Kevin stared at their clasped hands. This was the first time he felt connected to his father. He looked into his dad's eyes and thought he saw *hope*, and maybe a little *pride*.

Chapter Six

Three days disappeared in a flurry of activity. Kevin collected his check and prepared to leave Michigan the following morning. As he finished up his packing there was a knock on his apartment door. He opened it, and Bryce walked in.

"So, were you going to send me a postcard from Vegas or what? I'm your brother, and I have to find out *from Dad* that you've quit your job, and you're leaving town?"

"I'm sorry, Bryce. I was about to call you."

"Are you crazy or what? Leaving your job after twenty-one years--leaving your family and going off to where? What could you possibly want to do in Las Vegas?"

"I'm not moving to Las Vegas, just visiting. I've always wanted to go. I'm moving to Tucson and starting a business with Al Stewart."

"What's in Las Vegas?"

"A good time! You know, chase women, gamble, eat great food, be entertained, and drink. Probably in that order. I'm going to pull out the stops and enjoy life." Kevin swept his arms outward.

"Unbelievable!" Bryce threw his hands up and shook his head from side to side. His voice blasted at Kevin. "I'm *so* glad *I'm* not divorced."

Kevin smiled to himself. *There he goes again!*

Bryce softened his tone. "Brenda and I asked Jesus into our lives, and that has made all the difference. I only wish that you and Dana had gotten down on your knees and prayed for guidance. You'd still be married, and you wouldn't be about to destroy your life. I've tried to get you to come to our church and to meet our pastor, but you've never been interested. Kevin, I'm worried about

35

your soul. Don't do this. Stay here, and let Dad help you start a business. Let me introduce you to my pastor. He can help you."

"Thanks for the advice, Brother, but no. I'm happy you and Brenda have found a way to stay together, but there was nothing I could do to keep my marriage. I'm convinced she was planning our break-up for a long time--probably years. It's done--finalized three weeks ago. I have lamented my broken marriage enough, and now it's time to celebrate my freedom."

"You're going to spend your inheritance on women and gambling in Las Vegas?"

"Some of it. I have several thousand dollars of my own, too. I've already set aside college money for the girls. So, I'll spend my money where I please. But, most of it is going into this business with Al and starting over in Tucson."

"So what will you do in a couple of years when you come back here penniless? Are you going to ask Dad for more money?"

"If that happens, just don't say: 'I told you so!' I don't think that'll happen. Thanks for your vote of confidence!"

Bryce furrowed his brow. "Tell me you at least prayed to Jesus and asked Him for guidance."

Kevin's patience boiled over. "Back off, Bryce. You live your life, and I'll live mine. I'm not a 'Praise Jesus' kind of guy, and I can't make myself be--"

"Watch how you talk! You'll never get into Heaven with that attitude."

Kevin rolled his eyes. "So, are you going to Heaven, Bryce?"

"I'm saved, so of course I'm going to Heaven." Bryce folded his arms, his words carving a self-satisfied look into his face.

"Then why would I want to go there?" Kevin shot back. "Being lectured by you for all eternity sounds more like Hell. Quit trying to impose your views on me. All it does is piss me off!"

Bryce's eyes raked Kevin's face, and he clenched his fists. Kevin thought his brother would explode.

Music blasted from Kevin's pocket.

Wake me up. Wake me up inside.

Both Kevin and Bryce jumped. He reached for the phone.

♪ I can't wake up. Wake me up inside.

Kevin pushed the button, grateful for the interruption. The ringtone of *Bring Me to Life*, installed earlier that day, had become his theme song. "Hi Mom. Uh-huh. Okay. I'll be right there."

"Mom wants us to come over for dinner. Brenda and your girls are already on the way."

Bryce was still glaring at him.

"Look. Bryce. I'm sorry if I offended you. Let's not talk about religion anymore tonight. Okay? It's a contest neither of us can win." He reached out his hand to Bryce.

"Yeah. It's a contest between Heaven and Hell, and I know which side I'm on." He grasped Kevin's hand. Kevin let the comment pass, not wanting to continue the battle. They left the apartment, each driving in his own vehicle.

The gathering was warmed by family humor and genuine caring for each other. There was an unspoken sadness in the air. Kevin's girls had already moved back to their respective universities; Dana had left the family; and now Kevin was moving.

Kevin told Bryce and Brenda what he had learned about Tucson. Bryce excused himself and relocated to the kitchen to talk to his parents and his two daughters. Brenda turned to Kevin, "Are you sure about all of this?"

"I'm sure." He peered into Brenda's eyes. "*You're* not going to start talking religion to me, are you?"

"I can see that you've already talked to Bryce." She paused, waiting for Kevin's nod. "Forgive him. Bryce and I were lost, and it was through prayer and our church community that we got back on track. It's had a profound effect on him. So, now he thinks everyone should do it. Bryce cares about you and wants you to be happy. I know he comes on a little strong, but please don't be offended. He means well."

"Thanks, Brenda. So how come you aren't preaching at me?"

"You need to come to it on your own. No one pushed us into accepting Jesus into our lives. It just felt natural. You have to find your own way, Kevin. We're here if you need anything. I wish you well, and I hope you find whatever it is you're looking for." Brenda hugged him.

"How did my brother find you?" He smiled.

"We found each other." Brenda smiled back. "And recently, I think I've found myself."

Bryce and his family left, and Kevin found himself alone with his mother on the deck overlooking the back yard. The rising buzz of cicadas etched the air of an otherwise quiet evening. He thought about how cicadas live underground for years until they finally emerge as adults. *Kind of like me. I feel like I've been in the dark for ages, and now I'm crawling out.*

His mother touched his arm. "I still miss Dana, and now you're leaving, too. My family is falling apart." The tears in her eyes sparkled under the late August moon.

Kevin embraced his mom. "I'm sorry, Mom. A couple of weeks ago I had no idea I'd be leaving."

Still holding her son, she looked up into his eyes. "Then why so sudden? Don't you want to think about it?"

"I have thought about it. You know, for years I didn't think about much, and then suddenly I'm separated and then divorced. I'm not going to let life sneak up on me again. I needed to make a decision, or I was afraid life would make it for me."

"I understand, Honey, I do. I'll still miss you." She stepped back and wiped her tears with a tissue retrieved from her pocket. "You keep me in the loop." She kissed him on the cheek and hugged him again.

As he left, his father wished him well and acknowledged that it was a gutsy move. He offered his business expertise should Kevin and Al need advice. Kevin thanked his parents and told them he loved them. Driving back to his apartment, he was grateful for the love of his family, but had no regrets about his decision to leave. It was time.

Chapter Seven

At 7:00 a.m. Kevin was up. He dropped off his apartment keys and left for the far off city of Las Vegas, Nevada. His destination gave him a sense of purpose. His purpose gave him confidence. His confidence lifted him up. In Las Vegas he would feel alive again. In Tucson he would start over.

It took two-and-a-half days to drive to Las Vegas. Kevin used his driving time to prepare for his adventure by listening to CD's on how to pick up women, seduction techniques, and being an alpha male. He arrived at his destination late one afternoon, feeling a sense of confidence he had never before experienced, and ready to experiment with his new-found knowledge.

From the moment he checked into the hotel Kevin immersed himself in hedonistic pleasures--women, gaming, great food, entertainment. What he lacked in experience he made up for with money. Every night there was a woman, each one beautiful. He spent money on lavish dinners, drinks, shows, strip clubs, and gambling. After the first few nights and a slow start, he refined his techniques and became skilled at both the *chase* and the *kill*.

Two weeks later the constant pace of pleasurable pursuits took its toll on his body. The last two nights had been especially easy, and he was proud of his progress from Don Juan-a-bee to Don Juan. His head ached, and he was tired. He kissed his most recent date good-bye and fell onto the bed. Most of the day was spent lounging, napping, and drinking water. By the next morning he felt better, and he assessed his situation. Over $20,000 of his money was spent. *It's time to go. First a little brunch, and then I'm out of here.*

He decided on pool-side dining at his hotel. It was mid-morning, the sun was shining, and a dark-haired woman, sitting at a shaded table on the other side of the pool, caught his attention. She was wearing a loose fitting, off-white blouse, jeans, and leather sandals. *This lovely woman could be a good reason for staying just a little longer.* Kevin sauntered over to her table. "Hi. Looks like you have a lot on your mind. I'm a good listener. Would you like some company?" She was winding a shock of her long black hair around her finger, and seemed unaware of him at first.

Finally she looked into his eyes, holding her gaze for several seconds. *If she turns me down, at least there's no one here to see it. This place is dead!* Just as he began to feel nervous she motioned toward the empty chair. He took off his sunglasses to see her more clearly.

Her name was Rachel. Her eyes were green, and he found himself gripping his seat as if to prevent himself from falling--or leaping--into those two green pools and possibly never finding his way out. Forgetting his script, he told her his story of the past year. Strangely, it seemed as if they had known each other for lifetimes.

As he brought her up to date on his life she remarked: "So you've been on a roll these past couple of weeks. Lots of women and partying! Don't get your hopes up here. I've been in Vegas for seven years, and I'm leaving. Today."

The waitress brought Kevin a bagel and cream cheese, a glass of orange juice, and a cup of hot tea. Rachel had coffee. "Would either of you like anything else?" Both said they didn't.

Kevin masked his disappointment with a quick sip of juice. "I told you my story. Why don't you tell me yours?" He set down his glass and decided to relax and be patient. He took a bite of his bagel and wiped the excess cream cheese from the side of his mouth with his napkin. *That was smooth!*

Rachel looked at him. "This is my finale in Las Vegas--telling you my story. I'm an exotic dancer, or at least I was. I grew up in a nice home with good parents, and then went off to college. A friend suggested this line of work when I was a senior. I was struggling to make ends meet, and I missed the nicer things in life. So this friend and I went to a club on amateur night, and I gave it a try. At first I was shy about taking off my clothes in front of a group of people, most of whom were college guys. Once I started dancing it was a rush. It was like these guys couldn't get enough of me. I liked it! The manager of the club offered me a job."

Kevin had talked to a few exotic dancers his first two nights in Vegas. They wore glitzy outfits, five or six-inch platform heels and heavy makeup. Rachel wore no make-up that he could see. Her long dark hair was a finely woven tapestry with subtle variations in shades that reached half way down her back. After his failed chases on each of his first two nights in Vegas, the dancers had been very kind to him, which had soothed his feelings of rejection.

"I started off making a couple hundred a shift, and after a while I was making four to six hundred dollars every night, three nights a week. That was a lot of money for me. The admiration, money, and dancing were addictive. The club I worked for treated the girls decently and didn't allow guys to touch, so I felt safe.

"Good money for a college student!"

"Yes, it was. When I graduated, instead of going for my Masters in Psychology back in Indiana, I came here, to Vegas. I thought I'd dance for a few years, make great money, and get my Masters, too. Well, a few years turned into seven, and here I am. On the positive side, I did get the degree, and I learned a lot."

"Like what?" Kevin asked.

"I understand people. I understand men."

"So, I suppose you think you understand me." Kevin challenged. *Here we go.*

Rachel leaned slightly toward Kevin and looked into his eyes. "I can read a man's eyes and know what he wants. I know what you want right now."

Her movement unnerved him, but he recovered quickly. "Can I test that? What do you think I want?" *Now we're getting somewhere.*

"You think you want me. You think I can make you feel better, that you'll be more complete if you have me. I see the desire in your eyes."

"Big deal! You're good looking, and probably most guys feel that way. Tell me something I don't know."

"Usually when men are admiring me, they aren't really seeing me. They're seeing what they think I can do for them. But, you. You're conflicted. Part of you wants to be in control and sweep me off my feet. The other half is riding on a roller coaster, out of control, wanting to get to know me, but afraid of getting hurt."

Kevin stared at her, feeling as if he'd been undressed in public. The sun's reflection on the pool blinded him for a moment, and he reached for his sunglasses and put them on.

"I'm sorry, Kevin. I didn't mean to embarrass you, but you did ask. Look, this conversation isn't going where you hoped it would, but it could be going somewhere. Feel free to leave if you're not interested. I won't be offended." Rachel sat back, crossed her legs, and looked into the distance.

"I'm disappointed, but I'm not leaving. I want to hear your story."

"Read my body language, Kevin." She raised her brows and made eye contact. "It says, I really like talking with you, but I am totally unavailable to you sexually."

The past few nights the women had been into him--eye contact, feet pointed at him, moving closer, touching him, coming on to him--Rachel sat back in her chair, aloof, yet present. "I get it. Are you always this blunt?" He noticed that his shoulders and arms had tensed, and he made himself relax into his chair.

Rachel nodded. "Yes, because I don't want to mislead you."

"Please continue your story."

43

"About a year ago, I finally began to understand myself, which is why I'm leaving Vegas. I discovered that the woman who loved being wanted and admired didn't live here anymore." She tapped her chest with her first two fingers. "Money wasn't an issue. A fair number of women in this business are either supporting a kid or a drug habit. I've managed to avoid both. I paid for an education and put money away over the years. About eight months ago I came to work and gave away my outfits. I quit. I took a few weeks off, and prayed and meditated, looking for direction.

"I've spent the last few months cleaning out my condo, selling off stuff I didn't need, and deciding where to go. I'm due at a closing meeting in two hours, and then I'm gone."

A soft breeze rippled through her long hair. Her green eyes held him, as if under a spell. *I can't believe how confident she is.*

"I have no regrets. I did what I did. I learned how to manipulate men, but I'm not proud of that. That was the problem. I didn't want to spend any more of my life seeing how much I can get from other people. I'm pleased I've learned to *read* people, because that's a skill I can use to help others." Rachel sipped on her coffee.

"So, what changed you?" Kevin leaned in and looked directly into her eyes.

"Right. As I said, something happened. When I was on the stage I had influence. Every move I made, every look I gave, had an impact on my audience. I always felt in control. It took me almost six years, but I finally asked the question off-stage: How do I impact other people? I wanted to know how I affected people when I wasn't on stage or undressed.

"So I started paying attention. I could turn men on. I could make women envious or jealous. In the classroom I held some intellectual influence, but honestly, guys in my classes weren't interested in my brains. I asked myself if I could be influential when I wasn't using my sexuality as a means? The answer turned out to be *yes*. I talked to some of my colleagues about this, but most of them insisted that my body was the reason I had influence."

"How did you know that you had influence?"

"I observed people. I've known plenty of beautiful women who get beat up, abused, and taken advantage of. Many of the women I've known think they're worthless without their body. They're smart, and creative, but have very little confidence in who they are. In their personal lives they're disrespected. I don't have people disrespecting or abusing me. Do you know why?"

"I can't imagine anyone abusing you, but no, I don't know why." Kevin shook his head.

"Because I don't influence people that way. Everything I think, feel, say, and do has an effect. Whether I'm on stage or in the grocery store, I have an effect. The way I see it, I'm always teaching people how to treat me. I'm a center of influence, and I'm aware of my power. I don't see myself as a victim or someone wounded by life. I don't wallow in guilt or expect people to treat me special. I'm confident. My power is the ability to envision what I want and to be it. We all have that power, but most of us don't know it.

"Why is that?"

"Because most people see themselves as a center of attention. They look at others in terms of what others are doing *to* them, or in terms of what others should do *for* them. They see the world not as something they affect, but as something always affecting them."

"Really? I don't think I'm a center of attention."

"Yeah, well, most people aren't aware of it. You'd like to think of yourself as a man who respects women and who is a good listener, but your body language gives you away."

"What do you mean?" Kevin suddenly became self-conscious and shifted in his chair.

"Every time you think I'm not looking, your eyes are checking me out. You think I don't see you, but I do."

Kevin's face flushed, and he quickly added, "But I thought you liked being admired?"

"On stage, I liked being looked at. In a personal conversation where I'm expressing what's important to me, and maybe important to you, it's damned annoying. I thought we were clear where this conversation wasn't going."

"Sorry." Kevin offered sheepishly. *Damn, I forgot to control my eyes.* "Men look at women. I like looking at you. Is that so wrong?"

"Yes, it is in this context. It's not about men looking at women or you liking the way I look. It's about you being a center of attention. You're focused on *your* needs and wants. You're playing a listening role, but that's probably because you learned that technique in some book about how to pick up women. Do you think you're the first guy who's played that on me?"

Kevin was stung by her comment. He thought about his success with women in Vegas. "Being a sensitive listener *has* worked. Obviously it doesn't work that way with you."

"Well, aren't you proud of yourself!" Rachel glared at him.

"I used to be a nice guy, but that didn't work so well." He met her glare.

"So don't be nice, and don't be a jerk, either. Try being you."

Kevin looked at her, not knowing what to say, wondering *who* he was.

"Look, maybe I should go. I don't want to play this game!" Rachel stood up. "I'm going to the restroom." She walked away without looking back.

Images of Dana closing the bedroom door flashed in his mind while anxiety turned his stomach upside down. He hoped she would return.

Chapter Eight

Kevin breathed a sigh as Rachel returned to the table.

"I left my cell phone." She reached for the phone, concealed behind her coffee cup, looked at it, and dropped it into her purse.

Kevin stood up. "I'm sorry, Rachel. I really do want to get to know you. Please sit down."

Rachel studied his face for a few seconds, then sat down.

"You're so direct--and maybe a little bit controlling."

"Yes, I'm direct and assertive, and controlling, and not afraid. I've seen it all, so don't try to manipulate me. I don't always have to be controlling. When I meet a man I can trust, one without ulterior motives, I get very relaxed. Back to my question: Do you have any idea of the effect of your intentions and behavior on me?"

"It makes you angry. So have you met a guy you can trust?"

"Other than a minister I talked to, no, not here in Vegas. I had hopes for you."

"Sorry to disappoint. You're right." Kevin shrugged. "I thought I was listening to you, but my attention was drawn to your body."

"Bullshit!" Rachel calmly gazed at him. "Take responsibility. You weren't *drawn* to looking at my body. You *chose* to look at it, because that's how you think. For you, this isn't a real conversation. It's foreplay--a means to an end. I'm not saying it's bad that you think that way. Lots of people do, especially in this town. People are focused on their own needs. If I wanted to hook up with someone I might be willing to play the game. But I've already told you I'm not. So your behaviors tell me that you don't really care what I need or want. To you, I'm an object, a potential conquest, a possible vehicle for your pleasure. If you operate as a center of attention, you're just a child in an adult's body."

Kevin felt himself shrinking as if he really were a child being reprimanded. *I'm shrinking. The CD's said to always come from a position of strength--confident body language.* He sat up straight, breathed deeply, and reestablished his confidence. "Wow. That was harsh."

"Little kids see themselves as centers of attention. They think everything should revolve around them. When things don't go their way they react. They cry, stomp their feet, whine, yell and scream, or pout. So-called adults do the same things. You expect other people and the world to meet your needs. You think that if you behave right you should be rewarded. Or, you think that just because you want something, you should have it. That's partly why your wife left you."

"Wait a minute! You don't know what went on in her mind."

"I don't need to know. Tell me, Kevin, how do feel toward your ex-wife?"

"I told you very little about my ex-wife and my divorce. Where are you getting this?"

"You told me a lot. Your face and your voice changed when you talked about her. How do you feel about her?"

"I try not to think about her. When I do, I guess I'm still a little angry with her."

"Why?"

"She left me. She broke up our family."

"How did she feel?"

"What do you mean, how did she feel? How would I know?"

"Kevin, what did she need when you were married? What was it like being married to you, raising two girls, and managing a career? What was best for her?" She fired her questions like bullets, each one a direct hit.

"I don't know. As for leaving me, I guess she wanted freedom. She wanted a new life. But, we had a *good* life." He heard the whine in his own voice and made himself stop.

"Well, there it is. You have no idea what she felt or needed and no clue what was best for her. You were focused on you. Think about what it took for her to make that decision. She blew up her life so she could start over."

"She blew up my life, too. And I didn't ask her to."

"Maybe you did--by being unaware--you asked her to do what she did. If you were paying attention and if you were a center of influence, somewhat aware of your effect, you would have seen it coming. There would have been time to change it, or at least to be prepared for it. Maybe instead of being angry you should consider being grateful to her. Her chance to start again is also yours."

"I didn't want to start again."

"I get that, Kevin, but here you are talking to a strange woman in Las Vegas instead of teaching school. The question is, what are you doing with your new life? Years ago you crawled into this comfortable little space and fell asleep. There was life out there to be had, but you mostly slept through it, like the majority of people. Now you have this great chance to live, to figure out what you want and to do it. You have this opportunity to become a real adult--to look inside yourself and find what's there. Instead, I see you looking outside yourself for ways to make yourself feel good-- partying, women, gambling, shows. Instead of grabbing life by the horns and riding it, you're avoiding it. You're still a center of attention, looking at people and situations for how they might benefit you."

"I wasn't expecting to get my butt kicked today." Kevin shook his head.

"I know." Rachel smiled sweetly. "You thought I was placed here to make you feel good."

Kevin threw his hands up. "All right. I give up. Even after you told me you weren't interested I was still hoping."

"Look. It's not your fault the marriage ended. It's not hers either. It happened. Blaming her diminishes you. You can't really move on until you let go. You can't let go until you take full responsibility. Once you let go, you need to see the possibilities and go after them." Rachel finished her coffee. "Uck! It's cold!"

Kevin noticed his own cup was empty. He waved to the waitress and pointed to their cups. "How did you become so all-knowing?"

"I'm not all-knowing, just observant. My success as a dancer depended on my ability to read people. I've spent my free time reading and learning. I watch people, and I reflect upon myself. The last two years I've been hiking in the desert. It's a great place to think and meditate and pray. I looked at myself and at my life, and I didn't like what I saw. I recognized that nothing in my life was anyone's fault, and it was up to me to change it."

The waitress refilled Rachel's cup. "More tea or juice, Sir?"

"Please." He slid his teacup toward her.

Kevin handed her a ten and thanked her. He turned to Rachel. "How did you change?" He looked into her eyes, searching for the source of her confidence.

"I decided what was valuable and what wasn't. I paid attention to the stories I was telling myself, and I tossed out what wasn't true. That was hard, but worth it. I had so many beliefs about myself and the world. I looked at every situation and every relationship in my life and asked myself who I was being in that situation and what was my effect."

"What do you mean by stories?"

"We all tell ourselves stories. I treated the women I worked with nicely, but I saw myself as better than most of them. That was my story. I read books on psychology, philosophy, spirituality, and religion, and they didn't. I earned a Masters' degree in Psychology, and they didn't. I'm smart. Some of the girls were getting degrees, too, but I still thought I was better. Competition between dancers can be brutal, but I found ways to create some peace and cooperation. I had the skills and awareness to do that, and a lot of them didn't.

"I saw myself as smarter than the men who came to the club, because I could easily manipulate them. That's another story. The male ego is easy to build up, and just as easy to break down. I know how to get a man to want to spend his money on me. When I saw myself, I didn't like the person in the mirror, and the stories weren't enough to rationalize my lifestyle."

"That one about men is probably true, but I've found that women are easy to manipulate, too."

"How did that feel?"

"Well, honestly, I felt in control, powerful, attractive. I may not be attractive to you, but I was to several other women."

Rachel laughed. "Who said you aren't attractive? You're very attractive. I'm just not interested in casual sex or playing games."

"What *are* you interested in?" Kevin removed his sunglasses and hooked them on his shirt.

She sipped on her coffee, staring into her cup. "Being alone. A closer walk with Spirit. Beginning a new life. High quality friendships."

"Thanks for telling me that. I interrupted your story. You were talking about not liking what you saw in yourself. What didn't you like?" Kevin focused on what she was about to say.

"Okay." Rachel looked up to the right as if retrieving something from her memory. "There's nothing wrong with the skills I have with people. The skills are good, but the motive behind them didn't feel right. I was a center of attention. Every client was a mark, a target, and I prided myself that I could spot the guys who could deliver. I told myself that we were consenting adults and that there was nothing wrong with what I was doing. It wasn't wrong in any moral sense. Guys and sometimes couples came to the clubs for a good time. I delivered, and they paid me for it. That seemed fair."

Kevin nodded. "It does sound fair."

Rachel shook her head slightly from side to side. "It became wrong for me. I had to ask: 'Is this the person I want to be?' It wasn't. I started changing, doing my best to connect with each person who came to the club. I saw each man--his sadness, his insecurities, his anger, his loneliness, his need to be touched, to be noticed. I turned from being entertainer/actress/manipulator to more like a counselor and healer. To some degree, dancers played a counselor role with at least some of their clients, but I took it further. I spent extra time without expecting to be paid. I asked questions to help them clarify their thoughts and feelings. You know what really surprised me?"

Kevin shook his head.

"I was making just as much money. The demand to see me, to have a private dance with me grew. The other girls started accusing me of doing anything and everything sexually to make myself popular, but it wasn't true. I was connecting with people. Actually, if anything, I was being less sexual. I saw inside them, and they could feel it. For a lot of them, it may have been the only time they'd ever felt that kind of connection."

Rachel paused, curling a lock of her hair with her thumb and forefinger, staring off into the distance.

Kevin gently touched her other hand. "So what did you do?"

"Well, the demands were so high that I couldn't keep it up. More and more I needed time alone. I went to the desert every day, hiking, reflecting, asking myself: 'Who am I being?' I liked who I was being. Not just at the club. I saw that I could easily connect with people at stores and restaurants, and any place where I met them. It became easier outside the club because the expectations weren't there. I wasn't being paid, so I was free to be myself."

Kevin asked himself what it was like to be Rachel. He grew sad as he imagined her doing her job. "You know, I went to a couple of clubs last week and paid for private dances. It was fun for me to have these beautiful women dance for me and *pretend* they were into me while gyrating in my lap. But the experience lasted a short time, and then they went to the next guy. It couldn't have been much fun for you to do that dozens of times a night, every night."

Rachel looked at him and breathed deeply. "Like you, I enjoyed the control and being attractive. And the money! But, yeah, it got old. I learned to steel myself and become someone else when I was dancing. Several years took their toll on me. When I reflected on my life, emotions bubbled up. Then they flooded my mind and body, and I spent many of my hikes sobbing. Years of repressed anger and hurt came out. It wasn't all mine. It was the energies of hundreds of men, most of whom were unhappy, that I had taken on. When you make close physical contact you can tell yourself it has no effect, but it isn't true."

"Maybe I should avoid strip clubs altogether." Kevin shook his head from side to side. "I'm sorry."

"For what?"

"For seeing you that way--for seeing those women at the clubs as non-persons. I mean, I wasn't unkind to them or disrespectful, but I wasn't interested in who they were either. I'm not being patronizing. I just imagined being you and having to entertain one person after another and pretending to be into them."

Rachel smiled and nodded. "That was cool. Thank you. It has taken some time to heal from all of that. I have to re-learn to be sensitive to touch, and to let myself feel. I took a break from romance and sex and men. This is the first real conversation I've had with a man in months."

"You're welcome. And thanks for picking me to be the one you talk to. Now, back to your story."

Rachel fixed her look on Kevin as if seeing him with new eyes. "As I was saying, I stepped back from my life and asked who I was being with my parents, my friends, with boyfriends. Mostly I'd been a center of attention, expecting them to meet my needs. That's when it became clear. I needed to grow up. I *wanted* to grow up.

"One day I had an argument with a friend of mine. We said some mean things to each other, and I was angry. So I applied what I'd been thinking. I asked myself who I was being in that argument. It wasn't hard to figure out." Rachel stopped, and looked into Kevin's eyes, as if deciding whether to continue or not."

"So, who were you being?" Kevin leaned in a little, his elbows on the table.

Rachel leaned in, also, her face about two feet from his. "I was being the victim. I was self-righteous--focused on everything I thought she was doing to me. I gave no thought to what effect I had on her. I justified myself and added up all the reasons I was right, and she was wrong. When I looked at it, I was arrogant-- convinced I was smarter and better than her. Then I saw how I acted when I was telling myself that story. I couldn't believe what a conceited bitch I'd been--talking down to her, being critical, and then wondering how she could be so upset with me."

"What did you do?"

"I baked her some chocolate chip cookies and apologized. I told her how much she meant to me, and that I valued our friendship. We both cried and hugged each other. Then we talked and laughed and ate cookies. I love her so much." She sniffed and blinked, her eyes wet. "I'll miss her."

Rachel picked up her napkin and dabbed her eyes. She smiled. "It wasn't enough to ask myself who I was being in each situation in my life. That was a valuable and revealing question. It still is, but I needed to go deeper. I asked myself who I am. I've asked that question hundreds of times. 'Who am I?' Mostly I've come up with who I'm not. Still asking. I'm growing up, and I know I'm not done yet. I have further to go, but it won't be in Vegas."

"Where are you going?"

"I'm heading east to visit my parents. After that, I'm going to Atlanta. You know what *Atlanta* means?"

"No, I don't." Kevin shrugged and slid his chair deeper into the shade as he felt the sun heating his skin.

"It means *balance*. I could use some balance in my life. I'll miss the desert, but I think I'll like the trees. I have friends there, and it looks like a good place to start over. It's more intuitive than that. I can give you conscious reasons for why, but I really don't know. Atlanta is calling me."

"I'm sure you'll do fine."

"What makes you say that?"

"You're strong and confident, and you know what you want. You also got my attention. I've been listening, and I forgot to check you out." Kevin smiled.

"Thanks for that," Rachel smiled back. "I do feel confident. I think people draw to themselves life situations that reflect their inner thoughts and beliefs. We don't just influence the people in our lives; we influence what happens to us. I know that the universe will provide what I require. It may not always be what I want, but it'll be what I need. I see myself succeeding in Georgia."

Kevin heard Mick Jagger singing in his head: *You can't always get what you want...* "I wish I had your confidence," Kevin looked down at the table. *You can't always get what you want...* "I'm heading to Tucson because that was the only possibility I saw outside of staying in Michigan. If this restaurant deal doesn't work out, I don't know what I'll do." *But if you try sometimes, you just might find, you get what you need...* He looked at her again, his eyes questioning as if she might have an answer.

"You might try hiking in the desert. Give yourself a break from the partying and women and reflect." She paused, studying him. "Who are you, Kevin? What do you want?" She touched his hand with two fingers and searched his face with her green eyes.

Kevin resisted the magnetism of her eyes and concentrated on his thoughts and feelings. "I'm just a guy. I want to feel better. I want to belong somewhere."

"You're not just a guy. You're more than that. Take a good look at yourself. Start asking yourself who you are and what you really want. Get quiet and listen."

"I haven't listened like that very often. I learned to meditate, but I don't do it much." Kevin raised his eyebrows.

"You're here. You reflected on your life, decided you didn't like it, and made a change. Something inside called to you--said it was time to move on. You listened. It took courage to listen and more to act. So many people ignore their Inner Voice. Give yourself credit, Kevin."

"Thanks. I'm still not too sure about all of this."

Rachel reached across the table again, and this time squeezed his left hand. "You'll be okay. Take it one step at a time and see what develops. Trust."

Kevin felt electricity flowing from his hand up through his arm. "Trust who, or trust what?"

"Trust God or Spirit or whatever you call it. Trust yourself."

"I'm a little lukewarm on God right now. Never been a big believer. I don't go to church."

"Doesn't matter." Her voice was crisp and certain. "The answer's not in a church, nothing against churches. The answers you seek are within you. Churches, preachers, books--all they can do is support you and help point out a path. Look inside. Pray, meditate, contemplate, breathe--listen. My church is the desert. My fellow congregants are the succulents, the birds, and the other creatures.

When I'm in the desert and I think about being alive and being connected to God--when I see all the beauty around me--and I look at the life before me, I feel incredible joy. I feel loved and blessed, and more beautiful than ever. My best prayer is 'Thank you.'" Rachel's face shone like a sun, giving off its own light and warmth.

Kevin's heart quickened in excitement. He felt a bond forming between them. It was the first such connection he had made since being in Las Vegas. "So you've been praying and meditating for eight months? You didn't work or do anything else?"

"That's all I did the month after I quit. After that I took a job at a hospice. I emptied bed pans, changed linen, helped the staff and the patients. It felt good to get down off my high heels and do something humbling that comforted people. I looked forward to each day caring for them. *I* was doing the care, but the patients were caring for me. It was my way of shedding all the glitz and glam of the past several years. It was healing. Yesterday was my last day. I visited each of my patients and cried with them. I was so happy to have met and loved the people there. I was so sad to be leaving them." Her eyes teared up again.

"Why did you leave? Why not just stay if it made you happy?"

"It was time to go. I knew all along it was a temporary situation--my transition job. I helped people to make their transition, and they helped me make mine."

Kevin and Rachel sat quietly, basking in the moment. He watched her playing with her hair again, curling it up and straightening it out with thumb and forefinger. She noticed him watching and broke the silence. "It helps me process."

Kevin ran his fingers through his own hair. "I'm curious. Why did you let me sit with you? I mean, if you knew I was hitting on you, and you had no interest in that, why let me sit down?"

Rachel's gaze was soft, yet penetrating. "I looked past the surface. You were a predator on the outside, but something in your eyes, your tone of voice, something in the way you moved, told me there was more to you. My Inner Voice said okay. Also, you went off script right away." She grinned.

Kevin smiled back. "I did, didn't I? I guess you've heard so many scripts that no one could manipulate you anyway.

"No person is immune to manipulation."

"Maybe not. Do you think we might see each other again, sometime in the future?"

"When and if I create a relationship with a man, he'll have to be an adult. The girl who danced for everyone has become the woman who is very picky. Right now you're a friend. We can email each other or do Facebook. You may feel an urge to see me again. If I feel the same, we'll get together. We'll see what happens."

"Thanks for calling me your friend. I like that."

Rachel studied him for a few moments, nodded slightly, and softly sighed. She reached for a napkin, retrieved a pen from her purse, and began writing.

"What are you writing?"

"Something for you to remember me by." She continued writing. Next, she turned the napkin around so he could read it.

> Kevin,
>
> You are a center of influence.
> Everything you think, feel, say, and do
> has an effect and determines your future.
> Who are you? What do you want?
> Love and Blessings, Rachel Lindsay.

Kevin read the napkin. "Thanks. I'll keep this." He folded it and put it in his wallet.

Rachel picked up another napkin and wrote her e-mail address on it. She handed it to him. "Let me know how it goes in Tucson. My sense is that you're going to have a more exciting life there than you had back in Michigan."

"I hope that's a good thing."

"Of course it's good. It's all good." Rachel stood up. "It's time for me to go, Kevin. May I have a hug?"

"Definitely."

They embraced, and Kevin felt her warmth. He felt the heartbeat in her temple next to his jaw. Although he couldn't put it into words, he saw her. He understood what she meant about knowing that she was beautiful. They stepped back from each other and made eye contact. No longer fearing being lost in those green pools, he knew her as a friend, and that somehow, somewhere, they would meet again. They strolled into the hotel lobby

Rachel faced him, taking both of his hands in hers. "Good-bye, Kevin. Take care of yourself, and get out of this town. Go start your restaurant." She squeezed his hands, kissed him on the cheek, smiled, turned, and walked away.

"Good-bye, Rachel." He said as she turned. He sighed and watched her disappear through the entranceway. For a short time he had unexpectedly brushed against someone real, and just as quickly, she was gone.

Kevin returned to his room and gathered his things. Within the hour he checked out and headed toward Tucson, Arizona. Rachel was firmly embedded in him, the indentations of her handprints on his back and hands still emanating her energy--the feel of her kiss still on his cheek. He tried to think about the women he had bedded, the gaming, the shows, and the food. None of it seemed worth recalling. Just the same, he was glad he'd done it. And, glad he'd stopped! He smiled to himself. *No regrets!* He thought about Al, the restaurant, and Tucson. It was time to do what he came out west to do.

Chapter Nine

Kevin contemplated being a center of influence, as he entered US-93 and headed toward the state line. Certainly he had cared about his wife, his daughters, his parents, his brother. He had cared about his students and his colleagues. It wasn't that he didn't care, but he had usually thought of them in terms of his needs, not in terms of their needs. He had failed to see his impact on them.

Hadn't he practiced being a center of influence when he taught classes? He knew how to make his students laugh, and how to get their attention--had always been considered one of the "cool" teachers, but had he truly sensed what was going on in their minds and hearts? Did he really *see* his students? Doubt and regret punctured his self-image as a good teacher. Perhaps Mr. Neill, High School English Teacher, had not been as good as he'd assumed. Maybe he should have spent less time trying to be cool and more time being warm.

"How did Dana experience *me*?" He asked himself out loud. He really didn't know, having never asked that question. He thought about his daughters. He had been a good father, provided for them, and had been protective--helped them with their homework, coached them in soccer, attended their high school sporting events and their concerts. He had driven them to several campuses when they were deciding which college to attend.

Despite all the "good dad" things he had done, did he really know who they were as people? What did they want out of their lives? He didn't know their respective views of the world. *Hell, I don't even know my own view of the world anymore. Dana was right and so was Rachel. I've been asleep.*

He had always thought of himself as an adult. Although fourteen years older than Rachel, she seemed more an adult than he was. *I'm a failure. For twenty-one years I was supposed to help high school students, and my own two children, grow up, and I hadn't grown up myself.*

He tried to think of his colleagues at the high school and which of them might have been true adults. There was Ted Johnson. Ted was well-liked by both students and staff--genuinely kind and seemed to always be aware of what people needed. Ted knew the right thing to say in any situation. Whenever students or staff members were in conflict, they usually went to Ted. He would listen to both sides without judging, acknowledge how each person felt, and make helpful suggestions. "I never really appreciated Ted for all that he did." Kevin spoke out loud again.

When Kevin and Dana split up, Ted understood what Kevin felt. He was one of the few people to whom Kevin could express his anger. Ted's directness cut through Kevin's stormy thoughts and fantasies. One day last spring Ted came into his classroom after school and asked him how he was doing. As he told Ted about his separation, he mentioned driving by the house most nights, to see if Dana had any visitors. Ted put his hand on Kevin's shoulder and looked directly into Kevin's eyes. "What would you do if you saw a strange car in front of the house?"

Kevin stammered in response saying that he probably would just park and watch awhile.

"You want to know if he's spending the night. I understand. You had over twenty years with Dana, and you still love her. But, will that bring Dana back to you? Do you think if you spy on her or if you confront her--make her feel guilty, that she'll want you?"

Kevin admitted it would not bring her back.

"Then, Kevin, one more question. This driving by her house or sitting in a car outside watching, does it make you feel better or does it make you feel worse?"

"It doesn't feel good at all. It feels like I'm obsessed."

"It's understandable that you feel compelled to check on Dana. My concern is, where will it take you?"

"I've imagined catching her with someone and telling them both off." Kevin stared into space, focusing his vision inward. The scene played out in his head--yelling, self-righteous indignation, defensiveness--the imaginary sequence causing pain but also being somewhat satisfying, then spiraling downward into torment and suffering. "Maybe it's not a good plan."

A rueful grin unfurled across Ted's face. "You think?" His smile softened. "Let her go, Kevin. Let her live her life, and you start living yours."

"I know. You're right." He wiped the dampness from his eyes.

"I think you'll not only feel better, but stronger for it. Appreciate the good times you had. She's still the mother of your daughters. Love her by letting her go."

Kevin noticed he was already in Arizona having unconsciously crossed the state line while lost in the past. *Letting go.* Those had been wise words. Kevin had stopped feeding his jealous fantasies and given up driving by the house. He'd held on to his anger. Using Rachel's question, he asked: "Who am I being when I'm angry at Dana, and how does that affect the people around me?"

His mind fast-forwarded from Michigan to Vegas--his second night and the dinner date that had seemed perfect. Alicia was a lovely redhead who had been in Vegas for a convention. About halfway through the three hundred dollar dinner and too much champagne, Kevin began talking about his divorce. Hoping to garner some sympathy, he blamed Dana for breaking up his family.

The strategy had backfired. Alicia told him she doubted Dana was such a bad person, and he was obviously feeling sorry for himself. Then she wanted to leave, and she would find her own way back to her hotel. He was angry and thought Alicia had used him to get a free dinner. He had soothed his bruised ego at a nearby strip club where he could pay for some attention.

That was pretty rude. She didn't even say thank you. Wait. The question was who was I being? Not, who was Alicia being?

He had stopped telling his divorce story after that. Reviewing his material on picking up women, Kevin decided to stay on script, and he successfully wined, dined, and slept with several women. *So, who was I being that night with Alicia, when I told my story? Rejected. Poor me--cherishing my anger and my victimhood. Not very attractive! Why would Alicia want to spend her evening with a guy like that? She wouldn't!* Kevin shook his head as he recalled making the incident all Alicia's fault.

He thought about the man he'd been with Dana. He had always seen himself as a liberated male--helped around the house, took care of the girls; and had been very good at doing little favors for her. In the early days of their relationship he had wanted to know everything about her. He delighted in learning about her thoughts and feelings on everything. *But what happened? What happened was she started losing interest. Over time our love life faded to almost nothing. She stopped giving me attention, and I didn't feel like listening to her.* He couldn't remember the last time he'd asked her what she thought or how she felt about anything--couldn't remember when he'd last shared his own thoughts and feelings with her. Dana wanted aliveness. She wanted a spark, and he had become spark-less. *I wanted love and affection, and she... she rejected me.*

The last ten years or so were spent avoiding contact, avoiding life, content to play and watch sports, sit in front of the TV, socialize, go to work, and keep up house maintenance. A few years ago she had asked him to go to counseling, and he'd belittled the request. *Why did I do that?* He remembered avoiding her when she wanted to talk about their relationship. *Was I afraid of looking at us--at me? What was I afraid of? Growing up? I guess that was convenient. The relationship sucked, and it was her fault. No responsibility on my part.*

Maybe Dana wanted to grow up, to be responsible, to have an adult relationship, and he didn't. She wanted to become a woman while he was still a boy--still a center of attention, expecting the world to revolve around him and his needs. The realization flashed like lightning, illuminating the dark skies of his mind.

Gravel crunched beneath his tires as he pulled off the highway into a rest stop, and skidded to a stop. He turned the key, silencing the engine, but the cooling fan continued whirring.

Grateful he was the only person there, he stepped out of his car, put his hands in his pockets, and ambled down a dirt path. The bright sun cooked his body, and he was thirsty. Grabbing a bottle of water from a vending machine, he sat on a bench in the shade. Except for the intermittent sounds of cars and trucks rushing by on the highway, the desert was silent.

Who was I when I was picking up women? Cool, calm, confident, detached, good listener, game player. Expressing admiration one moment, slipping in a little criticism the next, keeping them off-guard. Was that really me? Definitely a center of attention, but playing like a center of influence. Meeting their needs for the sole purpose of meeting my own needs. It was fun, though! And I feel a lot more confident with women. And it wasn't like I was forcing anyone to do anything they didn't already want to do--just manipulating.

Elbows on knees, he put his face in his hands. *I wasn't a nice guy after that second night. But I don't want to be nice. I was nice to Alicia--whiny, but nice. After that, not nice, but not cruel either.* Rachel's words were etched in his mind. *Don't be nice; be you. Who are you, Kevin?*

"Who's the real me? Who would I be if I wasn't a center of attention? Who would I be if I fully participated in life? What if I saw other people in terms of their needs? If I took the risk to be myself and speak with honesty?" He was quiet for a few minutes and the answer appeared across the screen of his mind. *You'd be a man. You'd be grown up!*

"Yes." He said to himself. "I'd be a man, the kind of man that a woman like Rachel would be attracted to. I wouldn't be casting myself as a self-righteous victim in some sorry drama concocted to solicit sympathy from my audience. I wouldn't be playing games to get laid. At least, I don't think I would."

Kevin felt both ridiculous and relieved. Both Ted and Mike had tried to tell him. Derek had offered a good example of self-reflection and owning up. And now Rachel. For months this realization had been sitting in the outskirts of his mind, waiting to be discovered. He'd paid it lip service. He felt foolish for the years he'd spent being such a boy, and a victim--but relieved that he'd faced the truth. He resolved that he'd do better.

He stood up and stretched, reaching upward, as if connecting the brown earth with the bright blue sky. Pulled outward into the vast, rocky landscape, he could no longer find a reason to be angry with Dana.

The rest of the drive to Tucson was uneventful. He stopped in Kingman for food and gas, and called ahead to a resort on the west side of Tucson. A quiet night and some golf in the morning would feel good. After making his reservations and tee time, he texted Al and invited him to play. Al called him just after he passed Phoenix and accepted the invitation.

Kevin arrived in Tucson at about 8:00 p.m. As he exited his Escape, the wind picked up, and he noticed what appeared to be a whirlwind. It wound it's way across the terrain just outside the parking lot, whipping up dust and pebbles. *What is that thing? That's life in Vegas. Chaotic! Always on the move. Spinning in circles.* The whirlwind lost it's momentum as it hit one of the fairways. Kevin grabbed his bags and checked into his room.

The next morning Al joined him for breakfast. Kevin felt underdressed in his shorts and tee shirt as Al strode in with his Boss golf shirt and cotton gabardine pants. Al shook his hand and greeted him with a professional smile. Al's curly black hair and mustache were streaked with grays rendering him suave and sophisticated. Although they were the same height, Kevin felt shorter next to him. They shook hands and carried their clubs to the golf cart.

Golf was unspectacular, but rolling fairways, and the well-kept greens in front of a backdrop of brownish-red hills and mountains dotted with cacti, cast a spell on him. At first, it was difficult to focus on Al as his eyes constantly drifted across the landscape. Noticing that Al wasn't saying much, Kevin forced himself to start a conversation.

Kevin asked him questions about the past twenty years, and Al proffered mostly one word answers. He thought back to their college days. *He didn't really talk about himself back then, either.* A prickly coldness chilled his internal organs. *I guess that's just the way Al is.* He heard his father's words again. *Make sure you have an attorney look over your agreement with Al. Keep your eyes open.* He tried to dismiss the feeling by telling himself that he was committed to this venture. No way was he driving back to Michigan now.

He thought back to his conversation with Rachel and her honesty and directness. As they rode their cart along the ninth fairway, Kevin hit the brake.

"Why are you stopping?" Al lifted his sunglasses and peered beneath them.

Kevin swallowed his nervousness. "We're talking about going into business together, and I'm investing a lot money--just about all I have. If you're not going to talk to me I'm pulling out."

"What do you mean? I *am* talking! God, you sound like my wife."

"One word answers is not what I call talking. If I'm going to trust you and be in business with you, I need more. I can't trust a guy I don't know."

"I'm not a big talker."

"No shit! Here's an example; I asked you how things were going with Jenny and you said, 'Fine.' That's not enough. I need to know if you guys are stable. I want to know if you still love her."

"I usually don't talk about personal stuff like that. It's none of your business."

"Well, you need to talk to *me* about it. If you two were divorced in a year that could affect our business. If you aren't getting along that will affect your mood at work. So it *is* my business."

Al stared at Kevin for a minute and then shook his head. "I love my wife. We're good. We've been married for twenty plus years, and we're doing well. Jenny supports me one hundred percent in this business. There. Is that better?"

"That's a start. No more one word answers like *fine* or *good*. I want explanations. I want the truth. Am I clear?" Kevin surprised himself, but he felt his confidence growing.

"Yes. You're clear. You didn't used to be like this. What the hell happened?"

This is ironic. "A friend taught me the value of being direct and honest."

Finally they discussed the restaurant. Al spoke more, but his tone was all business. He made it clear that he would handle the financial matters--payroll, purchasing, bank relations, taxes, marketing, and repaying loans. Kevin was not strong in business, accounting, or marketing, so he ceded those tasks. They would each put in fifty-thousand dollars and borrow the rest. Kevin would oversee the hiring, train and manage the staff, take care of room set-up, and be accountable for customer service. They would work on the menu, together, with the chef and with some assistance from Al's wife, Jenny.

Finishing up around noon, Al softened a little and suggested: "Why don't you follow me and have lunch at my house. Jenny will be there, and you can meet her."

"Sounds good." Give me a few minutes to clean up, and I'll be right down."

Kevin followed Al's blue Lexus out of the resort. They headed toward the north side of Tucson. In Michigan, leaves prepared to turn from green to a rich array of reds, oranges, yellows, and browns. Here, Sentinel Peak, also known as the "A" Mountain, rose up like a pyramid on his left, and Tucson was surrounded by mountains and desert. He vowed he would take time to hike and reflect. *It worked for Rachel.*

The ride took almost forty-five minutes. As they entered the Catalina Foothills, Kevin noticed the spectacular views of mountains to the Northeast and the city center to the South. Many of the homes were set on one and two acre lots, and there was a wide variance in sizes and styles. As he pulled into Al's circular drive he was surprised at the luxury. The masonry was washed with mortar and had a rich, yet earthy look to it.

He stepped out of his car and joined Al on the walkway. The courtyard entry was landscaped with beautiful desert plants, the names of which he had no idea. Brightly colored flowers were arranged in circular patterns in pots and in hanging baskets. The walkway was bordered by reddish-brown gravel, neatly raked, reminding Kevin of the little Zen garden he used to keep on his desk at school. Al opened a wrought-iron gate beneath an archway, and led Kevin to a pair of oak doors under an arch.

The doors opened, and Jenny appeared with a smile. She stood about five-feet-seven, with light brown hair, slightly tanned complexion, and bright blue eyes. Kevin instantly felt at ease.

"Welcome, Kevin. It's so good to finally meet you in person." Jenny stepped forward and embraced him. She was dressed simply, yet elegantly in mid-length white cotton shorts and an olive, short-sleeved blouse. She carried herself as the owner of the space in which she lived.

Kevin followed her toward the back of the house, and over her shoulder she asked questions about his family. They passed through a large vaulted-ceiling living room with two cream leather sofas and two chairs to match. The mahogany dining room table, with its inlaid tiles, was large enough for eight people. He noticed the kitchen to his left, across a large granite counter. It contained both a stove and a grill as well as a large butcher-block table in the center of the room. The sweet smells of onion and spices hung in the air, arousing both his curiosity and his hunger.

The dining room peered through sliding glass doors onto a deck. "You have a beautiful home, Jenny." Motioning toward the doors he added, "And great views!"

"Thank you." She handed Kevin a bottle of water. "I'm sure you'll want this. We're very blessed to live here. Al has been quite successful in his businesses over the years, and that has made all this possible."

"She's being modest." Al added as he entered behind them. "Jenny is the queen of multilevel. She's built up a huge business organization over the years. Now she rakes in the money without having to work too hard."

"I wouldn't say I'm raking it in, but I do well. I have a strong downline that I've built and nurtured over the past twenty years. They take good care of me. I started the business so I could work and be home for our son, Matt. He went off to college a few years ago and is now living in San Francisco. We're very proud of him. Of course, I miss him."

The conversation continued with talk of children and colleges, the differing climates between Michigan and Arizona, and ideas about the restaurant. Kevin and Al moved to a table on the deck overlooking the swimming pool and in the distance, downtown Tucson. The smell of grilled seafood drifted from the kitchen as Jenny prepared their lunch. Kevin's mouth watered.

Jenny served Nicoise salads with freshly grilled tuna and baby red-skinned potatoes, along with French onion soup and French bread. There was a bottle of Tavel wine on the table. Al poured it, and Kevin took a sip of the dry, crisp, rose' that seemingly evaporated off his tongue. He worked his way through the salad, layer by layer, tasting each item and enjoying it thoroughly. The tuna was charred on the outside and pink in the middle. The juices exploded in his mouth, causing him to pause and shake his head.

"Are you okay, Kevin?" Jenny leaned toward him with concern in her eyes.

He slowly swallowed the remnants of tuna. "I'm great. This is incredible! I've never tasted fish like this. What did you do to it?"

"Ah, that's a secret recipe."

Kevin sipped the soup from his spoon. "Wow! This French onion, also, is the best I've had! Jenny, this is magnificent. Will you cook for us?"

"Thank you, Kevin. I won't cook at the restaurant, but I'll let you use my recipes."

"Please do. Al, we are definitely putting this salad and soup on the menu."

Al smiled and patted Jenny on the back. "Now you know why I have to work out every day. She's been feeding me like this for twenty years."

The food, the wine, and the conversation made for a delightful afternoon. Al warmed up, and they shared memories of their college days. "This is my new life." Kevin made a sweeping motion with his hand. "Beautiful people, tasty food, great scenery, and a warm climate. I think I've made the right choice!"

Jenny and Al smiled, and they toasted to new beginnings. Soon it was late afternoon, and Kevin wanted to drive back to the resort before dark. Al and Jenny conferred privately for a few moments.

"Kevin, why don't you stay here tomorrow night. We'd love to have you until you find your own place. Besides, that'll make it easier for us to work together. You could meet me here around eleven thirty, and we'll drive into the city and get some lunch. While we're there, we can visit our future restaurant site. What do you say?"

Jenny nodded and smiled. "The guest bedroom has its own bath, so I think you'll be comfortable."

The time with Jenny and Al had eased Kevin's initial discomfort. *It's like there are two Al's.* He pasted a smile over his concern. "Thanks. What a generous offer!"

Kevin hugged them both and turned to leave. He stopped. "One more thing. A good friend suggested that I hike in the desert, you know, to clear my head, reflect. Do you know any good places?"

Jenny looked at Al. "We like Pima Canyon. It's north of the city--not hard to find and not far from here. We'll take you there."

"Thanks. I'll see you tomorrow."

Chapter Ten

Kevin moved into the guest room at the Stewart's home, and over the next few months, immersed himself in the business. Jenny took him to Pima Canyon. She told him to take plenty of water. "This isn't Michigan where you have abundant water and humidity. Also, there are lots of rocks, so wear good hiking boots."

Kevin listened to her on the water, but insisted on wearing his old basketball shoes for hiking. They trekked in about two miles and then back. She told him it would be less effort with good shoes, but he insisted that the extra struggle was good for staying in shape. Kevin felt a kinship with the canyon that he couldn't explain, and promised himself to hike there every week. He didn't keep that vow, but managed to return occasionally.

At the end of October he rented a condo on the north side of Tucson, and Jenny helped him furnish it. In December he flew back to Michigan for a few days at Christmas to visit his parents and his daughters. While spending time with Jessica and Melissa, he ran into Dana. She looked him over. "How are you, Kevin? The Arizona sun has given you a nice tan."

"Thanks. I'm doing well." He noticed her hair was cut short, but she looked stunning--and younger. "I like the haircut. Very attractive! How are you?"

"Thanks. I'm doing well." She smiled and approached him, stopping a few feet away.

Why not? He stepped forward and embraced her, and she received him. They held each other for several seconds, and Kevin confirmed that his anger had fled.

"The girls told me about your restaurant in Tucson. I'm happy for you." She nodded, then raised her eyebrows.

"Thanks. We're opening next month. I heard you were promoted at work. Congratulations!" They chatted awhile, his daughters within earshot, obviously pleased their parents were speaking to each other.

* * *

The holidays passed pleasantly, and Kevin was eager to return to warmer temperatures and the January opening of the Calico Grill. He had prepared during the past few months by visiting dozens of area restaurants, observing the behaviors of managers and their staffs, noticing how he felt as a patron in each establishment, and taking notes. When he discovered good service he returned to see if it was consistent. He wrote down the names of outstanding waiters and waitresses, and attempted to lure them to the Grill. Some of them accepted.

The day before opening, Kevin stood with Al before their waitstaff, bartenders, hostesses, and kitchen staff. The dining room hummed with hushed voices. Like the first day of school, a room full of fresh, curious faces, all wanted to know what this new experience would be like. "The guest is first. You are here to serve them, to meet their needs. Smile; greet them; ask what you can do for them; and do what you can to make their experience great. Your guests are the people who will visit us because they want to feel good, and they are also your teammates here at the Calico Grill."

He studied their faces for traces of understanding, pleased that everyone made eye contact with him. "Great food, great service, and a beautiful environment add up to an awesome dining experience. If we can give that to our guests and to each other, people will come, and they will return again and again." As he nodded and smiled Al began to applaud, and the whole staff joined in. The applause energized him, and he was absolutely certain they would be successful.

The success they enjoyed was a little less than expected during the first few months, but enough to keep them in business. Kevin continued engaging with the staff, being a center of influence, always clarifying the vision and enrolling his staff members in it. Those who got it performed their roles with enthusiasm. The few who did not understand or care to perform the high level of service he expected were asked to leave.

Within six months the restaurant's reputation for great food and service captured the public's attention. Word of mouth, local articles and reviews drew customers to the Grill, and it became a popular place on weekends. Profits increased. Kevin hired an assistant manager, which freed him to enjoy more of a social life.

Al never asked him about employee matters, and Kevin asked very little about their finances. Money was coming in, the employees received their paychecks every week, and the bank and the suppliers were paid on time. Al gave him a quick summary, but Kevin was lost whenever he mentioned payables, withholding taxes, and other financial details. When it came to quality and customer service, Kevin focused on the specifics.

Kevin purchased his condo with the thought that he would eventually buy a house like the one Al and Jenny had. He dated several women over the first two years and enjoyed quarterly trips to his favorite spots in Mexico--always able to find a date for a weekend in Puerto Vallarta or Cabo San Lucas. He kept his work life and his social life in separate packages, the focus being on the work. Several of his dates held promise, but none of them blossomed into a relationship. He left behind his seduction techniques and approached each woman as himself, trying to offer the kind of honesty he had experienced with Rachel. She was his new standard, and no one could compare to her.

Then he met Veronica. Ronnie, as everyone called her, was a successful real estate agent, and Jenny's friend. The Stewarts hosted a party with *hors d'oeuvres* and drinks on a Friday evening. Kevin left the restaurant early to attend. Upon arrival, he opted for the frozen peach margarita over the usual beer. Gradually making his way to one of the Italian leather sofas, he settled in on the end to enjoy his drink and watch people. They were gathered in twos and threes, and there was a friendly buzz throughout the rooms, with intermittent peals of laughter.

It was as if he were simultaneously watching several scenes from a play, as an audience of one. *Cocktail parties are not my thing. Maybe I'll finish my drink, say hello to Jenny and leave.* From his sofa Kevin could see Jenny smiling and talking to two guests. She was the consummate hostess: relaxed, having a good time, and on top of everything. *I'm the same way at work.*

"Do you mind if I sit down?"

She appeared out of nowhere. Jolted from his musings, he was instantly held prisoner. Sensuality wafted from the pores of her skin. He breathed in her scent and felt it warming his body from the inside out. He wondered if this was what Whitman meant by the phrase, *I sing the body electric.* His own cells sang; his blood crackled; his brain disconnected; and his body was in charge.

"Well, if you're not going to say anything I'm going to sit somewhere else." She stood over him, smiling.

Her voice cut through the paralyzing mist. As if groping for a light switch in a dark room, he frantically searched his mind for clarity. Forcing himself to stand up, he offered his hand. "I'm Kevin."

"I'm Ronnie" She smiled again, taking his hand in both of hers. She eased them both onto the couch, Kevin landing first, and Ronnie gliding onto the soft leather next to him.

Kevin was captivated by her brown eyes, her golden tanned skin and her off-white, linen, strapless, summer dress. Her hair was black, parted in the middle, layered and curly down to her shoulders. Ronnie slipped her left hand behind his neck. "Kevin, put your right hand on my left shoulder."

Kevin's hand moved of its own accord to her shoulder. Ronnie gently pulled him to her, and their lips met with a kiss, long and sweet. The gentle suction sent waves of pleasure through him. He felt the heat in his groin. As the kiss ended, Ronnie smiled. "I thought we should get that over with. We both felt the attraction, so why not act on it?"

"Yeah." Kevin breathed, still unable to think.

"Let's have some *hors d'oeuvres* and get to know each other." Her eyes sparkled with promise. "I'm afraid if we keep sitting here things might get out of control." Ronnie paused, grinning, then stood up and offered her hand. "C'mon, Kev." He took her hand and rose from the couch.

They nibbled on tapas and sipped on margaritas while sharing the high points of their histories. She often touched his arm or his chest to make a point. She stood close, brushing him with her body then slightly pulling away. Kevin was reeling, yet managed to hold his own in the conversation. In his recent dating history, the signals had never been this clear. Ronnie excused herself to use the bathroom, and his mind cleared.

Jenny approached him with a big smile and lilting voice. "How's it going, Kevin?"

It was as though all the people at the party had faded and then suddenly re-materialized. For the past hour-and-a-half Ronnie was all that had existed for him. "Great party, Jenny."

"Looks like Ronnie and you made a connection. I saw you two kissing."

Kevin smiled. "I think she likes me."

"Be careful. She's my friend, and so are you. She may seem easy, but she's not. Don't assume anything, and definitely don't push. You won't have to. Ronnie knows what she wants, and she goes after it, whether it's a man or a business deal. She usually succeeds."

"Okay." Kevin raised one eyebrow.

"Just so you know, she won't go home with you tonight. She'll play you a little to see what you're made of. Don't get disappointed when she cools off.

"Really?"

"Yes, really; she absolutely hates neediness in guys, so she'll be testing you. If you want her, I recommend you tell her how beautiful she is, and be clear you'd like to see her again. Then leave."

"Thanks for the advice. Does it show that I'm drooling?"

"Yeah, it does, to me anyway, but I know you. Ronnie's a challenge, and she likes to be in control. More than that, she loves a man who won't give her control. Hey, it's up to you, Kevin. I'm just trying to help. I think you're strong enough, and I have to admit, I'd love to see you two together." Jenny squeezed his hand.

"Why do you want to see us together?"

"I think you two would make a great couple! Besides, we can double date!" She winked and walked away to attend to the other guests, leaving him with his resolve.

Feels like I'm back in Vegas, only--Who's the manipulator? Maybe both of us! This is the first time I've met someone who really turns me on. I can play this game and still be myself.

Kevin looked across the room and saw Ronnie talking to another man. A twinge of jealousy pricked his gut. *Let's not go there.* He yanked his attention from her and scanned the room. He didn't think of himself as shy, yet he was uncomfortable approaching people in social situations. Why was that? At the restaurant he had no problem talking, bantering, or engaging others. It was different, because he owned it. He set the tone. *I guess I'll have to pretend I'm at the restaurant.*

He conquered his urge to head toward Ronnie and made his way around the room, introducing himself, engaging in conversation. Most of them had been guests at the Calico Grill and recognized him as the manager. *Smile, and make eye contact. Tell each person something you like about them, especially the women.*

The next half hour passed quickly, and Kevin enjoyed meeting new people. Jenny approached him again. "What's come over you? I've had three people tell me what a charming guy you are."

"What, you didn't think I had it in me? I can be charming."

"That's what I just heard" Jenny nodded and smiled.

"What have you heard?" Ronnie gently squeezed in between Kevin and Jenny.

"I heard from some of my guests how charming Kevin is."

"I already knew that. I find him very charming." Ronnie entwined her arm in his.

Jenny rolled her eyes. "I'll leave you two to be charmed by each other while I go talk to some of my other charming guests." She smiled at both of them and glided toward the *hors d'oeuvres* table.

"Jenny is great! Al is lucky to have her." Kevin nodded.

"It won't last." Ronnie tensed her grip on his arm.

"Why do you say that?" He couldn't keep the surprise out of his voice.

"I know Jenny. Al is secretive and doesn't share much. Jenny is alive and enjoys life. People like her because she's confident and caring. All Al cares about is going to the casino and watching sports. Even now he's in the other room watching a game." She gently pressed his chest with her fingers and said: "But I'm sure he cares about the restaurant, too."

Kevin focused his mind on the conversation. He could feel her left hand wrapped around his right bicep and the softness of her breast pressing against his arm. *Stay in control!*

"Jenny gets him to go places, but I don't think he enjoys it. He's in his own world, and it might as well be in a far-off galaxy. He's not really unfriendly, just closed off."

"I didn't know Al liked casinos. He's never mentioned it."

She tilted her head and smiled. "That doesn't surprise me. You should go with him some time. But, enough about Al. I'd like to hear more about you."

"Sure." Kevin lightly touched her upper arm. "You're the most beautiful and intelligent woman I've met since I came to Tucson." Kevin looked at her and wondered if she believed him. It wasn't a line. "I have to head home in a few minutes, because I have an early day at the restaurant tomorrow. I want to see you again." He studied her face, and noticed a momentary look of surprise--or maybe it was disappointment.

Whatever it was, it shifted to a small smile and a nod. "Yes, let's get together." She reached into a small, almost invisible pocket near her hip and retrieved a business card. She grabbed a pen and wrote something. "That's my personal cell number. Why don't you give me a call tomorrow?"

Kevin handed her his card and said, "Write this down. 555-4948. That's my cell just in case I don't get through to you."

Ronnie stepped in closer and kissed him on the cheek. They embraced, and again her warmth ignited his desire. He held his breath, as if that could quell his hunger.

"I'll talk to you tomorrow then." Ronnie grinned. "Bye, Kevin." She turned and walked.

Kevin watched the sensual swaying of her hips as she sauntered toward a group of several people in animated conversation. Like an expert diver plunging into a pool, Ronnie smoothly entered the conversation and instantly emerged as the center of attention.

Kevin called her the next day after the lunch rush. They dined that night at Janos, where they talked and laughed and enjoyed the cuisine and drinks. Ronnie suggested Salsa dancing. This was unfamiliar territory for Kevin, but he reluctantly agreed.

The music was loud, and the club was crowded. A twelve piece Salsa band, complete with several brass, propelled colorful couples across the spacious, narrow-planked wood floor. They sat down at the last empty table. "How do we talk in here?" Kevin shouted over the unremitting throb of the speakers.

Ronnie gently reached for the back of his neck and pulled him close so that her lips were tickling his ear. "In this place," she said speaking very clearly, "you talk with your body and with your eyes. That's all you need." The kiss on his ear sent chills through him.

A waitress approached, and they ordered drinks. After a few sips, Ronnie reached for his hand. "Come on. Let's dance. I'll show you how."

Surprising himself, Kevin picked up the basic steps quickly, and he liked the music. It took several songs until he learned enough to lead. As the steps began to feel comfortable and automatic, he focused on Ronnie.

They surrendered to their mutual gaze, lavishing unbridled attention upon each other. Looking into her eyes he sensed a melange of shades and tones--strength, beauty, tenderness, sadness, love, joy, tenaciousness, ferocity. In Ronnie's eyes he saw every woman in the world. He saw goddesses, and women of every size and shape and color. She was Woman. She was beautiful, ravishing, stunning, and he couldn't resist her gravitational pull--didn't want to. He immersed himself in the music, the moment, and the woman.

As she predicted, they spoke little while they danced, yet the message was clear between them. The warmth, the heat Kevin had felt earlier, intensified as their bodies shared a language of their own. As if they were in a bubble, the other dancers faded. The music and the colors swirled around them, and they merged and moved as one. They danced until the band took a break, but stayed on the floor, gently swaying and talking, then danced the next set.

When they sat down to rest they continued the dance with their eyes--gazing, then glancing away, then looking again. Their skin glistened. Weary, yet energized in each others' presence, their hands connected across the table.

Beneath, Kevin felt Ronnie's knees on either side of one of his own. As they talked about the dance, they leaned closer. Her hand left a hot trail of tingles and tremors along his thigh. He stroked her knee. Her warm, damp skin delighted his fingertips.

At once, they withdrew their hands, as the band began the next set. Ronnie opened her legs to release his knee. They rose from their seats and exited the club, walking quickly, arm in arm, toward the car. Kevin let her in, raced around to the other side, slid in, and then thrust his key into the ignition. Ronnie reached for his face, and they kissed, passionately. He pressed his hands on her cheeks, and looked at her resolutely, "I'm driving you home, now."

They listened to more Salsa music on the radio during the half hour drive. Ronnie directed him with one hand, and with her other hand, massaged the back of his neck. As they arrived in her driveway she inquired: "Coming in?" She raised her eyebrows.

"Yes."

They entered the house, and Ronnie locked the door behind them. They slipped off their shoes and embraced again, kissing deeply, as if exchanging life forces. Ronnie took his hand and led him toward her bedroom.

When they made love Kevin was not self-conscious as he usually was during first times. He was fully present with the most beautiful woman on earth, and absolutely nothing else mattered. He savored touching and being touched. They talked into the early hours of the morning, and made love again.

As long as he held her, kissed her, talked to her, listened to her voice, made love with her, he felt full, complete. When he left her the next morning to go to work, the hunger for her returned. That was how it was that first week, and that was how it continued throughout their time together.

Chapter Eleven

Whenever Kevin was away from Ronnie she permeated his thoughts. Her touch, her scent, her look, her laugh, her eyes, her voice, her body, her smile, her strength, her softness--everything about her consumed him night and day. Although he still enjoyed his work at the restaurant, he focused on it less, and counted on his assistant more.

When cooler temperatures arrived in January, the two lovers flew to Puerto Vallarta for a few days. On a padded lounger under a palm on a quiet beach, Kevin lay on his back with Ronnie curled up next to him, asleep. *Is this Heaven? How did I manage to find this perfect woman and to live this perfect day?* Ronnie's right leg was draped over his right leg. Her right hand rested on his chest with her head nestled just below his chin. Her white bikini shimmered in contrast to her deeply tanned skin. He kissed her gently on her forehead, and his eyes slid along the curve of her hip, over her leg, and down to her feet. His visual journey continued, pulled from the tips of her toes onto the white-capped waves, to the point where blue ocean splashed up against blue sky. The gentle rising and falling of her chest and the heat of her breath softly buffeted his ribs. He loved everything about this woman.

His mind followed the path that had begun yesterday and led to this moment. After staying out late, dancing, and falling asleep as soon as they hit the bed, he was awakened in the morning with gentle kisses on his face and a smile. The kissing gradually turned into slow and easy lovemaking. They cuddled for a while. *I feel so loved with her!*

Afterward, they had gone for a walk along the beach, holding hands, splashing in the surf. The air was warm. A breeze tickled their skin, and they talked about the cobalt color of the Pacific and the beauty that surrounded them. Kevin told her that she was what was most beautiful in his life, then she smiled and kissed him.

Later, they had brunch and mimosas at a restaurant by the ocean. Kevin pictured it in his mind--the sweet, yellow-orange, fizzy drink in the stemmed glass, Ronnie's face framed by a background of palms, white tablecloths, and other couples smiling and talking.

After brunch they swam with dolphins. He was a little nervous when the trainer suggested they place their hands on the dolphin's tongue. Rows of sharp little teeth in a three hundred pound animal concerned him. Ronnie, without hesitation, placed her hand on the tongue. "It's grainy like sand paper. Go ahead and touch."

He felt the tongue and then petted the dolphin's head. Ronnie laughed with delight when the dolphin led her around the pool. He loved her belly laugh. It told him that she was happy, and he wanted so much for her to be happy. After the dolphin they came back to the hotel and found this lounger. *If I had a scrapbook of my life this day would have a page to itself. It doesn't get better than this.* He returned to the present moment and sighed.

He wanted to stay an extra day, but Ronnie insisted on getting back. She had meetings scheduled. Back in Tucson, they decided to move in together. Ronnie suggested that they live at her place, but that didn't feel right. "Why don't we get a new place, together?" Kevin asked.

"Kevin, I already have a great home. I don't want to buy another. I'm very attached to the one I have."

"Then how about I buy a new home, something bigger than this condo, and you can just live with me?"

"That doesn't sound fair to you, Sweetie." She placed her hands on his shoulders and looked into his eyes. "Keep the condo for yourself. Rent it out, or use it as a place for your stuff. Just move into my house with me."

"I'm not attached to this condo. I want a home, and I want my name on it. I can afford it." He pulled her close into an embrace. "I don't know why it's so important to me, but it is. I want a house. Will you stay with me? You can keep your place, too."

She helped him sell the condo and buy a house. He put all of his cash into the new place and took on twice the monthly payment he had at his condo. Ronnie kept her own home and moved in with him.

The restaurant thrived. Kevin, although distracted by his relationship with Ronnie, still maintained high quality food and service along with happy employees. Kevin and Al saw each other a couple of times a week, and everything seemed to be going well. Kevin received a profit check which helped to support his increasingly expensive lifestyle.

Ronnie had a big appetite for life. They traveled to Europe and to South America, interspersed with short breaks in Mexico. There was fine dining, parties at the house, and shopping for clothes at Louis Vuitton and Bebe. For Kevin, it was life in the fast lane. For Ronnie, it was the way she had lived for the past twenty years.

He had never known a woman with such energy. She spent many of her evenings with prospective clients, showing properties. In between there were yoga classes, Zumba, networking meetings, cocktail parties, and her meditation group. Whenever he could get away from work Kevin joined her for those functions. They worked out together at a health club most mornings or went for early hikes. On one such hike near Sabino Canyon, Kevin saw whirlwinds moving across the desert. He pointed. "I saw one those when I first came here. What is it? Looks like a small tornado."

"It's a dust devil, and it *is* a small tornado. It's created by hot air rising to meet lower pressure and cooler air. Most are harmless."

"Sometimes I feel that's what our lives are like, Ronnie. We're like little dust devils spinning and stirring up energy. I'm not complaining. I love my life, and I love that you're in it. It just seems like we never stop."

"As I remember, we slept in yesterday."

"That was wonderful, but we were up by 7:30 a.m. That's not sleeping in!"

"It is for me, Sleepyhead." She gently pushed him and smiled.

"Yeah, well you run on five hours of sleep, and I need more than that. You never seem to get tired."

"Life is to be lived, not slept through. I'm afraid if I sleep too much I might miss something. Besides, I've never needed much sleep. We can relax Saturday when we see Al and Jenny at the club."

"I'll be relaxing. You'll be talking to potential clients." Kevin laughed and gave her a playful shove.

"Meeting clients *is* relaxing for me." Ronnie smiled. "Speaking of which, I have an appointment at 10:00. Pick up the pace!"

"Yes, my little dust devil." Kevin smiled and twirled her around. Ronnie laughed and pushed him again.

On Saturday morning Kevin and Ronnie played eighteen holes at the country club with the Stewarts and then relaxed by the pool. Ronnie asked Al to introduce her to some friends of his who were on the other side of the water. They left Kevin and Jenny in their lounge chairs. Music was playing in the background and Jenny looked at Kevin with a big smile.

"What are you smiling about?" Kevin frowned.

"Kevin, they're playing your song." Jenny sang along: "They had one thing in common, they were good in bed. She'd say, 'Faster, faster. The lights are turnin' red. Life in the fast lane.'"

"Very funny." Kevin recognized the lyrics to the Eagles' song. "But, I don't think I'm a cruel dude."

"No, you're a good guy. That's why I'm worried about you. You're running in the fast lane with Ronnie. Are you sure you can keep up?"

"Where's this coming from, Jenny? I've never been happier with a woman than I've been with Ronnie. We love being together, and we're always touching each other."

"Is that what happiness is? I know the sex is good with you two. That's obvious. I know you have fun. I also understand business, and you don't make enough money to pay for your house and keep up with Ronnie's lifestyle."

"Look, Jenny, it's none of your business. Has Ronnie said something to you?"

"You're my friend, Kevin. I care for both you and Ronnie. You know that I speak my mind. I'm sorry if it hurts your feelings, but I can't just say nothing when I see that you might get hurt. And no, Ronnie hasn't said anything."

"Good, because I can't lose her. She means everything to me."

"Don't place your happiness on Ronnie. She can't bear the weight. I never should have introduced you two." She stared at the ground and shook her head.

"Why do you say that?

"Because you've lost your edge." Jenny's voice pricked him.

The words bled from his mouth, dripping with unease. "What! I have not!" He heard the defensiveness in his tone.

Jenny thrusted again. "When you first came to Tucson, you were focused, and you were in the zone at work. Now, you do what you have to do to get by. Also, I remember you going to the canyon to reflect and meditate. Are you still doing that?"

"The Grill is still running, and I reflect!" His parry was weak, encumbered with its lack of veracity.

"When was the last time?"

Kevin searched his memory files, picturing Pima Canyon in his mind. "Probably several months. Between the restaurant and Ronnie, I haven't had time."

"Maybe you should start going again, because you've changed. Also, there's a difference between real love and being obsessed with someone. I thought you knew that."

"I'm not obsessed. I love Ronnie."

Jenny fixed her eyes on Kevin, and then softened her tone. "Look, I just want you to be careful. You've done well for yourself, but that could change."

"I have done well, and I plan to continue."

"You know what they say about *best laid plans*. There are things you don't know."

Kevin's tensed as currents of fear hurtled through his body. "What don't I know?"

The brightness disappeared from Jenny's face, as sadness moved across her eyes like clouds before the sun. "I'm leaving Al. I'm leaving before he destroys our finances just like he's already destroyed the trust in our relationship."

"I don't understand. What happened?"

"Al gambles. He's gone through all of his money, and he's been taking mine. I've had to open new accounts and transfer all of my funds away from his greedy little hands. I'm filing tomorrow, and he'll be served this week. I'm going for half the house, but I'm leaving your business alone. As long as my business is off limits to him, I'll stay out of the restaurant business."

"I'm sorry Jenny. I didn't realize things were so bad. Why haven't you told me about this before?"

"You're a good friend, and I'm usually very honest with you-- but Al is your business partner. I didn't want to hurt your relationship with him."

"Well, I've been so involved with Ronnie, I guess I'm not surprised I didn't see you two were struggling. How can I help?"

"I'm fine. It's *you* I'm worried about. I don't think Al would steal from the business, but he's not the same man I married twenty-five years ago. He's an addict, and I think that eventually, it's going to affect the restaurant. Your life as you know it is at high risk. You've got Al who's unstable and not making good decisions. You've got Ronnie who runs hard and holds your heart in her hands. You guys have done well at the Grill, but I've seen the numbers. You spend more than you make."

"I can take care of myself, and you don't need to worry."

"Kevin, Ronnie is a good businesswoman. If you told her that you needed to slow down, she'd understand."

"She thinks buying the house was a mistake. Maybe it was. The problem is, if I sell it now, I'll lose the cash I put down on it."

"So maybe you need to cut your losses and live within your means. Why don't you two talk it over?"

He had tried several times to discuss his finances with Ronnie, but kept putting it off. He'd hoped that more money would come in, and the problem would be solved. They each paid their own way in the relationship, except for the house. She had agreed to stay there with him, but she made it clear she would not help pay for it. Jenny was right. He couldn't keep it up.

"I probably should talk to her about it." Kevin said.

"You're afraid of losing her, but you need to trust her enough to be honest. Al would never sit down and talk with me about his gambling. He just kept hoping for a big win that would solve everything, and then he wouldn't need to admit he has a problem. He's still hoping, but I'm not into hope. I believe in action. Don't be like Al. Face your problems. Take action."

"I'm *not* like Al." He said it with a little more emphasis than he intended. "Am I?"

"Depends. If you take more responsibility in the finances of the restaurant and in your personal life, I think you'll be okay. Make Al show you the books. Meet with him and the accountant. Talk to

Ronnie. Give her a chance to work with you. Will you do those things, Kevin?"

"Yeah, I will."

Ronnie and Al came back to the table. Ronnie was laughing. "Great guys, Al. Thanks for introducing me."

"I'm ready to go," Al directed toward Jenny. "You ready?"

Kevin stood up. "Me too."

When they were settled in the car Ronnie turned to him. "Looks like you two were having a serious talk."

Kevin let silence hang in the air between them for a minute while he shifted into gear and began driving out of the parking lot. "Jenny's leaving Al."

"Didn't I tell you so? I knew it would be soon. She told me she'd about had it last week. How did she seem?"

"Calm and resolute."

They reached for each others' hands over the console. Kevin felt reassured.

When they arrived home they showered. He dried himself and approached her, kissing her on the neck and face. Caressing her back, he whispered in her ear, "I want you. Right now."

"I love it when you talk that way to me."

They fell on the bed together--their hands touching their bodies in pleasing patterns memorized over the past several months. There was no thinking, no planning. It was as if their bodies knew what to do while their minds followed, immersing themselves in the pleasure of the moment. The thought of losing her intensified his passion. He found himself kissing and touching her as if it were the last time.

* * *

Jenny and Al split. Jenny moved to San Francisco, but her words of advice remained in Tucson and nagged at him. He knew that he should discuss his monetary issues with Ronnie, but he couldn't bring himself to do it. One day she asked him how he was doing financially, and all he could come up with was, "Fine."

Finally, he found a way to talk about it. "Hey, Ronnie. What could I get if we put this house on the market?"

"You could walk away with thirty-thousand."

"I put twice that down on it." His eyes narrowed, and the tone was one of protest.

"I know, but the market isn't going up. Sometimes you need to cut your losses."

"Yeah, that's what Jenny said."

Ronnie thought she could move the house quickly. Within the next few days she had several possible clients lined up. Kevin stayed silent on the topic, so Ronnie confronted him.

"Do you want to sell the house or not? I've got buyers."

"I haven't decided. Don't you think the market will rise again?"

"I told you NO. Sell it now, and you'll get some of your cash back. Sell later and you may end up owing when the deal closes. Why don't I bring in some clients, and we'll see what kind of offers they make?"

"I'll think about it." Kevin squirmed as if in a trap.

Ronnie shook her head.

"What?" He flung his frustration at her, as if it were her fault.

"I don't get it." Ronnie faced him, feet apart, palms facing upward, her tone an indictment. "You're losing money on this place. I've told you we can move into mine. You can pay half the utilities, and you'll be way better off than staying here. You need to act. Now!"

He felt his defenses rise. "I said I'll think about it!"

"Is it pride? You have to have your name on it?"

"Something like that. You know that's important to me."

"Then find a way to make more money. As for the house, I'm done trying to sell it. Let me know if you change your mind. I have a meeting." She turned and left, slamming the door behind her. Kevin felt Ronnie's logic tugging at him, but losing the battle. *My house is my success in Tucson. I have to keep it. I can't go backwards.*

Kevin met with Al and the accountant twice. The business was doing well, so he stopped checking. Profits were up, and Kevin realized a small increase in his income. He relaxed and told himself that everything would be okay.

Chapter Twelve

"I'm moving back home." Ronnie announced. It was Saturday morning, and Kevin had just come in from his front yard. Six months had passed since the last conversation about the house.

Kevin felt like she had pushed him under water. Mentally he struggled toward the surface. "Are you breaking it off with me?"

"No Sweetie, I just miss my house. You can sleep over any time you want. I need to be in my own space."

He let his breath out, not realizing that he had been holding it. "What's this about, Ronnie? Are you unhappy here?"

"No and yes. I'm unhappy living in this house, but I'm not unhappy being with you. You can bring some of your things to my place if you want. I'm not breaking up with you, just your house." She laughed and kissed him. "Will you help me move my stuff?"

"Sure, but are you telling me the truth?"

Ronnie gave him a hard look. "I *always* tell you the truth. I'm moving back because that's what I want to do. You want to be in this house, because that's what you want to do. Pretty straight forward, I think." Her voice was tinged with a little sarcasm.

"If you want to be with me tonight, you're invited." She placed her hands on her hips. "So, do you want to come over tonight?"

"Yes, I do." Kevin's voice sounded smaller than he liked.

Ronnie relaxed her stance. "Then, let's get this stuff in the car."

Kevin helped Ronnie move her things. He couldn't help but think their relationship had just suffered a demotion. They stayed together most nights, but always at Ronnie's home. They spent Thanksgiving and Christmas together. Kevin thought about selling his home, but the market continued to decline. *If I'd listened to her six months ago, and acted, I could've gotten thirty-thousand out of it.* He brought up the topic, but she refused to talk about it.

On New Year's Eve they celebrated quietly. Ronnie seemed more passionate, holding him tightly and kissing him hard. In bed she clung to him. He asked if she was okay.

"Of course I'm okay, Sweetie. Sometimes I just can't get enough of you." She pulled him closer, and Kevin felt the warmth, both familiar and exciting.

He felt moisture from her cheek upon his. "Are you sure you're all right?"

"I'm okay. You don't need to keep asking."

* * *

Kevin went into the restaurant on New Year's Day, and called Ronnie that night. She didn't answer, nor did she return the call. He called her several times the next day with no results. He drove by her house. No one was home. He checked at her office, but no one knew where she was. Her assistant assured him that yes, Ronnie was okay, and that yes, she had passed his message on to her. "I guess she'll call you when she's ready. I don't know where she is, and I'm sure she'll call you when she gets back."

Kevin waited for her call, constantly checking his cell for voicemails, texts, emails--anything! The week slowly dragged by, and then the phone rang. "Kevin, it's me."

"Ronnie I've been so worried about you. Are you okay?"

"Yes, I'm fine. I'm sorry I haven't called you. I needed some time alone, and I didn't want to answer any questions. Are you free tonight around nine?"

"I could get free. What did you have in mind?"

"Come over. I'll see you then."

The line was dead before Kevin could respond. Worry seized him, making it difficult to breathe. A sense of impending doom fell like a dark curtain over his mind. He recalled when Dana had told him she wanted a divorce four years ago. Kevin feared the worst, but held to the hope that there was still a relationship.

He arrived at Ronnie's house at 9:05 that evening. She greeted him with a hug and asked him to sit down. *She didn't kiss me. She's going to break up with me!*

"I can't believe it's already been a year-and-a-half since we started seeing each other. Can I get you something to drink?"

"No. Thanks." He had hastily drained a glass of pinot noir as he left Callico, and the taste lingered in his mouth. *Not a good choice! Sex in a glass! Probably a good thing she didn't kiss me.* He looked into her eyes. "What's going on, Ronnie? Suddenly, without a word, you're gone for a week?"

"Could we sit down?" She opened her right hand. Reality distorted as her fingers unfurled toward the sofa like time lapse photography. He forced himself to move to where she had pointed--his body battling gravity with every step. The image of a firing squad flashed in his mind. He swallowed as if he were the prisoner refusing the blindfold, rather than a guy getting dumped.

Ronnie sat down, and he remembered the first time she sat down next to him and kissed him. He shook off the memory. They were seated across from each other on twin teak sofas--the room softly lit by matching teak floor lamps. Kevin was again reminded of the difference in their incomes.

Ronnie crossed her legs and folded her hands on her knee. "Something has bothered me for quite awhile, and I needed time away from you, and from my life. So I went to Mexico."

"Why didn't you just tell me you needed to get away?"

"I was afraid if I told you, I wouldn't do it." She paused and inhaled deeply, her breath escaping quietly. "I did some thinking, trying to imagine my future with you."

"And what did you see?"

"Kevin, I couldn't see a future for us. It makes me sad to say, but I don't see this relationship going anywhere. I still care about you. I love you. I still think you're hot." Her mouth smiled, but her eyes were sad. "It has to end. I'm sorry, Kevin. You are still my dear friend, but I can't be your lover. I hope you can forgive me. This is what I need to do."

Her words rushed into his mind, like a dust devil, sweeping his thoughts into chaos. He struggled to find his voice. "I don't understand, Ronnie. I mean, I hear what you're saying. It just doesn't make sense. We were together on New Year's Eve, and it seemed like everything was great. The next day you disappear, and now you're saying it's over. I don't get it."

Ronnie plucked a tissue from a box on the end table and wiped the tears from her cheeks. "I don't fully get it myself. When I was alone in Mexico and thought about us, and thought about the future, I knew." She wiped two more tears that escaped from her eyes. "Maybe in time, I'll be able to tell you more specifically. All I can say is, I feel strongly that this is what I need to do. I feel terrible dropping this on you, but I don't know any other way. I'm sorry, Kevin. Sorry, but also grateful for what we've shared together. Grateful for your friendship and love."

Kevin thought he would explode. He stared at her. "I'll miss you." It took all of his strength to refrain from falling on his knees and begging her to stay with him, asking her for one more chance. But, he knew he would regret it. He didn't want Ronnie's memory of him to be pathetic. So he kept his chin up and dug down deep for his calmest voice. "I should get going."

"Just a minute." Ronnie quickly exited the room.

Kevin stood up, the reality of what just happened slapping him in the face. An impulse to yell at her strained like a leashed dog in his throat. *NO!* He commanded himself to stay.

Ronnie reappeared moments later with a cloth bag. "Your things." She held it out to him.

"Thanks." His tone was muted. He headed off another crescendo building inside, forced himself to look directly into her eyes, and said, "Ronnie, I'll be okay. If this is what you need to do, then so be it." The hurt and angry Kevin watched as the gentleman Kevin spoke much more generously than he felt.

"I appreciate how you're taking this. You're a class guy." She walked him toward the door. "Can we hug before you leave?"

"No!" The word cut abruptly between them like a sliding glass door.

Ronnie's face fell. "Okay."

He softened his voice again. "Maybe some other time."

She reached for his arm, gently grasping his elbow. "I know I hurt you. I hope we can talk after some time passes." Another tear rolled down her cheek. "I'll miss you, Kevin."

Kevin thought to gently dab the tear, but stopped himself as sorrow and anger both spoke at once, rendering his true voice impotent. He turned and fled through the front doorway. Walking quickly toward his car without looking back, he slid into the seat and turned the key. Holding his breath, it took all of his concentration to back out of the driveway and accelerate on the street. As he rounded the first corner tears broke through the carefully constructed wall of his face. Unable to stop sobbing, he pulled over to the curb and surrendered to the waves of emotion throbbing through him. Eventually, with no conscious recollection of driving, he made it home.

The door slamming shut echoed through the rooms of a silent and solitary house. Kevin paced the floor, turned on some music, tried the television, but nothing soothed him. His life support had been unplugged, and he was now gasping for air. Longing for unconsciousness, something to end this misery, he searched his kitchen for an answer. Finally, after downing a bottle of merlot, he put himself to bed and fell asleep.

Chapter Thirteen

He awoke by 8:00 a.m. and messaged one of his assistant managers to cover for him for a few days. Eating a little granola, he packed a sandwich and a water bottle in his backpack, and headed for Pima Canyon. *Why haven't I come here more often?*

It was sunny, as usual, with the temperature in the low sixties. He climbed the incline toward the canyon and the sun. The strain on his muscles was a welcome distraction from his inner pain. Thoughts about the past week and about his relationship with Ronnie hijacked his mind. Memories of walks on beaches, of lying in bed talking and touching, and of seeing her face each morning flooded his mind. *I've lost her.* He questioned whether there was anything left for him in Tucson.

Two young women passed him as they hiked down the path. They smiled and wished him a good morning. He hoped that no one else would cross his path. The last thing he wanted was to be saying nice things to people. His mind was on fire, and his painful thoughts and emotions threatened to consume him.

In the canyon there were no cover-ups or distractions. It was his place for complete honesty. He came here, not to escape his pain, but to confront it. About two miles in, he stopped at a small clearing.

He thought back to his first two years in Tucson, and how he compared every woman he dated to Rachel. Then Ronnie came into his life. Was she the equivalent of Rachel? Was the honesty and depth he found in Rachel also in his relationship with Ronnie?

No. So, did I lower my standards? I was just so overwhelmingly attracted to her. I love her, don't I? And what Jenny said--there's a difference between love and obsession. Do I know the difference? I miss her. What about that? Maybe it's not love, but it hurts not to be with her.

Some of his pain lifted, and like a phoenix, he rose from the ashes of loss. Breathing deeply, he felt some of his strength returning.

Eventually the restaurant intruded upon his thoughts. He saw the faces of his staff encircling him, supporting him, and believing in him. Thoughts about his regulars and how much he enjoyed their presence flickered across his mind. He smiled a little, recognizing that there were other people he cared about and who cared about him. He would get through this. Somehow he would move on. It was impossible to make all the hurt go away right now, but it would gradually dissolve.

* * *

Kevin was depressed most days over the next few months. Often his phone drew his hand like a magnet, thinking to call Ronnie. Each time he pulled it away. He worked late every night, avoiding the inevitable loneliness of his house. Remembering his experience in the canyon, he spent time feeling his longing, and the emptiness that served as his new bed partner. Dishes and glasses piled up in the sink and dust bunnies collected in the corners. There were papers and bills strewn across the dining room table. It was 1:00 a.m. on a Friday morning when he found himself drinking wine and listening to Elvis.

Are you lonesome tonight?

Do you miss me tonight?

Are you sorry we drifted apart...?

He hit the off button and laughed. *This is pathetic. I'm done feeling sorry for myself.* He started washing and cleaning and sorting. By 5:00

a.m. he had managed to put his house in order. He shouted at the house. "I'm sick of being down. I'm going out tonight, and I'm going to find a woman who really wants me." *Careful what you ask for!* He dismissed the voice in his head.

That night he left the restaurant early. Feeling nervous, he walked into the dance club for Friday night salsa. Sitting down at a small round table, he ordered a Corona. It had been several months since the last time Ronnie and he had been here. Sipping on his beer, he scanned the room for available women. Most were there with dates. Two beers and several dances later he was about to give up and go home. He made eye contact with an Asian woman wearing a white dress with a pink belt. She smiled. He walked to her table and leaned toward her. "Would you like to dance?"

She smiled and nodded her head.

Kevin offered his hand, and they walked onto the dance floor. Within seconds they fell into the rhythm of salsa. For the first time in months Kevin enjoyed what he was doing. He surrendered his thinking and let the music move his body. She followed him, flawlessly. After several numbers the band took a break, and Kevin invited her to his table. She asked him to wait as she grabbed her purse and said a few words to a female friend. The friend left, and his dance partner walked back toward him.

He stood up and offered her a seat. "My name is Kevin."

"I'm Marianna."

"Where are you from, Marianna?"

"The Philippines. I came to the United States twelve years ago to go to college at U of A."

A waitress approached. Marianna ordered a Daiquiri, and Kevin ordered another Corona. They asked the usual questions. Marianna was divorced and had two children. Her ex-husband had custody, and they lived in California. She worked an I.T. job during the day and at a health club most evenings. Friday was her usual night off.

She asked if he would drive her home later, because her ride had left. She lived only two miles from the club.

Straight black hair flowed over her right shoulder and lay delicately across her collar bone. Spaghetti straps held her dress in place and pointed toward her nipples which rose slightly beneath the fabric. Kevin tried not to look but found himself stealing quick glances whenever Marianna looked away. She was pretty. She stood about five-feet-four in her short heels, and she moved gracefully. Kevin enjoyed the feeling of attraction. She smiled; she touched him on the leg and the arm as she talked. The game was on.

Later when they left the club, Kevin suggested they go to his house. He was silently grateful for his cleaning spree earlier that day. When she hesitated, Kevin said it was a mild evening, and they could go for a walk.

Marianna scrunched the middle of her forehead and slightly moved her head from side to side. "I'm not spending the night with you."

"Okay. Is a walk all right with you?" He felt unconcerned about outcomes. He had already enjoyed the dancing. Anything else was a bonus. Besides, if not tonight, he knew he would be with her eventually.

"Yes. A walk is good."

When they arrived at Kevin's home, he gave her a quick tour. "Let's go for that walk."

They held hands and strolled for several blocks, stopping to enjoy a view of the mountains in the moonlight. Kevin studied her face. Her almond shaped eyes rested on high cheekbones framed by her dark, wavy hair. "You look absolutely gorgeous in this light."

She looked at him and moved slightly toward him. Leaning forward, he kissed her, the suction of her lips, sensuous and soft. They embraced and he continued to kiss her on the lips, and then her face, and then her neck.

"We should go!" Marianna scrunched her forehead again. "Let's go back."

"Okay." Kevin reached for her hand, and they walked toward his house. The sounds of distant traffic offered a backdrop to an otherwise quiet evening.

When they arrived, she retrieved her purse from the car and asked to use his bathroom. They spent several minutes in the house, and she complimented the framed photographs of his daughters that were on the wall in the hallway between the bath and the bedrooms. Kevin locked the house on the way out, and he opened the car door for her. Sliding into the driver's seat, he closed the door and started the engine.

As the car rolled backwards, Marianna shouted "Stop!"

"What's the matter?"

"I forgot my purse."

They abandoned the car halfway down the driveway and reentered the house. She took his hand as he walked across the living room toward the purse, which sat on a chair by a window. She stopped halfway there, resisting his movement toward the purse. Kevin turned and looked at her, and she rose on her toes and kissed him. She kissed him again and then again. He took her hand and led her to his bedroom.

* * *

The next morning, Kevin dropped Marianna off at her apartment on his way to work.

"Call me." She smiled and kissed him. "Please?" She kissed him again and exited the car.

He had enjoyed the night with her. She was an eager lover, but maybe too eager to be with him. Being with a woman again was delicious, but he wasn't attracted to *eager*. He told himself that he probably wouldn't call her.

His thoughts turned to Al. In the three months since Ronnie had ended their relationship, he had rarely seen him, and when he did, they had not talked. At Calico that morning, he asked his employees if they had seen him. No one had seen Al for a week.

He called Al and left a message. He texted him and then emailed him. Monday morning he called the accountant.

"Hi George. This is Kevin Neill. Have you seen Al?"

There was a pause. "No, I haven't. Why are you asking me?"

"You're our accountant. He usually meets with you weekly."

"Al fired me three months ago. Don't you guys talk?"

Kevin's voice stuck in his throat. "Oh, uh, I didn't know. Why did he fire you?"

"I have no idea, Kevin. He just said that you two had decided to go in a different direction."

"I'm sorry George. Al did that on his own. Can I call on you if we need your help?"

"Sure. Give me a call."

"Thanks."

Fear trickled into his body, and spread like a virus. By Tuesday night he was edgy. To avoid snapping at employees he went home early. He finally received a text from Al: I'll be in later this week. He wished he could call Ronnie and talk about it. He called Jenny, but there was no answer. He didn't leave a message. Unable to think of anyone to call, he found himself tapping Marianna's name on his cell. *Not a good idea. You weren't going to see her again.* His indecision decided for him.

"Hello."

Marianna's voice felt soothing. *You need to find Al and talk to him, not set up a date.* "Hi. This is Kevin."

"Oh, hi!" He could hear the eagerness in her voice.

"Would you like to get together Friday night?"

"Oh yes! Yes!"

"How about dinner?"

"I will cook for you. I'll bring dinner to your house. Okay?"

"Um, well, okay. That sounds fine. How about 7:00 p.m.?"

"7:00 p.m.. I will be there with dinner. See you then!"

He hung up. "And breakfast, too." He said out loud to himself.

For the next few days he alternated between imagining Marianna's sweet body and worrying about Al and the restaurant. On Friday morning he caught Al leaving his office.

"There you are. We need to talk."

"No time right now. I have a meeting." Al brushed past him without stopping.

Kevin followed, his heartbeat increasing, and he could feel his blood racing. "Al, we need to talk. What's going on with the restaurant? Why did you fire the accountant?"

Al turned on him, taking a step forward, his chin jutted out. "Look. Everyone got paid today including you. You don't need to worry. I have it under control."

Kevin's words burst into the space between them, without forethought. "I don't believe you!"

Al stared at him, and the scene was suspended for a few seconds. He wanted to believe Al, to think that Al was in control, but his gut disagreed. Kevin wanted to cash his check, go home, sleep with a beautiful woman, and wake up to a carefree world.

"I don't care what you believe." He turned to leave, then turned back to Kevin. "I'll talk to you tomorrow morning. You'll see that everything is fine. All right?"

"You look stressed out. At least tell me what's going on."

"Tomorrow!" Al placed his hand on Kevin's chest, pressing him backward. "Back off. Everything is fine."

"What time?"

Al turned back again. "Eleven."

"You'd better be here."

"Yeah. I'll be here." Al pivoted and left.

When he left for home, Al's exit was still gnawing at him. *Are the restaurant's finances okay? I can't afford to miss any paychecks, especially with the state of my finances.* He hadn't moved on selling his house. He was living within his means at the moment, but still carried substantial debt. *At least my date tonight won't cost anything.*

Marianna arrived on time with hot dishes in a box. She called it *adobo.* It was braised chicken along with vegetables and rice. She set down her boxes and kissed him, twice. "Now I will finish making the dinner, and we will eat in forty minutes."

Kevin poured the wine and sat at the table, as directed, to await dinner. About forty minutes later she served him, waited until he tasted it and said it was good, then sat down and served herself.

He enjoyed the meal as they talked and flirted. He forgot about Al. Marianna insisted on doing the dishes while Kevin relaxed in the living room. When she finished she stepped into the room and glided onto his lap. Kissing him and touching his face she asked: "Would you like a massage?"

"Yeah. You are really spoiling me tonight, Marianna!"

She smiled and nodded.

As they stood up from the sofa, Kevin's cell phone rang.

♪ Wake me up inside.

Al's name showed up in the display. "Al. What's up?"

"I'm sorry I left so quickly today, but I'm ready to talk."

"Now?"

"Well, yeah. Unless you're too busy."

"Al, I'm on a date. I…"

"Oh sorry. Hey, don't worry about it. I'll see you tomorrow."

"At eleven?"

"Yeah. Sure." The phone clicked.

Guilt shot through Kevin, like an arrow in his chest. Marianna kissed him, unbuttoned his shirt, and pulled him toward the bedroom. It was like college. Whenever either of them had a chance to be with a girl, the other would take his cue and disappear. *But, I'm not in college anymore.* Marianna's affections anesthetized his self-inflicted wound.

She took the lead as if her only goal in life was to please him. Sensual pleasure and sexual release pushed him out of his head as endorphins raced through his body. An hour later Kevin was completely relaxed and had fallen into a deep sleep.

The shrill ring of his landline next to the bed startled him awake. As if reaching through a fog, he grasped for the phone, if only to stop the noise.

"Uh, hello."

"Kevin? Is that you?"

"Yeah. Who's this?" He knew that voice. He was at once groggy and panicked.

"It's Ronnie. Are you okay?"

"Uh, yeah. I, uh fell asleep, and I wasn't expecting your call and uh..." He speech trailed off as there were no words to rescue him from this awkward moment.

"Is someone there with you?"

"No. I said I fell asleep. Uh, you woke me up!"

"Someone *is* there with you! You don't need to lie to me, Kevin." She hung up.

"Oh, shit!"

Marianna pulled him into a comforting embrace. She kissed his face and stroked his back. He surrendered to her soothing touches.

Chapter Fourteen

In the morning he awoke thinking about Ronnie as Marianna carressed him again. His cell phone rang. He was afraid to see who it might be. It was Chip, his assistant manager. Briefly the urge to answer the phone competed with Marianna's attentions. He set the phone down. Later as he lay in bed while Marianna showered, the landline rang again. It was Ronnie, so he didn't answer.

Marianna emerged from the bathroom wearing jean shorts and a white halter top, her damp, black hair brushed back into pony tail. "What are we doing this morning, Kevin?"

"We're going to have some breakfast. Next, I'm going to get some badly needed tires for my car, and then go meet with my business partner. What are you doing?"

"I work at the health club this afternoon. Go take your shower, and I'll start breakfast."

He headed toward the shower while Marianna scurried to the kitchen. Again the cell phone rang. Thinking it was Chip, he picked it up and froze. Bryce's name flashed on the display. "Oh my God, who else is going to call? The last person I want to talk to right now is my moralistic brother!"

After the shower he gave Chip a call back. "What's up, Chip?"

"Are you sitting down?"

Kevin sat down. "What happened?"

"Bad news, Kevin. Al was in an accident last night. He was drunk and drove through a guard rail into a ravine."

"Is he okay?"

"He's gone."

Kevin was silent, replaying what Chip said in his mind, attempting to understand the word *gone*.

"You mean he's dead?"

"Yes, I'm sorry."

Al dead? How could that be? The arrow of guilt thumped into his chest again and embedded itself.

"Are you still there, Kevin?"

"Yeah, I'm here. I can't believe it. I just talked to him on the phone last night. We were supposed to meet this morning. Does the staff know about this?"

"I'm the only one who knows. What do you want me to do?"

"Get the whole staff in for an 11:00 a.m. meeting. We'll make the announcement and probably close the restaurant for the day. I'll be there in a few minutes."

"I'm sorry to tell you this, Kevin. I feel so badly."

"There isn't anything you could've done. I never thought Al would do something like this. Just try to be calm for the staff, and I'll be there soon." *I could've done something, but I didn't.*

"Breakfast is ready." Marianna called from the kitchen, but Kevin had no appetite.

"I'm sorry, Marianna. I have to go."

"You don't want breakfast?" She moved toward him, embracing him, and then kissing him.

He gently pushed her away. "I'm sorry. My business partner was killed in an accident, and I have to get to work. Now!"

"I'm sorry." She scrunched her forehead, and the sides of her mouth turned downward. "You go, and I'll clean up. Then I will wait for you here."

"Thanks, Marianna, but please don't wait for me. You need to go home. Go grab your stuff from the bedroom, and I'll get your utensils together. We need to be out of here in five minutes."

Marianna frowned again, but did as she was told. Kevin threw her utensils into the box, and carried it to the front door. He yelled toward the bedroom. "Let's go, Marianna."

The doorbell rang.

"Now who?" Praying that it wasn't Ronnie at his door, he cautiously peeked through the peep hole. It was Bryce and Brenda.

"What the hell are they doing here?" He thought about not answering or sneaking Marianna out the back door, but her car was in the driveway. His car was in the garage, and the garage door was open. *There's no escape. Aw, screw it! I don't owe Bryce any explanations.*

He opened the door. "Bryce, Brenda. What a surprise! What brings you here?"

Brenda hugged him. "Sorry to drop in on you like this. We called about an hour ago to let you know we were coming, and Bryce left you a message."

"Oh, sorry. I didn't hear it. Hi, Bryce." They shook hands.

"Brenda's sister moved to Phoenix, and we were helping her get settled. Thought we'd see you while we were out here. Looks like you're getting ready to leave."

Kevin's pasted-on smile disappeared, and his brow furrowed. His shoulders contracted under the weight of Al's death.

"What's wrong?" Brenda reached for his shoulder.

"My partner was killed in an accident last night, and I need to get to work to tell the staff."

"Oh, Kevin, I'm so sorry." Brenda embraced him.

Bryce reached for his shoulder. "Yeah, sorry Brother. We--"

"I'm ready." Marianna sang from the bedroom. Brenda and Bryce raised their eyebrows.

They dropped their jaws as Marianna entered the living room, overnight bag slung across her shoulder.

Kevin cringed.

"Who are these people?" Marianna walked up to Kevin and put her hands on her hips.

"Marianna, this is my brother Bryce and his wife, Brenda."

"Hi." She shook Brenda's hand. As she extended her hand to Bryce he curled his lip and stepped back, as if avoiding something contagious. Marianna narrowed her gaze at him. She looked at Kevin. "What's his problem?"

"Why are you here?" Bryce stared at Marianna.

"I'm Kevin's girlfriend." She smiled and snaked her arm through Kevin's, leaned into him smiling, her breast pressing up against his arm. She looked up at Kevin, "I thought you had to go to work?"

"I do. I need to talk to my brother and sister-in-law and then go to work. Let me help you to the car." He untangled his arm and reached down for the box. Without waiting, he backed out the door.

"Nice to meet you." She smiled at Brenda and returned Bryce's curled lip. She passed Kevin and walked to the car, leaving them a view of her mostly-bare back and swaying hips.

She unlocked her vehicle, and Kevin placed the box in her back seat. Marianna reached for him. He turned his face causing her kiss to land on his cheek.

"Hey. I want a real kiss." She grabbed his cheeks with both hands and attempted to wrestle his face into position. He grabbed her wrists and firmly held her at arms reach.

"Not now, Marianna!"

She scrunched her forehead, her lips pushing outward into a pout.

"I'll talk to you later. I've got to go." Kevin turned and walked back to see Bryce and Brenda watching out of the doorway.

Marianna stood by the car, then started to follow him. Kevin froze and turned. She frowned again, and opened her car door. As Kevin approached the doorway, he turned, and they watched her drive away. He motioned them in. "That was awkward. Come in."

"I thought Ronnie was your girlfriend." Bryce's eyes surgically searched Kevin's face. Kevin led them into the living room.

"Have a seat, you two. Do you want anything? I'm thinking about a stiff drink right now for myself, but I'll settle for a Diet." He turned and studied Brenda and Bryce as worlds collided in his mind. *They have never visited me in Tucson, and now they arrive at the worst time possible.*

"Nothing for me." Brenda broke the silence.

"I just want an answer." Bryce glared at his brother.

Kevin quickly moved out of the line of fire and into the kitchen. He grabbed the can out of the refrigerator, opened it, retrieved a glass, put ice in it, and slowly poured. Looking out the window he realized that he hadn't been breathing. He inhaled deeply and exhaled slowly. He took a swallow and reconsidered his decision not to drink alcohol. In his mind he saw the staff and knew that they needed him to be on. They were the priority today, not his brother.

Back in the living room, Brenda was sitting on the couch, and Bryce resumed his glare. He sat down, the ice tinkling in his glass. "Ronnie broke up with me three months ago."

"Because of this girl we just met?" Bryce sat next to Brenda on the couch.

"No. I met Marianna last weekend." The fizzy liquid both refreshed and burned his throat.

"Where did you meet her, Kevin? She's really cute." Brenda raised the pitch on her voice to soften the inquiry. Bryce turned his glare on Brenda.

"At a club."

"What do you mean a club? A hiking club? A tennis club?" Bryce screwed his face and shrugged.

Is that sarcasm or is he naive? He's naive.

Brenda leaned into Bryce. "Honey, he means a dance club."

Bryce's squinted as if someone had turned the brights on. "You picked her up at a bar?"

"It's a club. A dance club. It's a classy place. Not some dive."

Kevin shifted in his chair.

"They serve alcohol, right?"

Kevin was silent.

"*Club* is just a nice name for a bar. You picked her up at a bar, and what, slept with her last weekend? Last night was round two?"

"You're really quick, Bryce. It's none of your damn business who I date or who I sleep with!"

"You're not only immoral, but stupid. You picked up a complete stranger and had sex with her. What do you know about her? What's her background? I can't believe you brought home a woman like that!"

Kevin's embarrassment lifted like a mist, leaving the part of him unwilling to be pushed around by his brother. "It's my life, Bryce. I didn't ask you to show up and surprise me. I don't owe you any explanations except this: My business partner died last night, and I need to get to the restaurant and talk to my staff. Some people are going to be very strongly affected by Al's death, as am I. So, your concern about my morals doesn't mean shit right now."

He stood up, and looked at Brenda. "Brenda, I'm sorry the timing is so bad here. On any ordinary Saturday I'd be happy to see you, and we'd tour the city. I can't be much of a host today."

"It's okay. Bryce and I were planning to check in at a resort and stay the night. Maybe we could have dinner tonight?" Again she raised her pitch on the last two words.

"I can't promise you anything. If I'm available, I'll try. I'm not really in a social mood." He aimed his next words at Bryce. "And I won't be interrogated."

Bryce ignored him and turned to Brenda. "Maybe we should just go back to Phoenix."

She gave Bryce a disapproving look and turned toward Kevin. "Is there anything we can do to help?"

"Thanks for asking, Brenda, but no."

"He definitely needs help. You're a lost soul, Kevin. I'm embarrassed to be your brother right now. It's no wonder bad things are happening to you. God isn't pleased, and he's showing you. You'd better get down on your knees and ask for forgiveness."

Anger arose from grief and fear, like molten lava pressing upward, about to erupt. Kevin felt energy pulsing through his arms, urging him to swing at Bryce. He squeezed his hands into fists and then flexed his fingers. As if from somewhere on the ceiling, he watched himself turn red with rage, and then release the energy like steam from the big pressure cooker at the restaurant. He silently thanked Brenda for her presence which helped him to avoid pounding on his brother.

"It's just like you, Bryce, to have your shorts in a knot about who I sleep with and think that's more important than Al's death." He turned to Brenda. "There *is* one thing you can do. Get my god damn brother out of here! Pull the door shut on your way out. Sorry about dinner." He grabbed his keys and escaped.

Chapter Fifteen

The staff was assembled by 11:00 a.m. and the *Closed* sign placed on the door. Kevin announced to everyone the news of Al's death. There were many questions and few answers. Staff members consoled each other and expressed their shock and sadness. They also seemed anxious about their own job security. Kevin assured them the restaurant would continue. The group agreed that they would open again on Sunday and close on Tuesday, the day of the service. By 12:30 p.m. Kevin was alone. He had two difficult phone calls to make. Ronnie would be the most difficult.

Jenny messaged him that she and her son had flown in that morning and were being picked up at the airport. Kevin called Ronnie next. She answered, her voice slipping into his ear, coursing through his veins to his heart, pressing, squeezing, seemingly bleeding him. He took a breath and exhaled.

"Ronnie, it's me, Kevin."

"I'm glad you called back."

"Al was killed in an accident last night!"

"I know. I tried to call you this morning. How are you?"

"Shocked. Concerned about the staff. Sad."

"I'm so sorry. Please let me know if I can help."

"I'll be okay. You might want to see Jenny. She's in town."

"I'm going to see her right now."

"Good. She'll need your support." His voice was more crisp than he intended.

The line was silent. Kevin wondered whether the call had been dropped.

Ronnie spoke. "I'm sorry about the phone call last night. It's none of my business."

"Thanks. I really was half asleep--and I did have someone there. It felt so awkward. Why did you call?"

"I thought it was time we talked about the break-up and why I did it. That is, if you want to."

"Let's talk after this whole thing with Al is over. We need to focus on Jenny."

"Sounds good." Ronnie sounded calm.

They said good-bye and Kevin sighed, relieved that the call had been quick. He returned to the reality of his, at this moment, unreal day. It all seemed like a dream. Arguing with Al, spending the night with Marianna, Al's phone call and death, Bryce and Brenda and Marianna in the same room, talking to the staff and closing for the day, and Ronnie, all in twenty-four hours.

He set his cell phone on the table and scanned the room. Tables were set neatly with silverware and turquoise cloth napkins. Small vases, each holding a rose, served as splashes of varying colors against the white table cloths. He remembered how much he loved this place. It was Al's and his baby, and he didn't know if he could be a good single parent. He spoke to the restaurant. "I've lost my significant other, and now my business partner. I don't know where we stand financially at this moment, except that Al said we were stable a few months ago. Now you're at risk. You're all I have. I've forgotten how much you mean to me. I've let you down, and the staff, too. Jenny was right. I lost my edge. I've changed, and not for the better. I'm sorry."

He spent the afternoon going through records on the computer and whatever paper evidence he could find. Spreadsheets and balance sheets were another language to him. *It's a language I should've learned. A businessman who can't read his own financials. Ridiculous!*

By the time he returned home dusk was deepening to darkness. He wondered whether Brenda and Bryce were still in Tucson, but didn't want to talk to them. The garage door was still open. He noticed dark shadowy objects along the wall as he parked his vehicle. Black plastic was wrapped around the objects, and a red bow was perched on top of one. He slowly peeled back the plastic and discovered four brand new tires. They were the right size for his car. *Who put these tires here?* The answer popped into his mind. *Marianna! I don't believe this!*

* * *

On Sunday morning Kevin met with Jenny to plan the memorial luncheon at Calico that would follow the service on Tuesday. They sat in the bar. Kitchen noises drifted from the swinging doors in the back.

Jenny's voice sounded hollow, and the color seemed to have drained from her face. "Chip helped me find out what happened to Al on Friday night. He lost big at the casino and left there between 8:00 and 8:30."

"Al called around that time asking to meet with me. We had planned to get together Saturday morning. I told him I was with a date, and he hung up. I should've called him back right away. It might have made a difference."

"Well, you don't know that, Kevin. His cell phone shows your number was his last call, just before he crashed. There wasn't time for you to get to him. He was driving too fast, and he'd been drinking. So, don't beat yourself up. Al made his own decisions."

"And I made mine. He should've been my priority. My priorities have been out of whack."

Jenny reached for his hand and held it. "Kevin, all of us who knew Al have some level of responsibility here. He definitely took a turn for the worse when I left Tucson. I wish I could've done something to help him."

"I should have been talking to him a long time ago." He pulled away from Jenny's hand and stared at the floor. She gently moved her hand in circles on his back. He felt her concern but found little comfort in the gesture. Still, he looked at her appreciatively. She was the sister he'd never had. More than anyone she had made him feel at home in Tucson. Kevin looked at the floor again.

"What is it, Kevin?"

"I know we didn't talk a lot when I moved here, and maybe we weren't that close, but you're like a sister to me. I miss you."

A tear streamed down Jenny's cheek. "I miss you, too. I was happy you were Al's partner--and my brother, too." She reached for him, and they embraced. "I'm so sorry it ended this way."

"Me too."

On the way home Kevin thought about the past few years and how he had abdicated so much of his responsibility at the restaurant. They were partners, but they lived in two different worlds. *Worse than that, I was too focused on me to notice what was happening. All I cared about was being with Ronnie, and then all I could think about was not being with her. I screwed up.*

That evening Kevin arrived home, and found Marianna on his front porch.

"What are you doing here?"

"I came to see my boyfriend."

"We need to talk." He opened the door and let her in. Kevin flicked the light switch. "Have a seat please."

Marianna plopped on the couch, and Kevin sat in the chair across from her. She wore the white dress with the pink belt, the same outfit she wore the night they met. She was innocently pretty sitting on the edge of the cushion, all of her attention on him.

"Marianna, I can't do this anymore. I can't be sleeping with you. You are a gorgeous woman--and I know we had a good time together, but it's over."

"You don't like me? I'm not beautiful enough?"

"It's not about how you look. It's me. This isn't right for me." Ronnie's break-up speech echoed in his mind. *I'm a jerk!* "Thank you for the tires, but I think you should take them back."

"I won't take them back. They are for you. Why don't you want me?" She pushed her lips out.

"I'm not the right man for you." He stood up and reached for her arm to help her up.

She resisted a little, than allowed him to pull her forward. She wrapped her arms around him, placing her forehead on his collar bone. "Yes, you are."

"No, Marianna. You need someone who can love you and be dedicated to you. I can't love anyone like that--not right now."

"But, I want to be with you."

"I can't. It's time for you to go." Grasping her elbow, he took a step toward the door.

She wouldn't move. "At least let me kiss you."

"Okay, fine. Then you have to go. Okay?"

"Okay." She reached her hands behind his neck and pulled him to her lips, mashing his lips, before breaking the kiss. Like a cat, she rubbed her body against his and kissed him again. She gazed into his eyes. "I want to go to bed with you, one more time. Please."

Before he could speak, she kissed him again, her hand slipping below his belt. Her touch jolted him from the depression of the day, and he began to feel excited.

Kevin watched the scene as if from a distance. The mind in his body considered her request. *Why not? It would feel good?* The mind that was observing countered: *This doesn't feel right. It didn't feel right when you called her for a second date. It didn't feel right when you slept with her instead of going to see Al. Now here you are again.* His thoughts shifted back to his body. *It may not feel right but, damn, it feels good. What's the matter with a little pleasure?* His mind shifted to his observer voice again. *How many times does this have to happen before you learn? You'll regret this.* He felt his ability to make a rational decision slipping away. *I shouldn't do this!* Some part of his rational mind called out.

He grasped both her arms. "No! Marianna. It's over. Please go!" He released one of her arms and gestured toward the door. She stomped her foot on the floor like a rebellious little child. He relaxed his grip with the other hand, and she moved toward him again.

"I said NO!" The force behind his voice surprised him. He watched Marianna jump backward as if pushed by his tone.

"You are mean, Kevin. You shouldn't treat me this way!"

"I know. Good-bye, Marianna."

She stepped sideways toward the door, not taking her eyes off of him, as if waiting for him to suddenly change his mind.

"Do you have the receipt for the tires? I'll take them back."

"No receipt. I threw it away. You need the tires anyway."

"At least tell me how much they cost so I can give you a check."

"No. Good-bye." She left him standing at the door as she walked toward her car.

He breathed a sigh as he watched her drive away. "Thank God I didn't tell her where I work."

* * *

The next few days were a blur. Emotions swirled like dust devils around and within him. Guilt seized him--guilt for his failure to respond to Al; for rejecting Marianna; and for the restaurant. Seeing Ronnie again recalled the pain of her leaving. He remembered a time they hiked off the main trail at Sabino Canyon. He had sat on the ground, bracing himself against a rock. Planting both hands in the sand for support, he didn't notice the danger beneath him. Moments later pain shot through his left hand. Ants were crawling on him and stinging. Ronnie helped him brush the little creatures off. "What kind of ants are these?"

"Those are pogo ants. We need to get you out of here, Kevin, and have you checked. Are you allergic?"

"I don't think so, why?"

"Their venom is powerful. Some people are allergic, and some have died from it. Even if you aren't allergic, it's still very painful."

For the next few hours his hand and arm throbbed. He checked out okay at the Urgent Care, and they gave him something to ease his pain. Later, as he was healing, the bites scabbed over. They itched, and he scratched without thinking. It offered temporary relief, but breaking open the scab just made the healing take longer. That's how he felt about seeing Ronnie again. It was like scratching. It felt good at first, but mainly it just reopened the wounds.

The service was held at Santa Cruz Parish. Al and Jenny were married there and had maintained loose ties over the years. It was large enough to accommodate the two hundred mourners who attended. The post-service luncheon at Calico filled all the tables. The staff took care of everything, and Kevin was grateful to be busy managing the event.

As the afternoon wore on the crowd slowly dwindled. Later, Kevin sat with Jenny and Ronnie. The crew had cleaned up and gone home. The two women carried the conversation while Kevin tried, without success, to relax. Both women looked at him. Jenny said, "How are you, Kevin?"

"Okay."

"It's going to take some time. I wish I could've helped Al, but wishing doesn't do anything now."

Ronnie held her hand. "Jenny, you did everything you could."

"We were married twenty-five years. I still cared about him."

Ronnie took both Jenny's hands and squeezed. "It's okay, Sweetie. You can't help but feel sad. No one expected it would come to this. Not you, not anyone." She looked to Kevin for agreement.

"I'm still shocked that Al's gone. Whatever was going on with him, I don't think it had anything to do with you, Jenny."

"Thanks, you guys." Jenny grasped a hand from both Kevin and Ronnie. "I miss you both." She glanced at the clock. "My flight leaves in two hours. We'd better get going." She turned to Kevin. "Ronnie's taking me to the airport, and we need to pick up Matt." She took his right hand in both of her hands, tightening her grip to make her point. "Kevin, dig into the financials immediately."

"I have a meeting with the accountant in the morning. He'll help me straighten this out"

Ronnie touched his left hand, sending small ripples up his arm. "Call me if you need help. I mean it."

They all rose from the table. Jenny embraced Kevin and kissed him on the cheek. "Let me know what happens."

"I will. Safe flight."

Ronnie approached him and wrapped her arms around him. He held her loosely, trying not to hold too tightly, trying not to squeeze her in desperation. Whenever they had been in each others' arms, the world had felt right. He wanted the world to feel right again. She kissed him on the cheek.

"Thanks, for being here, Ronnie. It was good to see you again, despite the circumstances. Take care."

Ronnie smiled, turned and walked out the door with Jenny. He watched through the window as they drove away.

Everyone's leaving. In his three-and-a-half years in Tucson, the three people he had been closest to were now out of his life. *At least I still have the restaurant.*

Chapter Sixteen

Early Wednesday morning Kevin unlocked the front door of the restaurant, determined to put the business in order. He walked back to the office and sorted every financial document into one pile. He turned on the computer and copied the Quicken files onto a jump drive. On impulse, he lifted up the keyboard and found an envelope addressed to Al from the U.S. Department of Treasury.

Sentences jumped off the page at him.

> Withholding taxes and FICA have not been paid for 180 days. This is your third notice.

Tension flared in his stomach. He put the letter on top of the pile and left for his appointment with the accountant.

The next few weeks were excruciating. Working with the accountant, he discovered that Al had taken all available cash plus the money that should have been paid for taxes. He was also behind six months on the building mortgage. When Kevin first came to Tucson, Al owned the building outright. He didn't know his partner had taken a substantial equity loan a year ago. Vendors called, saying they hadn't been paid. The money problems of the restaurant attacked in waves, and Kevin was drowning.

Ronnie recommended an attorney who could sort out his personal liabilities. Between the IRS and other debts, the restaurant owed over half a million dollars. Kevin committed himself to making the Grill solvent, but his long hours and titanic effort weren't enough. After three weeks he had little cash and no available credit. He was forced to close. All money gathered from the sale of equipment was to be paid to the IRS, with the rest divided among the vendors. Ronnie promised to find a buyer for his house.

After paying the staff, Kevin was left with two hundred dollars and plenty of personal debt. He had no idea what he would do next, with a month to move before the closing on his house.

Throughout the process he had ignored daily texts and voicemails from Marianna. Several times he had approached his street only to see her car in his driveway, and Marianna sitting in front of his door. Each time he had continued driving, arriving at home after she had gone. One night the phone rang at 2:30 a.m. Startled out of sleep, he picked up the phone. "Hello."

"Hi, Kevin. I have been calling you. Why won't you talk to me?"

"Marianna, why are you calling me in the middle of the night?"

"I want to take you to Vegas. Some friends and I are going tomorrow. I will pay your way if you come."

"No. Stop calling me."

"But, Kevin. I love you. You are my boyfriend."

"Please stop calling and texting me."

"I love you, Kevin. I would do anything for you."

"Then I want you to do one thing for me."

"Yes. What is it?"

"Leave me alone. Live your life, and let me live mine. Will you do that for me?"

There was no response. Kevin hung up.

At dawn he was awakened by knocking. He pulled on his sweats, splashed water in his face, and dragged himself to the front door. It was Marianna. Depression changed to anger as he opened the door. "What are you doing here?"

"I just wanted to see you, Kevin. Please. I promise to go away after this. I promise."

He looked at her, debating whether he should close the door or let her in. He stepped out of the house and closed the door behind him. "What do you want?"

"I just want to hug you, and say good-bye."

She wrapped her arms around him, squeezing him, her nose pressing his chest. Her hair smelled of the sweet, fruity shampoo she had used the last morning they were together. Having had no human physical contact for several days, the hug felt good. He returned it. *She just wants to be loved like everyone else.* A minute passed when he grasped her shoulders and gently pushed her away.

She looked at him with sad eyes and quickly kissed him on the lips. "Good-bye." She ran to her car.

Kevin watched her drive away. She didn't look back.

There had been no contact with his family in the past few weeks, as he couldn't bring himself to face them. He was convinced they were as disappointed in him as he was. The phone rang. Kevin hesitated, thinking it might be Marianna again. It was his brother.

"Hello, Bryce."

"I expected an apology for how you treated us. I guess that was too much to ask." Bryce's tone was coarse, like sandpaper on flesh.

Kevin was tired, too weary to argue. "Bryce, I'm sorry."

"What happened to the girlfriend?"

"I don't have a girlfriend. I'm not seeing anyone."

"Good."

"And the restaurant?"

"It's gone. Out of business."

Bryce was quiet for a few moments. "I knew you'd fall on your face. Remember, I said you'd come crawling back to Michigan broke? You never should've left, and you shouldn't have wasted that money. Don't expect Dad to give you a job. You don't deserve it. You're being punished for your sinful life. Maybe if you got down on your knees and prayed for forgiveness, God might help you."

"You're right. I did fall on my face. It's my own fault. I don't expect Dad to give me a job, so don't worry about that. As for God, I don't think He or She would punish me, because I'm doing a good job of that on my own."

"Well, definitely God is He. You need help--spiritual help."

"You're right. I do." The line was silent. "I need to go, Bryce. Thanks for calling and checking on me." He hung up without waiting for Bryce's good-bye.

Kevin spent the rest of the day pacing, searching for solutions to the mess his life had become. In his mind's eye he recalled the last meeting with the employees at the grill. He had announced that the business was bankrupt. Their faces transformed into a mishmash of fear, anger, and sadness. He made himself hand each staff member a final paycheck, scraped together from the last week of business. He shook each person's hand and thanked each one.

He felt powerless, unable to change the past, and unable to create a better future. The hopelessness of his situation penetrated his bones like an osteoporotic disease, crippling his ability to move forward. *Move forward to what? Homelessness? Guilt over letting the people go? Financial ruin?*

Depression wrapped its stiff, bony fingers around his chest and crushed him. He did nothing for a week. Finally, he talked himself into looking for employment. He searched for a week, hoping to find a management job. There was nothing. Going to bed was somewhat of a relief. At least, during the night, nothing was expected of him. He spent less time searching and more time lamenting his situation. He was paralyzed, and he knew it. Early one Sunday morning in June he found himself wide awake, but not wanting to get up. *You have got to do something. Get your ass out of bed!*

He rose from the bed, ate a bowl of cereal and drank some orange juice. While sorting old papers, he came across a flyer for Mike's meditation class back in Michigan. *When was the last time I tried to meditate? Pima Canyon?*

There was plenty of work: packing, organizing, cleaning, looking for a job, but it could wait one more day. Kevin drove to Pima Canyon and ascended the path that took him to his desert retreat. Listening to the sand and stone crunch beneath his feet, the familiar strain on his muscles felt good, but his thoughts still tortured him.

Why does life have to be so difficult? Had a great job--was a good manager with a fantastic staff. Could be intense at the restaurant, but everyone had each others' backs. We laughed. He cared more about his people than he'd realized. His income was way better than his best year as a teacher. *But, was I really that good? I was dedicated the first two years. Fantastic service--reputation. With Ronnie I lost my focus. Calico was still good, but not growing. Being with Ronnie was more important. Still, I got the job done, didn't I? Why is this happening?*

He rejected Bryce's theory. One of Jenny's friends told him it was probably his negative thinking that created this mess. She had invited him to her prosperity group. He said he'd think about it. *Just what I need--to sit in a group with a bunch of other losers! Maybe I should have done better, but I didn't deserve all of this.*

He climbed higher on the trail. A pinion jay squawked at him. *Stupid brown-headed bird!* He tripped on a large rock embedded in the trail and fell to his knees. *God damn it!* His jeans were torn, and he wiped blood from his knee on his pants. His skin burned as he brushed the dirt from the wound. Ronnie came to mind. *What kind of woman just walks out on a two-year relationship without a word? I was good to her. And what about Al? What an ass! He screwed up, died--left me holding the bag. I have to pay for his god damn mistakes.*

Consoled and energized by his anger, he picked up the pace. Accompanied only by the sound of his footsteps, he pressed on. Mountains dotted with saguaro surrounded him, isolating him from the rest of the world. The knee hurt, and more blood oozed out.

He couldn't decide if he liked the desert or not. Sometimes it looked dry and barren, and at other times it was teeming with life. It depended on the light in which he saw it. Today it appeared dry and stark, and his parched mouth pleaded for water. He took a drink. *That takes care of my body. Wish I could refresh my head.* His thoughts drifted toward the rest of the day. There were errands to run. The car needed gas. *How much money do I have?*

Kevin reached for his wallet, opened it, and found a ten and two ones. *That's sad.* He wondered if there were any other bills hidden within. From somewhere beneath the now useless plastic he found a cocktail napkin, neatly folded. He opened it and could not help but smile. It was Rachel's napkin.

> Kevin,
> You are a center of influence.
> Everything you think, feel, say, and do
> has an effect and determines your future.
> Who are you? What do you want?
> Love and Blessings, Rachel Lindsay.

I'm a center of attention. Here I'm talking about what a raw deal life has given me. What am I giving to life? Self pity. Poor me! I'm blaming Al and Ronnie, but what about me? Our business was falling apart, and my concerns before Al died were about getting laid and having enough money.

I've been here before. Remembering the car ride to Tucson when he had reflected on his center-of-attention tendencies, the promise to become an adult lay back there on US-93. *How could I have forgotten?*

Reading Rachel's words again, his true intentions were elusive. Ronnie always seemed to know what she wanted. Rachel knew what she wanted. Even Marianna knew what she wanted. *Are women better at knowing this than men?* He wondered how Rachel was doing. He had only occasionally thought of her since the day he met Ronnie.

Messages had been exchanged infrequently over the past few years, and he remembered her words about relationships--that she would only be involved with a real adult. *I don't think I'm qualified yet.*

There's so much I don't get. You'd think a guy in his mid-forties would have it together. I don't. Six months ago I was a big success, but it was a cardboard cutout. I spent more than I made. No wonder things fell apart. I felt pretty good about myself, but I wasn't an adult. I depended on Ronnie, my income, and my home to make me happy. Always seeing life in terms of what it's doing to me--or what it should be doing for me.

So who am I anyway? Whiny. Angry. Life sucks. Disappointed in life--disappointed in myself--don't really know what to do about it. Not an adult--more like a sixteen-year-old with thirty-one years of experience. I'm responsible. I get it. Now what?

He remembered Rachel telling him that her life began to change when she sought solitude in the desert. She said her best prayer was "Thank you." He took off his shoes so he could feel the earth beneath his feet and prayed the way she had taught him.

Facing the sun as it rose over the canyon wall, he closed his eyes, breathing in the warm air, drawing it down deeply. Exhaling slowly, he continued breathing deliberately. With each exhalation he gave thanks for breath, for life. He looked to the universe, to whoever or whatever was the source of life. Was it within him or around him, or both? Did Rachel call it God, or Spirit, or by some other name? He spoke to that which was nameless. "Thank you. Thank you for everything that is now happening in my life." *Really?*

Anger and regret poured into his mind, and he allowed himself to feel the agony. Diving into the pain, embracing it, *wanting* to feel it, he surrendered to the moment, and stood in silent atonement.

When the emotion had run its course, he said aloud: "I did this. No one is to blame." He continued to breathe slowly and deeply, trying not to think, but only to feel. For a few moments he felt acceptance. He accepted the mess his life appeared to be. *This is all my responsibility, not Ronnie's or Al's or anyone else's. I'm the one who needs to act. Help me. Whoever or Whatever is the power that created me, help me.*

There was no burning bush--no big voice on the cosmic intercom. Just stillness. Tears streamed down his cheeks. His body shuddered as a sob bubbled up from deep within his chest. More sobs shook his body as he gave up control and allowed them to come. The release purged him of resistance to responsibility. Eventually the sobs subsided, and emptiness and quiet filled his inner space. *Whatever it is that I need to learn right now--I want to learn it.*

In silence, he joined with the desert, grateful for the little peace he felt. Several hikers walked past, and he paid them no mind. No words came, nor any urging to a particular action--just a small sense of trust--that all would be well. He allowed himself to bask in this small confidence.

Breathing and giving thanks, he noticed everything around him--the heat of the sun on his face, the songs of birds in the canyon, the solid ground of sand and stones beneath his feet. The desert appeared different now, not so harsh and dry, but beautiful. *This place is amazing! Funny, how my appreciation for the world increases when I stop focusing on me.* It was like watching a great movie, losing himself in the surrounding beauty, and time passing without him.

♪Wake me up inside. Wake me up inside.

The ring tone of his cell phone startled him. He looked at the screen, surprised that he had service this deep in the canyon.

"Hi, Jenny."

"Hi, Kevin. How are you?"

"Okay. I'm in Pima Canyon baking in the sun. How about you?"

"I'm doing well. I was thinking about you. I heard how things turned out with the restaurant. Are you managing all right?"

"It's a struggle. I was praying when you called. I'm standing here trying to figure out what to do next. The money is running out, and there are debts to pay. Everything you tried to warn me about that day at the club--it happened."

"Well, I hope this helps. I have a name for you. There's a couple in town, delightful people, old friends of mine--Michael and Sarah.

They really *are* old, but energetic people. Michael owns a diner, and he wants to spend less time there and more time with his wife and great-grand kids. He needs someone to manage the place, and I told him about you. It doesn't have to be a career, but it might be just the thing to keep you going until you figure out what you want."

Kevin thought a moment and felt a wave of gratitude toward Jenny. "Thanks, Jenny. Give me the number, and I'll call him."

After Jenny's call, Kevin typed the name and phone number into his cell. He uncapped his water bottle and held it to his lips. The water felt cool as it flowed over his tongue and into his throat. "Thank you." He squatted down to watch a gecko scurrying across his path, and gently touched the pink flowers on a little hedgehog cactus with his index finger. *Life!*

* * *

"Hello. This is Michael." The voice was clear--sure of itself.

"Hi Michael. This is Kevin. Our mutual friend, Jenny Stewart, said you needed a restaurant manager." Kevin sat at his kitchen table looking at the website for the Butterfly Diner.

There was a pause for several seconds on the line. Finally, Michael responded, "Can you start tomorrow?"

"Ah, don't you want to interview me and check my references?"

"You were just interviewed, and I already checked your references. Do you want the job or not?"

"Yes." Kevin answered quickly. "I can start tomorrow."

"Good. Be at the diner at 4:00 a.m. We'll begin breakfast prep and your training. I'll see you then." The phone clicked.

He had accepted a job, with no idea what was required, the salary level, or what hours he'd be working.

Monday morning he was up and showered by 3:30 a.m. He put on jeans and a blue denim shirt, but no cowboy boots. They were uncomfortable. His blue Ford Escape arrived at the diner's back parking lot just before 4:00 a.m.. It was an adobe-style building illuminated by a pair of floodlights. A black Jeep Cherokee was the only vehicle in the lot, and Kevin parked his car next to it. He approached the back door and reached for the doorknob. *Behind this door is a new beginning.*

The door pushed outward, and Kevin stepped back to avoid being hit. "You're here! Good morning, Kevin. I'm Michael." He reached out his hand, and Kevin shook it. The grip was strong. "Please come in."

Kevin stepped into the brightly lit kitchen, and Michael closed the door softly. He invited him to sit at a small wooden table on one of the two round stools. "Now that you're hired, I should interview you." Michael smiled. "That was a joke, Kevin. Relax."

Michael stood about five feet nine inches, but seemed taller. He had a noble look with high check bones and a straight, broad nose. His white hair was combed back on the sides and reached to his collar. His smile was calming. There were a few small wrinkles on Michael's reddish tan face, mostly around the temples. As if they had just witnessed something splendid, his brown eyes seemed to be celebrating. Kevin wondered how old he was.

"I'm eighty-seven." Michael offered a wide grin.

"Excuse me! How did you do that?" Kevin leaned on the table and squinted at him

"How did I do what?"

"How did you know I was wondering how old you are?"

"Everyone wonders how old I am. Nine times out of ten when I meet someone, they're wondering about my age. I was born in 1925. My father was Mexican and my mother was Hopi. I grew up around Tucson and spent my summers on the Hopi reservation. Most of my adult life I've been in the restaurant business. That's it! Tell me about yourself, Kevin."

Kevin cleared his throat and collected his thoughts. "I've been in the restaurant business for almost four years. I was part owner of the Calico Grill which was shut down several weeks ago. Before that I was a high school teacher in Michigan and a basketball coach. I've lost everything, so I really need this job."

"I know about the Calico Grill. It was a very successful place, and I enjoyed dinner there a few times."

"I don't remember seeing you."

"I saw you. You were busy, and you were good. You have a job here if you want it." Michael looked at him with confidence, as if he had known Kevin for years and had no doubt in his abilities.

"I don't know anything about the position. What hours do you need me? How much is the salary? What will I be doing?"

"Monday through Sunday, 4:30 a.m. to 3:00 p.m. Wednesdays are off. Six hundred dollars per week plus meals. You'll do whatever needs to be done. Make sure all the roles are filled--cooks, waitresses, dishwashers. Take up the slack where needed. Talk to the customers, and make sure they're delighted. Count the money, and take it to the bank. Anything from seating a customer to taking out the trash to grilling vegetables is your job if it needs to be done."

Kevin tried to hold back his disappointment at the salary. He had made more than three times that at Calico. *Since I don't have any other prospects, I'd better take this.* "I can handle that. Thank you, Michael."

"All right then, Kevin. Let's get you trained."

Chapter Seventeen

"Thanks for your help, Ronnie." They were at Ronnie's office, and they had just planned the closing meeting on the house. "The only reason I have any equity to pay off some of these bills is because you didn't take a commission. Your friend, the lawyer, has been very helpful in dealing with the IRS."

"Sorry you had to go through all of this."

Kevin glanced at her once, twice.

"I know you've got something going on there. Just say it."

"Why did you leave? Was it about money?"

Ronnie closed her eyes, and nodded her head as if having a conversation with herself. Her eyes opened. "That was a part of it. I admit I like to spend, and travel and have nice things. I don't think that's wrong. At one time it would've been okay with you moving in with me and you not buying this house. I don't care that I make more money than you. But, you care. You didn't want to live in my house, and it didn't make sense. I'm a businesswoman, and supporting two houses was wasteful. So, yes, part of the reason I left had to do with money and attitudes about money."

"Not the only reason?" Kevin tilted his head toward her.

"It's a small part of it. I'm a great salesperson. I should've persuaded you to move in with me." Ronnie smiled. "As long as you were gainfully employed and enjoyed your work, and felt confident in doing it, that was enough for me. I wouldn't have minded being the one who had to cover more than fifty percent of the expenses. But, we had a much deeper issue. Our relationship wasn't healthy."

"What do you mean by that?"

"Our relationship was mostly physical--about attraction and chemistry. Those things are wonderful, but I want more than that.

You wanted me; you needed me; and I could feel that; but your appetite for me never seemed to be satisfied. For a while, I enjoyed it. I admit, I liked feeling wanted and needed. Then I realized it had little to do with my soul. It was like you were addicted to me, and I didn't want to be your drug. I didn't want to be the object of your love. I don't want to be an object at all."

"I thought you wanted me just as much as I wanted you." Kevin challenged.

She was silent for a few seconds. "You're right; I wanted you, too. You were the object of my desire, especially when we first met. But, we never really solved problems or dealt with our emotions. We had sex. We avoided real intimacy and chose dopamine. So in a way, I guess you were my drug, too, and that bothered me. It's not what I want."

"What *do* you want?"

"I want a relationship where there's intimacy and connection, where my partner and I are sensitive to each others needs, where we face our difficulties together. I want sex to be a sacred connection, but I don't want it to be the center of the relationship."

"So, because of my neediness for you, and yours for me, you stopped loving me?" Kevin faced his palms upward.

"Kevin, I haven't stopped loving you. You're a beautiful man, and I'll always think well of you. I hope you can forgive me for leaving you in a way that was abrupt and hurtful. My other hope is that you'll see my leaving as something good."

"Why didn't you tell me this when we were together?"

Ronnie shrugged and shook her head. "I don't have an answer. I couldn't explain it then. It just felt wrong to me. For us, the chemistry dominated everything. I didn't think we were capable of changing that. There wasn't much substance to our relationship-- not much honesty, or sharing from the heart. It was physical intimacy but not emotional or spiritual."

Kevin looked across the table at Ronnie, gazed into her eyes, tried to see into her soul. In his mind's eye she was eclipsed by an image of Rachel. He remembered sitting across the table from Rachel looking into *her* eyes. He recalled her honesty, and how she refused to allow him to be dishonest.

He thought about the year-and-a-half with Ronnie, and how obsessed he was about being with her, and fearful of losing her. He thought back a few months to how distraught he was at not having her. *Is that the person I want to be? Jenny was right. I don't know the difference between love and obsession. I was a slave to my desire, and it helped to destroy my business.*

"Hey, Kevin, are you still there?" Ronnie smiled.

"I'm here. I was just thinking about what you said. Thanks for answering my question. I guess our relationship was mostly one-dimensional. I hope you can forgive me for that."

"There's nothing to forgive. You know how I feel about the past. You and I have a connection, and I honor and love that. You will always be in my heart." She patted her chest.

Kevin held her in his gaze, searching behind her eyes. He saw both her pain, and her potential for greatness. "I see you."

She glanced away, then quickly returned. "I see you, too."

He sensed they would take different paths, and he let her go.

They stood up and embraced. The usual physical excitement was gone. He felt love, but no sense of desire or need. He kissed her on the cheek. "It's okay, Ronnie. Be happy."

"Thank you." She spoke softly. "I'll see you at the closing."

Kevin turned and walked toward the door. He let himself out.

Chapter Eighteen

"Good morning, Michael." Kevin arrived at work at 4:30 a.m.

Michael held his forefinger to his lips. "Shhh. Today is piki bread day. Come with me."

They stepped into the doorway of a small room, about ten by ten feet, where a woman was spreading blue batter on a rectangular, flat stone. A fire burned beneath it.

"How does she do that? She's using her bare hands!"

"She's been doing this for years. That's my cousin, and she grew up in a Hopi village. Piki bread-making is a sacred tradition."

"I hope you're not expecting me to do that!"

"If I did she would have a fit. Only Hopi women make piki bread. Once I dared to help, and she threatened to break the piki stone and quit. That sandstone slab has been in the family for over fifty years. She lets me grind corn, and sometimes build the fire, but bread making is strictly hers. She makes it every Tuesday, and there will be a line out the door at lunch. Everyone loves her piki bread-- great with lamb stew or corn soup."

"How many pieces does she make in one sitting?" Kevin watched as she peeled the thin piece of blue-grey bread off of the stone. She rolled it and placed it on a brightly colored plate.

"Up to one hundred pieces. We only allow one per customer. I asked her to make an extra piece for you."

"Thank you." Kevin felt honored.

"Come." Michael led him back into the kitchen.

Kevin's second day was more difficult than the first. On the first day he had followed his new boss around and was shown the elements of his job. On this day Michael asked him to do each task while he watched and coached. It all looked easier when Michael had done it. As customers arrived Kevin found himself in more familiar territory, welcoming and seating them. By day's end he was tired. As they were locking up, Michael invited him to his home.

Kevin followed the black Cherokee as it turned onto busy Speedway Boulevard. They drove to Colonial Solana, an historic area near Reid Park and the zoo. It was a different world. The car paths were dirt with stones lined along the side in places to distinguish yards from avenues. An arroyo snaked through the neighborhood. Other than a few palm trees, he noticed that most of the plants were native. There were no lawns or exotic, tropical flowers as were sometimes found in upscale neighborhoods.

They turned into the gravel drive of a white adobe-style home. A large Palo Verde tree replete with yellow blossoms shaded the driveway. As he exited the car his attention was drawn to the bright reddish, orange flowers along a trellis in front of the house.

"You'll want to see this. Walk softly." Michael led Kevin toward the flowers. They were trumpet-shaped, and there were dozens of them. Michael pointed to the right, and then Kevin saw it. A hummingbird floated over a blossom, then inserted its bill inside. Several more hummingbirds alternately darted and hovered.

"The flower is called a hummingbird trumpet. I think you can see why we grow them. They've just begun to bloom."

Kevin nodded, mesmerized by the birds and flowers. Michael tugged on his arm and led him toward a wooden gate near the back of the house. The back yard was enclosed by a seven foot adobe barrier, and a variety of colorful, flowering plants grew along the inside wall. Sunlight reflected off an L-shaped swimming pool set in the center. Dark blue ceramic tiles sparkled beneath the surface, and the corners of the el were slightly rounded, giving a relaxed look to the pool. A few round tables with umbrellas and wicker chairs surrounded the pool. Another Palo Verde stood at the far end of the yard providing shade to a pair of lounge chairs. Brilliant yellow blossoms adorned the tree and its canopy which hung about six feet from the ground.

Michael nodded toward it. "There are a few hummingbird nests in that tree as well."

Looking to his left, Kevin beheld a tree, probably eighty feet tall, towering over the yard. "What kind of tree is that?" He grasped Michael's arm and pointed at the giant.

"That's an Aleppo Pine, also known as a Jerusalem Pine. It was here long before I arrived."

"What's that at the base?" Kevin gestured toward a series of concentric circles made from small stones encircling the trunk.

"That's Sarah's labyrinth. She walks it when she needs to think."

Kevin's face blanked. "A what?"

"Let's save that until you meet Sarah. She'll explain it better than me."

As Kevin approached the pool, a colorful mosaic face appeared, embedded in the bottom looking up at him. Its turquoise, red, and yellow face was framed by purples and reds woven together. It looked like a sun catcher.

"That's Dawa, the sun kachina. Sarah made it. All of our tables have kachinas, too.

"What's a kachina?"

"It's a spirit being. Kachina dolls represent spirit beings from Hopi lore. Most are benevolent, but some are not."

"Do you believe in these things? I mean, is this part of your religion?"

Michael laughed. "I don't *believe* in anything. I only know what I experience. This is art--Sarah's art, and it's good, don't you think?"

"Yes." Kevin nodded and admired the figure in the pool.

Michael motioned toward the loungers. "How about a cold beer? We'll sit here and enjoy this little piece of heaven."

"Sounds good."

Michael pointed to a rectangular structure with sliding glass doors at the back of the yard. "That's our poolhouse. There's a bathroom inside. Feel free to use it and look around." He turned and proceeded toward the main house.

Kevin slid open the door and walked into what looked like a large studio apartment. It was appointed with a queen-sized bed, desk, chest of drawers, small sitting area, and a kitchen. At the far end he found a full bath. The place was simple and homey, and he was tempted to lie on the bed and take a nap. Resisting the urge, he returned to the yard. Michael waited with two beers, a bowl of chips, and salsa.

Side by side they relaxed into the loungers, angled toward each other, the drinks and chips on a small table between them.

"So, Kevin, let's hear your story. And don't leave anything out." He sipped his beer, and then set it on the table.

Kevin downed half the bottle, and sighed. Each swallow cooled him degree by degree. The gentle scent of the Palo Verde blossoms seemed to relax him. Peering up into the canopy, he was unable spot any hummingbird nests. Closing his eyes, Kevin reached back to the year of his divorce and began his tale.

Michael listened quietly as Kevin's story poured forth. He kept his eyes softly focused on Kevin, occasionally savoring a swallow of beer or nibbling on a chip.

Kevin looked at his watch, surprised that an hour had passed.

"Don't worry about the time. For me, this is like watching a full length film: *The Life and Times of Kevin*. I enjoyed it. Thank you. Bravo!" He clapped his hands.

"Are you being sarcastic?" Anger and hurt seeped in behind Kevin's eyes.

"Oh, no, Kevin. I enjoyed your story so much. It's beautiful."

"Yeah, like that old Bob Seger song, *Beautiful Loser.*" Cutting himself on his own voice, a tear bled from his left eye. Quickly, he wiped it with his finger.

Michael closed his eyes and started playing the table like a snare. Next he sang, as if he were on stage:

Beautiful loser.
Read it on the wall. And realize.
You just can't have it all.

He raised his right arm and pointed to the sky. His left hand held an invisible microphone. Michael opened his eyes and peered at Kevin; his lips unfurled into a grin; eyes danced; eyebrows arched; he shook his head; and he swayed his long white hair.

Unable to contain it any longer, a laugh exploded from Kevin's belly and rocked his body. The laugh multiplied, completely disregarding his intention to remain serious and offended. He squinted through teary slits and saw Michael doubled over, hooting and roaring in obvious delight.

As the laughter subsided, Kevin spoke first. "So you think my life is entertaining?"

"Very."

"I don't understand how you can find my failures so delightful."

"I don't understand why *you don't* find them delightful."

"Easy for you to say; you're not the one going through this. Why should you care?"

"Oh, Kevin, I care very much. When Dana left I felt sad. When you changed your life and moved out west, I was excited. I was intrigued by Rachel. I felt attraction when you described both Ronnie and Marianna. I grieved when Al lost his life, and you lost the restaurant. I was absolutely joyous when you had an epiphany in the desert. I loved your story."

"Yeah, well, it's different when you're the one the story is about."

"Why?"

Kevin raised his eyebrows in disbelief. "Because of all the pain, and the unhappiness I feel with myself."

"What *is* happiness, Kevin?"

"It's, I don't know, being successful, I guess." Kevin had assumed he knew what happiness was, but now, it seemed as though he didn't. "I thought it meant being successful and making money, and feeling good about it, but now I'm not so sure."

"There is no joy without sorrow. There is no up without down-- no happily ever after where you never feel sadness or hurt or anger again, at least not as long as you're living on this planet."

"Well, I thought success waited for me out here, and I just had to grab it."

"You were tired of teaching school and not finding much in life that meant anything. You wanted an adventure."

"Yeah, I did."

"So, you're having one, aren't you?"

"I didn't expect to fail like this."

"I know. You thought you'd move out here, get rich, find the woman of your dreams, live happily ever after, and then go back to Michigan and tell Bryce and your father you told them so. Right?"

Kevin nodded slowly.

"Most stories don't go like that. If your instant success story were made into a movie it'd be a real yawner. Personally, I like the way *you're* doing it. It's delightful."

Kevin furrowed his brow. "Who gets delighted at failure?"

"I do. It's not the failure itself. It's the story. Your story. Stop taking yourself so seriously and live it. Haven't the past three or four years been rich in experience?"

Kevin had to agree.

"You could have stayed in Michigan, secure but bored. It's wonderful that you stepped out. Aren't you excited to see what happens next? You and I have met, and now I wonder what adventures we'll have."

"I'm not even sure *why* I'm here with you." Kevin gazed into Michael's eyes.

"Me neither." Michael grinned and finished his beer.

They were quiet while Kevin searched for answers.

Michael reached across the table for Kevin's arm and fixed his eyes on Kevin's eyes. "You are the manager at my diner, and we are now friends. Choose to step into those roles, or make another choice. It's up to you. Have you considered that the universe led us to each other?"

"I'd like to believe that, but I don't know how long I can stay. I mean, I'm grateful for the job and to be invited to your home, but the money I make here is not enough to cover all of my payments and to rent a new place." *I have to be out of my home in a little over a week. I don't know what I'll do then.*

"I understand. Why don't you just let things unfold and see what happens? Be patient. I know you have financial pressure, but don't let fear take over."

* * *

Kevin thought about Michael's words on the way home. *Be patient. Let things unfold.* With six figures in debt and no place to live in a week, he felt anything but patient. His minimum payments were almost as much as his salary. Tension grew in his gut and infected the rest of his body. *What am I afraid of? I have a home for the moment. I can eat at the restaurant.*

His father came to mind. He was embarrassed to tell him the money was gone. He *was* a failure--a failure in business and a failure in love. Afraid to face his daughters, he worried that they would see a father who had nothing. What if one of them decided to get married? He couldn't offer anything. Bryce knew what had happened, and no doubt had told everyone everything--the restaurant failure, Marianna, Ronnie.

Focus on what's going well, Kevin--your new job, Michael as a boss and a friend, good health. There are things to be thankful for. You're alive! Outside of the basketball court, he had seldom felt alive his last few years in Michigan. He spoke out loud to himself. "It *has* been quite a ride since I came to Arizona." As he pulled into the driveway, the image of Michael drumming and singing *Beautiful Loser* flashed across the screen of his mind. He burst out laughing.

Chapter Nineteen

Days flew by as Kevin immersed himself in the work of the diner, but the nights inched along as he worried and pondered where to live and how to pay his debts. Michael began leaving him in charge for hours at a time, and after a week he pronounced him properly trained. They sat mid-morning of Kevin's eighth day enjoying the first two cups of lamb stew and a roll of piki bread. "What makes this so good?" Kevin savored a mouthful of lamb, potato, onions, and carrots in a tasty broth.

"It's the coriander, mixed with garlic, rosemary and thyme, and slow-braised lamb. I spent years getting the recipe right. Coriander is my favorite spice." A smile spread across Michael's face.

Tania, a part-time waitress, refilled their water glasses, and Kevin couldn't resist a quick look down her blouse as she leaned over. For a moment he enjoyed her well-shaped curves and felt the longing to touch and be touched. She finished filling his glass.

"Thanks, Tania."

She smiled as they made eye contact. A flock of blond hairs sprang from her hair-tie and fell, suspended across her left eye. Her face turned slightly pink as she tucked them behind her ear, and they continued their eye contact. Kevin watched her walk away, admiring the sensual sway, lost in fantasy. As he returned his attention to his stew, he noticed Michael staring at him. "What?"

"Don't even think about it, Kevin." Michael's face darkened. "Anything between you two and it's over."

"I was just looking." Kevin's eyes widened.

"Don't even look." His tone pierced Kevin's defenses. "Did you date any of your employees at Calico?"

"No. I didn't think it was a good idea for an owner to date an employee."

"Not for managers either. So make the choice. If you start seeing her, the job is out." Michael studied Kevin's face, waiting for his response.

Kevin shifted in his chair. *I can't believe I forgot where I was for a few seconds there.* "Nothing will happen. You don't need to worry, Michael. I want the job."

* * *

Later, as they finished cleanup, Tania approached. "Kevin, could I get a ride home with you today?" She smiled and scrunched her shoulders, her right foot lifted, toes touching the floor.

Kevin cleared his throat. "Who usually drives you home?" He asked more abruptly than he intended.

Tania pursed her lips and clasped her hands below her waist. "Well, Mary has been driving me."

"Tania, I need to meet with Michael. Why don't you ask Mary again?"

"Well, maybe another time then?"

"I don't think so, Tania."

Her eyes narrowed; lips closed.

Inwardly he rolled his eyes, reprimanding himself for leading her on. *This isn't her fault.* As she walked away, he spoke. "Hey, Tania."

She turned, looking at him, eyebrows lifted.

"Thanks for your good work today. You were a real professional with that party on the patio at lunch. You should be proud of yourself."

"Oh, yeah. Thanks." Her face brightened. "I'll see you Thursday."

A few minutes later, Michael passed Tania and Mary in the doorway and gave each one a quick hug as he entered the restaurant. "Kevin, are you free for dinner Friday? Sarah will be home, and I'd like you to meet her."

"I'd love to. What time do you want me there?"

* * *

The closing on Kevin's house took place the next day--his day off. He had no place to go for the night, and it was two days before his first paycheck. He had meant to ask Ronnie if he could stay in her spare room for a couple of days until he could pay for a room on his own. Unexpectedly, she was called out of town and missed the closing.

He spent the night in his car, behind the restaurant. Having slept intermittently and uncomfortably, he stumbled out of his vehicle at 3:30 a.m., muscles stiff and sore. *Hang in there, Kevin. A few more days and you'll have your own place.* A lizard scurried under a rock. *'The foxes have holes and the birds of the air have nests, but the Son of Man has nowhere to lay His head.' Why did that quote come to mind? Probably because I have no home.*

Once he entered the kitchen he brewed and iced some black tea. He hoped the caffeine would get him through the day. Michael called and said he would not be in, leaving them shorthanded, so Kevin waited tables for part of the day. By 3:00 p.m. everyone had gone, and he stayed, sipping on another tea and surveying the restaurant, debating whether to sleep in his car again or camp out on the couch in the office. The couch won.

Fatigue took hold, and his vision blurred. He lay down and quickly fell into a deep sleep. A few hours later he awoke and used the big pots and pans tub to bathe himself. Putting on clean clothes, and pocketing the $26.50 accumulated from waiting tables, he decided to take a walk.

He left the diner with no destination in mind. Traffic had eased, but an old red pickup rumbled by and belched a cloud of exhaust that drifted into his path. Covering his nose with the crook of his arm, he continued eastward down Speedway Boulevard.

Kevin had read that back in the seventies, *Life Magazine* named Speedway the ugliest street in America. Twenty-five years later it was awarded "Street of the Year" by *Arizona Highways*. *A street of contradictions! Perfect for me: a man of contradictions!* How many hundreds of times had he driven up and down this main artery? He watched the traffic, and wondered if the drivers were like him: traveling down the road to an unknown destination. The sun set behind him, lending a reddish-orange hue to his three mile trek. He found himself in front of Oasis, a gentleman's club, and went in.

The friendly young woman at the counter let him know that his $26.50 would pay the price of admission plus one drink and a tip and assured him he would have a good time. A well-proportioned blonde woman approached and took his hands, placing them on her hips. She gently grasped his shoulders, and swayed from side to side as if they were about to dance. "Are you coming in, Sweetie?"

He felt a rush of warmth. His internal debate lasted seconds, before shaking his head. "I'm sorry. I should go." He turned quickly, not wanting to see her reaction. Staring at his feet, he exited the doorway. *I can't believe I was even thinking about spending every cent I have in there!*

Hands in pockets, he walked through the parking lot angling away from the main road. Realizing his misdirection, he turned suddenly and collided with two pairs of muscular shoulders wearing black tees.

"Hey, Buddy. Watch where you're going." They stood, chests puffed out, blocking his passage.

"Sorry. Didn't mean it." Kevin put up his hands in surrender, and backed away.

They were both twenty something and smelled of alcohol. The taller one had a scar across his right cheek. The shorter one had a skull on an anchor tattooed on his bulging upper arm.

"Yeah, well, we think you did mean it," smirked Scarface.

"You owe us! Give us your money, and we might let you go." Tattoo glared at him.

"I don't think so." Kevin challenged.

"Yeah, who says it's up to you." Tattoo lunged at Kevin and slammed his fist into his stomach. As Kevin doubled over in pain, Scarface moved behind him and grabbed his arms with a firm grip. "Check his pockets."

Tattoo reached behind for Kevin's wallet and emptied it on the pavement. "No money. Just a few papers and a driver's license."

"Check his front pockets," ordered Scarface. Kevin squirmed and attempted to kick Tattoo. Tattoo punched him again, leaving Kevin breathless and hurt. Scarface yanked Kevin upright, pushing his knee into his lower back, while Tattoo reached into his front pockets. He rooted out the cash and change.

"It's not much, you son of a bitch, but we'll take it." He stuffed the money into his pocket. Looking at his partner, he nodded, "Let's get out of here." Scarface pushed Kevin against a parked car, and he fell to the ground. By the time he straightened up they were gone. *Did they go into the club? They can't get away with this!* He leaned against the car to steady himself, his entire midsection in pain.

He stumbled toward the club, intent on reporting the incident and finding the two thugs. Entering, he asked the young woman to see the manager. She squinted at him, hesitated, then picked up the phone and asked for the manager to come to the front. She looked at Kevin. "Just some friendly advice, Sir. You might want to leave *before* he gets here."

"What?" He raised his voice. "No, I'm not leaving. I was attacked! In your parking lot! The jerks could be in here!"

She shrugged and looked away, busying herself with counting bills. Kevin noticed his reflection in the mirror on the wall behind her. His hair was tousled, dirt smeared over the right side of his face and across his shirt, his eyes red. The sorry-looking reflection seemed to be a different person--someone he didn't know. The manager approached. He stood about six-feet-five with a stylish dark, blue sport jacket hung on his large frame. The young woman spoke to him privately and then pointed to Kevin. He stepped around the counter and advanced toward Kevin.

"What's the problem?"

"I was walking in your parking lot and--"

"Are you a patron of this club?"

"Well, not exactly. I thought about--"

"So you were wandering around our parking lot; you got into trouble; and you want me to fix it? Are you homeless?"

Kevin shoulders slumped as the comment punctured his anger, deflated his nerve and turned it to shame. "Hey, I didn't deserve what happened." His voice whined, and he hated it.

"Look man, I'm sorry for whatever happened, but I can't have you walking around my club looking for whoever might have jumped you. This is gentleman's club, not a lineup. My girl tells me this is the second time you've been in here tonight. If you want to come in, you need to clean up and pay."

"I was trying to tell you that two guys took my money in your parking lot and--"

"Everybody has a story. Listen, don't make me walk you out." He stood, like a concrete pillar, arms folded, waiting.

Kevin shrunk, and melted into the floor, defeated, disappearing from reality. As if in slow motion, he turned and shuffled away from the manager and the club.

Halfway back to the diner he was exhausted, but his mind was poised for attack. *I'll file a police report tomorrow. They won't get away with this.* His thoughts were interrupted by an explosion of lightning and thunder. Looking up and behind himself, he gaped at an army of angry clouds bearing down on him. Towers of rain raced swiftly across the city, and in moments, he was engulfed in the storm.

He ran for several minutes. Noticing a store with lights up ahead, he launched himself across a north-south avenue. One step forward and the beleaguered runner was battling to stay on his feet in the fast-moving current of a river. The *Don't Walk* sign flashed, and he tripped on a crack in the road and sprawled face-first in the water. He crawled to the curb. Urging himself up, Kevin stumbled toward the store entrance. The door was locked.

He peered inside the lighted room. No one was there. Banging on the door produced nothing. He cringed in the portal and waited for the storm to pass. *I hate monsoons. I hate my life.* The storm left as quickly as it had appeared. *One more mile.* He pushed himself to return to the diner.

Back at the diner, he bathed again and changed into a tee shirt and sweatpants. His stomach still tender, he laid out his blanket and pillow, and lowered himself onto the couch. The incident at the club would not let him sleep.

The evening seemed surreal. If it weren't for his aching midsection and the scrapes on his knees and elbows, he wouldn't have believed it happened. He had to be Tucson's biggest fool.

What's the matter with me? Why did I walk into that parking lot? Did I bother to check the weather forecast for tonight? No, I never check the weather. Is the universe conspiring against me? Homeless, penniless, drenched, and stupid! Even the club manager could see what a loser I am. Dear God, save me from myself. What do you want from me? My life sucks! I could do better than this back home. I should ask my father for a job--a plumber's helper or carpenter's assistant. I'd make just as much money, and I could stay with them.

What would my daughters think? I'm a failure! Bryce would have a field day with this! I'm thinking I'm so spiritual because I prayed a few times in the desert. A lot of good it did! Who's listening anyway? I'm talking to the air, and there's nothing on the other side. You're pathetic, Kevin. And if you're there, God, you're pathetic, too.

This thinking went on for hours. Finally, he reached through the darkness and twisted the radio knob, hoping music would ease the pain, and help him sleep. Percussion blasted into the room.

> You got mud on yo' face
> You big disgrace
> Kickin' your can all over the place. . .

Kevin reached again, fumbled for the power button, and knocked over the radio. It fell on the floor.

> We will, we will rock you . . .

"Where's the damn button?" He searched with his hand, feeling for the radio.

> You got blood on yo' face . . .

"Damn universe has a mean sense of humor." He found it, and struggled to turn it upright and find the button. The lyrics hurt, as if they were more blows to his stomach.

> We will, we will rock you. . .

"Shit!"

> Somebody better put you back in your place . . .

He found the button--spun it. Silence! "Unbelievable!"

Shifting and turning, he searched for comfort and rest. His thoughts took up where Freddie Mercury and Queen left off--continually replaying the events of the past few months. Every few minutes he turned, or sat up, or held his head in his hands. Unable to find peace or sleep, he looked at the clock and noticed it was 3:00 a.m. In an hour he needed to get up.

Seemingly in the next moment, Michael's voice startled him. "Hey, Kevin. You need to get up. It's almost 4:30, and the crew will be here any minute."

Kevin attempted to sit up quickly and moaned, the ache reminding him of last night's misadventure.

"Come on, Kevin. Let's get you some tea."

He told Michael what happened.

Michael listened without comment and then checked Kevin's stomach. "Nothing broken. You'll need to move a little more carefully today. Good thing it was just a micro burst and not a full blown monsoon. Rest in here for awhile, and we'll see how you feel when the breakfast crowd comes in."

"Thanks. You must think I'm a fool, getting into such a mess last night." Kevin gently lowered himself back onto the couch.

"I'm not your judge. What happened last night needed to happen." Michael left him to rest.

Kevin blinked around the small office. Papers were laid in neat little piles across the mahogany desk, and a Mac computer and keyboard sat on a matching credenza next to the desk and against the wall. He puzzled over what Michael had said. His eyes snapped photos of the office, but the pictures blurred. His thoughts muddled into nonsense, and within seconds he was asleep.

The sounds of Friday morning breakfast, a mixture of dishes clanking, jovial conversation and staff members calling out orders, pulled him up and out of sleep. The office door opened, and Michael walked in.

"How are you? Feeling any better?"

Kevin sat up slowly and rubbed his eyes. "I'm awake. Stomach is still a little tender, but I'll be okay. As for last night, I'm pissed off. I want to find the assholes who did this to me."

"If you find them, what will you do?"

"I'll report them to the police."

"What if they say they've never seen you before, and that you're making it all up?"

"Damn it. What they did wasn't right. There must be something I can do to make them pay for this."

"You're in pain, and as much as you want them to pay, there 's not much you can do. If you want to file a police report, go ahead."

"Well, what would you do if it happened to you?"

"I'd say: 'Thank you.' And take a good look at myself."

"What! Are you kidding me?" Kevin's eyebrows raised, his jaw jutted forward, and his hands flashed out from his sides. He froze in that position for a moment.

Michael continued. "No, I'm not. Everything that happens in my life is for my good, including the painful things. It's up to me to find the gift and move on. Those two guys gave you a gift, Kevin."

"Yeah, some gift. Two punches to the gut, took all my money, and then threw me to the pavement. I was humiliated when I tried to report it in the club. It shouldn't have happened."

"Why shouldn't it?"

"Are you trying to tell me I got what I deserved?" Kevin stood up and began pacing. "I didn't deserve that."

"Why not?"

"Because I'm, because... It was stupid for me to go into that club and then go wandering around in the parking lot. So, maybe I did deserve it."

"Kevin, don't take this as a judgement. Your sense of self-importance is bristling at what happened. You're filled with self-righteous indignation at how you think you've been treated--at how you think the world is treating you--you, who doesn't deserve this treatment--and two strangers crash into your life and assault you. More reasons to be indignant and angry. You can keep building up that anger and resentment, or you can let it go. Your choice. What do you want?"

Kevin stood there staring at Michael, as if attempting to digest his words. "So what you're saying is that the reason I was on their radar was all the anger I have."

"It's your sense of self-importance that creates the anger--your belief that none of this should happen to you. Who are you?"

Kevin inhaled deeply, held his breath, and let it out slowly. He thought about Rachel and the napkin that was still in his wallet. "It's me focused on what the world is doing to me. I'm not thinking about what I'm doing to the world. I'm the center of influence. The world is responding to how I see myself."

Michael smiled and patted Kevin on the back. "So, are you ready to get back to work?"

Chapter Twenty

Kevin and Michael were sitting at a table by the pool. Kevin ran his forefinger over the smooth tiles, admiring the kachina in the surface. It was late afternoon and hot, but the table umbrella shaded them from the sun.

"That's Kwahu, the eagle kachina. He represents strength and power, and he can carry your dreams up to Heaven."

"Sarah does amazing work. How long have you two been married?"

"Sixty-five years. We met one summer when I was visiting my grandfather. He was an elder, and I was sent to him to learn. He told me that I would marry Sarah one day. Sarah was a beautiful young girl, also of mixed lineage, and I hoped he was right. Even at fourteen, I knew I wanted to marry her."

"You've been together since you were fourteen?"

"No, I stopped visiting during the last two years of World War II, because I was in the navy. When I returned home, Sarah was at U of A. I moved back to Tucson, and we started seeing each other. Within two years we were married."

"How did you do it?"

"Do what?"

"How did you manage to stay married for sixty-five years?"

"It was our intention. As Sarah and I grew closer, I knew I wanted to be with her for life, however long that would be. She told me that was her intention, too."

"Weren't you ever tempted to be with anyone else?"

"There have been many beautiful women in my world, and being a successful businessman, there were many opportunities. I was single-minded about Sarah, and I've never been tempted to be with anyone else."

"I thought I would be married to one person for my life, too. It didn't work out that way. She left me."

"Why do you think that happened"

"She said that I was asleep."

"Were you?"

"If by asleep, you mean not really doing anything to nurture the relationship, then yes, I guess I was."

"What did you want when you were married?"

"To stay married. I wanted to teach and coach, take vacations every summer. I wanted my girls to grow up healthy and go to college. I wanted to pay my bills. I wanted what most people want."

"You say that you wanted to be married, but your behavior shows you wanted other things more."

Kevin lurched forward, as if to speak, but Michael held up his hand in a gesture to stop. "If I plant a garden in May, then walk away, don't come back until August, and then expect to have a rich harvest, did I really want a garden?"

Kevin settled back in his chair. "Maybe. You just didn't have time to work on it."

"If I don't make time, do I really want it?"

Kevin was sweating, both from the heat and Michael's words. He wiped his brow with a napkin. "So you're saying I didn't really want my marriage?"

"We can move under the Palo Verde if you want. Might be a little cooler--or inside the pool house."

"No, I'm okay. After almost four years, I'm used to it." He wiped his brow again.

"I'm saying your intentions were conflicted. When there were opportunities to connect with your wife, you chose other actions. When there were conflicts you chose avoidance. If you really

157

wanted to be married, you would've done all that you could to build and maintain a marriage relationship."

Kevin's shirt was soaked. "That's no guarantee that she wouldn't have left me. She might have had different intentions."

"True, but your intention would have made a difference for you. Intention needs a healthy sense of detachment. My intention is to love Sarah, but she is free to leave at any time. If she leaves I'll still love her. I have lived every moment loving and cherishing her, yet also being myself.

"I've risked divorce every day. Sarah always knows who I am and what I want. I know that about her, too. We talk. We agree and disagree, but as long as we're together, I am true to her in all ways-- thought, words, actions, intentions. I am true to myself, as well."

"You and Sarah are rare. I don't know any married couples like you. We all have conflicted intentions."

"Why?"

"I don't know. It's the way of the world?"

"It is the way that you choose. Just ask yourself what you want, and listen. I love Sarah, and I always act like I love her, even if I'm not pleased with her. If I were tempted to leave or to treat her poorly, I would ask myself what I want. That thought eliminates the conflict and helps me know what to do."

"You make it sound so simple."

"It is simple."

"But, it isn't easy."

"It's easy if you know what you want. You demonstrated that a few days ago."

"You mean with Tania?"

"Yes. I asked you what you wanted. You made a choice."

"You made it clear that I needed to choose between playing with Tania or working for you. Tania asked me to drive her home, and I wouldn't do it."

"I only made clear what you already knew."

"I probably would've known better with Tania, too. I was just looking."

"Looking is communicating. If you look down a woman's blouse, what are you communicating to her?"

"It's more about me than her. I was just enjoying the view."

"It still communicates something. Your look has an effect. I noticed it. Tania noticed it, and thought you were attracted to her. Other women might be pissed off at that behavior. Do you think you'll look at Tania that way again?"

"Only if I could be sure she wouldn't notice." He paused. *Really?* "No, I'm not going to be sneaking any looks."

"Why not?"

"Because I want to be the manager at the diner, and that behavior will distract me from my intention."

"So, will it be difficult not to look at her in that way?"

"No. I've made a decision, so I'm not interested. If I want romance or sex, I'll find it outside of work."

"Is that your intention? To get sex?"

Is that what I want? "I feel a need for it, but I don't know. I was thinking about that last night when I went to that club. The whole relationship, romance, sex thing isn't clear to me right now." Kevin grabbed his wet shirt and pulled it over his head and off.

"Take the time to get clear, then decide what you want."

"What you're saying makes sense. So many times my intentions have been conflicted, and I've made poor choices. How did you learn this in your twenties? I don't think there were too many self-help books when you were young."

"You're right. When I was a young man intending to love my wife, Wayne Dyer was barely in kindergarten. I learned in the navy."

"Really? How?"

"You want another beer?"

"Yeah, I do. Thanks."

Michael stood up and walked toward the poolhouse. Kevin returned his attention to Kwahu, outlining the figure with his index finger. *I want to know my real intentions.* He looked up at the Jerusalem Pine. It's upper branches were swaying in a gentle wind. It's trunk stood solid, immovable in the midst of the labyrinth. Michael returned with two bottles and a bowl of nuts. He handed a beer and a towel to Kevin.

"Thank you." Kevin mopped the moisture from his bare skin.

Michael eased into his chair, tipped the brown bottle to his lips and set it on the table. "I was on a minesweeper in the Pacific. Perfect duty for me, because I didn't want to shoot people. We were in the business of saving people by marking and removing mines. I was eighteen years old and eager to do well. I was still a recruit.

"One day I was told to stand on the forecastle, the deck above the deck. A senior petty officer was on the bridge. Seamen were positioned port side, ready to drop buoys into the water, and I was the messenger. The senior petty officer was supposed to yell down to me and say when to drop the buoy. I, in turn, was to tell the sailors on the deck to actually drop it. So the senior petty officer yelled: 'Drop the buoy.' I eagerly yelled, 'Drop the buoy!'. Then the petty officer yelled, 'When I tell you.' Well, it was too late. They had already dropped it. I was reprimanded for that one. Extra cleaning duty in the kitchen."

"Funny story, but not very fair to you."

"Doesn't matter. I was accountable. I thought about that mistake for the months I was at sea. I thought about acting with clarity rather than acting impulsively, and about not wanting messages that were unclear. I decided that I would always give clear messages, both to myself and to other people. If you want to give a clear message you need to have a clear and unified intention.

Otherwise, people don't know what you want. The universe doesn't even know what you want."

"So I need to intend for a woman to share my life with?"

"Don't ask me. It depends on what you want. If you want that, decide for it. If you want sex with a variety of women, intend for that. What does your Inner Voice tell you?"

"I don't know. Maybe I'm just not ready to decide."

"Maybe that's what it's telling you."

"Yeah, but I miss sex."

"Who are you in regard to sexual desire?"

"Hungry. Maybe stupid, too, and careless."

"There's nothing wrong with sexual desire. It's part of life. But, you have to manage it, like any other desire."

"Who I am when sexual desire takes over is a center of attention. It's all about me and getting my needs met." Kevin stared at his feet.

"Is that who you want to be? A man controlled by his desires?"

Kevin pictured himself earlier, staring at Tania. He thought back to his addiction to Ronnie. Rachel appeared in his mind as she told him his conversations with women were just foreplay, and not real. He expressed his thoughts to Michael.

"Sex isn't good or bad. Like any other part of life, it has polarity. On one side it's the joy of loving connection, and on the other extreme it's obsession and then the sex industry, and trafficking, and violence toward women and children. Where do want to be on that continuum?"

"Good question. Definitely not on the dark side. What should I do?"

"Ask your Inner Voice."

"I'm afraid to ask."

"Because you might not get the answer you want?"

"What if my Inner Voice says: 'No, you can't have it?'"

"It doesn't work that way. Your Inner Voice is not a higher being up in the clouds deciding what you should or shouldn't do. It's your essence. It's will is your will, and your path to freedom and fulfillment. What it indicates is what you *really* want to do."

Kevin looked down at Kwahu and moved his finger in a circular motion around the eagle eye.

Michael placed his hand over Kevin's. "Your dreams are being carried up to Heaven as we speak. Listen. You'll know what to do."

"Thanks. Besides I have other more pressing needs to consider. Like finding a home. I noticed you have a shower in the pool house. I'd really like to clean up before Sarah gets here."

"Go ahead. She'll be home in half an hour."

Kevin stood to go, hesitated, and turned back. "I'm thinking about this Inner Voice. I've heard it these past few months. Haven't always listened. I keep hearing this verse in my mind: 'The foxes have holes and the birds of the air have nests, but the Son of Man has nowhere to lay His head.' I think it's because I'm homeless."

Michael touched Kevin's chest with his index finger. "That's your home, Kevin." He gestured toward his house and yard. "This isn't my home. My home is here." He touched his own chest with the same finger. When I follow this, I am safe, I am clear, and I am who I am."

Kevin nodded, turned, and headed for the shower. He envisioned Jesus saying to his disciples exactly what Michael just said. *Why am I thinking about Jesus? And why isn't it okay to think about him? I've never been big on Jesus. I think Bryce ruined him for me. Okay, let's not think about Bryce. Think about what Michael said.*

After his shower, Kevin stepped out of the poolhouse, his flesh cool and clean. He walked toward the Aleppo and entered the labyrinth. After his first visit to Michael's home, curiosity led him to explore labyrinths and their usage, by way of articles on the internet. Bowing his head slightly, and folding his hands in front of his belt, he trod slowly and purposefully along the path. *I'm listening.* Distracting thoughts flowed through his mind. Ignoring them, he focused his attention on his feet and the path. *Seek ye first the kingdom. All else will be added.*

Kevin worked his way around to the center until he was standing next to the tree. *At the center of my soul is my home.* He placed his hands over his heart. *I have everything I need.* He imagined himself protected, provided for, at ease. His body responded to the thought as a calm confidence rippled through him. *All is well. Thank you.*

He retraced his steps, walked back toward the table, and sat down to wait for Michael and Sarah.

He felt them, like a wave flowing over him, before he saw them. He stood up to meet Sarah.

"Kevin, I've heard so many good things about you. Welcome to our home." Sarah embraced him, lingering a few seconds. The air around them sparkled and fizzed, enlivening his awareness.

They stepped back and studied each other. Sarah stood about five-feet-three. Her long, silver-white hair was pulled back, flowing almost to her waist, and dark brown eyes danced above high cheekbones and a straight, broad nose. Her smile filled the lower portion of her face, and with her eyes, traced a glow on her countenance. Like Michael, there were few wrinkles except at the temples.

"Michael said you were beautiful. I have to agree." *Her skin is so smooth. Just a few lines around her eyes.*

"Thank you, and that's because I laugh so much."

"Pardon me?"

Sarah let out a musical laugh. "You were noticing that all of my wrinkles are around my eyes. It's because I laugh so much."

"How did you know I was thinking about that?"

"I'm an eighty-six-year-old woman, and everyone I meet wonders why I only have wrinkles near my eyes. The answer is laughter. Right now I'm enjoying the look on your face and feeling joy that you're here. You know, most Hopi women tend to wrinkle up at an early age, but you see, I still feel young, and I don't spend as much time out in the sun as the women on the Mesa."

Rising on her toes, she took Kevin's hand and lifted his arm. She glided under and turned, moving toward Michael, and repeated her dance move with him. She and Michael both laughed, and Kevin could not help but smile at this most-unique introduction.

Michael pulled her close, kissing her on the temple. She wore a bright turquoise, cotton blouse tucked into her ankle length blue skirt, both complemented by a turquoise and blue scarf, splashed with orange, wrapped around her waist. She gently reached for Michael's chin, turned his face slightly and kissed his cheek.

Not knowing what else to say, Kevin bowed to Sarah. "You're quite the dancer."

Sarah made a slight curtsey. "Thank you. Why don't you two sit down, and I'll prepare dinner. How does a big salad sound?"

Both men signaled their approval as Sarah turned toward the house. "Knocks your socks off, doesn't she?" Michael nodded toward her.

Kevin looked at her retreating form. "Yes, she does. It feels like her presence is still here, even though she's gone into the house."

"Ah, Sarah is so completely Sarah; you can't help but feel her."

Kevin leaned in and placed his arms on the table. Suddenly something within became clear. "I want what you two have. I want to feel that comfort with myself and share it with someone else who has it, too."

"There's nothing stopping you, Kevin. Just let go of all of your conflicts. Decide what you want, and be single-minded."

"Yeah but, how do I do that?"

"We'll talk about that soon enough. That's a long conversation by itself." Michael waved his hand sideways.

Kevin stared at Kwahu. "I have this other thought: 'Seek ye first the kingdom, and all else will be added.' What does it mean?"

"From the New Testament."

"I didn't know you studied the Bible. Do you belong to a church?"

"I've studied many books, and I don't go to church. Never have. Your question is a distraction. If your intention is to understand the relevancy of these thoughts, wondering about my religious roots won't get you there."

"But, I'm curious."

"Every thought and every behavior has consequences. At the very least, your mental wanderings delay the results you seek. Single-mindedness, Kevin."

"I'm trying."

"Don't try. Do it, or don't do it. Succeed or fail. Anything in between is just a story, another drama." He paused, and then looked back at Kevin. "I have an idea. Why don't we hike together at Pima Canyon on Sunday? You can show me your prayer place, and we can teach each other how we pray. Also, we can learn a little about dealing with distractions. Is it okay if I join you at your spot?"

"Let's do it. I'd like for you to go there with me." Kevin was excited. "What about *seek first?*"

Michael held Kevin's gaze for an endless moment. "It means to set aside all desire and follow only the will of your Spirit. Surrender everything you think you need or want, and you'll receive what you need."

Kevin nodded. "How do I know what the will of Spirit is?"

"You listen and you learn to hear the Inner Voice. You will learn to know it, or to feel it. It takes practice."

Chapter Twenty-One

"Salads coming right up." Sarah called from the house. Michael moved to assist her with the trays of food.

"Three to choose from. Kevin, you are our guest. You pick first." All three salads were arranged in identical turquoise and orange ceramic bowls. Sarah pointed to the salad closest to him. "This one features tahini and eggplant and has a poppy-seed dressing. The next one is a spicy black bean salad. The last one is spinach and artichoke."

"Spinach and artichoke sounds good."

"Here you go." She handed the bowl to Kevin. "And Michael, I know you want the spicy black bean." She passed the salad to her smiling husband.

Kevin took a moment to enjoy the still-life before him-- spinach, artichoke hearts, chicken salad, bacon, egg, cheese, and sunflower sprouts. He grouped as many food items as he could, pierced them with his fork, and driven by both hunger and curiosity, lifted the unique mix to his mouth. Mediterranean and poppy-seed dressings merged with the ingredients, creating a blast of flavor that momentarily focused all of his attention on taste. He savored a few more bites before he returned to the people around him. "This is incredible, You made all this yourself?"

"Of course. I call it my eclectic dinner."

Michael let out a laugh.

Kevin creased his brow, and pursed his lips. "Really? I mean, most people just make one salad, but three! And this one--it's amazing!"

Sarah and Michael both broke into laughter.

"Okay. What's so funny?"

166

Michael looked at Sarah with a grin. "She didn't make the salads. She picked them up at the Eclectic Cafe and put them in these bowls." Both giggled like small children.

Kevin shook his head. "You two had me going for a moment."

Sarah beamed at Kevin. "My story was partly true. I made the bowls." They laughed again, and Kevin joined in.

"Kevin, I so enjoy you. You're a delight." Sarah touched his forearm, her silver bracelets clinking on the ceramic tiles.

"Yeah, well, you're pretty delightful yourself."

"I heard you were walking in my labyrinth." Sarah tapped his hand.

"Yes. I hope that's okay with you."

"Oh yes. Do you understand labyrinths?"

"I read a little on them. You do a walking meditation as you move along the path to the center. There, you stop and give thanks, continuing the meditation. Then you make your way out the same way you came in."

"Yes." Sarah brought her hands together as if in prayer. "The center of the labyrinth is called New Jerusalem. It is the home that we are seeking. Labyrinths were built in many Catholic churches in the Middle Ages."

"What made you build one here?"

"It helps me focus. Michael sits down and meditates. He's very disciplined. My mind and body love to move. When I sit and meditate I get restless. Sometimes I dance my way to the center and then back out." Sarah lifted her hands up and danced in her seat.

"I probably won't dance, but I like walking." Kevin set down his fork, placed his elbows on the table, and propped his chin on his knuckles. "Is it important to follow the path out of the labyrinth?"

"Yes. You walk in to join with God. You walk out to share what you have gained with the world." She nodded her head.

Michael spread his hands to either side to emphasize his words. "It's the same with any prayer or meditation. You enter the silence, and then you come back into the world, bringing to the world what you've gained from your union with God."

"Makes sense." He wanted to ask if he could use her labyrinth sometimes, but deemed it too soon to request such a gift.

They finished dinner. Michael and Sarah returned the empty dishes and trays to the house, leaving Kevin by himself. He looked toward the Palo Verde and noticed the blossoms had fallen. It was several minutes before his friends returned to the table with ice water.

"Now for the evening's business." Sarah sat down and placed her hands on the table.

Kevin looked at both of them, attempting to discern what was next. "Is this another joke?"

"No joke." Michael said. "Kevin, you need a place to stay. We'd like for you to stay in our poolhouse."

Kevin's eyes widened. He had forgotten about his homelessness and where he would stay that night. "Thank you. That's very kind."

"No, Kevin, thank you." Sarah grasped his hand. "In Hopi culture, it is a great privilege to give something of value to another. You honor us by accepting our gift. Thank you for allowing us to give to you."

Kevin waited for the punchline, but nothing came. He noticed both Sarah and Michael nodding almost imperceptibly. "Then you are welcome. I would be most pleased to live here, at least for a short while until I can get a decent place for myself."

"Stay as long as you need, Kevin." Michael nodded toward the poolhouse. "Do you want any help moving your things?"

"All of my things are in my car, and no, I can get them myself. Thanks"

Sarah stood up. "Well, then, we'll leave you to get settled." Each in turn hugged him. Together they walked toward their house. Kevin watched them disappear into the entrance.

Later, as he settled into a stuffed chair in the small sitting area, he remembered the previous two nights sleeping in the car and in the diner. *Life changes so quickly sometimes.* He thought about being assaulted and robbed the night before. *I know I should let it go, but it still pisses me off.* Anger flowed into his arms and clenched both his fists. *If I ran into them tonight it would be a different story. Yeah, right! They were stronger, and there were two of them, Macho Man.* The sound of knocking punctured his thoughts. "Come in!"

Michael entered the house. "Kevin, I thought we should revisit the events of last night. How are you feeling about it?"

"Well, I'd forgotten until a few minutes ago. I'm still ticked."

"Would you be willing to work on that with me, right now-- attempt to resolve it?"

"You mean like some kind of process or something?"

"Yes."

"Sure. Okay"

"Before we can begin, you need to take responsibility. You talked earlier about being a center of influence. Can you accept that you influenced what happened last night?"

"You mean the attack was my fault?"

"You're talking about their effect on you. What about you?"

"Sounds like you're blaming the victim."

"You decide, Kevin. Are you the center of influence, or are you the center of attention? Are you a cause in life, or are you just an effect? How do you see yourself?"

"I don't want to be a victim, but I didn't ask those guys to beat on me."

Michael was silent, his gaze steady as Kevin struggled with his victimhood.

Images of Dana, his parents, Bryce, Al, and Ronnie flashed in his mind. He remembered his conversation with Mike four years ago. *Who's responsible for your life?* "If I don't take full responsibility, I'll always be the victim, won't I? I'm the one who chose to visit that club and walk through the parking lot not paying attention. I suppose I could've avoided the physical damage by giving them the money in the first place. So, okay, I see how I'm at least partially responsible for what happened."

Michael said nothing.

"I know what you want me to say, but how can I be one hundred percent responsible?"

"I don't *want* you to say anything. I'm waiting for you to be ready to move forward. That can happen tonight, next week, or next year, or never. You cannot truly grow up until you take full responsibility for your life and everything in it, exactly as it is. Nothing is anyone's fault, nor are you to blame. What happened last night happened. Your life is what it is. The real question is what do you want? Are you responsible or not?" He waited a few seconds. "Would you like me to leave?"

He again remembered what Mike said: "Do you want to spend the rest of your life being angry, or will you take responsibility for your own happiness?" *It's about time I did that.* "No, I want to resolve this. Could you explain to me how this is my responsibility?"

"Think of it as a chain reaction. First comes being. Your experience begins with who you are being in this moment. Your mind is filled with hundreds of identities that you have created through the course of your life. For example, *I am powerless.* is an identity, or *I'm not good enough.* or *I'm stupid.* are identities that most of us carry."

"So, it's like a story that I tell myself about myself?"

"Exactly. But, it's more than a story. You become it, and you're convinced that it's real."

"It's not?"

"No, it's a story, a role you play. Who you were last night is not who you really are."

"Then who am I?"

"Good question. For now let's just say you are the ultimate decision-maker for you."

"Okay. How do I decide which identity to be?"

"The identity is triggered by whatever is happening--someone's behavior, a specific situation, or something you imagine. You react to the trigger automatically and step into an identity. Last night, the events at the club triggered an identity in you. That identity led to how you felt. That set off a chain of thoughts. The identity, feeling, and thoughts led to your behaviors, and all of it created the result you experienced. Let me show you." Michael grabbed a pad of paper that was on the table and a pen from his pocket.

Be -- Feel -- Think -- Do -- Have

Kevin shook his head, half in bewilderment, and the other half in self-condemnation. "Doesn't seem like I have much control over which identity I become."

"At this point you're right. You can change that by taking full responsibility. Experience happens on the inside, and you live from the inside out. Despite the fact that most humans are searching for external things to affect their experience, it's all created on the inside. That's the difference between being a real adult or just a child in an adult body."

Kevin frowned, and brought his finger to his lips. His eyes defocused. "So, something happens, and an identity is triggered. That creates my emotion and my thoughts which lead to my behavior and the results I see."

"Very good."

"All right, I'm willing to assume responsibility. Going by this concept, I created the experience of last night."

"Good. Let's begin. This process will help you dis-create the negative identity. Close your eyes if you wish. Bring up the anger you were just feeling."

After a few minutes Kevin again felt the energy coursing through his blood--fists clenched--throat tensed. "I am definitely feeling angry now."

"Good. Who are you that you're so angry?"

"What do you mean? I'm still Kevin."

"The identity. Why are you so angry?"

"I'm angry because they beat me up and took my money. I was embarrassed."

"At what moment did you feel the worst last night?"

"When the manager at the club asked if I was homeless."

"How did you feel then?"

"Humiliated, and then angry. Angry at those guys, at myself, at life."

"Who were you that you were so humiliated?"

"A loser, a failure."

"So, you are such a loser that you don't even have enough money to get into the club, and two guys beat you up because you're such a loser, and you lost your restaurant, your home, and your girlfriend. You're a loser!"

"Yeah. That sums it up. Is this supposed to make me feel better? Shouldn't I be cultivating the positive?"

"I don't want you to feel better. At least not yet. I want you to experience being the loser right now. Your power is in the negative. Negative identities obstruct the positive that is already within you."

Kevin opened his eyes. "What?"

"Trust me on this. I'm asking you to become that loser, just for now. Let yourself experience it. Don't analyze it. Just be it."

Kevin dove into being a loser again. He felt shame, as if he had no value, then anger. "Now I'm starting to feel anger, again."

"Let yourself feel it. There is nothing wrong or right about anger or shame. It just is. There's nothing wrong with being a loser. We live in duality. You win some and lose some. The problem is you're judging yourself. You think it's wrong or bad to be a loser."

"I don't want to be a loser."

"Go into that state of: It's bad to be a loser. Experience it."

Kevin sat with his judgment. Anger and sadness performed a duet in his body. He stayed with it for a while. "It's easing a little."

"Good. Now go back into the experience of being a loser. Tell me when you feel complete."

Kevin played the role and breathed deeply. After several minutes, he noticed a shift. "I feel lighter."

"One more thing. How do you want to feel about last night?"

"I want to feel confident and free. Not like a loser."

"Who would you be if you felt confident?"

"I would be, well, a person who has value. I'd have worth."

"You're already worthy. Being valuable means that by your very presence, you offer value to the world. Last night, you became worthless, so worthless, that you sought out people who confirmed your lack of value--who would punish you for it. You were so effective that you believed others were devaluing you."

"Well, I definitely want to be valuable--to be a center of positive influence. How do I become valuable?"

"Use your will. Make it your intention to be valuable. It may help to change your posture. How would a valuable center of influence sit? Breathe, and become valuable. Feel your confidence."

Kevin willed himself to be valuable. He sat up straight. Confidence penetrated his chest, slowly at first, then it grew, and emanated throughout his whole body. It surged through his being. He recalled feeling this when his basketball team won the league championship, and when he had taught an effective lesson in High School English. He remembered the feeling when he first saw people lined up to get into the Calico Grill on a Friday night. "In this state, I can accomplish anything."

Kevin opened his eyes, and Michael was smiling.

"Good work. Now, call to mind the incident in the parking lot last night. How does it feel?"

Kevin re-imagined the scene. Instead of seeing two bullies pushing him around he saw two lost young men, confused and searching for something they couldn't find. He saw himself as potentially able to help. He explained what he saw to Michael. "How did I achieve this?"

"By resisting being a loser, you made it stronger. By experiencing it and accepting it, you discharged the negative emotion. You dis-created the negative identity. Now the event doesn't trigger a negative response. You are in space."

"What is space?"

"Clarity. Free of fear. Not triggered in any negative way. In space, your decision-making ability is enhanced. Also, you have greater access to your inner wisdom--to the Inner Voice."

Kevin enjoyed his space for a few minutes and then turned to Michael. "Thank you. It feels like events would unfold differently-- better, if I were to see those two guys again."

Michael nodded. "Let's pay a visit to the club and see what we can do about that."

"What are we going to do, challenge them to a fight?"

"No. We won't need to fight. We're going to help them."

Kevin noticed that over an hour had passed. "Okay, let's go."

They drove to the club and found a parking place. Michael asked him to back in. Kevin turned off the engine. "So now what?"

"We watch and wait. Was it around this time when it happened?"

Kevin noticed the clock on the dash--9:30. "Almost exactly."

They observed patrons of the club coming and going. After a few minutes Kevin spotted the two men, several cars over, heading toward the entrance. His heartbeat accelerated. "That's them!" He pointed.

"Draw your window down and stay here. I'll talk with them." Before Kevin could say anything Michael slipped out of the car and sauntered into the parking lot, crossing in front of the two men.

Lowering the window, he heard Tattoo speak. "Hey old man, watch where you're going."

Michael stopped in front of them and made eye contact with each man. "Good evening, gentlemen. How are you?"

"You're either a fool or a helluva fighter, cuz you wouldn't be blocking our path otherwise." Scarface folded his arms. "What do you think, Jack?"

"I'm leaning toward fool. No way can this old man take us." Tattoo Jack shook his head.

"Tell you what, old man. If you have enough money we'll let you go and forget about this. How much do you have?" Scarface mashed his left palm with his right fist.

"I don't have any money." Michael looked at Jack's arm. "I like the tattoo. U.S. Navy. I'm a navy man myself. World War Two. Michael Santos, Seaman Second Class." Michael held out his hand to shake. "When did you serve?"

Tattoo Jack froze. Dazed, he slowly moved his hand to Michael's. After a few seconds words tumbled out like ice cubes from a cup. "I--I enlisted four years ago. I got out two years ago."

"Jesus, don't bring that up!" Scarface squeezed his eyes shut. "He doesn't like the Navy."

"I like the Navy! All right?" Tattoo Jack flung his words at Scarface. "They weren't fair with me." The parking lot lighting reflected off the moisture gathering in his eyes.

175

"Tell me about it, young man." Michael gently placed his hand on Jack's shoulder.

"I really did like the Navy. I was on the USS Ronald Reagan, aircraft carrier out of San Diego. I made CS Second Class."

"Ah, a Culinary Specialist. Excellent!"

"It was excellent until I got into trouble."

"What happened?"

"I signed some documents without reading them. A couple of buddies of mine used the paperwork to steal supplies. They got caught, and then they said the whole thing was my idea. Two against one. I was dishonorably discharged. Being in the Navy was my dream, and the day I got kicked out was the worst day of my life." Tears flowed down Jack's face, and his shoulders sank.

Michael gently pulled him to his shoulder and held the back of his neck. "I'm sorry, Jack."

Jack's body convulsed as he sobbed on Michael's shoulder. Scarface shuffled his feet and looked at the pavement. Kevin's eyes teared, and he wiped at them with his fingers.

"I don't care about the discharge, Jack. We're Navy men, and we need to have each others' backs." Michael grasped both of Jack's shoulders firmly and looked into his eyes. "You made a mistake, but it wasn't criminal. You were caught not paying attention, and it cost you. You also trusted the wrong people. Tell me what's going on with your life right now."

Jack wiped his eyes. "I get odd jobs here and there. Who wants to hire a dishonorably discharged sailor? No one. Unless I lie. Lost my girlfriend, too. She said my dishonorable discharge was embarrassing. I'm living in my mom's basement. All I got is my mother and sister and my cuz here, Daniel." He hooked his thumb toward Scarface.

"Hi, Daniel." Michael shook hands with him. "You weren't in the Navy. What's your story?"

"Not much to tell. I live with my girlfriend. She works nights. I work the graveyard shift as a custodian. Quit college a couple of years ago--couldn't afford it. Jack and I really are cousins--good friends, too." Daniel put his fist toward Jack, and they bumped knuckles.

Michael pulled a card from his pocket, and he handed it to Jack. "Come see me around noon, Monday. Can you cook?"

He read the card. "Hell yes, I can cook. You own this place?"

"I do."

He looked at Daniel. "I can't believe we were thinking of beating this guy up!"

"And stealing my money." Michael smiled. "That reminds me. I want to introduce you to a friend of mine." Michael waved to Kevin to join them.

Kevin exited the car and slowly walked toward them.

"Kevin, this is Jack and his cousin, Daniel." Michael motioned them toward Kevin. They shook hands. "Kevin manages my diner. So, if things work out, Jack, he'll be your boss."

"You look familiar. Do I know you?" Jack stared at Kevin. Michael nodded to Kevin.

"Yeah, we met last night. You hit me in the stomach and took my money." Kevin managed to keep his tone even.

Jack's eyes opened wide. He looked at Daniel who shook his head and shrugged. He turned back to Kevin. "I'm sorry, man. I owe you $26.50." He looked at Daniel. "Hey, man. Give him his money back. Give him what you were going to spot me tonight."

Daniel fumbled in his pocket for a few seconds. I don't have the change. I got thirty."

Jack rolled his eyes. "So what! Give it! We more than owe it."

Daniel handed the money to Kevin.

Jack nodded at Kevin. "I wouldn't blame you if you didn't want me to work for you."

Kevin studied Jack, whose face now looked more human, more real, than it did yesterday. "I'm fine, and let's see how things go. I won't hold last night against you."

"Thanks, Man. I owe you." Jack shook Kevin's hand and turned to his cousin. "Let's go." He hugged Michael. "Thank you. For the job offer and for whatever you did to me. I feel a lot better." He turned to walk away.

Daniel stood still, staring at his cousin. "What about the club?"

Jack turned, walking slowly backwards. "Are you kidding? I can't afford it, and your girlfriend doesn't want you in there anyway. Let's go."

Kevin watched them walk away. "How did that happen?"

"It's called being in the flow. When you allow it, life unfolds perfectly. What do you think about last night's encounter now?"

"Like it was supposed to happen."

"It was one of many possibilities awaiting you, depending on who you were being."

"Last night I felt insignificant and worthless, a loser. In my mind I wanted to make those guys even more insignificant. I wanted them to suffer like I suffered, because they deserved it. I wanted to see myself as better than them."

"And now?"

"Now I care about them, especially Jack. I see myself helping him." Kevin stared, his eyes unfocused. His mouth flared into a small smile. "Amazing!"

"Kevin, you're amazing. It wouldn't have been possible without you taking responsibility. You've done well."

Chapter Twenty-Two

Early Sunday morning Kevin drove Michael to Pima Canyon. Michael wore hiking boots, long cotton pants, and a light, long-sleeved shirt. Kevin wore shorts, a tee shirt and old basketball shoes. When they arrived at the canyon parking lot, Michael looked at the shoes. "No hiking boots?"

"I like these better. Ronnie used to ask me the same thing, but it works for me. We're not hiking very far, just a couple of miles in."

Michael nodded. "Let's go." They set out on the trail. Michael led the way, and Kevin worked to keep up.

"Wow! You're in great shape!"

"Should I slow down?" Michael asked without looking back.

"No, you're fine." He felt the familiar strain in his thighs as he climbed toward the canyon. As morning illuminated the landscape, hundreds of saguaros saluted them with three fingered hands welcoming them into the gorge. They hiked until Kevin stopped where he had prayed two weeks ago. "This is my spot." They were in a clearing just off the trail, and the canyon walls on either side towered above them.

Michael pointed toward the ground. "Help me gather small rocks and place them in a circle. When you pick one up, ask it if it's okay to use it. If it feels right, move it. We're going to make a medicine wheel." They placed the rocks at one-and-half foot intervals in a circle about seven feet in diameter. Other stones were placed inside, marking a small cairn in the center. Four spokes were created dividing the larger circle into quadrants, one for each of the four directions.

When the wheel was completed, Michael asked, "Kevin, what is your intention with this prayer?"

Kevin looked toward the East where the sun was still hidden, just below the rim of the canyon. "I want guidance. I want to hear the Inner Voice more clearly."

"Select a stone for yourself, then follow me around the outside of the wheel. This is your heart stone. We'll enter the wheel from the eastern point after three circuits." They each selected a heart stone, spiraled around the wheel three times and entered the medicine wheel. "Go to the place in the wheel where you feel drawn." They each found their spot and faced toward the direction of the rising sun.

Michael led them, as they greeted each of the four directions with a slight bow, hands, prayer-like. He explained, "The East represents air and the mind. It's for the adolescent stage of life. Now, let's face the South." Michael turned to his right and Kevin followed. "The South holds the heart and fire. It's for the adult stage of life. The West is for the final stage of life, and the North for childhood, and beginning again. Hold your stone to your heart, fill it with love, and think upon your intention as if it were already accomplished."

Kevin imagined himself hearing his inner guidance clearly and moving through life with confidence. They stood there for several minutes in silence until Michael spoke again. "Place your heart stone on the earth in front of you, and give thanks." They placed their stones on the ground, and Michael turned toward him. "Show me what you do when you come here to pray. I will follow you."

Kevin placed his hands palm to palm in front of his heart. "Let's face the East." He raised his hands together still pointing upward toward the sky while inhaling deeply. When they reached their zenith, his hands came apart, each arcing downward and around, until they touched in front of his hips, exhaling along the way. Fingertips met, and then he spread his arms, palms open, out to the sides, inhaling again. Exhaling, they positioned their hands, again, in front of the heart. They repeated the movements continually until the sun rose over the rim. Next, they closed their eyes to the blinding light and stood still, breathing deeply, silent, basking in the warmth upon their faces, listening for guidance.

When they were complete, Michael gestured in a circular motion. "We moved counterclockwise to enter the circle. Let us move clockwise three times when we exit." When they left the circle, Michael brought his hands together in front of his heart, and bowed slightly toward Kevin. "Thank you."

Kevin did the same. "Did you receive guidance?"

"Yes. I should continue to help you. I do this because I like to, and I want to."

"That's it?"

"That's the part for you. The rest is for my own path. Did you receive what you needed?"

"My guidance was to stay the course--I'm on the right path."

Michael nodded. "Pay close attention to that--staying the course." He pointed at the sun. "The Hopi word for sun is *Dawa*."

"Like Sarah's sun kachina on the bottom of your pool."

"Yes. Right now on the other side of the earth, in Tibet, two men are praying in the moonlight. They call the moon *Dawa*. If we drilled a hole through the earth and came out in Tibet, it would be dusk. Daytime in the Hopi world is called *Nyma*. In Tibet, *Nyma.* is night. The universe is constructed of polarities and patterns. Opposites define each other. Joy and sorrow, pleasure and pain, light and darkness. You must experience both. You can learn to navigate this world of opposites and flow with it. Listen to your guidance."

They walked slowly in silence for half an hour, climbing, twisting and turning along the irregular trail. Passing a few hikers, they nodded and said good morning. The day was already heating up, and beads of sweat appeared on their faces. Both were about

181

two-thirds through their water bottles. A rushing sound came from somewhere to their left as the trail temporarily spread into a flat area. "That sounds like water." Kevin pointed toward the sound.

"I don't think so." Michael shook his head.

"I want to check it out."

"Are you sure you shouldn't stay on the trail? That's what I recommend."

"Thanks, but I'd really like to see the water. I've never noticed it before. I'm curious. Come with me."

"No. I'll stay the course. If you feel you must go, be careful. You only have a little water left. I'll meet you up ahead."

"I'll be fine. See you in a few minutes." Kevin picked his way across the terrain, avoiding the prickly pears and giving wide berth to the saguaros. Most of the plants had prickers or needles, but he was driven by the rushing sound and chose to endure the scratches and pokes. After several minutes, he came to a fence with a privacy sign. He looked ahead trying to see the water, but saw only a small building. It dawned on him that the sound was not water, but an air conditioning unit. *Michael was right. I should have stayed on the trail.*

Instead of retracing his steps back to the trail, he tramped a new path that angled downward to meet up with Michael. The new path dead-ended after fifty feet. Kevin continued forward, but groups of cacti and prickly thickets slowed his progress. The canyon walls indicated his direction was correct, but in relation to the main trail, he was lost. Stepping by another prickly pear, he lost his balance and fell backward, landing in a dried-out bush and smacking his head on the ground. He lay there for a few moments sensing his body, fuzzily trying to determine whether there were injuries. Shaken but not hurt, he slowly rose to his feet. *I can't believe how stupid I was. Why did I get off the trail? What's the matter with me?* He yelled. "Michael!" There was no answer. Voices murmured in the distance, promising that others were near. No one appeared.

He stumbled through several areas of dense vegetation, stopped twice to remove needles from his bleeding shins, and to drink his remaining water. Finally, a dry arroyo filled with boulders came into view, and he climbed over the rocks, working his way downward. He hoped that the arroyo would come out somewhere near the parking lot. Climbing across the rocks was difficult, but at least his legs weren't being stabbed by a gang of needled succulents.

After about forty-five minutes into his unpleasant diversion, an opening appeared that looked promising. Climbing out of the arroyo, he made his way along the path. *Is this it?* It looked somewhat familiar as it merged with a wider trail. Blood smeared on his fingers as he stooped to pick more needles out of his shins. His mouth was dry. *Am I still lost?*

"There you are! I was beginning to worry about you." Michael walked down the path toward Kevin. "How was your adventure?"

"Not so good. Didn't you hear me calling you?" Kevin splayed his hands outward and jutted his face forward.

"No. The trail moved upward at first, after you left it, and you must have angled downward."

"No wonder I couldn't find it!"

"I knew we would meet up eventually." Michael smiled and patted Kevin on the shoulder." Looks like you had some run-ins with the plant life."

"Yeah. No kidding." Kevin stared at his bloody legs.

"Be happy you didn't meet any rattlesnakes or scorpions."

"Okay, this is the part where you tell me: 'I told you so.'"

"No, this is the part where you recognize that when you set an intention, and veer off into distractions, there are consequences. You did nothing wrong. This is life. It's what happens. Now you have a story to tell."

"Yeah, I'm sure this will get more humorous as time goes by."

"Whatever you intend, Kevin, it's all about what you really want. Decide what you want, and stay the course. If you don't stay your course, eventually pain and discomfort will help you decide, as it did today. When you were searching for the path, your sole intention was to get to the main trail and then to the car. Nothing else mattered."

"Yeah. If I would've been clear about that sooner, I could've saved some time and pain."

"Without a commitment, there will be distractions and consequences. Come on. Let's get you home. Sarah is an expert with tweezers. She'll help you with the rest of those needles."

* * *

A few days after the desert adventure, Kevin was sitting with Kwahu by the pool. The daytime heat was slowly easing into the evening coolness. Having showered and gone for a swim, he munched on cheese and crackers and drank a glass of iced tea. It had been a successful day. Jack was a quick study and had endeared himself to the rest of the staff. Kevin had begun his third week, and he had already seen the level of service improve.

He ran through the day in his mind and could find nothing wrong. It had been a good day. *Why then am I feeling so depressed?*

A dark cloud had gathered around him as the week progressed. Hadn't he been blessed this past week? Michael and Sarah had given him a home The violent encounter with Jack and Daniel had become a blessing. Except for the needles in his legs, he had enjoyed a Sunday hike and prayers with Michael. His days at work were satisfying and successful. Yet, yesterday, his day off, he'd spent in darkness.

Kevin lay in bed most of the morning unwilling to get up. When he finally dragged himself out, he swam in the pool. Later there was lunch with a couple of friends he had met through Ronnie. He prayed, meditated, watched TV, tried to read a book, and took a walk. Nothing helped to lift the cloud. It was a relief to get back to the diner today, because he could at least set aside his desolate mind and involve himself in work.

He traced an outline around Kwahu with his finger. *How can I break through this fog?* A list of potential remedies ran through his mind. Food, sweets, sex, alcohol, more caffeine, action adventure movies, anything to take away this feeling! He knew the items on his list would be temporary escapes. He told himself that the darkness was somehow good, but that was hard to believe. *How can something that feels so bad, be good? Just say thank you. Right?*

He stared at the Jerusalem Pine. He had already walked the labyrinth several times this week--tried to think happy thoughts, but his happy thoughts--picturing himself with money, or sharing emotional intimacy with a beautiful woman, or traveling around the world. Those dreams failed to spark joy.

"Sometimes the only way out is through. May I sit with you?"

Kevin hadn't heard Sarah enter the yard. "Yes, of course. But, I'm not very good company today. What did you say to me?"

Sarah glided into a chair. "I said sometimes the only way out is through. You've been fogged in all week."

"I don't like feeling this way. I have so many reasons to be grateful and joyful, but instead I don't want to be around myself. No escape though. I'm stuck with me. I don't understand."

"It just means you're getting close. Congratulations!" Sarah smiled, her eyes danced in the sunset as she reached across the table and squeezed his arm."

"Close to what?"

"To who you are. Michael must have taught you about experiencing your feelings rather than running from them."

"Yeah." Kevin stared at her still-smiling face.

185

"So feel it. Love it. This is life." She grabbed his hand and gently pulled him into a standing position. Facing him, she began a dance, something between a waltz and salsa.

He felt the energy in his body shifting as they moved.

"Let yourself go, Kevin. Feel that hurt rushing through your body. Stop thinking and analyzing, and just be. Dance."

The dance forced him to concentrate on his body, and to stop thinking about why and how and when. Sadness and hurt intensified at first, and then dissipated. He began to feel lighter. Soon the two were laughing.

"Okay, that's good for me." Sarah was breathing hard and raised her hand to stop. Why don't you sit down and do the process Michael taught? You know, dis-creating the negative identity and creating something more in alignment with who you really are." She turned and headed for the house. "I'll see if I can find Michael."

"Okay." Kevin sat down.

He tried to quiet his mind. Tales of conflict and struggle competed for airtime in his head. One moment he was focused on being in his feelings, and the next he was worrying about money, or the diner, or thinking about being single. The harder he worked to push away his thoughts, the more insistent they became.

The sound of glass on ceramic startled him. He opened his eyes as Michael set two glasses on the tiles.

"I thought you might like some water." He sat at the table.

"Thank you." Kevin grasped the glass and drank half the water as Michael slowly sipped his.

"How are you feeling?" Michael put his glass down. The sun had dropped below the walls, turning the aerial landscape into an Impressionistic canvas of peach and purple. He looked up. "It's beautiful isn't it."

"It is. I still don't understand why I feel so bad when there's so much good around me to appreciate."

"Maybe you should stop trying to understand. Just go with it."

"I know. I was hoping to a few moments ago, but I couldn't get all the dark thoughts out of my mind. Do *you* ever feel depressed."

Michael raised his eyebrows. "Brief moments. It doesn't stick."

"How do you and Sarah manage to stay so happy?"

"I'm in love."

"You mean with Sarah?"

"Of course I love Sarah, but that's not what I mean. I'm in love with myself. I delight in myself. Things happen. I'm sad or angry or impatient. I feel emotion, and life is one story following another."

"I'm happy for you. Really."

"But, you're not feeling happy for you right now, and that's okay. Let yourself be depressed. The weight of your sadness is strong, and you'll be tempted to find relief. Be present with it. Who are you when you're depressed?"

Kevin stared at him, and struggled to make sense of his words. "I don't know."

"Let go, Kevin. Feel; don't think. Ask yourself who you're being. When the answer comes, be it. I suspect this has something to do with being powerless. If that's it, then be powerless."

"Why do you think that?"

"Because depression is hopelessness, and hopelessness is about not having the power to change anything."

"Do you dis-create *your* negative identities?"

"I've spent many hours doing just that."

"Would you sit with me--guide me through this?"

"Sure. I'm here."

Kevin stared into the pool. Dawa blurred as a light breeze stirred the water's surface. He closed his eyes and allowed the darkness to encompass him--centering his awareness on his powerlessness. The darkness permeated his mind as he split his psyche--simultaneously watching a play and acting in it.

It was his play. Moments of embarrassment and hurt mixed with moments of victory and pride appeared as scenes from a movie stitched together into a trailer depicting his forty-seven years. He felt two impulses: one to hold on to the memories, to be the star of the movie; and the other to detach, to let go of the importance he assigned to his story.

He saw a Kevin who had been selfish and foolish, a Kevin who had struggled to get what he wanted, a center of attention. It was a small Kevin who was like a leaf, whipped about by winds, soaked by rains, and powerless as it drifted onto a pile with everyone else. He desperately didn't want to be *that* Kevin.

He tried to make the small Kevin disappear. Fear invaded his body, as his arms and legs began to shiver. The image of little Kevin persisted, so he took a deep breath and accepted the fear. *Don't fight it.* Zeroing in on small Kevin's eyes, he saw a frightened little boy--unsure of himself, unable to handle his current difficulties. He told Michael what was happening.

"Who are you that you can't handle your money issues?"

Childhood images appeared across the screen of his mind--a father who ignored him--a brother who always outperformed him in sports, academics, and dating--the time when the teacher and all the students in his sixth-grade class laughed at him when he gave a wrong answer. Adult images flooded his mind--his wife leaving him--Ronnie--the bankruptcy--two men beating him up. *I'm small. Powerless. There's nothing I can do to change anything!*

He became small, powerless. Shoulders slumped, and he trembled in his nakedness and vulnerability--as if the entire world could see his imperfections. He was standing on a stage, alone, unprotected, as the audience ridiculed him. Embarrassed to the core, he dared to raise his head, open his eyes slowly, and peer into the crowd. Every person there was Kevin, gaping at him, judging him, and criticizing him. He stared at himself--at the cowed eyes and cringing body, the quivering limbs and shaking hands--and he felt tenderness toward this frightened being.

All at once an insight flickered in his mind. *It's not really you.* Kevin looked at this little self and saw it was a hologram, not real. *It's a part I've played. I created it, and I can dis-create it.*

Judgment hijacked his process. *You shouldn't be powerless or small. You should be better than that.* Kevin sat with his judgment, feeling it, both observing and being it at the same time. Time passed, and his negative opinion melted into his memories.

He again sought out the small Kevin and became powerless, playing the role, unable to change anything, subject to the whims of the world. He continued to tell Michael of his experience until he no longer felt any negative emotion.

"Now focus your attention on who you want to be--powerful, capable, and confident--and how that would feel."

A half hour passed, then Kevin breathed deeply, and took stock of his emotional state. The depression had lifted, and a lightness presided over him. He felt stronger, more confident, and almost fearless. A verse from Corinthians came to mind. "When I was a child, I spoke as a child, I understood as a child, I thought as a child: but when I became a man, I put away childish things."

It was dark, and Michael was still sitting in the chair, asleep. The stars shimmered brightly and through a quarter moon, the heavens smiled down upon him. He took another deep breath, stood up, and faced the celestial sphere. Hands folded in front of his heart, he inhaled and raised them to a peak, then arms arcing downward, he exhaled. Somewhere in Tibet, a man like him was paying homage to the sun.

Chapter Twenty-Three

Summer temperatures ran as high as one hundred and ten in Tucson. During those hours, Kevin, like many people, lived in air conditioning. The grill at the diner would have been unbearable without it. Early mornings and evenings were pleasant, and the pool proved to be a blessing after work every day.

On the following Sunday morning Michael and Kevin sat in the yard, and Michael was speaking. "You live between love and anti-love--between positive and negative identities. You vacillate between God and ego. To become an adult you must discern between negative identities and the clarity of the Inner Voice."

"Well, until these past couple months, I wasn't all that aware of my Inner Voice."

"But, it was there, and you listened. When you were teaching and coaching there were times when you knew exactly what to do. There were times with your daughters when you made decisions that were in their best interests."

"I did what needed to be done."

"When you listened, and acted on it, who were you being?"

Kevin picked up his glass and sipped on his smoothie.

After work he had come home, changed, and jumped into the pool. He had swum a few lengths, then floated and gazed at the brilliant blue sky. After a quick shower he had changed into shorts and a tee shirt. When he exited the poolhouse Michael was sitting at Kwahu's table with a couple of mango smoothies.

He sipped slowly, since he had already suffered from brain freeze on the first gulp. Thinking back over his years as a parent and teacher, he sought out his most successful experiences.

His basketball team won a game no one thought they could win. He recalled being in the zone, believing in his players, as he delivered his half-time talk. A former student came to mind, who returned two years after graduation to thank him. The scene was as poignant in his mind now as it was then.

Mr. Neill, I just wanted to thank you for teaching me how to write. I've decided to be an English teacher. I want to be like you.

He remembered times he had taught and coached his daughters and times when they just had fun together. Moments at the Calico Grill showed up, when he had everyone working together, serving the customers and each other.

"It felt good, joyful. It meant something. Some kind of positive change took place." He re-ran the scenes in his mind and attempted to access how he felt in each one. "I was confident, and that came from knowing exactly what to do."

"Who were you being when you knew exactly what to do?"

"Wise."

"Wisdom is part of who you are. When you listen and act in alignment with your Inner Voice, you are in the flow. In the flow you are wise--you know what to do. Out of it, you're conflicted, fearful, and prone to mistakes."

"So how do I stay in the flow all the time?"

"You're doing a good job at the diner. I've noticed a change in the past two days. Things are going so well that I might have to open another location." Michael lifted his glass in salute.

"I've been in the zone at work, at least since Friday morning. I see what needs to happen, and I make sure it occurs."

"You're not worried about your needs or your concerns. The focus is on the people and the general environment. Everything you say and do is for the good of all."

"I hadn't really thought of it that way, but you're right. I only have one focus, and it's doing whatever it takes to make sure everyone has a great experience." Kevin felt a wave of joy throughout his body. "This is *better* than I was at Calico. I was distracted there--stuff with Al bothered me, and my obsession with Ronnie. At the diner, I'm single-minded, focused."

"So perhaps the next step is to become this wise in all of your life. You aren't going to feel good all the time. That's not the goal. The goal is to open up to the Inner Voice as your guide, or if you prefer, to do what the universe indicates you should do. Call it whatever you want. It's seeking first your Source, following its lead, and enjoying and accepting what unfolds. These past few days at the diner are an example of what it means to be an adult."

"I'm forty-seven. It's about time." A rueful expression crept across Kevin's face.

"Not an easy task in this world. People have their moments, instances when incredible wisdom and creativity come forth. Usually their fears are running things. You've had many instances when you performed as a successful adult, but now you're building consistency. I'm proud of you, Kevin."

"I am, too." Sarah appeared, and placed her hands on his shoulders and kissed him on the cheek. "I'm so pleased for you."

Kevin stood up and hugged her. "I couldn't do this without you two. I was stumbling on the edge of complete failure, and suddenly I'm in this dream where I have a job, a home, and two incredible people as friends and teachers. I'm afraid to pinch myself. I might wake up."

"You're right on all counts, except the pinching part." Michael laughed. "You were stumbling, and now you're well-supported-and you *are* dreaming. We all are."

"Can't say I understand that. It doesn't seem like a dream. It feels real." Kevin shrugged.

"That's okay." Sarah squeezed Kevin's arms and turned toward Michael. She leaned down, kissed her husband on the lips and embraced him. She caressed his cheek and held him in her gaze.

Kevin shifted his attention toward the Jerusalem Pine. The tree stood tall and vibrant despite the dryness and the heat. He rose to his feet and stretched, feeling taller, more confident.

"What happened last Thursday night, Kevin? You seemed to be doing fine, and I nodded off." Michael gestured for Sarah to sit next to him.

Kevin looked into Michael's eyes for a few moments. "I thought about who I've been and who I am now." He told them about seeing a small version of himself and dis-creating his resistance to it, then dis-creating his powerless reality.

"Good work. We feel the difference in you." Michael turned to Sarah, and she nodded.

Kevin looked at the two people sitting with him. *I'm so lucky to have these two. Even though they laugh at me sometimes. What did I do to deserve this?*

"The universe always connects people who need to be together. It may sound trite, but it's true. We're here for you. You're here for Jack and the other staff members at the diner." Michael reached for his drink and finished it.

"There you go again, reading my mind." Kevin pointed to his forehead.

"Don't ascribe special powers to me, Kevin. When I speak to your thoughts it's just logic. If you watch someone and listen to them closely; and if you're not focused on yourself, you can become aware of the other person's needs and to the patterns of their thinking. Understand?"

"I think so. My awareness is not as sharp as yours."

"Not true. At work you see your customers. You know exactly what they need, even when they don't tell you. Does that make you magical?"

"No. Just good at my job."

"Me, too. You are not my first student. One more thing..."

"What's that?" Kevin straightened to attention.

"Don't get too comfortable. Awareness is wonderful, but it's nothing without action."

"What is it I need to do?"

"I think we'll know the answer to that soon. As for now, this may be a good time to ramp up your practice of dis-creating your negative identities and your resistance."

"What did you have in mind?" Kevin leaned forward, curious.

"Daily practice with me. One to two hours every day. Dis-creating and then creating your positive identities."

"I would be grateful for your guidance."

"There are three broad areas in human experience: Value, power, and wisdom. We worked on value the first night. Value includes your ability to love yourself. On Thursday we worked on power. Today we were talking about wisdom. Are you with me?"

"Makes sense. When do we start?"

"Tomorrow, after work."

Chapter Twenty-Four

The summer passed quickly, and the diner thrived. Good service became great under Kevin's leadership, and he taught each staff member to be a center of influence with each other and with their customers. He met with his employees every day between breakfast and lunch to talk about how to create positive experiences for their guests and each other. Using a program developed at the Calico Grill, everyone practiced their ABCD's (Always Be Collecting Details.) Waitstaff and cooks became adept at reading people, understanding their needs, and meeting them.

If customers were cranky, they received both empathy and service. If a customer was in a hurry, they were served quickly. Kevin asked the staff to treat each person as if they were among the most important people in the world, and offer the same high level of respect, empathy, and service to each other.

People came back for more. A customer approached Kevin one day, shook his hand, and offered a comment: "I couldn't put my finger on it, but somehow I knew I was going to get great food and service the moment I walked in." Kevin smiled and thanked him.

It was rewarding to see staff members grow in confidence and skill. Jack became a full-time short-order cook and grill man. His joy at finding a place to work and to belong overflowed. Customers loved to banter with the cook with the anchor-and-skull tattoo. He gained his own following who sat on the stools facing the grill.

Since business was booming, Kevin received raises and profit-sharing as did everyone who worked there. He was still making considerably less money than Calico, and with interest rates, his progress on reducing indebtedness crawled. Gratitude for a salary and living quarters consoled him. His daily sessions with Michael were often difficult, but he felt himself maturing. He liked being focused and disciplined both at work and at home.

One August evening he prepared dinner for Michael and Sarah by the pool. Using his kitchenette and a small outdoor grill, he made *Nicoise* salads with grilled tuna. As the reds, oranges and yellows gave way to a black and purple sky, Kevin lit several candles. Three plates of vegetables awaited him as he seared the tuna, leaving black stripes on the browned steaks. He carefully sliced the end off one, and tasted it. The interior was still red, but hot, and the exterior was sizzling and flavorful. Quickly he slid his spatula under each piece and placed one on top of each salad.

"Here you go." Kevin stepped back to observe the first taste.

"Mmm, Kevin, this is incredible!" Sarah pointed at her salad with her fork. "What spices did you use? It's delicious!"

"Salt and pepper mostly. One other spice that will remain a secret. I love hot seafood on a cold salad." He wore a self-satisfied smile on his face. It was a pleasure to be the one doing the giving. "I learned this recipe from Jenny, and we served it at the Grill."

"How's she doing?" Michael asked as he took his first bite.

"She's still in San Francisco and doing okay. She emailed me today and said she may be coming back to Tucson. She wants to see you two again--says she has a business idea for you, Michael."

Michael nodded--his mouth full. "Mm-m. Excellent taste! Thank you."

"You're welcome." A pleasing chill ran up Kevin's spine.

"Jenny stayed in the poolhouse for a couple of months before she moved to San Francisco." Sarah cut off a piece of tuna with her knife and speared it with her fork. "We'd love to see her again."

"I didn't know that. So, she was your student, too?"

"This salad is definitely as good as Jenny makes it." Sarah took a bite, chewed slowly and closed her eyes.

"Okay, well I guess you don't talk about who's your student and who isn't."

Sarah shared a grin with Michael. "No, we don't, but it's okay if you know that we love Jenny and her salad very much." They both nodded and smiled.

"I guess you've had other people stay here over the years."

"Only if they can make a decent *Nicoise* salad." Sarah broke into a laugh. Michael laughed, too.

Kevin shook his head and smiled. He reached for his own plate and sat at the table.

"So, Kevin, have you had any contact with your family?" Michael forked a slice of potato.

"Talked to my daughters a few times. They're both doing well."

"And your parents?" Michael continued eating.

"I haven't talked to them or Bryce. My mom and I email once a week." Kevin took a moment to admire the look of his creation-- tuna in the center on a bed of lettuce, surrounded by cut green beans, slices of red-skinned potatoes, tomatoes, and quarters of boiled eggs--a homemade vinaigrette drizzled over the top.

"Maybe it's time you visited." Michael paused from eating, setting his fork on the table.

"I can't afford to fly to Michigan, and I don't have the time to drive." The words cut sharper than he meant.

"Labor Day weekend is coming up in two weeks." Michael tilted his head toward Kevin. "I'll buy your ticket, and you can have a few days off. Think of it as a bonus for work well done."

The tuna called him, and he dodged talk of his family. He savored a bite of the fish while it was still hot before he responded. "Well, I don't know." A trip to Michigan did not sound like the ideal way to spend the holiday weekend. His stomach muscles tensed, and the discomfort radiated into his chest. He set down his fork.

Sarah placed her hand on his forearm. "Kevin, it *will* be okay. I'm sure your parents would love to see you."

His arm warmed to her touch, while the rest of his body remained on edge. "To be honest, I'm afraid to face my father. I lost all the money he gave me. I'm sure he's disappointed in me." The intensity of his fear surprised him.

"Maybe he is, and maybe he isn't," Michael said. "Either way, you won't know until you see him. I know this is difficult, yet I can tell you're ready. We offered this poolhouse as a place to live, not as a place to hide. See if you can get clear on this."

"Can I think about it and tell you tomorrow?"

"Of course." Michael nodded and returned to his plate.

* * *

Kevin considered Michael's offer as he lay in bed that night. *Here I thought I was making all of this progress, and now I feel like a little kid. I'm not too excited to see Bryce, either. Maybe Michael and Sarah are right. Is it time to go back?* Random thoughts flitted about as he slid in and out of consciousness for several minutes. Confusion gave way to weariness, and his questions faded into unconsciousness.

* * *

In the morning he awakened anxious, yet sure it was time to visit Michigan. The picture of his father being displeased and his mother being upset flashed in his mind. He dismissed the thoughts, but dove into the feelings. For a few minutes he sat on his couch, a little boy in trouble with his dad. His embarrassment felt like a toxic fluid injected into his body, and his system tensed to fight it. Over a half-an-hour the sensations peaked and then dissipated. He accepted it. *I created this little boy. Who do I choose to be now? A man.*

What does that mean? A man wields power with compassion, and is unconcerned with the opinions of others. He sat on the side of his bed and became a man.

He thought about his many conversations poolside with Michael and Sarah. Their home had been a retreat, a place of healing. Gratitude suffused his mind and body, and with that he slipped into his suit, opened the door and dove into the pool. The cool water embraced and enlivened him as he glided along the bottom. Emerging on the other side, Kevin blinked into the first rays of sun as they sprayed the yard with streaks of light.

* * *

Thursday morning before Labor Day weekend, Sarah offered to drive Kevin to the airport. "We're leaving early. Mind if I take the long way? I want to show you something."

"No. What is it?"

"You'll know it when you see it. Are you feeling a little nervous about seeing your family?"

"Yeah. Any suggestions besides to breathe?" Kevin clicked his seatbelt together as they backed out of the driveway.

"Breathing is good. Think about your family instead of yourself. Just be helpful."

"And Bryce?"

"Bryce is a pain in the ass for you, isn't he?" Sarah laughed. "What do you think he needs from you?" Sarah stopped at a stop sign, then merged into the early morning traffic.

"Yeah, he's a pain, and I don't know what he needs. To be right. He needs to think he's the better brother."

"Is he better?" Sarah raised her eyebrows, and her eyes smiled.

"In high school he was--first-string football, basketball and baseball--almost all A's. My athleticism was more modest, and I was a B student. I wasn't motivated to excel."

"And after high school?"

"His stardom ended there. He wasn't good enough to get a scholarship at a big school. I remember both my dad and Bryce being disappointed about that." Thinking about Bryce as just a student at Michigan State, and not a star, Kevin tapped on his knee with his index finger. "He probably needs to make sure he's still the favorite, and needs me to think like he does."

"Those aren't needs." Sarah braked for a mother with a baby stroller crossing Country Club Road. "Maybe he needs to be valued and appreciated, and maybe it's not you that he needs it from."

"What do you mean?"

The crosswalk was clear, and Sarah tapped on the gas pedal. "Do you think you're the only one who has father issues?"

"So, you think Bryce's anger toward me is about our dad?"

"It's possible; isn't it? Let that thought help you in not taking Bryce's words so personally."

"I'll do my best."

"You must be excited to see your daughters."

"I am. I haven't seen them in over a year. Ronnie and I went to Jessica's graduation. I was proud of her and to be honest, proud of myself. I was a successful entrepreneur, and I had a beautiful, intelligent woman on my arm. Everyone congratulated me, except Bryce. He wanted to know where we were sleeping."

"So what's the difference between the Kevin who visited last year and the one who's visiting this year?" Sarah skillfully wove through the traffic like a race car driver, but within the speed limit.

"This year I'm the guy whose business went bankrupt, lost his inheritance, lost his home, and his girlfriend left. I feel humbled."

"You're talking about the trappings of life, and not about you. What's different between Kevin then and Kevin now?"

They drove in silence for awhile as Kevin considered Sarah's question.

"Look over there." Sarah pointed.

Kevin looked out the window as they passed the Boneyard, an airplane graveyard east of the Tucson Airport.

"It's the Boneyard. I've read about it, but never saw it before."

Sarah nodded. "Thousands of flying machines set in rows, all remnants of battles fought and earlier forms of aeronautical evolution. Preserved by the desert climate, some will be repaired and see action again. Some will end up in museums, and others will be used for parts. Over four thousand aircraft stored here."

"I think it's the biggest aircraft storage facility in the world."

"That it is."

"Why did you want me to see it?"

"Once upon a time all of these aircraft were useful. Now they are sorted according to whether they are useful or not. It reminds me of growing up--also a sorting out process. When you visit your family, you'll be a different person than the last time you saw them."

Kevin thought how he had retained some parts of his personality--his friendliness and his skills with people. Other parts he had sorted out to be left behind--his selfishness, need for approval, and his tendency not to pay attention. Through his work with Michael he had sorted out the part of him that identified with being a loser, and the part that claimed to be powerless.

"When I visited Las Vegas four years ago, I met a woman who impressed me. She talked about sorting out what she wanted and didn't want in her growing up process."

What was her name?"

"Rachel."

"Beautiful name. Think you'll see her again?"

"Yes. I don't know when, but we'll meet again."

"Maybe sooner than you think." Sarah smiled, as if she knew something he didn't. "Now, how about my question. What's different about you?"

"I'd like to think I'm wiser. More observant. Aware. Although I have significantly fewer things, I'm more grateful. More confident. This year I'm more of an adult."

"Where does the confidence come from?" Sarah slowed the vehicle around a curve, and then accelerated quickly. He felt the tug of the seatbelt holding him in his seat.

"Well, last year, my confidence was about what I had and how that looked to others. I hadn't really thought about it until now. My confidence comes from me, not from stuff, or having a romantic relationship, or professional status."

Sarah veered right following the sign for departing flights. "Who you are has never been about your stuff. Stuff comes and goes. Think about your daughters. Would they rather have a dad with a beautiful girlfriend and who delights in his own success, or an adult father who is interested in them?" Her white Jeep Cherokee glided to a stop curbside. She reached for his left hand with her right, silver bracelets clinking, and squeezed.

"You're probably right. Thanks for the tour." He squeezed her hand back.

"You're welcome. See you next week." Sarah let go.

Kevin looked at her, memorizing her features so he could easily recall her warmth if the family situation became difficult.

"Get going, Kevin. Michael and I are just a thought away, or a phone call if you need us."

He grabbed his carry-ons and opened the car door.

Chapter Twenty-Five

Kevin's plane landed around 6:00 p.m. at Metro Airport near Detroit. He rented a Malibu for the hour-and-a-half ride to his home town in Okemos. Each time his father came to mind he told himself everything would be okay. *I just have to trust that Michael was right. I'm ready for this. Let me be keenly aware of my effect on others. Let me connect with my family and be helpful.*

He arrived at his parent's subdivision just before dusk. Parking in the street in front of their Tudor-style home, he exited the car. The smell of recently cut grass brought back memories of summers in Michigan riding his dad's mower. His parents had moved into this four bedroom home when he was a freshman in high school, and he remembered the excitement Bryce and he had felt when they discovered that the whole basement was a recreation room complete with projection TV, pool table, ping pong and foosball. Kevin imagined revisiting the scene of their adolescent competitions. He grabbed his carry-ons.

The closing car door echoed throughout the neighborhood like a hymnal being dropped in church. The area seemed deserted, the only sign of life being a cat sitting under a red Lexus SUV parked two driveways down. As he stepped onto the walkway, the front door opened. His father emerged from the house with his mother behind him. They approached with ebullient smiles and met him halfway up the walkway. "Welcome home, Kevin." His dad embraced him, surprising Kevin with his passion.

I think he's glad to see me!

His dad stepped back so his mother could greet him.

"Oh, Kevin. We've missed you so much." She hugged him and then looked him over. "You look healthy and well."

203

They each seized a bag and escorted him into the house. As he was whisked through the living room and into the kitchen, his mother chatted excitedly about his visit. Within minutes they were comfortably seated on the deck sipping wine coolers.

The yard was carpeted with a rich green, neatly trimmed sod. Pink and purple impatiens filled the flower boxes around the deck. The yard, bordered on each side by a high rough-sawn, cedar fence, ran up against a beech-maple woodlot. A small opening between the trees revealed a path into the woods. Along the fences, his mother's roses thrived offering brilliant colors now dimmed by the onset of dusk. He used to play catch with Bryce in this backyard. The memory of his brother throwing him a pass triggered a smile.

"Kevin, I'm sorry we haven't been out to visit. You were here a year ago with Ronnie, and we know lots has changed for you since then. Why don't you catch us up." His mother touched his arm.

"Well, you know I'm not with Ronnie anymore."

Both his parents nodded. "That must have been difficult. I know you cared about her very much." His father made eye contact and held it, then quickly reached for his wine cooler.

Kevin paused a moment, struck by his father's empathy and interest. "You know that Al died, and the restaurant went out of business." He continued his story, leaving out many of the details, yet providing enough that his parents understood what had happened.

His father asked many questions about the business, how it went under, and what liabilities Kevin had. He simply nodded his understanding with each fact that Kevin offered.

"Dad, I'm really sorry the money you gave me is gone. I have a job now, but I don't earn as much as I did at my own restaurant."

"Don't worry about it. Over eighty percent of businesses fail to make it past five years. For restaurants, it's even higher. You guys had a good run for a few years. I don't care about the money. I gave it to you, hoping you would start a business, and you did that. Think of it as an investment in your business education."

"Costly investment. I thought you'd be disappointed in me."

"Not at all. I'm proud of you."

"You're proud of me?" *Really?*

"Sure I am. You're an entrepreneur. It took guts and vision to do what you did. I couldn't be happier with you. It's like that old saying about love." He looked to his wife, for help.

"'Tis' better to have loved and lost, than never to have loved at all." His mother beamed, squeezed her husband's hand and gave him that look that Kevin remembered, the one that said *I'm so glad we're married!* "That was Tennyson." She grinned, proud of herself.

Jim Neill returned his wife's look and turned toward Kevin. "Well, it's better to have started a business and lost it than never to have made the effort. I'm proud that you succeeded, and I'm proud that you failed."

"What do you mean?"

"Most people don't succeed or fail. They give up, or they don't make the attempt. You went for it, and you did all you could. So learn from it and move on. I see you making a comeback soon. You're already running Michael's diner. Obviously he thinks highly of you to put his business in your hands."

"Thanks. That means a lot." Kevin felt like a little boy again, but this time it was akin to the first time he successfully rode his bike. *Oh, Kevin, You did it! You know how to ride a bike! Way to go!*

His mother smiled. "I'm proud of you, too, Kevin. My boy has grown up, and that pleases me." She squeezed his arm.

"Kevin, I have something for you. Remember this ring?" His father grasped the ring on his right hand middle finger.

"Your entrepreneur ring. You were *Michigan Entrepreneur of the Year*, maybe ten years ago?"

"That's right. Now there's a new entrepreneur of the year in my book. That's you. I want you to have this ring, so you can remember how proud I am of you."

"You do? Are you sure, Dad?" Kevin cleared his throat to cover his breaking voice, then took a breath and held it, keeping his tears in check. "I mean, this is an honor, but it was a big deal for you when you got it."

"I always hoped one of my sons would be an entrepreneur." He placed the ring in Kevin's right hand. "It'll be a little loose, but we can get it resized."

Kevin looked at the ring. "Wow! I didn't expect this."

His mother dabbed the tears on her face. "I love it when my boys show their love for each other."

Both men looked at her and simultaneously, smiled and grunted like Tim Allen, and laughed until her face showed her disapproval.

"Now don't you go and ruin it!" She smacked her husband on the arm.

Jim flinched. "Ouch! That hurts!"

"No, it doesn't." She turned to Kevin. "I hope you're not feeling too tired, Dear. Most of the family is coming in about half an hour. Would you like to freshen up?"

"Yeah, Mom. I would."

"You can have the guest bedroom on the first floor."

Kevin finished his cooler. "I'd better get ready then."

His mother stood up. "Better fire the grill, Jim."

Kevin opened the sliding doors to the house. *So far so good.* He could not remember a time when his father had been so complimentary or affectionate. That kind of warmth and acceptance usually came from his mother. He showered and slipped into shorts, knit shirt and sandals. Other voices were in the air as he combed his hair in front of the large mirror on the dresser. His daughters were talking, and apprehension about seeing them fluttered about in his stomach. The conversation with Sarah repeated in his mind. *Would they rather have a dad with a beautiful girlfriend and who delights in his own success, or an adult father who is interested in them?* He breathed deeply and opened the door.

"Dad!" Jessica ran toward him and gave a him a hug.

Melissa followed behind. "So glad to see you, Dad. Tell us all about Michael and Sarah, and the diner."

He barely had a chance to ask them about their lives before Brenda and her two daughters walked in. While the cousins reconnected, Kevin talked to Brenda.

"Brenda, I'm really sorry about what happened in Tucson. I was upset and took it out on you two. You didn't deserve that."

"Well, I told Bryce we should've called you sooner. If we had called you the day before it wouldn't have been so awkward."

"I wouldn't have had a guest for the night. That's for sure."

"Let's just move on, okay." Brenda hugged him.

"Is Bryce ready to move on, too?"

"You'll have to ask him about that. You two have other issues."

"Where is he, anyway?"

"He's been at a convention in California." She looked at her cell. "His plane was supposed to land at 7:30. He should be here in an hour or so."

"Does he know I'm here?"

"I hope so. I didn't know you were coming until this afternoon. I think your father emailed him, and I texted him." Her cell phone rang. "That's him now. Excuse me."

He watched her take the call, holding the phone in one hand and explaining something with the other. He approached her when she was finished. "Everything okay?"

"He's tired, and he didn't know you were coming. He said he'd stop by at least for a little while."

"Good!"

Brenda looked at him, her head tilted a little. "Are you sure about that?"

"Yeah. We don't always get along, but he's still my brother. Let's check out the food." He gestured toward the back of the house.

The family gathered on the deck for dinner. The table was laden with salads, barbecue ribs, and corn on the cob. Sweet smells permeated the air. Time raced as they enjoyed the tastes of summer and stories from their shared history. Most of the way through dinner Kevin noticed that Brenda was missing. He was about to check on her when she came out and leaned toward his father's ear. Jim nodded and went into the house.

Brenda sat down. Her eyes looked worried.

"Is everything okay, Brenda?"

"Bryce is here, and he wants to talk to your dad."

Kevin ejected from his chair and headed toward the door. Brenda called to him to wait, but he continued in forward motion. His father and brother were talking in the front room, and he decided to hold up before seeing Bryce.

Bryce raised his voice. "You could've called!"

"I sent you an email this morning."

"Come on, Dad. You knew he was coming a few days ago. You should've told me."

"Okay, you're right. I should have. But, now he's here, and you're here. So, come in and enjoy the party."

"You're throwing him a party? This is rich! My brother blows his inheritance on women and gambling and comes home with his tail between his legs. Now you're celebrating?"

"I don't know about women and gambling, but yes, I'm happy your brother has come home. We've missed him."

"Yeah, well I don't remember you throwing me a party, and I *never* left you. I've been a loyal employee for thirty years, but my brother, who hasn't worked a day at the family business in over twenty-five years, gets a big celebration."

He placed his hand on Bryce's shoulder and made eye contact. "Son, you always have me. We see each other almost every day. We've gone fishing together every summer for forty years. You live three miles from here, and you're always welcome in our home. Your brother has been gone for four years. Of course we make a big deal about him coming home. Why wouldn't we?"

Bryce grabbed the hand and firmly removed it from his shoulder, then grabbed it again. "What happened to your ring?"

His father looked at him without speaking.

"Your ring, Dad. Where is it? Did you lose it?"

"I gave it to Kevin. It was a gift from one entrepreneur to another. I'm proud of him, and you should be, too."

Bryce let go of the hand as a pained look took charge of his face. He opened the door and walked out.

"Bryce, come back." His father called, but there was no response.

"Maybe you should take this back if it's going to cause problems." Kevin entered the room and took off the ring.

His father turned toward him. "No. I gave it to you. Bryce is not an entrepreneur. He's a good man, and he's done good work for me. I just sent him to California for a week to represent our company. So put it back on your finger. I won't pander to pouting. I'm going back out on the deck. Coming?" He gestured toward the back of the house.

"I'll be there in a few minutes, Dad." Kevin stepped out onto the front porch to be alone. He inhaled deeply and then exhaled. The air was warm, but not as hot as Tucson. He sat on the front steps and gazed into the darkness, absently turning the ring on his finger. There were no street lamps on this part of the street.

Headlight beams pierced the night as a vehicle hurried into the driveway. Someone got out of the car and walked toward the garage. The door opened, and he saw Bryce standing in the light. Kevin put the ring in his pocket and walked toward the garage. "Hello, Bryce. How are you?"

Bryce turned and said nothing.

"How was your trip?"

"My trip was *fine*. What are *you* doing out here? Shouldn't you be at your party?" His question sliced through the air between them, walling them off from each other.

"I could ask you the same. It's not really *my* party. Just the family; no one else."

Bryce picked up a chain saw case. "I'm borrowing this from Dad. Tell Brenda I went home." He walked past Kevin.

"Bryce, I'm sorry for how I treated you back in Tucson."

Bryce stopped. "You think that's what this is about? I don't care about that."

"What do you care about?"

Bryce set the chain saw down. "I care about how screwed up this family has become. I've worked my whole career at the business. I've managed to stay married to the same woman for twenty-seven years. I'm a good Christian and very active in my church. You, on the other hand, are divorced. You lost your inheritance. You've spent the last four years having extramarital sex with who knows how many women. As far as I can see, you have no spiritual base, no connection to God and definitely no allegiance to Christ who died for your sins."

"So what's your point, Bryce?" Kevin worked to keep the sarcasm out of his voice but knew he wasn't successful.

"The point is that in spite of your unchristian behavior this family welcomes you with open arms and a party. I really thought that when you came home Dad would lay into you about what you've done. Instead, he rewards you with his special ring."

"Well, I'm surprised, too. I've struggled this past year, and I was amazed to feel so much support from my family, especially Dad."

"Your struggle was completely of *your* own doing." Bryce pointed his index finger toward Kevin several times as if pushing an invisible button in the air.

"Yes, I'm responsible. I've also learned some things." Kevin took a step toward Bryce and looked into his eyes. "I don't understand why you're making a big deal out of this dinner. We're all here. It makes sense to get together."

"You don't get it. Sin is not to be celebrated. You should repent, and ask Jesus to come into your life."

"That will make everything better?"

"It's a start. Then you have to start acting like a Christian."

"How does a Christian act, Bryce?"

"Well, he doesn't sleep around or associate with pagans!"

"What the hell are you talking about?"

"Idol worshippers. Those Indians you live with who have pictures of their gods on tables and in their pool."

"Bryce, you are so full of shit. You've made some huge leaps here. I mentioned the artwork in the backyard to Mom, and my friends are not idol worshippers. Why am I bothering to defend them to you?" Kevin took a deep breath. "They are good people, and they have helped me a lot."

"Are they Christians?"

"What difference does it make? They're *good people*."

"You really don't understand, and I can't explain it very well. Maybe I should have you talk to Reverend Mason."

"Who?"

"The pastor at our church. He could make you understand."

"What about Reverend Turner?"

"Retired. Reverend Mason is new."

Kevin thought a few moments and was curious. *Is he a hard liner like Bryce and Turner?* He felt an urge to meet the minister. "Okay, I'll do it on one condition."

"You'll meet with the pastor?" Bryce peered at his brother suspiciously.

"Yes, I will." Kevin nodded.

"Oh!" Bryce dropped his arms to his side, as if he were setting down his weapons, and assumed a more relaxed stance. He pulled his cell phone from his pocket. "I'm calling him. What's the condition?"

"You come back and sit on the deck with the family as if none of this happened. Don't do it for me. Do it for your wife and daughters."

Bryce hesitated, taking his eyes off the phone and aiming them at Kevin. He waved Kevin toward the house. "You go on. I'm going to call him, and then I'll be there, at least for a little while." He began pushing the buttons on his phone.

Kevin returned to the deck, feeling satisfied. He seated himself at the table, and everyone went silent. "Bryce will be here in a minute. He has to finish a phone call." Brenda sighed and began a conversation with his mother. His dad shot him a puzzled look to which Kevin shrugged and turned his palms up.

Bryce arrived a few minutes later to a warm welcome, which seemed to soften him. He looked at Kevin. "11:00 a.m. Saturday, here at the house."

Kevin noticed his mother's puzzled look. "Reverend Mason, Mom. He's coming here to meet with Bryce and me."

Chapter Twenty-Six

On Friday morning Kevin slept until eight. Losing three hours traveling east made it difficult to wake up early. It was 10:00 a.m. when the *whoosh* of the front door alerted him that his daughters had arrived, ready to go to the beach.

Jessica and Melissa were talkative on the hour-and-a-half drive, but Kevin could barely stay awake. He asked Jess to drive. By the time they arrived in Saugatuck he was rested. They parked on the road high above Douglas Beach, a small, public stretch of sand on Lake Michigan.

They had come here often as a family when the girls were growing up. It was the only free beach in the area and usually quiet. They changed into swimsuits in the restrooms a few steps from their car. Descending the steps through the woods and down to the beach sparked memories of sand castle building, laughing, and splashing in the waves with his wife and daughters.

Once blankets and umbrellas were set up, Jessica challenged them: "Last one in is a rotten egg." She sprinted for the waves. Melissa and Kevin followed. They stepped carefully through the first ten feet where the lake floor was covered with stones, but once they hit the sandbar the trio high-stepped through the whitecaps and dove in. He knew better than to delay getting wet. His daughters would have splashed him unmercifully. The girls were ten years old again as they charged the three-foot rollers with their dad.

Swimming and diving both refreshed and rejuvenated him, and he tingled with energy as the brilliant sun quickly vaporized the water droplets from his skin. It felt like dry champagne on his tongue, and the sensation spread over his whole body. One thing

Tucson didn't have was the abundant waters of Michigan--but more than lakes and rivers, he had missed his daughters.

They returned to their blankets and umbrellas. Several other families and a few singles fanned out across the beach, and he hoped it wouldn't become more crowded. Most of the people were at Oval Beach, just north.

He sat between them as Jessica passed out cold cans of lemonade and tea. She looked a lot like Dana with short, dark, brown hair and brown eyes, and a shapely, firm body. Boys had started calling the house when she was thirteen, and it never seemed to stop. He had worried about her in high school, with all the athletes pursuing her. But, she had a good sense of herself and like Dana, was not intimidated by males.

He considered Melissa, who looked more like him. Her medium-brown hair fell just below the shoulders--her gray eyes mirrored his. She had been the more intellectual of his daughters. She played the cello and earned good grades. In high school she occasionally went on a date, but seemed to have no envy toward her more popular younger sister.

"Okay, Dad. What's up?" Jessica said. Melissa nodded her head in agreement.

"Nothing. I'm just admiring my two beautiful daughters. I'm thinking about the good times we had at this beach and of how proud I am of both of you."

"And?" Jessica looked at him directly.

"I was thinking that maybe I was a little distant the years I was married to your mom, but here at this beach, I think we all connected. How does it feel to be here again?"

He noticed both his daughters staring at him. "What's up with you two? Why are you looking at me like that?"

Jessica shook her head and laughed.

Melissa shot her a disapproving look. "Dad, you've never talked to us like this. I mean it's usually 'How are you?' or 'How's school?' You know, basic stuff. You played with us when we were kids, and we both liked that. You never tried to find out how we feel."

That stung.

Jess poked him in the ribs, and he jumped. "So what happened to you in Tucson that you're doing this bonding with the daughters thing?"

"I don't want to analyze the past. I've always loved you both. I hope you know that. I was just too self-involved to learn more about you. I'm sorry."

"Hey Dad, if you want to get to know me better I'm cool with that." Jessica gave him a gentle shove on the shoulder.

"Thanks, Jess. What about you, Melissa?"

"I'm fine. I mean, I did miss you when you were away. It's like you went off to Arizona and forgot about us. I've seen you what, once or twice a year in the last four years? I'm glad you created a new life for yourself, but it didn't include me." Melissa looked out over the lake. A tear rolled down her cheek.

"I'm sorry, Melissa. You're right. I didn't include you. I thought about you, and everyone in Tucson knows I have two great daughters. But, I didn't share much with you."

"Hey, you brought Ronnie to my graduation. She was cool, an inspiring woman. I'm taking real estate classes because of her. One more to go, and I'll get my license. Did she dump you or did you dump her?" Jessica asked.

"Just a minute, Jess. Melissa, anything else?"

"I'll let you know if anything else comes up. It's not like I was planning to talk about this."

Kevin re-situated to his knees and embraced her. "Thank you for telling me that. I love you." She squeezed him a little tighter, and he kissed her on the cheek.

"So, tell me what's going on, you two. Boyfriends? Anything you want to say?"

"I have a boyfriend. That's all you get until Monday. I'm bringing him to the family Labor Day picnic." Jessica smiled, enjoying her secret.

"Wow! This must be serious if you're introducing him to the family." Melissa raised her eyebrows.

"What about you, Lissy." Kevin asked.

"I'm still with my boyfriend, Greg. It's been a year-and-a-half now. We're both so focused on our careers, I don't know how serious it'll get. We're good friends, and we're comfortable with each other. We'll see what happens. He'll be at the picnic, too."

"That's it? That's all I get?"

"Oh, we're saving the big news. Should we tell him now, Sis?" Jessica asked.

Melissa nodded. Jess put her hand on Kevin's shoulder. "Not sure how you're going to take this Dad, but Mom's getting married!" She studied his face, no doubt waiting for his reaction.

Although he didn't expect to hear this news, he felt nothing. It seemed Dana was two thousand miles away, and she usually was. He had let her go. It wasn't that he wished anything hurtful for her--he didn't. It just didn't matter. *Should it matter?*

"Cool! How do you feel about the guy? It is a guy, right?" Kevin's eyes twinkled.

"Da-ad! Yes, he's a guy." Jessica took her towel and gently snapped it at him. "His name is Jarred, and he's all right. Mom's been seeing him for two years. So we've had plenty of time to get used to him. He's rich, too. Mom's done well for herself, and that isn't why she's marrying him."

Kevin felt a twinge in his stomach as he compared himself as the failed restauranteur to this rich man. Now it seemed to matter. He caught the thought, remembering again his talk with Sarah on the way to the airport. He tried to let it go, but the residue lingered in the pit of his stomach.

He looked up at the clear cerulean sky. It looked more like a Tucson sky than one he'd see in Michigan.

"Dad?" Jessica touched his arm.

"Yes, I'm happy your mom has found somebody she loves." He made eye contact with each of his daughters.

"Which brings us to you, Dad. Do you have a girlfriend?" Jessica brushed sand off her feet. "What *did* happen to Ronnie?"

Kevin related the story about Ronnie leaving, the restaurant closing, and then told them about Michael and Sarah. He couldn't remember sharing so much information and feelings with his daughters. He realized that while they were still little girls in his head, they had grown into amazing young women.

They followed their old practice and took a long beach walk, had dinner at their favorite restaurant in Saugatuck, and returned to the beach for the sunset.

They sat on a blanket watching the sun sink below the Lake Michigan waves. "Dad, I didn't realize that you'd been through so much. I'm really sorry."

"Please don't be sorry. It's okay. Everything has helped me to grow and understand life better." He put his arms around his daughters and pulled them close.

* * *

Kevin was up early on Saturday. He entered the kitchen and found his mother finishing up the dishes. "What's going on, Mom?"

"I have a hair appointment and will be gone all morning. Your dad's golfing. Honey, would you make sure the living room is straightened up before Reverend Mason arrives. I hope it goes well with you and Bryce."

"No problem, Mom."

"Do you want some breakfast?"

"Granola is fine for me. And orange juice. Do you have to leave right away?"

"I have a little time."

"Why don't you sit with me?" It was a large kitchen with a bar and stools on either side. Part of the family business was selling kitchens, so they had one of the best. From his stool he could see out through the garden window into the yard. Herbs and small flowers grew in little pots on the spacious window ledge.

"Mom, I'm sorry I haven't communicated much this past year."

"It's okay. I know you've had a tough year."

"Thanks, but it's not okay. I should've called. I'd like to say that it's because I was embarrassed over losing Ronnie and then Al and the restaurant, which was true, but I was self-involved."

Madeline looked at her son and reached for his hand. "I know you love me, and I know you need to live your own life. I always want to hear from you, but I won't make you feel guilty about that. I'm grateful whenever we can talk or spend time together. Why don't you tell me more about the people you're living with?"

Kevin told her about Michael and Sarah. She asked questions, especially about Sarah's artwork. "I don't remember you being that into art, Mom?"

"Oh Kevin, that's one of my secrets. But, right now I've got to get to the salon, and you have some cleaning to do."

* * *

By 11:00 a.m. Kevin had the living room looking presentable. The doorbell rang. He opened the door to find a forty-ish-looking man in blue dockers and a white dress shirt.

"I'm Reverend Mason." He smiled and extended his hand. "Jeff."

"I'm Kevin. Good to meet you, Jeff. Where's Bryce? I thought he was bringing you."

"He said he'd meet me here. May I come in?"

"Sure." *This isn't right.* Queasiness seeped into Kevin's stomach. "Why don't you have a seat. Would you like something to drink?"

"Just water. Thanks."

He brought two glasses of water, and they sat down across from each other. Kevin asked about the church and how long Jeff had been there. After several minutes, Kevin peered at Jeff. Irritation began to supersede queasiness. "I'm starting to feel like this is a setup. Bryce isn't coming, is he?"

"If it is, I'm not in on it. Do you want me to leave?" Jeff slid forward to get up.

Kevin thought about something Michael said: *Whatever is happening is happening. Find the flow and go with it.* "No, please stay. You came here, and we planned for this time. Let's see where it goes."

"As long as you're okay with this." Jeff slid back a few inches in his seat, still poised, as if ready to rise at any moment.

"I think Bryce wanted you to fix me. He wants you to talk sense to me so I'll drop everything and ask Jesus to be my savior. If that's your goal, you'll leave here frustrated." Kevin lowered his chin and raised his eyebrows, challenging the minister.

Jeff tilted his head slightly and looked at Kevin. After a few moments he settled back into the chair and crossed his right leg over the left. His arms floated onto the fabric of the armrests. "That's not my goal. My goal is whatever God wants. He brought us together for a reason. My first objective is to understand why."

His calm tone chafed at Kevin. "So you're not here to proselytize?" Kevin's query rushed at Jeff like waves against a break wall. *Back off, Kevin. This guy isn't your enemy. Who is my enemy? Do I have an enemy?*

Jeff breathed evenly, his eyes seeming to massage Kevin's aggravated mind, as if absorbing and transmuting his energy. Silence hovered between them. The minister spoke, slowly at first, each word crisply stepping forth, as though on parade. "The only way I know to share the good word is to live it." He picked up the pace, smoothing his words. "Of course I preach it on Sunday, but it's what I do between Sundays that makes the real difference. So rather than preaching to you, how about you share something about yourself. Maybe if I understand you, I'll have an idea why I'm here."

Kevin felt ridiculous, like a warrior, all dressed for battle, and then the war was cancelled. It was as if he fired off his best shot, and Jeff had sidestepped it. "I don't have much interest in sharing my history. Maybe we could talk about spirituality." *I am my own enemy here. Who am I, that I feel so threatened?*

"I'd like that. I'd be honored to hear what you have to say."

"You don't sound like a preacher my brother would follow."

"Well, my predecessor was much more traditional. I inherited Bryce, and the whole congregation from him. I'm doing more listening than preaching--until I get a good sense of where people are and what they need. So, please, tell me about your spiritual perspective."

He's different. He has nothing to prove. Kevin found he liked this minister, and relaxed into the conversation. *If more ministers were like this I might have to reconsider my opinions about Christianity.*

Kevin cleared his throat. "I think spirituality and religion are two different things. Religion is rules and beliefs--rituals, and I'm not interested in that. Spirituality is relationship and connection and what you are. It's about growing up and allowing yourself to hear the Inner Voice."

"I'm with you so far." Jeff sipped on his water, set the glass down, and leaned in toward Kevin. "Who or what is the Inner Voice?"

"God or spirit or higher self. When I pray or meditate and listen, life seems to work better. In your context I guess that would be to say *Not my will, but Thy will be done.* I don't need rituals. I don't need beliefs, and I don't worry about going to Hell. I just need to be myself and listen."

"Is there a book or a specific path?"

"If I feel drawn to reading a book, I'll read it. I've read parts of the Bible. My last girlfriend was into *A Course in Miracles.* It's good, but I can't say I'm a follower. I don't want to follow anyone, except my Inner Voice. I don't need an intermediary."

"I'm not familiar with the miracles book, but the Bible, of course, is my guide. I think I understand what you're saying. Please go on." Jeff's eyes shone, like students in a classroom who are learning. Shining eyes were always Kevin's goal as a teacher.

Encouraged, he continued. "I'm not judging other people. If you want to be a Christian and teach Christianity to people, that's fine with me. From what you've said, you probably do a great job. I think everyone has their own path. I've had some miracles on mine. One day I'm empty-handed, praying in the desert and the next, I find myself working for an amazing man who hired, housed, and mentored me.

"He doesn't want me to put him on a pedestal or ascribe any religious authority to him. He doesn't expect me to have specific beliefs. He accepts me without judgment and tells me to look within. When I compare that to all the rules and bullshit I hear from Bryce, I know I'm on the right path." Kevin looked at Jeff for a reaction and saw none.

"When I hear Christians condemning gay couples and a host of other things they don't like, and then say that God doesn't approve, my bullshit detector lights up. People use religion and scripture to promote their personal point of view. Those views have nothing to do with doing God's will." Kevin felt himself pushing, as if trying to convince Jeff of his rightness. He made himself stop talking.

"Sounds reasonable." Jeff nodded. "I'm not disagreeing with you. You have to follow your path. I can understand why the more extreme expressions of modern Christianity would turn you off."

"That's putting it lightly. How do *you* see those more extreme beliefs?" He bit his tongue and reminded himself that he wasn't talking to Bryce.

Jeff took his time again. "My path is clearly based on the teachings of Jesus and the inspiration I find in the Bible. I pray to God for guidance every day. It's true that people use Scripture to condemn others. I don't use the Bible as a weapon. I have opinions about gay marriage, politics, and other topics, but it's not my job to express them. My job is to counsel, to teach, to listen, and to help people find their connection to Jesus and to God. I help people to learn how to live his principles, and to put God first in their lives. My opinions mean nothing."

"You didn't really answer my question. How do *you* feel about gay marriage and Creationism and abortion, all of which seem to be strongly expressed Christian beliefs?" He pushed the question in spite of his better judgement, as if the response were a test, and he wanted to know if Jeff would pass.

Jeff looked at him, as if considering what to say. "It's not my job to judge. If a gay couple wants to attend our church I'd accept them. I don't think our board would, but *I* would."

"You would stand against your board for that couple?"

"I would speak for not judging and for the gospel message of love. I would welcome everyone as Jesus did."

"You still haven't said how you feel about it personally."

"And I won't." Jeff's tone shifted and stood like a shield between them. "I received the call to minister to others. It didn't say to force my opinions on everyone or to condemn those who live differently. It simply said to love people and help them. Part of that is doing my own work. Growing up as you say, and learning to do God's will. You and I are on similar paths, just different pages."

Kevin tilted his head. "How are we on similar paths?"

"We've read different books, but both of us are seeking to hear the Voice of God in our lives. Besides the Bible, I've learned a lot from Phillip Gulley, a Quaker minister from Indiana. I feel he represents what Christianity is meant to be. Jesus' message is a message of love and Reverend Gulley emphasizes that love. My favorite quote from Gulley is this: *In the end, what I'm hoping for is a church a little less full of itself, and a little more full of love. It wouldn't take much, for love and grace and kindness have a way of multiplying.* That's my goal, too. I want a church and a minister--me--with less pridefulness and more love and humility."

Jeff's face brightened, and he gestured with his hands as he spoke. "I'm from the 'Love God and love your neighbor camp' in Christianity. Love means acceptance, compassion, deep appreciation for others, and not judging. I care more about love than sex, and more about helping people than condemning them for behavior I may not agree with. I care more about the example that Jesus set than about making him an object of worship. I'm for prayerfully studying Scripture and applying it to my life, not quoting it at others. As you can see, I have some passion about this."

"I can see that. How does Bryce feel about this?"

"Bryce is doing fine. I haven't given him all of this message in words. It's much more important I live these truths rather than preach them."

"I wish you luck in presenting your truths to Bryce. I've seen no evidence that he is anywhere near your point of view."

"I disagree." Jeff's tone was firm. "When I look at Bryce I see dedication and commitment to being a Christian.--a man who's willing to serve for the greater good. Bryce is on the church board. He takes an active role in making sure our building and facilities are running well. He's highly respected in our community. My job isn't to change him. It's to support his growth in Christ. I don't judge him. Rather than searching for his flaws, I prefer to build on his strengths. That usually works better with people."

Neil Young's *Heart of Gold* played in Kevin's mind. *I am a miner for a heart of gold...* "You dig deep for the positive, and you don't let appearances put you off. I've never met a minister like you." Kevin shook his head.

"How many ministers have you met in the past several years?" Jeff smiled.

"Maybe two or three."

"I might not be so unique. I always try to put God first. That's a core teaching of Christianity: 'Seek ye first the kingdom.'"

"I appreciate that you're not pushing your beliefs. Now tell me what you really think. Bryce thinks I'll go to Hell unless I accept Jesus as my savior and believe he died for my sins. What about you?"

"It's not my job to make you believe as I do. Jesus is my teacher, and I am doing his work. I do what I can to help others whether they agree with my beliefs or not. I don't believe in an angry God who sends people to Hell. There's plenty of hell right here in this life."

"Do you believe in Hell?"

"Can you keep a secret?"

"Yeah, sure."

"I don't. I can't reconcile it with an all-loving God. The idea that there is a literal place called Hell is not even in the Bible. Hell is a spiritual condition of feeling completely separate from God."

Kevin smiled inside wondering what Bryce's reaction would be to this news. "I'm glad to hear that, but I think Bryce might be disappointed that you're not giving me a fire and brimstone talk."

"I do my best, and God does the rest." Jeff grinned.

"Are you married?"

"No."

Kevin felt a shift in the mood, as some of the brightness drained from Jeff's face. Kevin veered away from personal questions. They sat quietly for a few minutes, each lost in his own thoughts, yet Kevin was aware of Jeff's presence.

"Did you figure out why you're here?" Kevin asked.

"Not really, but it doesn't matter. We talked, and the conversation went where it was supposed to go." Jeff stared into the distance, a hint of sadness in his eyes.

"Are you okay?" Kevin leaned forward, his elbows on his knees.

"Yes, I'm fine. I should be going." Jeff pasted a smile across his face and stood up. "I have another appointment. Thank you for this. I enjoyed talking with you, Kevin."

"I enjoyed it, too. Probably would have been a very different conversation if Bryce had been here." Kevin searched for his sweet spot inside, the place where he felt total confidence and well-being. He couldn't find it. He felt disconnected from the moment, from himself, even though he was comfortable with Jeff.

"Let Bryce be Bryce. Don't judge him even though he seems to be judging you. He's a good man, and with God's help, he'll learn and grow."

They shook hands and said good-bye.

After seeing Jeff off, Kevin reflected on the conversation. He cringed as he saw himself on the attack, and Jeff calmly parrying his words. He turned his head from side to side and felt humbled, foolish. *Maybe I'm not as grown-up as I think. I couldn't let go of the idea that Bryce set me up.*

He shifted his thoughts from self-criticism and remembered the things Jeff had said about a loving God and there being no Hell. He knew Jeff was right about the message of love. He needed to love his own life and the people in it, whether they met his human expectations or not. Maybe it was time to love this era of his life, this period of seeming failure and foolishness.

Kevin sat down and allowed himself to feel the pain and frustration of being a fool, to become the person who felt stupid, and ignorant about life. *So many mistakes! I'm a fool. But, I shouldn't be a fool. It's wrong! I should be wise.* He listened to his resistance and joined with it as Michael had taught him. It felt like a concrete wall of judgment, erected to keep him safe from his own foolishness.

After half an hour the resistance dissolved. Next, he assumed the role of a fool, and he accepted it. *Sometimes I'm foolish, and sometimes I'm wise. Who do I want to be? I am wise. I make good choices. Clear. Insightful. Just like I am at the diner. I can handle this.* He became the wise person who could discern the best options. Kevin surrendered his opinions and judgments to the Inner Voice. He asked for wisdom and to see himself and others as spiritual beings, children of God.

Time passed, and the good feelings he generated subsided into a neutral state. From there he became drowsy and nodded off. The swoosh of the front door jolted him awake. Bryce burst into the room. "So, did Jeff come? I meant to be here, but I was held up on a job. Jeff was here wasn't he?"

Kevin jerked, rubbed his eyes, and struggled to reclaim his reality. He yawned, stretched his arms and sighed. Slowly, the blurry figure that was Bryce came into focus. "Yeah, he was here. I liked him. Said some good things."

"Good." Bryce nodded once. "About time someone talked some sense into you. Did you accept Jesus as your Savior?"

"It wasn't that kind of conversation, Bryce. We didn't hold a revival meeting here in the living room. We just talked." Kevin's adrenaline-laced words aroused his senses.

"If he knew the stuff you've done, wasting Dad's money, screwing around with women outside of marriage, and rejecting the Lord, he would've had you on your knees. I can't believe how everyone is letting you off the hook. Dad, Mom, Brenda, now Reverend Jeff. They don't really see you." Bryce stood over Kevin, shaking his reddened face and furrowing his brow.

Kevin, now fully awake, fired back. "*You* really see me?" He rose and faced Bryce, inches away.

Bryce's eyes were on fire. "Yeah, I do. I see you for the sinner you are. I see you for the fake who has the wool pulled over everyone's eyes except mine. I see you. You don't fool me for one second. You're in league with Satan, and I'll not let you pollute this good Christian family with the influence of the devil!" Bryce's eyes bulged. His voice grated on Kevin, like rough sandpaper on soft skin. Obviously energized by his own fervor, Bryce paced back and forth, reminding Kevin of a tiger in a cage at a zoo.

Kevin closed his eyes and imagined another reality. *Struggling to prevent his face from contorting into rage, he grabbed Bryce around the neck with both hands and shook him--then raised his right hand and smacked him on the cheek. His brother fell to the floor.*

Bryce--oblivious to Kevin's imaginings--continued to rant.

Kevin pulled himself from the precipice of losing control. Taking a breath, he waited until the pacing ceased. He measured his words and tone. "I'm sorry you have so much anger toward me. I don't know what to do about it. I care about you, Bryce, but I can't change to be what you think I should be."

"This isn't about what I want, Kevin. It's about the salvation of your soul! Jesus says you can only be saved through him." Bryce's breaths were short and rapid.

"Thank you for caring about my soul." Kevin said through his teeth. He breathed deeply and exhaled. The anger eased slightly as he consciously relaxed his muscles from forearms to fingers.

"Maybe you're just ignorant." Bryce nodded, as if agreeing with himself. "I feel sorry for you. Satan has his hand up your ass; he's working you; and you don't have a clue. I don't know which I feel more--pity or disgust." He resumed pacing. "I'm tired of pleading with you and trying to save you." Flecks of spittle sprayed with the word *pleading*. "You disgust me." He glared at Kevin.

Kevin rolled his eyes. "So you've made your choice. Good! I'd much rather have your disgust than your pity. Why don't you pray for me and leave it at that?"

"Don't roll your eyes at me!"

Kevin laughed.

"This is serious." He stepped toward Kevin but was distracted as Brenda came in the front door. Whoosh!

She looked at both brothers. "Oh! Oh! Bad timing?"

"It's good timing, Brenda." Kevin puffed a small sigh. "You came in at the perfect moment. We were just finishing this conversation. I'll leave you two to talk while I take care of some correspondence."

"This isn't over." Bryce promised.

Kevin ignored him and left the room. He walked into the kitchen and turned on the flame beneath the kettle. Grabbing a tea bag and a cup, he listened for the whistle. He focused on the task, ignoring his thoughts as they blew past, dust devils eating up the terrain. The shrill whistle awakened his automatic response of pouring and inserting the tea bag. Holding his cup of tea, the battered warrior made his way toward the bedroom.

228

Chapter Twenty-Seven

He closed the door, cutting himself off from Bryce. Leaning back against the door, he breathed another sigh. Kevin imagined himself two thousand miles away, back in Tucson, where he belonged. He walked toward the bed, picked up his laptop, and Rachel came to mind. He stared at the screen as his tea steeped. As if his hands had a mind of their own, they began typing.

> Rachel, how are you? I could use a friend right
> now. My brother just accused me of being in league
> with Satan and bringing destruction on my family.
> It sounds humorous as I write this to you.
> At the time, I was ready to explode in anger.
> Somehow I kept my sanity and stayed cool.
> It's been a miraculous trip back to Michigan. My
> family has been wonderful to me, except Bryce, of
> course. Before I head back to Tucson, I'd like to visit you
> in Georgia. Just a quick visit. It's been a long time!
> Are you up for that?   In gratitude, Kevin.

He hit *Send*, and took another deep, cleansing breath. He continued to breathe deeply, consciously letting go of his angry thoughts toward Bryce.

They had written occasionally. He knew she had gone back to school to earn her doctorate in Psychology. *Did she complete it?* There was a relationship. *Did she still have a boyfriend?* Then he smiled. Rachel wouldn't have a *boy* friend. He would have to be a man. He wasn't sure how he felt about that. *Do I love her?*

He felt connected to her, and that was all that mattered. He would be happy just to see her again. It seemed best to have no expectations and therefore no possible disappointments. His computer dinged and woke him from his musings. An email from Rachel showed up on his screen. *Wow! That was fast!*

> Kevin, your timing is perfect. I'm visiting my parents in Indiana and would love to see you again. How about South Bend? I could meet you at Harrison Place, brunch tomorrow, 11 a.m. Do you know the place?   Love, Rachel

Kevin wrote back.

> I can find it. I'll see you at 11. Thanks.

His heart danced. In his mind he could see Rachel as she appeared four years ago, her dark hair, long and thick, draped over her shoulders contrasting her white chambray shirt. He remembered her green eyes seeing both into and through him. *Has she changed since then?*

Kevin wondered if the connection he felt with Rachel was only a memory. He recalled going back to his college to visit Dr. Markham, ten years after graduation. Markham's effect on him had been profound. Even now, the memory of his classroom made him feel excited about the beauty and wonder of language. Markham had inspired him, and he had made his professor's enthusiasm and techniques his own. Markham had taught him how to teach, and Kevin wanted to thank him.

Kevin saw him walking in the hall and greeted him as if it had been yesterday when they had shared a special teacher-student relationship. The professor didn't remember him. He thanked Kevin for coming and hurried off to class. Kevin was left standing there, deflated, disappointed. He hoped that if he ran into any former students while in Michigan, he would remember them.

His encounter with Rachel four years ago was wired into his brain. He felt close to her when he recalled their meeting. What if she didn't share that feeling? After all, most of their communications over the past four years were initiated by him. All of it had been by email. What if Rachel and he had changed so much that they felt nothing toward each other? *She did agree to meet me.* Tomorrow would take care of itself.

The next email was from Michael.

Call me this weekend. I have something to discuss with you. I think you'll like it! Blessings, Michael.

It was 2:00 p.m. That was 11:00 a.m. Saturday, in Tucson, which meant breakfast was just ending, and lunch would begin soon. Kevin reached for his cell, found Michael, and placed the call.

"Hi, Kevin. I'm happy you called. Give me a minute to get somewhere where I can hear you." People were talking in the background. "Are you there still?"

"I'm here, Michael. How are you?"

"It's a beautiful morning, Kevin. We should hit one hundred today, but you didn't call to talk about the weather."

"What *did* I call to talk about? You had something to discuss."

"That I do, Kevin. A group of people, investors, want to reopen the Calico Grill. They want to purchase the building and the equipment. They want you to run it, and make you a partner."

"Who are the people?" A chill ran through Kevin's body. This was unexpected, and he felt unprepared.

"We were talking about the restaurant scene in Tucson, and everyone agreed that we missed the Calico Grill. So we brainstormed how to bring it back. We decided that we couldn't do it unless you ran it."

"Who else besides you wants to do this?" Kevin noticed his breath had become quick and shallow.

"Ronnie, Jenny, Sarah, myself, and a couple of others you don't know. It was Jenny's idea, and we all agreed. You would be the manager and a full partner."

"But, you know I don't have any money to put in."

"We don't need your money. It's your leadership that we need. We want you to find your former employees and bring them back. None of us can do those things."

"This is, surprising!" Kevin breathed into the phone. "Uh, thanks for your confidence in me." A *Yes* stuck in his throat, and he couldn't get it out. "Can I think about this for a day or two?"

"Of course. Let us know when you get back to Tucson. How are things going with your family?"

"Better than expected. Everyone has been great except Bryce."

"Bryce is your teacher." Michael paused. "He's teaching you about love and forgiveness. It's not Bryce you need to forgive. Remember. His behavior is only the trigger. Who are you when you're with him? Work with that, Kevin."

Kevin thought about Michael's words. "I will."

"Good. No need to fight. You'd only be fighting with yourself. I should go now. It's lunch. I'll see you Tuesday."

Kevin was stunned. He could be resurrecting and running the Grill in a few months. With his new partners it would be better than ever! Wasn't this what he wanted? A voice in his head protested. *What makes you think you won't screw it up again. Only this time you'll be losing other people's money.*

That one hurt. Kevin stepped back from his thoughts and observed the *not good enough* identity that made that statement. He became it, feeling the frustration of reaching for unattainable goals, and bathing in the guilt of incompetence. He acknowledged that it was an identity he had created.

When it seemed that *not good enough* had played itself out, he constructed an image of success. He allowed himself to feel the satisfaction of working toward and attaining a goal. A flame of enthusiasm and confidence ignited in his mid-section and slowly radiated into his chest, and then into his whole body. He stood up, erect and powerful, becoming the passionate, influential leader he imagined himself to be.

The *yes* was no longer stuck in his throat, and Kevin said it out loud: "Yes! Yes! Yes!" He called Michael but connected with the voicemail. Not wanting to leave the *Yes* as a message, he promised himself to call later.

* * *

It was late afternoon, and Kevin sat on the deck with his parents. Bryce and Brenda had left by the time Kevin finished his emails and phone calls. He was confident he could maintain a peaceful and adult perspective with Bryce, but the effort demanded all of his awareness and energy. Also, his thoughts rebounded between Rachel and the Grill.

Kevin told them about his conversation with the minister. They were very interested in Reverend Mason's views. His mother said, "I had no idea Reverend Mason was like that. I knew Reverend Turner, and he was very strict on the Bible--too fire-and-brimstone for me. Now they have a minister who doesn't believe in Hell?"

She looked at her husband, her eyes seeking agreement.

Jim took his cue. "Well, I don't believe in Hell either. There's plenty of suffering in this life. We don't need an eternal place of suffering on top of that. It never made sense to me that God would create humans, put them through this test on earth, and then make them suffer for eternity if they fail. It's illogical. It's just stuff made up by the church over the last two thousand years to keep people in line. Don't you think so, Maddy?"

"I do. I can't stand the yelling and the threats. God, to me, is loving, not some eternal jailer."

"You're right about that." Jim looked at his wife and nodded.

Maddy raised her eyebrows. "What I don't understand is why Bryce became such a fanatic. He's a good son."

Kevin watched as his parents passed the conversation back and forth, as if playing catch. He had always admired their way of communicating agreement between their eyes and their words.

"He *is* a good son," Jim agreed. "Bryce has always been a rule-follower, the key word being follower. Your brother isn't a leader like you. In the years he has been at the company, he has never stepped up and led. He does what he's told. He comes in at eight every day, and he leaves at five. Not much initiative. On Fridays he leaves early unless there is a specific meeting scheduled. Other than that, I don't have to worry about Bryce breaking any rules.

"Don't get me wrong. I have always been happy to have Bryce working at our company, but I can't have him run it. When I retire I'll need to sell it, unless..." Jim paused, looking at Kevin. "Unless you would be willing to come in and manage it."

It was like being hit in the side of the head with a pillow. "You want me to run your company when you retire?" His eyes widened.

"No. I want you to run it now. I'm asking you, because I want to work less. I'm seventy-seven, and I've been doing this for fifty years. I'd like to be a consultant for the company and work when I please. I'd like to travel with your mom and enjoy life a little more."

Kevin couldn't believe what he heard. He had never imagined himself running the family business. "I don't know enough about HVAC and plumbing *or* home improvement."

"Once upon a time you worked with me, Kevin, and you learned a lot. Yes, the business has changed, but I don't need you for your plumbing or your home improvement expertise. I need you for your people skills and your ability to run a business. You know how to motivate people, and you can take risks."

"If you recall, Dad, my one and only business went bankrupt."

"You learned from that, didn't you?"

"I did. Maybe I'd be capable, but what about Bryce? He would never accept me as his boss."

"You leave Bryce to me."

"I'm not saying *Yes*." Kevin cautioned.

"What are you saying?" Jim raised his eyebrows.

"I'm honored that you would ask me, so I will consider the possibility. Also, I just talked to Michael, and he and some others want to reopen the Calico Grill and make me a partner."

"That's wonderful, Dear!" His mother gushed. "Such good friends you have in Tucson!"

"Thanks for your confidence in me. It means a lot. I don't think I'm the right person to run your company, but I will consider it."

His father eyed him. "Looks like your fortunes are turning, Son. Two offers in the same day." He nodded approvingly. Kevin guessed his father had given him more respect in the past few days than he had received from him in his whole life.

"Yeah, it feels good. You know Bryce is in a leadership position at his church."

"Not really." Jim said. "He mostly did what Reverend Turner recommended. He's doing the same with the new guy. That's fine, but it's *not* what my business needs." He sat back in his chair as if he were at the office and had just given an order.

Kevin recognized his father's characteristic silence that declared there was nothing more to say on the matter. "I'm going to meet a friend in South Bend tomorrow for brunch."

"Is this a *love* interest, Kevin?"

Kevin shook his head. "We don't know each other very well, and I haven't seen her in four years. She's a friend. That's as much as I can say right now. My girls are coming over tonight. You want to eat here or go out? We can talk about *their* love interests!"

Chapter Twenty-Eight

On Sunday morning Kevin drove west on I-96 and began his two-and-a-half hour journey to South Bend, Indiana. As he headed south on I-69, he turned on the radio.

> That's me in the corner
> That's me in the spotlight
> Losing my religion
> Trying to keep up with you . . .

Kevin sang along with R.E.M. until he drifted into thought. *I'm not doing this again. I'm not losing my religion over a woman. Gotta be two-way or it's no-way! If I want her and she wants me, great! If either or both of us aren't interested, that's fine!*

Getting ahead of yourself, aren't you? You barely know her. Just be cool. Be yourself. Don't try to impress. Listen to her. Let Rachel impress you. Nothing to get! Nothing to prove. Why am I even thinking about this?

I'm the creator. Whatever happens with Rachel--I'm creating it. My family being generous to me--just a mirror of who I am inside. That's what Michael says. Bryce kicking my ass--just a mirror of my own crap. Who am I when I'm with Bryce? Shit, the answer stings. I think I'm better than him--more enlightened, more spiritual. Damn it, Kevin.

But, Bryce is a prick! I am better than him! Like I'm never a prick--never selfish--never arrogant! Bryce is my teacher. That's what Michael meant. Bryce shows me who I'm being. He indicts and convicts me. And he'll continue to piss me off until I clean up whatever guilt I have.

So, if Bryce personifies my guilt, then I don't see him. What if I could see the real Bryce, without my negative stuff, without my guilt clouding the picture? Who would I be? Not the right question! Who would I be without guilt? Who would I be if I loved and accepted myself without conditions?

Never been without guilt or self-criticism. Never had that freedom. That's it! That's the answer. Without guilt, I'd be free. What would that feel like?

Kevin tried to let go. He imagined himself flying, exhilarated, unrestrained, soaring, joyful. The feeling was elusive. He caught the I-94 West sign out of the corner of his eye and quickly veered right. *Almost missed it!* A horn blared behind him. In his rearview mirror an angry Mercedes threatened to devour his rear bumper.

His mind wandered to Tucson with thoughts of the diner, Michael, Sarah, debts, Ronnie, and a series of what-if's. *Get focused, Kevin. Use this time. Since I can't create the feeling of 'I'm free,' I'll go in the other direction.* He thought about the things that Bryce had said--that he was a bad influence on the family--that he was in league with the devil--that he was going to Hell. He thought about his relationships, the women who had left him, and the ones he'd left.

He thought about how desire had motivated much of his behavior. *Ah--there it is.* Twinges of guilt bubbled inside as he thought about needing and wanting sex. *Who was I being when I most needed sex?* As guilt oozed from his cells, he felt it and observed it. A new thought flashed in his mind: *This guilt isn't about needing or wanting sex. It's about judging myself for it. I'm bad for wanting it. I'm a bad person. That's the identity.*

He became bad, despicable, of no use to the planet. He hated himself, and then despised himself for feeling such hate. Death sounded like a good idea. The pylons holding up a bridge invited him to end it all. *Maybe doing this in the car is not a good idea.* But, the Inner Voice kept him safe. *This isn't real, Kevin. You created this identity.*

Next, regret overcame him. *What a waste my life has been! So much I could've done, should've done.* Sadness seized his body, and he quickly pulled over at a rest stop. He stayed with his feelings.

Anger came next. His chest was about to explode, and he shouted to ease the pressure. He avoided thinking and stayed with feeling, wallowing in his wrath toward himself and the world. Kevin burst from his car, dashed across the grass, and then paced around the perimeter of the rest stop. Each step and each exhalation burned off more of the rage. Out of breath and mostly out of anger, he stopped at a picnic table.

"Are you okay, Sir?" A young woman stood a few feet away. She glanced back at the man standing behind her who nodded. "Are you all right?"

Kevin looked up. "I'm fine, thanks. Just need to be alone."

"Okay. Well, have a nice day." She turned and left with the man.

Kevin was grateful--that she left. *Back to the car.* He jogged to the car, plunged into his moving retreat, and started the engine.

He felt nothing, and spoke aloud. "I created the identity of being a bad person. Is it gone?" He intuited that everyone carried a sense of being bad and felt the guilt. "It's not gone, but I've chipped away at it. We live in polarity. I'm good and bad in my mind. I am imperfectly perfect. He drove the Malibu out of the rest stop, with a firm grip on the steering wheel, one foot on the gas, and the other foot hovering over the brake pedal.

Emptiness settled around his mind. It was not the emptiness of apathy, but more the echoing emptiness of space. His emotions spent, at least for the moment, the thought of freedom appeared again. *I am free.* Three deep breaths later he was flying. The joy that was inaccessible a half hour ago now came flooding into his mind and body. He accelerated to seventy-five miles per hour. The sun was shining, and the sky was blue. The trees along the expressway were green and strong. He was on his way to a new adventure, and the world was just fine.

* * *

He arrived at Harrison Place just before 11:00 a.m., parked his rental car, and walked into the restaurant lobby. The building, a former mansion belonging to an automotive magnate, was elegant. A wide staircase welcomed patrons to the second floor. Thick blue and red carpeting ran up the middle of the steps, with potted plants on either side of each step, and he was struck by the intricately carved wood on the ceilings and walls. The restaurant, itself, had mixed reviews on the internet. It was as if each customer had visited different restaurants on different planets. One said the food and service were fantastic. Another said both were terrible. There were plenty of reviews in between.

In his manager's mind, he knew that inconsistency was typical of many restaurants where service behaviors were not consistently communicated to the staff. At the Calico Grill, he had specified how patrons and fellow employees were to be treated. He set the example with his own behavior. Every customer was treated as an esteemed guest. There were no exceptions. They were valued regardless of their position and regardless of how much money they had to spend. He and his staff stood behind their food. Guests who were anything less than delighted were not charged.

It was rare at the Grill that a waitress or waiter was stiffed. He could confidently say that all guests left the Grill happy. That was the goal. All employees were happy, too. If not, they were either helped into a position where they could be happy, or helped out of the company. Employees who did not understand or care to offer excellent service usually didn't last more than a week. For a restaurant, his employee turnover was rare, and that's why it hurt so much to let everyone go when the restaurant folded. They were a strong team at the Grill, and he had treasured every one of them.

He wondered if the staff members here were treasured. A beautiful young woman, dressed smartly in a knee-length black skirt and crisp, white cotton blouse approached him, and asked if she could help. She moved with grace, obviously practiced at greeting customers. He hoped that this would be an excellent restaurant experience.

"I'm here a few minutes early, and I'm meeting a friend at eleven."

"Would that be Rachel Lindsay?" The hostess smiled and motioned for Kevin to look behind himself.

"Yes, thank you." Kevin turned around to find Rachel standing before him. Her long, dark hair was pulled back and flowed onto the back of her green, silk blouse. Makeup was subtle, just enough to accent her green eyes and tanned face. She wore an ankle-length wraparound skirt with swirling greens, yellows, and blues.

He saw recognition in her eyes, and they embraced.

"I'm so glad to see you, Kevin. Thank you for meeting me."

"You look absolutely gorgeous, Rachel. I've missed you."

The hostess stood by patiently until Kevin noticed her. "I think you may seat us if you're ready."

"Please follow me." She led them through a large area containing multiple buffet tables, abundantly appointed with a variety of breakfast and lunch choices. They were seated in a room that looked a little like a greenhouse, mostly enclosed by glass and filled with a variety of plants and flowers. No one else was seated there. "This is the garden room. It'll be a little while before it fills up. In the meantime, enjoy your time together."

"Thank you," Kevin was grateful for the hostess' sensitivity to their desires. They had a private room, at least for awhile. A waitress entered and took their drink orders. She invited them to visit the buffet. They decided to wait and talk to each other instead.

"Did you really miss me?" Rachel asked.

"Yes and no. I thought about you many times, but I lived my life. You were always there, in the back of my mind."

"Even when you were involved with Ronnie?" Rachel grinned.

Kevin blushed. "Maybe not as much, but even then there were times when I thought of you. I always knew I'd see you again. Yesterday when I wrote to you, I felt it was time. It's been four years; a lot has happened in both our lives."

"I didn't miss you, but I thought of you with confidence that you were becoming the man you were meant to be. Confident that you were safe and well. Confident that I would see you again one day. Looks like my confidence has been fulfilled. Here you are safe, well, and definitely the man I saw in you back in Vegas."

"Thanks." Kevin sat up a little straighter to compensate for feeling a little smaller, and at the same time he felt he was being assessed. *Let it go, Kevin. We're assessing each other. She looks great! But, subdued compared to four years ago.*

"I know bits and pieces about the last four years of your life. I'd love to hear more." She nodded and smiled, the tone of her voice was encouraging. "Tell me about the Calico Grill, and your walks in the desert and about the couple who asked you to live in their pool-house. I want to hear about your visit to your family."

"I want to hear about you, too. You went back to school for your Ph.D., and you were in a relationship."

"Both true." Rachel nodded. "You first!" The waitress brought them drinks, coffee and orange juice for Rachel, tea and orange juice for Kevin.

Kevin launched into a narrative about his years in Tucson. He talked about the successes of his restaurant, his relationship with Ronnie, Al's death and the closing of the business. He told her about hiking in the desert, and his time with Michael and Sarah. He related the history of the past few days with his family, but left out the parts about Bryce.

Rachel smiled at him, reached across the table and took his hands in hers. "You are beautiful! I am so proud of you for what you've become. I'm grateful to know you."

241

"Thank you. I'm grateful to know me, too. I didn't know me that well when I first met you. I'm learning--and you helped."

"How's that?" Rachel's brows raised like two question marks.

Kevin pulled his wallet from his rear pocket and opened it on the table. He retrieved a folded cocktail napkin from within and opened it in front of her.

Rachel smiled, and her eyes glistened. "You kept it!"

"When I was at my lowest point, after Ronnie was gone, the restaurant closed, and I didn't know where I would find money, work, or a place to live, that's when I found this napkin. I was checking my wallet for money. Your napkin had been there for three-and-a-half years. I was on the trail at Pima Canyon, and I re-read your writing about being a center of influence. It helped me let go of my sadness and fears.

"Then I prayed like I'd never prayed before. I felt connected to everyone and everything, to God and to my own self. I didn't pray *for* anything. Just prayed about being connected. I remembered your thank you prayer and I used it. I felt joy and gratitude just for being alive. I'd never felt so happy for no reason in my life before that moment. I can't tell you how long I stood there in the sun, being grateful for it all.

"Then the phone rang and snapped me out of my reverie. It was Jenny calling to tell me about an opportunity to work with Michael. That was a miracle!"

"I love that story. So happy for you! I have a similar story."

"Let's hear it."

"Let's get some food first. I think your story made me hungry, and I need some energy to tell you mine."

They stood up and went into the next room to explore the buffets. They had already been there half an hour, and Kevin hoped their privacy would last long enough to hear her story. They seated themselves back at the table with platefuls of tasty looking food.

The hostess approached them. "Good news for you. We have a large party that reserved all the other tables. They were supposed to be here at 11:30, but they've been delayed. You have another half hour of this room to yourselves. Enjoy!"

They spent a few minutes savoring their freshly made omelets along with fruit and toasted English muffins. Kevin closed his eyes and chewed slowly, flavors and textures of eggs, peppers, tomatoes, bacon and cilantro bursting in his mouth. It was so good, he forgot about Rachel for a minute.

Rachel sighed. "Mm...this is delicious! Okay, I can talk now."

"After we met, I closed on my condo, deposited the check and drove to Indiana to see my parents. My parents are a lot older than me, and I'm an only child. I'm thirty-three and they're both eighty. I told them the years in Vegas had been good for me, and I had learned to take full responsibility for my life--that I'd grown up.

"They knew I'd been working as a dancer, but they didn't realize I was an *exotic* dancer. Definitely a world my parents didn't understand! I was worried they'd feel that they failed me."

Rachel stopped to take a bite.

"So, did they feel that way?" *I wouldn't want my daughters stripping for a living! Yeah, but it's okay if daughters of other fathers do it. Is this because I'd be worried about them, or because I'd be embarrassed? Maybe both.* "Did they think they'd failed you--or you failed them?"

"Granted, it was weird, but I didn't see it as a failure. My mom was empathetic and proud of me. At first my dad said nothing, and I could tell he was not happy. Later, he said he was disappointed about the choices I'd made. He thought it was a waste of my education and talents. Then he said not to worry, that he'd get over it. He was glad I'd grown, and that I was making something of myself. I asked him what he meant by *something*."

"He stumbled on that and couldn't really explain. I said, 'Dad, I've always been someone, and I've always made something of myself. I don't feel guilty, but I don't want to do it again either.'

"He said that he loved me regardless of anything I'd done. I told him I could accept that. Mom gave him a little bit of a hard time about that, but then she started talking about me getting married and giving her a grandchild. I told her there were no plans at the moment." Rachel smiled and cut a piece from her omelet with a fork. "Love this food!"

Kevin's stomach tightened. He'd fantasized the possibility of being with Rachel, but that story never included a child. He'd already raised two. *Calm yourself. It's only a fantasy.* He felt connected to Rachel, but that didn't necessarily mean marriage. *I'm fourteen years older--probably too old for her, anyway.*

At that moment he noticed a man and a woman seated across the room. The man was obviously older, probably in his mid-fifties. The woman looked to be in her late-twenties. He watched them while Rachel enjoyed her eggs, and he sipped his tea. The pair rose from their table and moved toward the buffet room. The man placed his hand affectionately on her lower back and said something near her ear. *They seem to be getting on well!* She laughed. "Come on, Dad." He was taken aback, and then smiled to himself. *Very funny, Universe!*

Rachel looked up from her now-empty plate. "It turned out to be a good visit. They both hoped I'd settle down near them, but I told them I was going to Atlanta. My best friend from high school, Marcy, was running a cafe on Peachtree Avenue. She offered me a job and a place to stay. So I became a barista. Marcy and I hit it off, both at work and in our living arrangements.

"A whole lot more happened, like getting into the University of Georgia for the doctoral program, but can we get some more food first? I definitely want to sample some of the pastries." Not waiting for a response, Rachel stood up, and Kevin followed her lead.

A slice of peach pie whispered his name, and he couldn't say no to a couple of chocolate chip cookies. He secretly tested one to see if it was soft, the way he liked them. It passed the test, and he ate one on the way back to the table.

Rachel glided into her seat, and took a bite. "M-mm, blueberry pie. I didn't date for a year-and-a-half. Never crossed my mind. Guess I needed a break from men." She continued talking between bites. "You know blueberries are considered good brain food. They help increase memory. That might justify another piece."

Kevin relished the food, and savored Rachel. Her eyes twinkled as she told her story. The tone of her voice created a variation on a theme--speeding up, slowing down, raising and lowering the pitch, pausing, and then bursting forth--much like the musical score of a film. She was magnetic, and he was attracted. He thought back to his time with Ronnie, and the desire he felt. It was mostly sensual and physical. His feeling for Rachel was multidimensional.

"I entered the Psych program and focused on my studies. A year into my program I met Ben. He was about ten years older and had his Ph.D. in Psychology. He was one of my professors. It really surprised me when I fell for him. I was perfectly happy on my own and didn't want a relationship. I graduated last year, and then started my supervised practice."

"Congratulations, Dr. Lindsay!"

"Thank you. Just after I became Dr. Lindsay, that's when I moved out of Marcy's place and in with Ben."

Again Kevin felt a twinge. He knew that Rachel was involved, but didn't know the details. He reminded himself once more that his fantasies were not reality.

Rachel finished her pie, and dabbed her lips with her cloth napkin. "Do I have blueberry on my face?"

Kevin leaned in, looking at her lips. He pictured kissing her.

Rachel laughed. "So, you want a magnifying glass? Am I a mess or not?"

Kevin's felt his cheeks flush. "No. Your face is perfect!"

"Thanks. On with the story--unless you're too distracted?" She gave him a look and a smile that told him she knew exactly what he was thinking.

"On with the story." He swept his hand across the space between them and sat back in his chair.

"Ben was unique. He told me that life is a dream, and we're all asleep. He'd spent years studying Buddhism, Shamanism, metaphysical Christianity, and *A Course in Miracles*. He said that this was not so much a belief system as a discovery. Years of study, contemplation, and meditation had led him to this place of seeing life as a dream. I asked him if he was seeking enlightenment, and he said he wasn't. He explained that enlightenment meant *no-self*. Translated, that meant *no-Ben*. He said that for the time being he was content to become a spiritual adult. Does this sound strange to you? I should ask that first, because it's going to get more strange."

"It's not strange to me, but I can't say I understand it fully. Michael has talked about the dream. Ben sounds like him. What did he mean by a spiritual adult?"

"I'm glad it's not too strange. He said that a spiritual adult is someone who is a center of influence and who is driven by spirit, not ego. Does that make sense?"

"Yeah. That's what I'm doing, too. Or, at least I'm trying."

Rachel smiled and gave an appreciative nod. "You're doing more than trying. Anyway, everything was going very well. I was doing work I loved. I was with a man I loved. I felt such gratitude for how things had come together in Atlanta. Then right after the first of January, Ben told me he had some discomfort in his neck and chest. There was some swelling of his lymph nodes, but it hadn't been painful. I asked him to see a doctor. He said it probably was no big deal, maybe an infection he was fighting, but he would make the appointment. I could see he was losing weight, too.

"It took a couple of weeks before he got in. He was diagnosed with non-Hodgkin's Lymphoma. It was aggressive and advanced. We were both in shock!"

Kevin felt his eyes widening. "I'd be in shock, too."

"Chemotherapy was recommended, and Ben went for it. It made him sick, and we didn't see any positive results. He was looking at more chemo and possible bone marrow transplants. He became intensely fearful and sad. Then that changed to anger. He didn't yell at me, but directed his anger toward himself and life. That was hard for both of us. In one month's time we went from completely happy to angry, distraught and hopeless."

"I'm sorry. I had no idea you were going through that."

"Thanks. So one morning, it's late February now, and we've had four weeks of hell, Ben wakes up with a different perspective. He'd prayed most of the night, turned over his cancer to Spirit, and asked for guidance and strength. Ben said the extra time on the planet was not worth the treatment regimen nor was it necessary. His goal wasn't to live long, but to live meaningfully. At that point he became the strong one in our relationship, and I *really* started falling apart." Rachel motioned to the waitress to pour some more coffee. "Thank you." She sipped on her drink and looked at Kevin. "I feel like I need to tell you the whole story. Is that okay?"

"I want to hear it. Go on."

She nodded. "Ben and I prayed every day. It wasn't the kind of prayer where you petition God for a cure. We looked for peace and wisdom in the midst of chaos. Ben had shared his fears, regrets, and his hopes with me. He hadn't fully accomplished his purpose, but be was grateful we had found each other--cheated that the time was so short. He was disappointed in his emotional reaction to the cancer and thought he should've been more calm and centered. I told him it was okay. It's not every day you get a diagnosis of terminal cancer. He laughed at himself then." Rachel smiled, her vision defocused, as if viewing a scene from the past.

Kevin picked at a bowl of strawberries and blueberries, but the sweetness of the berries contrasted too much with the tone of Rachel's story. He made himself stop eating. The hum of human voices increased its volume as people streamed into the room. He looked across the table at Rachel who remained lost in her memories, absently sipping her coffee. "Rachel."

Startled, her eyes focused on his. "What?"

"It's getting crowded in here. It might be better if we continued somewhere more private." He thought about his car, or going for a walk. "Did you have enough to eat?"

"Yes. We can go." Rachel excused herself to use the restroom.

He thought of Ben, and a twinge of jealousy still lurked inside. He breathed through the emotion and dismissed the notion. In the corner of his mind where fantasies were hatched and nurtured, Rachel was supposed to be his. His what? Friend? Lover? Wife? Girlfriend? He saw the two of them together, but couldn't name it. She was honest, and he found himself wanting to be honest with her. He felt more free when he was with her--to be himself.

But, wasn't he free to be himself with anyone? It was always his choice to be himself or not, wasn't it? The difference with Rachel was that he didn't have to work at it with her. His thoughts shifted to her perspective. Imagining both the joy and the pain she felt in her relationship with Ben, he decided to be happy for her that she had experienced such love.

Rachel returned as Kevin paid the bill. She surveyed the room several times. Kevin watched her. "What are you doing?"

"I'm reading the room--a skill I developed in Vegas."

"What do you see?"

"Rachel nodded toward a couple with two young children. See that guy? He's stolen at least three looks at me in the last two minutes. On the last one he didn't turn away, but smiled at me. Look at his wife. She's gorgeous. Knows how to dress. When he looks at her, he doesn't smile--no desire or appreciation in his eyes. Also, he's got money. That suit cost over a thousand dollars, and those shoes--five hundred. If I were still in Vegas, he'd be an easy mark. Now I'm a therapist, and I see him differently. If he's not already having an affair, it'll happen soon."

Kevin confirmed her observations, although he couldn't verify the price of the suit or the shoes. "What about his wife?"

"She's totally taken up with the kids. She looks at her husband, and her face says: 'Will you please pay some attention to your children?' Then she shakes her head, subtly, and focuses on the kids. She still has hope."

"Could you help them?"

"I help people who want to be helped. She might want it, but he doesn't look ready."

Kevin thought back to his own marriage and his reticence in seeing a therapist. He shifted his eyes to a woman in a black dress with a large-framed man. He nodded toward the couple.

Rachel turned. "She checks out every man who walks in the room. She smiles at them when they make eye contact. When her husband talks to her, she gets this look of disgust. He's a nice guy-- adores her--would do anything for her. She doesn't love him-- probably never did. She's around forty; he's fifty or so. Their kids are over there." Rachel nodded toward them. "Early teens."

"So why the disgust when she looks at him?"

"She finds him unattractive. He doesn't pay a whole lot of attention to how he dresses. He's out of shape. But, loyal. No matter how badly she treats him, he'll stay with her."

"Do you always read the room?"

"I can't help it. It's automatic, and too often, painful. A lot people are suffering, and don't know what to do about it. I do what I can. Send them love. Start a conversation. Listen. See that guy there?" She gestured toward a man in a gray suit.

"Yeah."

"He's dying for a smoke--can't wait to get outside. His right leg is vibrating, ready to run. And that young woman over there--drugs. She's hurting--needs something to settle her down."

"Are there any happy people here?"

"Besides you and me?"

Kevin smiled. "Yeah, besides you and me."

"That couple over there." She pointed to an older couple.

"How do you know?"

"When she talks to their friends, he looks at her and smiles. He's listening even though he's probably heard the story before. When *he* talks, she gives him all of her attention. See them now? They're holding hands. I think they like each other. They're still in love."

"Michael and Sarah are like that. Married sixty-five years and still interested in each other."

"That's beautiful. Let's go. We'll end on a good-feeling one."

They took a brief tour of the mansion. The oak staircases and the intricately carved panels and balustrades spoke of another age when artisans constructed beautiful homes. Kevin thought about how people touched each other's lives through their works.

They thanked their waitress and hostess and walked out to the veranda. The breeze, now cooler, chilled them. It began to rain, and Rachel reached for his hand. "I have a suite at an inn near here. It's spacious, like an apartment. Would you like to follow me back there?"

Chapter Twenty-Nine

They settled on the couch. He sat on one cushion, and she on the other. Rachel had changed into stretch jeans and a sweatshirt and sat cross-legged facing him. Each held a glass of Chardonnay. The soft glow of a fire illuminated the room while rain beat steadily on the roof.

"One morning Ben told me that after praying through the night, he understood. The disease was his opportunity to let go of all attachments and to awaken from the dream. Cancer was an illusion, and it was also his cue to transcend his ego. He told me his goal was no longer to cure the cancer; it was to awaken spiritually. A physical cure was irrelevant.

"When Ben first started talking to me about this life being a dream, I resisted. How could this be a dream? It feels so real. He said most spiritual teachings and religions were elaborate dramas where the ego could tell itself it was being spiritual. It was a pretend game where we argue for beliefs that really aren't true. That morning he told me his spiritual practice had been a game, too."

Kevin thought about his own rejection of beliefs, and his desire to approach God empty-handed. He had little interest in beliefs. It was experience he wanted. "How did you feel about that? About religions just being a game?"

"Mostly true, but I'm not saying there isn't any value in religion. I think Ben outgrew religion. He wanted oneness with God. He admitted that he wouldn't take this step if he were healthy and had everything he wanted. He would see me and his career, his health, and his money and think that was happiness. Faced with losing all of that, there was only one place to turn--to God.

"I argued, saying I thought he wasn't interested in enlightenment. He said the goal had changed. I wanted a cure. I was researching natural remedies and looking at psychological factors that may have manifested as the cancer. He said it wasn't up to him or to me whether the cancer went away."

As Rachel paused to sip her wine, Kevin tried to see things from Ben's perspective. He couldn't imagine abandoning every desire, even the desire to live, to find God. *What would Michael think of that?*

Rachel continued. "He told me death was an illusion, but the love we shared would always be. He was determined to awaken from this dream, and I was invited to be his witness. The cancer was good for him, because otherwise, he wouldn't have committed to this goal. Awakening was his reason for being in this life.

"I felt like all my safety lines had been cut, and I was falling into an abyss. Anger was the only way I could get any sense of control. So, I ran into the bedroom and grabbed his stack of spiritual books from the bedside table. I told him what he could do with his f'in books and threw them on the floor at his feet. I grabbed my keys and left the house.

"As I drove toward the mountains, I knew I was strong, and capable of taking care of myself. I could be just fine alone--but I didn't want to be alone. I wanted him. I'd finally found an adult man, and I didn't see why I had to give him up. 'Life is a dream. Death is an illusion. The love we shared will always be.'--a lot of pretty spiritual words--right up there with 'He's gone to a better place.' and 'It was God's will.' I was inconsolable.

"I grabbed a water bottle and set out on a trail with no idea how long I'd walk nor to where. I cried, and argued with myself and with God--continued walking, crying, yelling, arguing for hours. Finally I came to a peaceful spot near a mountain stream, and I was so tired, I sat down. I stared at the water, and immersed myself in emotion. I was angry and hurt and didn't want to feel better. If someone had tried to console me then or offer me spiritual platitudes, I would have punched him in the face. At some point, exhausted, I curled up in a ball, and fell asleep."

Kevin watched her closely, as a tear rolled down her cheek. The tear told him that she trusted him, and for that he was pleased.

She reached for a tissue and wiped the tear from her face. "Sorry. I thought I'd already processed this."

"It's okay." He reached for her hand and squeezed it gently.

She returned the pressure and didn't let go. "I woke up on the bank of that stream to birds chirping. In the distance I heard a waterfall I hadn't noticed earlier. The sun had traversed the sky and changed the shadows so much that it felt like a different day. The rhododendrons were just beginning to bloom--purple flowers everywhere!" She swept her hand in front of herself.

"I sat there enjoying the peace and the beauty and saying *Thank you* for my surroundings. I gave thanks for Ben and all that he had meant to me. I gave thanks for the love we shared and the depth of our relationship. Strangely, you popped into my mind then, so I gave thanks for you and the connection we'd made back in Las Vegas. The thought of you made me smile, and I knew you were going to be okay."

She thought about me. Her comment simmered in his mind, the warmth spreading through his whole body.

"You had written me a few days earlier about the death of your partner. I didn't reply because I was caught up in the drama of Ben's cancer. I admired Ben for his strength and for being clear about what he wanted. I thought again about his words to me, about waking up being his only goal.

"He told me that in spiritual circles people talk about things like awakening all the time. He said there's a difference between talking about being one with God and making a commitment to achieve that state. Most of us meander along the path, or talk about the path, or read about it. Ben made it the most important thing in his life. He was seeking first the Kingdom, completely handing over his will, seeking only God's will."

Kevin touched her knee. "Wait. What do you mean, or what did Ben mean by God?"

"Ben said that God is all there is. There is nothing *outside* of God."

"What do you say?"

"God is love. So love is all there is."

Kevin nodded. Satisfied. "Please, go on."

"As I sat there by the stream, I got it. I understood. I also knew that I wasn't ready to climb the steep path Ben had chosen.

"I prayed, and in that moment by the stream I gave up all of my concerns. I surrendered my need to have Ben's physical body present in my life, surrendered my attachment to being with this wonderful adult man, and let him go. For a few minutes my mind was free. I was surrounded by love. I wanted to do whatever I could to help Ben in his quest. That's what I meant about having a similar epiphany to yours in the desert."

"Sounds like it occurred a little before mine." Kevin pictured Pima Canyon on that day in early June. He stared at the fire in the hearth, several feet from the couch, and wondered what fires a person would have to walk through to get to a state like Ben's. *I am such a long way from that.* A subtle retort whispered in his mind. *No, Kevin. You're just a thought away.*

"The next few months were intense. My mind would zigzag between surrender and stubbornness. Humanly, love to me was having him. Real love was about helping him do what he needed. I tried to explain what was happening to Marcy, and she thought both Ben and I were crazy. She said that if she had a guy like Ben she'd be trying every alternative cure in the world. I told her that even if I wanted to, I couldn't do that. I couldn't force Ben to look for a cure. Ben wasn't interested in the cure for cancer. He wanted the cure for life--the cure for all suffering. He found it!"

"When I said those few months were intense, I meant for me. Ben achieved this state of calm that was unbelievable. There was physical pain and discomfort, yet he smiled every day. He was the most loving man I'd ever met. It was like his body was sick, but his soul was well. Ben said that he'd never felt so free and alive, and that he was awake. Regardless of the physical state of his body, he was safe and whole.

"Near the end of this, Ben lost his voice. His condition was weak, and it was all I could do to keep him comfortable. I started crying one morning. I lost what little calm I'd felt, and watching Ben die was too much. He motioned for me to hand him a pen and paper and wrote to me: 'Ben is already gone. There is no Ben. But, *I* am here--will always be with you. Do not lament my death. There is no death.'" Rachel sipped on her wine. Another tear rolled down her cheek, and dropped into her lap. Kevin imagined he could hear the sound it made. He watched her stare into the space between them.

The rhythm of the rain on the roof had softened, as if it had progressed to the next movement in the symphony. Kevin attempted to grasp what it meant to be one with God and have no self. "I can't wrap my mind around the idea of no self."

"That's exactly how I felt! Ben was awake. It's kind of like being in a dream and you think everything is real, but then you wake up and you see how limited you were in the dream."

"So, someday I'll wake up and find that this Kevin role I've been playing is very small, and I'm much more than this?"

"Something like that. I've only had a glimpse because of Ben. I understood it at the moment I was with him, but I can't explain it. I can tell you this: When I was finally able to look at him without all of my fears and worries, I saw a face that radiated pure love. We were into the last few days at that point, and he became a mirror for me. I knew that all he saw was beauty, and love, and perfection. In his eyes I was God's perfect expression. I was innocent. It made me cry. I wept away all the guilt, all the self-criticism, all the fears that somehow I wasn't good enough.

"Ben gave me a great gift in seeing me that way. He made it possible for me to see myself. I had never loved and accepted myself so much. I felt fearless. I can't say I always feel that way, but most of the time I do."

"I thought you were fearless when I met you in Vegas." Kevin grinned.

"I was feeling bold that day."

"And now?"

"Sad. I've been holding it together, sort of waiting for someone to talk to who could understand--someone I could lean on for a moment."

"I'm glad to be that someone. Tell me the rest." Kevin stroked the back of her hand with his thumb.

Rachel held him in her gaze and pressed her lips into a straight line. She nodded and took a deep breath. "On the final day, Ben wrote to me that he was not afraid. He asked me to make sure his mother and sister and his closest friends were there. We were all sitting in the room when he passed. He looked at each one of us. He said, 'I love you.' With his eyes. We all felt it. Then he closed his eyes and left his body behind." Tears flowed down Rachel's face and she freed her hand to grab more tissue. She dabbed her face, soaking up the effects of her story.

She reached across the couch and squeezed Kevin's hand again. "Thanks for listening." Her voice broke.

"You need to be held."

She nodded, unable to speak.

Kevin slid forward and pulled her close, her face on his chest--his one hand pressing her back and the other stroking her hair. Her sadness burst forth, tossing her body like a swimmer in rough seas, and she held onto him tightly, as if he were a raft keeping her afloat. Kevin felt his power stirring inside, and he lent it to her. In that moment, he recalled his earlier thoughts of Rachel being about what she would give to him--her friendship, her wisdom, and maybe her affection. Now, he was giving, and he liked the feeling of his love and strength flowing into her. It seemed that the more of himself he gave--the more he had to give.

After several minutes the sobs subsided. She pressed her hands against his chest, lifted her head, and made eye contact. Kevin dabbed a stray teardrop from her cheek with his thumb.

She smiled, her hands suddenly holding his face. She pulled him toward her gently, nearer, closed her eyes, and her lips softly caressed his. He wrapped his arms around her as the kiss ended and then began again, this time harder and more passionate. A soft cry emerged from her throat as she kissed him a third time. Her arms slipped down his neck and around his back as she pulled him still closer, as if trying to merge their two bodies.

Kevin heard her breathing and felt the stirring of desire in himself. He wanted her, and he didn't. He longed for intimacy with a woman, this woman. Yet, something told him it wasn't time. For a moment, as they pressed their lips together again, the two voices spoke at once in his head. *I need to be in control here.*

Rachel kissed his neck and his cheek, her hands getting to know his back.

Kevin breathed deeply and spoke from within their embrace. "Rachel, we need to stop."

She locked on to his lips again. He received the kiss, without returning it.

She pulled back, hurt in her eyes and then a flash of anger. "Well, all right then!" She launched herself off the couch and headed toward the bathroom.

A twinge of regret nagged at him, but he shook his head. *No. I did the right thing. If we kept going I'd be sorry. I listened to the Voice, and I'm glad I did.* He felt an ache in his crotch, and he spoke to it. "You'll get over it." In a strange way, the ache felt good.

It was several minutes before Rachel emerged, silently headed for the kitchenette, and began preparing coffee.

Kevin stood near the fire, the warmth balancing the cold he felt from Rachel. He felt her pain, and her desire. He smiled, knowing that he was in control of himself. For most of his adult life, whenever he was confronted with the possibility of sex, he had plunged forward, often ignoring his Inner Voice. He had listened when he refused Marianna, but that was after he had already been with her. Now, he realized the power found in doing what he knew was best both for her and for himself.

Halfway through a cup of coffee, Rachel set it heavily on the counter. She strode up to him and gently grasped his hands. She closed her eyes and swallowed. "I'm sorry. You were right. After dealing with death these past several months, I needed to feel alive, and I thought making love would help me do that."

Kevin looked at her and kept his silence.

"Thanks for being the strong one. Everything I needed this afternoon, you gave to me."

"Including saying No?"

"Yes. You should know, with my history, I find self-control in a man extremely attractive!" A slight grin crossed her lips.

"I know." He returned the grin.

Her smile grew. She spoke softly. "Is it okay to hug you?"

"Sure." Kevin opened his arms, and they embraced.

"Thanks for putting up with my pouting." Rachel murmured into his neck.

A smile fanned out across Kevin's face.

They spent the remainder of the afternoon sharing stories and ideas. The conversation flowed--another musical composition with the rests in all the right places. As evening approached, they ordered a pizza from an Italian restaurant down the street.

Kevin talked about his brother.

Rachel set down the pizza slice she was working on. "I don't think it's about tolerance. It's really about understanding that each person is on their own path. Ben said that I shouldn't try to do what he did. He explained that everyone is called in some way. His path was more about surrendering to the goal rather than trying to achieve it.

"He said that the key was, 'Not my will, but thy will be done.' It may be that your brother has listened and knows his path. The problem is that he thinks he's right and everyone else should follow it. Expecting others to follow your path is a distraction. The expectation creates inner conflict, and that puts the ego back in charge."

Kevin nodded. "So what is your path?"

"It's day-to-day right now. My path brought me here to you. Tomorrow, I go back to Atlanta, and Tuesday, I have appointments with clients. After that, it's not clear. My friend Marcy is opening a second cafe and needs a manager. I told her I knew a good one. Are you interested? We could spend more time together." Rachel raised her eyebrows.

Kevin smiled. "That's the third job offer I've had this weekend. Michael offered me a partnership in restarting the Calico Grill. My dad offered me a job in his company. Now you."

"So what's your path, Kevin? Is it Michigan, Arizona, or Georgia? Somewhere else? What does Spirit tell you?"

"When you put it that way, Tucson is calling me. I love it there. You could visit. I know some great places where we could hike in the desert."

"I do miss the desert. I'll come and see you, but I don't know when. I'm still grieving. I understand spiritually there's no death, but emotions are a little behind the rest of me. Sometimes I can feel his presence around me. When I have questions or I'm having a difficult time with something, he's there for me. I hear his voice in my head."

"What does he tell you?"

"When I was at my lowest point, after the funeral and after the people left, he helped me move forward. I was in conflict. Why couldn't he awaken in a healthy body? Then I started thinking that everything he and I had talked about wasn't true. He was dead and that was that. Nothing made sense. My mind was in Hell. There was no God, no Ben, and I was this lonely person who would die one day, too. If a person seeks God first and lets go of the attachments to this world, then all else should be added--like health and abundance and love. Instead Ben got suffering and death. If there was a God, then I was angry at the way She did business."

"So how did Ben help you with that?"

"When I calmed down, I heard Ben's voice in my mind. He said, 'Rachel, I had pain but not suffering. I am not my body. As for my cancer, stop trying to figure it out. All is well. Would you rather have peace, or would you rather drive yourself insane trying to figure it out? Accept the peace of God, and you'll understand.'"

"Seems like you're still trying to figure it out."

"I go back and forth, but I'm doing better. Ben told me that figuring it out was an ego game. When I let go, it makes sense to me. So, I'm okay with what happened to some degree. I miss him, but I'm becoming less sad about it. You listening to me today has been a big help."

"How long has it been since he passed?"

"A month. I love Ben as much as before all of this happened. That will never change. In a way I don't yet understand, I love you, too, Kevin."

They were quiet awhile. Kevin let her words fill the space between his head and his heart. He knew that he had loved Rachel the moment he met her. Then he had seen her as unattainable. Now, he was content to love and felt unconcerned about outcomes.

He shared his thoughts with Rachel, and she told him she was sure they would see each other in the future. They talked for the next few hours, and she related her plans to expand her therapy hours, and to use her experience with Ben to help people transition through loss.

"Every time I assist someone in moving through a change in life, I experience healing, too. I'm excited to help people in this way. My supervising Psychologist and I think alike on this. We work with the whole person, combining the spiritual and the psychological."

He could feel her enthusiasm for her work. "You're on fire with this, aren't you."

Her eyes were shining. "Yes. It's my mission. I love it."

She needs to be in Georgia right now. I need to be in Tucson.

She looked at the clock. It was after midnight. "It's late! Why don't you stay here? The bed is a queen; we can share it. I want to be next to you when I sleep."

Kevin knew his face displayed the doubt he felt. "Maybe not."

"Don't worry. I promise to behave. Besides, I'm tired. All this emoting has drained my energy. Please?" Her eyes begged him.

"What are you wearing to bed?"

Rachel laughed. "Baggy sweats. Totally unsexy, but comfortable. How about you?"

"The best I can do is boxers and a tee shirt."

"Ooh. I do find boxers to be sexy." She held her head between her hands. "Put it out of your mind, Rachel." She looked at him. "I'm kidding."

He wanted to stay. Kevin walked to the window and looked out at the splash of light from a spotlight on the building. Rain was still coming down, but even softer now. Lightning flashed, and his mind was made up. "Okay. I'm staying."

* * *

The next morning Kevin awoke while Rachel showered. He lay in bed listening to the muffled splashes of water. His mind wandered into the bathroom, and imagined naked bodies embracing in a steamy scene. He saw himself kissing Rachel. Desire flickered and then flowed like electricity as sexual anticipation began to build. He stopped. "What am I doing?"

I miss sex, and touching and being touched, and the feel of a woman. Maybe it's not love, but it feels like love. I want that with Rachel--just not now. Not yet. He threw off the covers and slipped into his clothes. Within moments the kitchenette erupted in a clamor of clinking cups and saucers, running water, and the purr of a coffee maker.

Coffee for Rachel. Personally, he couldn't stand the taste of it, yet making it for her became a sacred act. He held her presence in his mind, and set about brewing. He was a restauranteur, and he knew a few things about making coffee. Enjoying the idea that this cup would bring her pleasure, the process became his meditation.

Just as the coffee was ready, Rachel appeared next to him. She was wearing loose-fitting white shorts and an oversized University of Georgia football jersey. Her wet hair was pulled back into a pony tail. She smiled. "You made coffee for me! Thank you."

He carefully poured it into the cup on a saucer. Rachel lifted the cup to her lips and sipped. "Perfect!" she smiled, "And so are you."

She set the cup on the counter and embraced him, and then kissed him on the cheek. "I am so happy you stayed all night. Thank you. This is the best I've felt in a long time."

Making the coffee and feeling her gratitude took the edge off the desire he had cultivated earlier. The need to find other ways of expressing love occupied his mind as he joined her with a cup of tea. That was what his Inner Voice was telling him that his body couldn't know. A physical relationship would have distanced them. She would have become a part of his past, but not his future. How did he know this? *I just know!*

She looked at him, her eyes asking him what he was thinking. He told her, without leaving anything out. The truth-telling freed him from fear. He could tell her anything, and she would accept him. No matter what form their relationship took, she would love him, and he would love her. There was nothing to fear because there was nothing to lose.

"I told you I'll visit you in Tucson. Wish I could tell you when, but can't. Just know I'll be there."

"I know. It's okay."

Later that morning they walked together, holding hands along the riverfront. The gray sky changed its mood, turning blue and smiling brightly upon South Bend. The sun cast diamonds over the surface of the St. Joe River causing the pair to squint as they gazed at the water. "This is where the city gets its name." Rachel led Kevin to a steel rail where they could lean and enjoy the view.

"What do you mean?"

"We're looking at the south bend of the St. Joseph River--hence the name of the city."

Kevin put his arm around her shoulders and pulled her close. "What other knowledge do you have for me O' Wise One?"

"Well, did you know that a lighter roast coffee has more caffeine than a darker roast?"

"No, I didn't. I don't drink coffee, anyway."

"No, but you serve coffee, so you should know that. See that snapper down there?"

Kevin scanned the surface of the water until he noticed a head poking up. "I see him."

"Turtles can breathe through their butts."

"You're making that up." Kevin laughed.

"I'm not. They really can. Speaking of water-life, did you know that most lipstick has fish scales in it?"

Kevin quickly kissed her on the lips, softly, lingering a few seconds. "Doesn't taste fishy to me!"

She laughed. "I'm not wearing any. I'll let you know next time I am, and you can take another sample."

He kissed her again.

She opened her eyes slowly. "So what's with the kissing? We spent the whole night in the same bed, and you didn't kiss me once. Now you get the urge?"

"I'm memorizing what it feels like because I may not see you for a while."

Her smile turned downward, and she kissed him, one hand moving behind his neck and the other to his back.

Kevin pulled her close. When they parted he looked into her eyes. "That was memorable."

She smiled. "I will never forget this time with you."

An hour later, Rachel headed toward Atlanta, and Kevin drove back to Michigan. *We're on parallel tracks, beginning new lives.* The weekend had created a wave of possibilities in him, and he rode that wave all the way back to Okemos.

Chapter Thirty

He arrived at his parents' home early afternoon on Monday. His mother looked at him. "What happened to you, Kevin? Are you in love?"

He didn't answer, and instead asked his mother for twenty minutes to get settled. They agreed to meet on the deck and talk over soup and sandwiches.

On the deck he found a bowl of homemade chicken noodle soup and a whole wheat grilled cheese sandwich. "Looks great, Mom. Thanks." He took a bite of the sandwich. "Real cheese. Mmm. You're the best."

"All right, Kevin. Tell."

He told her about the events in South Bend. As he finished his story he noticed her tears. "Mom, did I say something that upset you?"

"Oh no, Honey. I'm crying about all of it. Ben's death. You and Rachel spending time together. Her helping people. You caring about her so much. It's all so romantic. I hope you see her again." She left her chair and embraced Kevin. I'm so happy for you. I would love to meet her. She sounds like beautiful person."

"She is, Mom, but I don't know when I'll see her next." He shrugged. "or even if..." He heard Alicia Keyes singing on the radio.

Oh, she got both feet on the ground.
And she's burning it down.
Oh, she got her head in the clouds.
And she's not backing down.
This girl is on fire.
This girl is on fire.

They chatted more about relationships and Rachel.

"Bryce and Brenda and your daughters are coming over later for our annual family Labor Day picnic. You're leaving tomorrow, so it will be good for everyone to see you."

"That's fine, Mom, but I'm concerned about Bryce being there." He breathed deeply. "It'll probably be okay."

"Yes, it will." Her voice sounded firm. "I told him that arguing will *not* be a part of tonight's gathering. If he can't say anything nice, then he can keep his mouth shut!"

"You told him that?"

"I told him exactly that. I know he's unhappy with you, but I insist on civility in my home. Just to make sure he behaves, I invited Reverend Jeff to join us, too."

Kevin laughed at that.

* * *

The food was on the table, and everyone was filling their plates. Kevin bit into a piece of grilled chicken breast. "Mmm, Dad. What did you put in this chicken? It's amazing."

Jim puffed up and smiled. "Well, I can't tell you all my secrets, but I will say that I marinated the chicken overnight in orange juice and olive oil and a couple of confidential ingredients. The glaze, of course, has honey in it."

"We'd be proud to serve this recipe at the Calico Grill!"

"Really? Well, I might be persuaded to write it down. It's an old family recipe--"

"Oh, Jim. Please. You got it off the internet." His wife patted his shoulder.

Jim's face reddened. "Well, yeah, but I also experimented and added some of my own touches."

"You outdid yourself, Dear." Madeline tapped him again.

Everyone at the table nodded, their mouths too busy to talk.

It seemed like old times--good food, laughter, and everyone wishing Kevin well with the reopening of the restaurant. Bryce was quiet. When Jessica asked her dad about Rachel, Bryce gave Kevin a hard stare. "Who's Rachel?"

Kevin paused for a few seconds. "Rachel is a friend."

"You mean a girlfriend?" Bryce sneered.

"Bryce!" Brenda spoke through her teeth and nudged him in the side with her elbow.

"Rachel is a woman, and she's my friend." Kevin held his calm.

"She's the one you went to visit in South Bend, isn't she? You didn't get back until today. You slept with her didn't you? You and your loose women!" He addressed the whole family. "My brother wastes money, fornicates with whores, and feels no remorse. Yet, all of you think he's a great guy and throw him parties. Don't you people know the difference between right and wrong?"

No one responded. Madeline frowned at her son, but he didn't notice. A strained silence paralyzed the scene as Bryce's accusations echoed around the deck. Kevin intentionally kept quiet.

Bryce broke the silence. "Come on, Reverend. Back me up. What do you think of my brother?" He looked at Jeff, his tone petitioning the minister.

"Bryce, why don't you and I talk in private?" Jeff held Bryce's eyes in his gaze.

Bryce tried to look away. Finally he asked, "Why?"

"I'm here as a guest, and I don't want to embarrass anyone. Not you, and not your brother. I know that you're angry. Let's take a walk and talk about it."

"It's my brother who needs a talking to."

"Maybe, but it's you who's upset." Jeff stood up. "Let's go. Maybe we can get back in time for dessert. Please."

Reluctantly Bryce stood up, and they stepped off the deck, toward the gate.

"Thank God the Reverend was here." Madeline raised her eyebrows. "He delayed his own plans for the evening to be here instead. Bless him."

"Sorry, Dad." Jessica shrugged.

"Not your fault, Jess." Turning to the group, "It's not anyone's business, but I want to set the record straight. Rachel is a dear *friend*. We stayed together last night, but we aren't involved. I don't know when or even *if* I'll see her again. If I do, I just didn't want any of you to have a negative opinion of her."

"It's your business, Son." His father shook his head. "I don't think anyone else here thinks poorly of you." He looked at Brenda.

"I don't think people should have sex outside of marriage." Brenda spoke slowly, tentatively. "I didn't assume that about Kevin and his friend. God commands that sex should be within the confines of marriage, and Bryce and I believe in that. I'm sorry Bryce was so rude to you." Her voice broke. "Excuse me." Brenda hurried into the house. Her daughters and Madeline followed.

Jessica rolled her eyes. "Uncle Bryce sure knows how to end a party!"

"You got that right." Melissa agreed. "Why is he so rude to you, Dad?"

"I don't know."

"Maybe it's me." Jim sat back and folded his arms. "I've been bragging about your dad to Uncle Bryce." He turned toward Melissa. "I'm very proud of your dad for his courage and his confidence."

Melissa flashed a smile at her dad. "Why should Uncle Bryce be upset about that? Is he jealous?"

Jim cocked his head to one side. "I'm the one who's jealous." He aimed his words at Kevin. "I wish you were staying here to manage my company, but I'm proud that your friends think so highly of you and your abilities."

"Thanks, Dad."

Jim spoke, mostly to himself. "Bryce probably thinks I favor Kevin over him."

Kevin thought about all the years since his teens when his father and Bryce shared similar interests, and his brother was the obvious favorite. *No doubt Bryce is feeling his position has been usurped.* "Maybe you should talk to him, let him know how much you appreciate what he does."

"Yeah, maybe I should." Jim stared at the table, lost in his own thoughts.

The conversation shifted to Kevin's restaurant and then to the girls' lives and careers.

Madeline returned to the deck, and everyone looked at her expectantly. "She's trying to be a good Christian wife. I explained to her that being a Christian doesn't mean you have to let your husband embarrass himself and you at family dinners. The girls are with her, now. They'll help her."

Jim's face mutated toward distress. "Is their marriage okay?"

Madeline matched his mien. "Brenda feels she has to watch everything she says and does or Bryce will criticize her. When they first started going to church several years ago, Bryce treated her with great respect and loyalty. Their relationship was loving, and they started having fun. You know she was ready to leave him before they joined the church?"

"I remember," Kevin said. "It happened just after Dana and I broke up."

"Well, with each passing year, Bryce has become more strict in his observance of, what he calls, Biblical morality. Now Brenda is considering leaving him again. She says that as a Christian, it's against her principles to divorce. She doesn't know what to do."

Kevin flashed back over four years to his meeting with Bryce at the cafe. Bryce had expressed his concern and his love for Brenda.

Seeing that she had everyone's attention, Madeline continued. "I asked her to talk to Reverend Jeff, but she already has. She's afraid that if Bryce doesn't like what Jeff says, then he'll leave the church, and she *loves* her church community. I'm hoping that Jeff is making some headway with him right now."

"Just because Uncle Bryce leaves the church doesn't mean Aunt Brenda has to, does it?" Melissa grasped her boyfriend's hand.

"It is if you want church to be something you share." Madeline nodded to her.

"Where is Aunt Brenda?" Jessica peered into the house, through the sliding glass.

"She left." Jeff answered as he walked up to the deck. "We met her out front, and she asked Bryce to take her home. The girls left, too. They said to thank you, and Brenda will stop by tomorrow and pick up her food containers."

"How did your talk go?" Madeline grasped his elbow and looked up, studying his face.

"Hard to say. Let's just say he wasn't ready to come back and apologize to anyone, except maybe Brenda. He does love her."

"I'm sure he does." Madeline cast a worried look across the table to her husband. He nodded his agreement. Silence weighed on the gathering for several seconds before Madeline stood up. "When in doubt, serve dessert. Are we ready for pie and ice cream?"

All the heads at the table bobbed, signifying their assent. The evening faded with quiet conversations.

* * *

Later, Kevin loaded the dishwasher and washed the pots and pans.

"Hey, Dad. Want some help?" Jessica touched his shoulder from behind.

"That'd be great. You can dry." He turned, handed her a towel and pointed toward the large bowls he had already washed.

"Some evening, huh?" Jessica wiped the inside of a green plastic serving bowl.

"It was. In all the excitement I forgot to ask: Where's that guy you were going to bring?"

Jessica rolled her eyes and shook her head. "I don't know if I'm staying with him. I uninvited him to the picnic."

Kevin stopped washing and turned toward Jessica again. "You want to talk about it?"

She grabbed another bowl and quickly wiped it dry. "Where do these go?"

Kevin pointed to a lower cupboard.

Jessica opened the cupboard door. "We were at this party last night, and he's sitting on a couch with this blonde. She's wearing this short little dress, and they're sitting so close you'd need a friggin' crowbar to pry them apart." She placed the bowls on the shelf and closed the door. "So I go up to him, and ask, 'What's going on?' And he gets this sheepish grin and says, 'Nothing.'" Jess walked back over to the counter and picked up the towel again. "Doesn't even introduce me to the girl. I look at her and she gets this look like *Who are you?* So I give them both a look and walk away."

"Did he get up and follow you?"

Jess started on the pots. "No. From across the room I see that she's really laying it on, and he's eating it up. He's talking; she's laughing; and then she puts her hand on his thigh. So I wait to see if he's gonna do anything about it, and he doesn't!"

"Ooh. That must've really hurt. I'm sorry, Jess"

"Yeah, so here I'm thinking I've got something really good with this guy, and he pulls this shit right in front of me."

"So what did you do?"

"I walked over to them, and I told him I was leaving--and he asks why. And I said because you're a jerk, and I don't want to be around you. Then this girl rolls her eyes at me. I said: 'Roll those eyes again, and I'll rip them out.' That made her pause. Jerry just sits there saying nothing, so I left. Then he yells to me: 'Wait. How am I gonna get home?' I drove. I yelled back. 'Ask your girlfriend.'"

"Wow." Kevin placed his hand on her shoulder, and squeezed gently. "I can see why you didn't want him here. So what now? Did he call?"

Jessica reached into her shorts for her cell. "About six times today. I didn't answer."

"You're making him work aren't you?" Kevin smiled.

"Damn right, Dad. I'm not making it easy. If I can't trust him when I'm there, how can I trust him when we're apart?"

"You love him, don't you?"

"Yeah, apparently too much. I don't care how much I love him. No way am I staying with a guy who would embarrass me like that at a party with our friends, and no way am I gonna be with a guy I can't trust. I'll find someone else." Her eyes teared. She tossed the towel on the counter, shook her head and quickly wiped her face with a paper napkin.

Kevin pulled her into a hug. "I'm proud of you. You know what you want, and you won't settle."

"Thanks, Dad. You think I should take his call if he calls again?"

"Well, I think you should use your instincts. Pick up when you're ready. If he can't persist until that time comes, it's probably just as well. You think you'd be able to forgive him?"

"I can forgive him, but that doesn't mean I want to be with him. I'm tired of the bullshit, Dad. I mean the dating game. I want a guy I can be with, long term. Maybe Jerry's not the one. If he is, he has to jump through a lot of hoops now. I don't want him unless he really wants me. If he really wants me, he'll call again. Is that too harsh?"

"No. I think you're right. You should have the best. If that's not him, move on."

"Thanks." Her word flowed over his shoulder as she squeezed him tight. She let go, wiped her eyes, and grabbed the dish towel. "Let's get this done."

Kevin reached for the dish cloth. A smile inched across his face, and as he inhaled, a little bit of pride filled his lungs along with the air.

Chapter Thirty-One

Kevin awoke to the sound of chickadees outside his window. They were calling his name. "Ke ----- vin. Ke ------ vin." He sat up, swung his legs over the edge of the bed, dropped to his knees, and placed his elbows on the window sill. The late summer breeze wafted through the screen, caressing his face and gifting his nostrils with a mixed scent of loam and roses. He offered a prayer of thanks.

Twenty-four hours ago he had awakened in South Bend with Rachel. Tomorrow he would wake up in the poolhouse in Tucson. What would today bring? He asked in prayer that whatever happens, he would be helpful. He showered, dressed and packed, anticipating his afternoon departure. As the door to his room opened, the sweet smells of breakfast swept into his nose and mouth, activating saliva glands, reminding him that he was hungry.

Jim and Madeline sat at the counter that divided their kitchen and dining areas. "Just in time." His mother placed a plate of scrambled eggs and toast at the open place setting.

His father was reading the paper, closed it slightly to make eye contact, nodded, and resumed reading.

Now that's the dad I remember. Kevin sat down. "Thanks, Mom." He savored the eggs in his mouth--felt their firm, soft texture on his tongue; tasted their richness enhanced with a little salt, pepper, and garlic--before chewing, swallowing and satisfying his stomach's need.

"Put the paper down, Jim. Kevin will be leaving in a few hours, and this is the last you'll see of him for a while." She gently pushed on the newspaper to make her point.

"Same old crap anyway. Damn Democrats aren't worth a shit, and the Republicans think they're going to save the day. Who you for, Kevin?" He closed the pages.

Unwilling to hurry his second bite, Kevin was silent.

"Well?" His father tapped him with the open newspaper.

"Oh Jim, let him chew his food, for God's sake." His mother shook her head.

"I'm for the best leader." Kevin spoke softly, irritated at his father for the first time on this visit. *I almost forgot how rude he can be.*

"That's not an answer." His father folded the paper and set it next to his plate.

"That's *my* answer. I don't care about political parties. I'll vote for the best leader, and I haven't decided yet." Kevin held back on his tone as if his words were dogs on a leash. *Wow! I'm really getting annoyed with him.*

"Hmph." His father looked at him, seemingly holding back on his own tone, then plunged his fork into a mound of fluffy eggs, and thrust them into his mouth.

Madeline pointed her fork into the air. "The President isn't as bad as they say, and the Republicans won't work with him. I'm thinking we might be better off with someone who has a business background--someone who understands that you can't keep spending more than you make." She poked at the air with her fork to emphasize her point.

"I don't listen to the ads. All they do is criticize each other. To be fair, being the President is the hardest job in the world, and I have to respect whoever is willing to step up." Kevin scooped more scrambled eggs into his mouth. "Good eggs, Mom." The words were muffled having to share their space with the food.

Jim wiped his chin with a napkin and chopped the space between himself and Kevin with his index finger. "I'll tell you this . . ."

Whoosh! The front door opened, and all three turned their heads. "Who's here?" Jim called.

"It's me!" Bryce hurtled into the room, eyes wide, staring. "You won't believe what I just saw!" He paced, lips tight, hands wringing.

"Well, spit it out, Son. What's got you so upset?" Jim set his fork down, his eyes narrowed with concern.

"I stopped by the church this morning. Needed to take a few measurements for the remodel we're doing in the reception area outside Jeff's office. I have my own key." He panted between sentences, as if there were too many words to squeeze into too few breaths. "I heard voices so I moved quietly. Jeff was talking to some guy. They didn't know I was there. I couldn't hear the words, but then they hugged each other. Then I saw Jeff kiss him."

"On the cheek?" Madeline asked, her question sounding more like a statement.

"No. On the lips or right next to the lips--I don't know. I couldn't believe it!"

Kevin's words spilled from his mouth. "So, Bryce, was it a passionate kiss, a French kiss, or just a little smooch?" *Shut up, Kevin. Stay out of it.* Anger bubbled inside him.

Bryce glared at his brother. "It's not funny. They kissed. It was quick, but it was a kiss. I trusted him, and now I find out he's gay." He continued pacing.

Kevin breathed deeply before he spoke. "Bryce. You don't know that for sure. Even if he is, what of it?"

Bryce stopped and faced his brother. "What of it? I'll tell you what. I'm not going to a church run by a homosexual. It's a sin. It's an insult to God."

"I don't think God is that easily insulted. Jeff is a good man. That's all that matters." Kevin slid off the stool and faced his brother.

"It's not all that matters, and what do you know? You're not even a Christian!"

"All right boys. Let's not fight. I'm sure there's an explanation." Madeline looked at each face in the room. There was silence.

"What are you going to do?" Jim stood, and edged between his two sons.

"I'm going to talk to the other board members, and we'll confront him about it. I want him out. If he doesn't leave, then I'll--I'll go to another church." Bryce stood erect, arms folded.

"Why don't you just ask him yourself? You know, one to one, instead of spying on him and going behind his back?" Kevin searched Bryce's eyes for a way to get through to him.

Bryce turned toward Kevin. "The Bible teaches us how to live, and I follow the Bible. That's what a Christian does." He turned away. "The board members should know about this. If they want me to talk to him alone, I will. I gotta go. I'm going back over there, but first I'll see who I can get a hold of on the way." He kissed his mom, and turned to leave.

"Don't forget your torches and white hoods." Kevin said under his breath.

Bryce waved him off without turning back. They heard the door swoosh open and shut.

"That's not what I expected this morning." Jim picked up his fork and resumed eating.

Madeline looked up at Kevin. "Do you think he really is gay?"

"I don't know, Mom. I like him and don't want to see him attacked like this. I should probably warn him." Kevin sat down, and pushed his plate away, his appetite gone.

"How does he justify it?" Madeline eyed her husband and son.

"What do you mean?" Kevin squeezed his napkin, at first unconsciously, and then he wondered if it served as an effigy of Bryce. He let it go on the counter.

"She wants to know how Jeff can be in a gay relationship when the Bible says that it's a sin." Jim reached for Madeline's hand again. She nodded her head in agreement.

"I think people use the Bible as a club for beating on those they don't agree with."

"Your mother isn't saying she's against gay people. As you know, her Aunt Molly lived with Sandy for over thirty years. We always thought there was something between them, but no one ever asked. What your mom wants to know is, how a minister can justify a gay relationship given that the Bible says it's an abomination." Jim looked at Madeline, and she nodded again.

Kevin couldn't stop his smile, noticing again how his parents often spoke as one, and how his father protected her from any possible condemnation. "I think the Bible is far from inerrant, and it was written long ago in a context we can't even understand. I don't know how Jeff sees it. I'll ask him and let you know. I should tell Jeff that the posse is coming." Kevin patted his jeans pocket looking for his cell phone. "I don't envy what he has to deal with today." He pulled out his phone and found Jeff's number.

"Are you sure you want to get in the middle of this?" His father wiped his hands on his napkin

"I'm leaving in two hours, Dad. I'm calling him." He hit *Talk*. The phone rang until the voicemail cut in. Kevin hit the *End* button. "I'll try again in a few minutes. Thanks for the breakfast, Mom. I'm going to put my things in the car."

Fifteen minutes later, Kevin tried again.

"Hello."

"Jeff, this is Kevin Neill."

"Hi Kevin. I thought you were leaving today."

"I am. Something's come up, and you should know about it."

"What is it?"

Suddenly, the words were stuck in Kevin's mouth. "Um, well. Here's what happened. Bryce was at the church this morning, and he saw you talking to someone. He said you were kissing each other, so now he thinks you're gay."

The line was silent. Kevin looked at his screen and saw that the seconds were still counting. "Jeff! Are you there?"

"Yeah, I'm here. Thanks for letting me know."

"Are you all right?"

"I'll be okay. I suppose I owe you an explanation."

"You don't owe me anything. I just didn't want you blindsided. You'll figure out what to say."

"There's nothing to figure out. I don't advertise my personal life, but now I have to be honest. The man in the hallway this morning is a dear friend of mine. We don't see each other very often, because he lives in Phoenix. This is the first time he visited me here, and I wanted him to see the church before he left."

"This sounds like a lot of drama for nothing then."

"It's not nothing. He's my friend, and he's my partner. I love him, and I could never say that we aren't involved."

Kevin let that sink in. "I'm sorry you have to go through this."

"Thanks, but it's my responsibility. I knew this could happen."

"Maybe you need to find a more liberal church."

"I know." He paused. "I'm looking out the window, and two cars are arriving in the parking lot. Bryce and two others are getting out, and they don't look happy." He laughed uneasily. "I'd better go. Bless you, Kevin. Have a safe trip."

"Take care, Jeff. Call me when you're done; let me know how it goes. Don't let my brother get to you."

Kevin slid the phone into his pocket and looked to his parents who were watching him. "Well, he told me that he's gay. The guy that Bryce saw is his partner."

Jim and Madeline both shook their heads. Jim pulled his wife close. "Sometimes I feel very old, Maddie, and that I don't comprehend this world at all." He looked toward Kevin. "I don't understand this reverend and how he could preach the gospel and be involved with a man, too. Frankly this whole business of men sleeping with men turns my stomach."

Kevin stared at the floor, his thumbs hooked in his jeans pockets. "I don't understand why a man wants to be with another man. I've never felt that kind of attraction. It doesn't matter."

"It doesn't?"

"Look, Dad, I don't get why Bryce is such a fanatic. Frankly, the thought of eating liver turns my stomach, but you love it. That doesn't stop me from loving and respecting you, and Bryce, too. We're all wired differently."

"I don't think my eating liver compares to having gay sex." Jim glared at Kevin.

"I'd rather kiss a man than eat liver." Kevin glared back.

"Well, there's nothing in the Bible about eating liver, but there sure are a few things about proper sexual behavior."

Kevin folded his arms. "Dad, is Jeff created by God?"

Jim squinted at his son. "Of course he is."

"So you think that God put Jeff on this earth, gave him his same-sex preference, and plans to punish him for being himself?"

Jim cleared his throat. "I don't know. I'm not God."

"So maybe you can at least give him the benefit of the doubt, and not judge him."

Kevin's father studied his son for a moment, then picked up his newspaper.

Guess that means the conversation is over.

"Kevin, I don't want your visit to end on a sour note." His mother embraced him.

"It's okay, Mom. I still love you guys."

"We love you, don't we, Jim?" She gave him a look that said he'd better not disagree.

"Yeah, yeah. Of course." He returned to his newspaper.

* * *

The church parking lot was empty when Kevin pulled into a space near the side entrance. As he walked up the steps, Jeff pushed the door open and let him in. They shook hands, and Kevin gave him a hug. "How are you?"

"A little shaken, but okay." They walked toward the reception area outside the office, and Jeff motioned for him to sit down. The beige carpeting showed a trail of thousands of footsteps. 1960s wood paneling served as wainscoting around the walls. Kevin sat in a green easy chair, and Jeff eased onto a cream love seat. The smell of cleaning agents filled the room. Kevin thought it may be awhile until the room was remodeled.

"Sorry about the smell. People were here yesterday cleaning the place. It really needs work, as you can see."

"No problem. I hope Bryce wasn't too hard on you."

Jeff's tone was even, and he seemed to be choosing his words carefully. "Not as hard as he was on you. He was business-like, stated the facts, and then asked me if I'm gay."

"What did you tell him?"

"The truth. Nate is my closest friend and my soulmate. They asked me if I'd had sex with him, and I told them it was none of their business. My relationship with Nate is centered on love, not sex. Whether we make sex one of the ways that we express our love, or not, is our business. Bryce said it was God's business, too. He said that the Bible expressly forbids gay sex."

Kevin raised his eyebrows. "What did you say to that?"

"I told him that the verses from Leviticus he was referring to were about sex with temple prostitutes and not about a loving relationship between two men. I also told him that the Hebrews were against any waste of semen because they believed it was killing a child. They thought that the whole child was in the seed, and women just provided the womb. So, any seed that was not planted in a woman was a waste, and it was killing potential children."

"Bryce didn't buy it, did he?"

"No. He dismissed what I said and told me that he could read; that the Bible clearly said it was an abomination; and that he believed in the Bible. Then they called a meeting of the Board for tonight to decide my fate. Bryce made it clear what his vote would be."

Kevin shook his head and sighed. "So if they vote you out?"

"I'll forgive them. I think the lesson for me is that I have to be up front with people wherever I go. I have to be myself. One of the guys offered the possibility that I could go through a treatment to correct my gay tendencies." Jeff smiled. "I appreciated the helpful intent of the thought. I told him I don't have a disease, and I don't need to be cured."

Jeff scooted forward on the seat and looked at Kevin directly in the eyes. "Don't feel sorry for me. I'm not a victim. I trust in God, and I know everything will work out. My concern is with the church members and how this will affect them."

"I'm sorry, again, about my brother."

"Let's make an agreement, Kevin. You don't apologize for your brother, and I'll not apologize for who I am."

"You're right. I feel embarrassed, and to be honest, angry about what Bryce did. You, on the other hand, are handling this very well. How did you recover so quickly?"

"The lessons of the New Testament are clear. Seek God first. Forgive. Don't judge. Love everyone. Nowhere in the Gospel does it say that Jesus was pissed off or hurt when they arrested and crucified him. This is nothing compared to what he went through. My faith gets me through this. It allows me to see Bryce and be grateful for everything he has done for this church community."

"Don't you feel betrayed by Bryce's behavior?"

"I definitely feel hurt and anger. Part of me resents him. On the flip-side, he feels betrayed by me because I was dishonest. I could blame Bryce, but I'm the one who decided to keep quiet about my sexual preference knowing that many of the folks at this church would disapprove. So maybe I betrayed myself."

"Does that mean that everywhere you go you'll have to tell people about your sex life to be honest?"

"No. It means that if I hide my relationship with the person who is most dear to me, then I'm pretending to be someone I'm not. I don't want that anymore. I just realized that, and I have Bryce to thank for it."

Kevin nodded. "This isn't the first time you've had a confrontation like this, is it?"

"No, it's not, and in a way, I've been expecting it. I'm not that good at pretending. Even though there are some emotions swirling around in me, I'm determined to love through this and learn from it. I am responsible, and blaming people for their attitudes is not going to help me."

Kevin stood up and reached for Jeff's hand. "I guess if you can forgive him, I can, too."

"I'm glad to hear that. To love and to forgive--that's what a Christian does."

You're the real deal, Jeff, and I'm glad I met you." He looked at his cell. "I have a plane to catch."

"I'm glad we met, too. Don't worry about me. I checked on the internet and found there are 117 gay-friendly churches in Arizona.

There are even more in Michigan, but I'm thinking I'd like to be closer to Nate. Maybe I'll see you."

"I hope so. Come to the Calico Grill in Tucson. We'll be open in a couple of months."

They said their good-byes, and Kevin walked out the door. As he was entering his car, Brenda parked next to him. She turned off her engine and sat there. Kevin knocked on her passenger side window, and she opened it. He placed his elbows where the window had disappeared. "Are you all right, Brenda?"

Her eyes were red; her voice sounded hurt. "Bryce told me about Reverend Jeff. I trusted him."

"Now you don't?"

She undid her seatbelt and turned toward Kevin. "How can I trust a minister who blatantly disobeys God's word?"

Kevin held back his argument and decided to listen first. "What are you going to do, Brenda?"

"As much as I feel hurt and angry by all of this, as a Christian, I have to try to convince him to give this, this sex with another man up. I can't watch someone I care about go to Hell. I have to set aside my feelings and warn him."

"Brenda, he doesn't see it as a sin, and neither do I. Besides, there is no Hell."

"That's why I have to try to convince him. I know you don't believe in Hell, but he's a minister. He should know better. That's what a Christian does, Kevin. Out of love, we help each other to be saved." Brenda opened her door and stood on the other side of her Buick.

"Do what you feel you have to do, Brenda, but it doesn't sound like love to me."

She stared at him for several seconds. "Go ahead. Say what you're thinking."

Kevin hesitated. "I know you mean well, but it sounds more like arrogance than love. You're coming from this position of superiority, and you think you're going to *fix* Jeff. You think your way is better, and that you can save him. He doesn't need to be saved, Brenda. Love means that you accept and appreciate him as he is."

"I would be happy to accept him if he repents. So will God." Brenda closed the door gently. "I'm going in. Are you leaving?"

"Yes. I have a flight to catch. Take care, Brenda." He shrugged and shook his head.

"You, too. Be safe." She turned and marched up the steps to the church entrance.

* * *

As Kevin drove along I-96 toward Metro Airport, thoughts about his brother's actions nagged at him. He didn't want to be angry, but embers of irritation continued to glow inside his head. He looked forward to a quiet flight where he wouldn't have to deal with his brother's, or his sister-in-law's religious views.

It had been a good visit. *Dad seemed totally different today than the past few days. Even though he's proud of me, some of the old issues are still there. I'll focus on the good stuff I heard from him.* Traffic was light as he made it to the airport in just over an hour. He turned in his rental car and rode the bus to the terminal. He boarded American Airlines Flight 206 and found his seat. The young man in the middle seat moved so Kevin could sit near the window.

"Hi. I'm Jason." He extended his hand, and Kevin shook it.

Kevin settled in comfortably, and soon the aircraft began to move. Jason held a small *New Testament* in his hand. "Are you saved?" He smiled, eyes innocent.

Kevin hesitated, as the plane turned and positioned for takeoff. He felt himself sucked into the seat as they accelerated down the runway. "Yes, I am. Thank you."

The young man, still smiling, prayerfully enclosed the small Bible between his hands. "Praise the Lord. God bless you."

"God bless you, too." Kevin smiled back and closed his eyes as the aircraft lifted off the ground. *The universe has a sense of humor!* His anger toward Bryce dissolved. He opened his eyes and looked out the window. *I'm flying.*

Chapter Thirty-Two

"It feels like I'm in a dream." Kevin shared cold beers and snacks with Michael.

His Tucson world was both familiar and comforting. The Jerusalem Tree stood sentinel over the yard, its reflection distorted on the surface of the pool by thousands of tiny silver mirrors created by the sun and a breeze. He looked affectionately at the poolhouse that had been his home for the past few months. They sat at Kwahu's table planning the new Calico Grill.

Michael laughed. "That's good, because you *are* in a dream."

"It's a happy one!" Kevin smiled.

"What makes it happy?"

"I make it happy. You taught me that. The trip went very well. I enjoyed my family and Rachel. There were definitely rough spots with Bryce, but I'm okay. My brother hates me, I'm still in debt, yet I'm feeling pretty good. I'm less prone to conflict. Bryce still gets to me, but I recover quickly."

"What about Rachel? Do you miss her?"

"We made a connection, but I don't feel needy. She's right here." He patted his chest. "I'm still trying to get my mind around this life being a dream."

Michael sat back in his chair, and closed his eyes as the sun cast its light on his face. "Have you ever had the experience where you knew you were in a dream?"

"Once. I was a kid, and I dreamed I was flying." Kevin stared at the amber liquid in his glass, peering into the distant past. "Suddenly the thought came to me that I was dreaming. Since I knew that, I started doing loops and dives, taking all kinds of risks. It was fun."

"That's what it's like for me in this life. I'm a lucid dreamer-- awake within the dream. Knowing this isn't real, I'm never afraid to express truth or to do something I desire to do. I'm flying and achieving my purpose."

"Wow. Do you ever want it to end?"

"I don't want or not want it to end. My life's not about desiring to accomplish anything. I have one goal."

"What's that?"

"To be led by what some would call *God's Will*. My life doesn't belong to a body named Michael. My life belongs to God. All Life is one thing, and I call that one thing, God, or Spirit. My role is to play out my purpose. My purpose is to help certain people who show up. Right now, that's you. Maybe when we're done, it'll be time. I don't really have an opinion about it, and it's none of my business. I wake up in the morning, and I notice I'm still in this dream. I say *Thank you,* and I follow the promptings of Spirit all day. Whether this body lives or passes away, I am."

"So, you're unattached to specific outcomes or to having any particular thing."

"Yes."

Kevin contemplated living as a lucid dreamer, unattached to outcomes or things, and following his purpose. "How do *I* wake up?"

"Do you want to wake up?"

"Yeah. When I came out here my goal was success. You've taught me that success is more than money and position and having a beautiful partner."

"Life taught you that."

"True. My prayer is to live confidently as an adult, and to be awake in my daily life."

"To whom do you pray?"

"God. Spirit. The Source. I don't have a specific name."

Michael kept silent for several minutes, first closing his eyes, and then looking directly at Kevin. "When you pray, you are the one who prays. You are also the one you are praying to. You are the one who responds. Spirit doesn't need convincing or special rituals or crystals or prayer shawls or anything. It's you that needs convincing. What you ask for is *already* given. The world you experience is a projection of your mind. There is no cosmic arbitrator who determines if you are worthy or not. You decide."

"Then I've decided. I want to be awake and happy."

"The only thing that stands between you and your happiness is you. Happiness is not something you get, and neither is success, or money or love. Your world reflects who you think you are."

"So I attract experiences that coincide with my thinking?"

"There is no Law of Attraction. Nothing to attract. Nothing outside you." Michael faced his palms up and shrugged. "It's all inside. Let go of everything you've created that makes you unhappy, or that keeps you asleep."

"Then I should ask for the strength to let go?"

"Prayer is not asking for anything. There is nothing to ask for, given that you already have everything. It's joining. When you pray you *unify* with Spirit. When you see that you are linked to God, happiness and wakefulness are natural outcomes."

"Seems like I'd be happier if I was out of debt."

"You'd be out of debt more quickly if you were happier."

"That seems counterintuitive."

"I know. Become aware of each moment when you're worried, hurt, angry, or resentful. Accept your emotions and then tell yourself the truth."

"The truth is that I'm creating the emotion, not someone else."

"Yes. And who are you?"

"I'm--I'm a piece of God. A spark--a part of an eternal flame. I'm also Kevin, aren't I?"

Michael shook his head slowly. "There is no such thing as Kevin. Kevin is a point of view, a collection of memories and a state of consciousness. There is no Michael either. That's the only difference between you and me. I know this is an illusion, and you don't. In time, you will."

"That's reassuring, I think. The idea of not being real is a little disturbing." Kevin took another sip of beer and tried to conceive of *not being real*.

"Here's another way to look at it. I got this from a guy named Yogananda. Imagine a gas flame on a stove. You know the round piece with the little holes in it?"

"Yes. The burner."

"Okay. Imagine there is one flame. That's God. Then you put the burner over it, and you have many seemingly independent flames, one for each hole. Each little flame sees itself as separate, but that's an illusion. There's only one flame. Each of us thinks we are separate, but there's only one of us. One flame. One light. One Spirit, appearing as many."

"That image has possibilities." Kevin nodded, lips drawn tight.

"At first you knew your source, that you were part of the whole. Then you started comparing yourself to other flames, and seeing yourself as special and different. You have forgotten what you are. That's when the game began."

"What's the game?"

"The game is to go as far away from God in your mind as possible and then find your way back. The game is complex, too. You have created hundreds of identities, but they are all from you. You are an amazing creator, Kevin. You've created these identities-- Kevin the restaurant manager, Kevin the father, Kevin the son, and beyond that--Kevin the victim, and Kevin who isn't good enough, and Kevin who is a bad person. You slip into each of these roles, and you're convinced they're real. Your special effects are incredible. Give yourself kudos for making it so convincingly realistic, but know that it isn't." Michael's eyes twinkled.

"Whew! I think my head is spinning. Either that or you're just plain crazy!" Kevin eyed Michael with suspicion. *Is he toying with me?*

"Which is it? Is the world you see insane, or am I?"

Okay, that's a good question. Kevin chewed on his experiences in the world--divorce, bankruptcy, broken relationships, conflict with his brother, lack of money, being beat up, and chasing women. The taste soured in his mind. He pictured experiences with Michael and Sarah, the lessons and the laughter, and savored the blessings they had given him. "Definitely you have to be the sane one. The world is clearly insane."

"You are God expressing as you, as is everyone else." Michael made a sweeping motion with his hand. "As long as you see yourself as separate and real, you will have suffering."

"That reminds me of Ben, Rachel's friend. Even though he had cancer, he said that he didn't suffer. It wasn't real to him."

Michael grinned. "Now you're starting to see. Ben took a steep path."

"I can't see myself doing that."

Michael closed his eyes, as if contemplating. His eyes opened. "Most of us aren't ready for that. So the best thing we can do is surrender to the will of God. Seek God first. Have no other gods before God. Let go of everything you think will bring you fulfillment or happiness and choose the will of Spirit first. Non-attachment. You can see that Sarah and I lack for nothing. We live simply, and we live well. Our needs are always met."

"How do you know you're not attached? I mean, it really seems you love Sarah and the restaurant and your home. This illusion seems to mean a lot to you."

Michael smiled. "It's not either/or. I do like it in this dream. I like being with Sarah and spending time with you, and I like the

291

restaurant business. For me, the universe is one big amusement park. I play at being Michael, the restaurant guy, the husband, father, and grandfather and sometimes a teacher. Those are games. In each one, I maintain an awareness of what I am. For example, throughout this conversation, I'm mindful that I am spirit and so are you. I'm not worried or concerned about you or me or this restaurant business."

"Yet here we are planning for this opening."

"We're planning, but we're not worrying about it. Planning and visioning are fun. Just don't be attached to outcomes. Attachment creates fear. You love Rachel, but you don't seem fearful about losing her."

"I don't see how I *can* lose her. We love each other, but I don't know what form that will take." Kevin poured water into a glass from a blue ceramic pitcher. The cold liquid pleased his tongue and throat. He set down the glass with a clink. "I guess that means I'm unattached. I'm happy when I'm with her, and I'm happy when I'm not."

"You've done well. Now can you plan this restaurant and not be attached to how it plays out?"

Kevin nodded. "As far as gurus go, there are plenty in Arizona, from here to Sedona. I think you're one of the best-kept secrets."

"I like it that way. I don't desire fame, or to give speeches or sell books. I like the restaurant business, and I like working with individuals. If you create the right environment, hire the right people, train them well, and serve good food, people will leave their egos at the door and enjoy themselves and each other. When we get the Grill up and running, Kevin, people will be lined up to get in."

"I'm not so sure. Do you really think so?" Kevin's eyes widened.

"Yes. You've changed. There's a light shining in you that wasn't obvious a few months ago. You're growing up. You inspire people just by being yourself."

"My brother doesn't seem too inspired by me."

"Ah, your brother is very strongly affected by you. Your light is shining brighter, and some people will feel threatened by that. Your brother thinks he'll feel better if he can change you. What he really needs is for you to love and understand him, not to engage in his pain.

"This is where understanding the dream helps you. You see that none of it is real--that everything you invest your emotional energy in is yours. Your brother reflects your fear. He's a mirror. Just as Rachel reflects the love that is within you, your brother reflects your self-rejection. When you stop rejecting yourself, the dynamics will change."

"My mind and emotions want to see Bryce as a jerk, but you've told me he's my teacher."

"You don't see Bryce. You only see your image of him. When you forgive him, you are really just letting go of your image of him as a jerk, and more importantly, your image of yourself as his victim."

"I try to forgive, but then he does something else, like what he did with the minister." Kevin shook his head, and rolled his eyes.

"Forgiveness is not something you try, Kevin. It's something you intend, and then you do whatever it takes to get there. You do whatever it takes because your freedom and your peace are more important to you than holding Bryce hostage in your mind."

"I get it, at least intellectually. It's doing it that's so hard."

"Forgiveness is easy. It's not doing, but undoing that helps you forgive. Forgiveness is not something you give. It's a process by which you find your true self. The hard part is that you want something else more. You are the sole creator of your experience. Not Bryce. Not anyone else. It's you. So ask yourself who you are being when you're upset with Bryce, and then dis-create that."

"I have the power."

"Yes. I'll tell you a story. A minister was talking to his congregation one Sunday about forgiving one's enemies. He asked the group how many thought it was possible to do that. A few people raised their hands. Then he launched into a sermon on the topic, and his words were compelling. When he finished the sermon he asked them again if it might be possible for them to forgive their enemies. Almost all of them raised their hands--except one older woman near the front. He was curious so he asked: 'Mrs. Smith, don't you think it's possible that you could forgive your enemies?' To which she replied: 'I don't have any enemies.'

"Now this made him more curious, so he invited her up to the front of the sanctuary. She carefully and slowly made her way up to where he was standing, and he handed her a microphone. 'So, Mrs. Smith, may I ask, how old are you?' She brought the mic to her lips and said: 'I'm ninety-five.' He thought for a moment. 'Tell the congregation, Mrs. Smith, how, at the age of ninety-five, you don't have any enemies.'

"Mrs. Smith looked out over the rows of people, and again brought the mic to her lips and said: 'I outlived the bitches!'" Michael broke into a laugh, and slapped his knee. "So, you can wait until you're ninety-five, if you make it that far, or do it now."

Kevin's belly shook as he laughed.

"All right then. Now that I've got you relaxed: who are you when you're mad at Bryce?"

Kevin closed his eyes, the trail of laughter still imprinted in his body, but his thoughts swirled in confusion. *Bryce is a child of God. But, he's a jerk. And he's so self-righteous. Back in high school he thought he was so much better than me. Just because he was a good athlete. I got tired of being compared to him by Dad and by some of my teachers. He was the golden boy. Wait. What was the question? Oh yeah. Who am I being when I'm angry at him? I don't know.*

"Breathe, Kevin. Step outside of your thoughts and be in your feelings. What's going on?"

My thinking is all over the place. Have to stop focusing on thoughts. What do I feel? Kevin inhaled deeply and let it out slowly. Nothing.

"Who are you when you're with Bryce. What do you feel when you think of him, or when you compare yourself to him?"

"Disgusting. Bad. I worked on this in Michigan at the rest stop."

"Wisdom, power, value, love and joy are yours, Kevin. It is this illusion of badness that suppresses who you are in truth."

Kevin again brought his attention to his feelings. *Bad. Bryce is the good son, and I'm the bad one.* Anger flooded his body, tensed his muscles, creased his brow, and reddened his face. Kevin let it flow. The storm of anger passed, then anxiety seized his heart sending waves of discomfort throughout his body. He seemed to be shrinking, like an ice cube melting into a puddle of water. *Disgusting. I hate myself! Why am I even here?* He became nothing, insignificant, unwanted and alone--so alone. Next he was suffocating in the dark, as if imprisoned in a brown paper bag and punching, pushing, grabbing, trying desperately to tear his way out.

"Breathe, Kevin." Michael gently touched his shoulder. "Breathe deeply and stay with it."

Kevin wanted to escape the hurt, to distract himself somehow, to make it all go away, but he made himself stay with it. The anxiety shifted to his stomach, and he felt himself cowering, as if trying to hide from the world, from its disapproval, and from the fear it was flinging at him. "God, I feel like shit."

"Stay with it, Kevin. You're doing well."

Kevin pressed his back against the chair, but he was unable to conceal himself--unable to mask his many imperfections. He felt naked and unprotected, the world his firing squad, firing accusations, peppering him with blame. He cried out in a voice that seemed not his own, and tears rolled down his face. He covered his head with his arms.

"Breathe, Kevin." Michael's hand on his shoulder steadied him. "Tell me where you are right now?"

"I feel empty. Afraid to open my eyes."

"What will happen if you open your eyes?"

"You'll see me for what I really am."

"What are you, Kevin?"

"Bad. Despicable."

"How does that feel?"

Kevin listened to his body. "It doesn't hurt anymore. I feel deeply sad."

"Open your eyes. You have played both roles, good and bad, just like me, and everyone else. Who created the *bad* identity?"

Kevin opened his eyes and peered at Michael, who slowly came into to view. "I did."

"Was it real?"

"It felt real."

"That's how powerful you are in this dream--so powerful that you had yourself believing you were bad, and that you needed to defend that. It was your illusion. It had nothing to do with your brother."

"Bryce was a trigger?"

"Yes. Now I want you to try something different. I want you to integrate it."

"How do I accomplish that?"

"Will yourself to love the *bad* identity."

"You want me to imagine I'm sending love to it?"

"No. I want you to will yourself to love it, and then feel yourself radiating love from your heart to the *bad* identity."

"What if I can't feel it?"

"Use your will, Kevin. Intend to love it, and then focus your mind on sending love from your heart to the identity. This isn't a battle between love and anti-love. Your bad identity is anti-love. That is, it is against love. By believing you're bad, you are withholding love from yourself."

Kevin closed his eyes and willed himself to love the negative identity. Although he was still sad, he focused his intention on loving the sadness and loving the identity that created it.

Michael spoke: "You are the infinite power and presence expressing as you. This is the truth of you. You *are* love, Kevin."

For awhile he could not move beyond sadness. He increased his focus on loving even though he could not feel the love. After several more minutes something cracked inside his chest, and confidence spilled from his heart, transpierced his bloodstream, penetrated his cells. Life bubbled inside. Joy seized his face, compelling him to smile. He was more than Kevin had ever been. The universe no longer seemed ready to attack and destroy him. It was his amusement park, and he was ready to play. He opened his eyes again.

Michael sat across from him and mirrored his smile. They sat in silence for several minutes--or maybe an hour--as two gifted men, beholding each other--yet the lines between Michael and Kevin blurred--and Kevin saw himself in his mentor's eyes. Michael reached for a pen and paper. "So, let's talk about this restaurant, shall we?"

"Wow!" Kevin wanted to talk about what he experienced.

Michael touched his hand. "Let it settle, Kevin. If you put words to it you'll begin to forget it. Just let the experience sink in. The more you talk about it, the more you'll forget what you really felt. As old Lao Tsu once said: 'Those who know, do not speak. Those who speak, do not know.'"

* * *

Later that evening:

"I don't understand why my brother and other people are so hung up on gay partnerships. I think people are real uncomfortable with the thought of same-sex intimacy, and they use religion to attack it. People see it as unnatural. Including my parents!"

Michael laughed. "It's not that unnatural. There are plenty of examples in the animal world of same-sex partnering. Lions, bears, lizards, and even birds engage in it. We are a society preoccupied with sex, attached to who's doing it or not doing it, or reading and talking about it, and determining who should or shouldn't have it. It's just another drama to distract us from the real work of growing in Spirit."

"So you're okay with same-sex attraction?"

"I'm not for or against it. It is. I accept it as part of this dream. For me, it's not an issue."

"Is anything an issue with you?"

"Very little and not too often. How about you?"

"Obviously I still have issues to resolve. I'm happy to say I haven't thought about sex in the past few weeks, except for the night I was with Rachel. I hope I'm not losing my drive."

"Don't worry. I'm sure it will be there when you need it. As for issues--you are so used to having issues, I suspect you don't have as many as you think. As long as issues and conflicts are what you use to define yourself, you will have them. Continue dis-creating and integrating negative identities, and your issues will gradually go away." Michael patted him on the shoulder and stood up. "Okay, that's enough for today. I'm going in."

As Michael headed toward the house, Kevin removed his clothes and dove into the pool. Floating, raw, the stars sparkled over him, as if signifying their approval. The water carried him, and the walls around the yard protected him. Naked before the universe, for the first time in his life, there was no one to throw stones, nothing to protect or defend, no one to attack, nothing to get. Life rose above and around him, shaping itself to his needs and desires, reflecting the God-Self within. He could've fallen asleep on the water, but thought better of it.

He heaved himself out of the pool, and walked into the pool-house. He lay in bed, and faces flashed across his mind--Bryce, his parents, Jessica, Melissa, Michael, Rachel, Jeff, Jenny, Ronnie. Love poured forth toward all of them. It was a good feeling, and he hoped it would last.

Chapter Thirty-Three

"Life is complicated." Kevin pushed aside the laptop he had been working on. "I'm not complaining. My mind wants to go in every direction at once--the diner, the new restaurant, Rachel, my family back home, my need to pay off my debts, my personal growth, and all the financial stuff I'm trying to learn so I can be a good manager. It's hard to focus."

"Start with you." Michael sipped on a mango smoothie and sat back in his chair. A solitary cloud floated in front of the hot September sun and gave them respite. "You spend too much time thinking. Spend more time feeling."

"What do you mean?" Kevin placed one elbow on a knee and cupped his chin with his hand.

Michael laughed. "There you are, the thinker. Pay attention to how you feel. *Let* yourself feel."

"I can't just shut off my mind." Kevin shrugged with his hands facing upward.

"I'm not asking that. Instead of focusing on thoughts, focus on your experience, your feelings. I'll tell you a story.

"There was once a Hopi holy man who lived out in the desert by himself. It was said that he could leave his body at will and travel about as a spirit. A group of seekers spent several days tracking him down. They arrived at his cabin, and he asked them what they wanted. 'We want to be able to leave our bodies. Can you teach us?' The old man laughed.

"The seekers were a little offended when he said to them: 'You're already not in your bodies. You don't need me to teach you how to leave. You need to learn how to be *in* your bodies. They were puzzled at that, because they didn't even know they weren't in their bodies. Like most people today, they avoided their emotions, masking them with food and drink and television and sex and fantasies, and every other escape."

"I've always thought it was better to control my emotions."

"It's not about control, it's about *how* you control them. We're mostly talking about negative emotion here. If you avoid and resist your negative emotions, they smolder beneath the surface and get stronger. When you dis-create your negative identities the emotional charge dissipates--like letting the air out of a balloon."

Kevin shook his head. "I've been on edge for the last month since I came back from Michigan. I've sat by the pool every day after work trying to let go of thoughts and stay in my feelings. Not much progress. It's frustrating." Kevin folded his arms across his chest and stared at Kwahu, who stared back at him from the eagle eye in his mask.

"Your practice counts. It may seem like there's no progress, but don't let that discourage you. When you spend over forty years avoiding your feelings, you don't retrain yourself overnight. Have you practiced today?" Michael touched him on the knee.

"No. I was waiting for you and couldn't stop thinking about the restaurants."

"Let's give it a shot right now. Okay?"

Kevin nodded.

Michael sat back in his chair. "Close your eyes and focus on how you feel."

Kevin focused on his feelings. His thoughts were like thousands of people rushing about on a Chicago street. He watched them, resisting the impulse to be caught up in the rush. *Feelings, Kevin. Feelings.* He sent his awareness down into his body, and feelings, faint at first, increased gradually, then quicker, and soon his emotions were a subway train, growling and screaming beneath the surface. Anxiety, anger, fear, and guilt screeched on their tracks, and reached a crescendo as they raced through a dark tunnel beneath his chest. As the pressure increased he labored just to take a breath.

"Breathe, Kevin. Breathe in deeply and then let it out. Who are you being?"

He felt powerless, hit and run over, dragged by emotion. There was nothing he could do. He tried to think about who he was being,

"Stay out of your mind, Kevin. Don't think about it. Just feel it, and let it come to you."

He sank into helplessness, grasping at handfuls of nothing. "I'm powerless. I've worked on this one."

"You made great progress. Now we're going to use integration on it. Let yourself be powerless."

Kevin ignored his thoughts and concentrated on feeling. He lost all sense of time. Was it ten minutes? An hour? He stayed in his dark tunnel, carried by the force of his inner turmoil, facing it without judging or analyzing or thinking.

"Use your will to love this identity, your creation. Decide to love. Intend with all of your will to love this part of you. It's not an intellectual process. It's not about you coming to terms in your mind. It is you by-passing thoughts about it and literally sending love. You intend to love and then you do it."

Kevin willed himself to love this part of himself. At first he couldn't feel it, but eventually the feeling of love became evident. He felt a shift. His fear and anxiety dissolved into feelings of well-being and joy. He expressed what was happening to Michael.

"How much can you love? Push it further. Open yourself to feeling the love of your innermost being, your essence."

Kevin saw himself accessing that love--unconditional and all-encompassing.

"Open yourself to receiving the full love and support of the universe."

Kevin felt the universe supporting him, loving him.

"Further, Kevin. Further. How much love can you express?"

He pushed it further. Immediately fear rushed in, terrorizing his mind, filling his body with unease. He described it to Michael.

"Let it flow. Don't resist the fear, or fight it. Continue to will yourself to love."

Kevin was shaking. The fear was like a wall of ice, isolating him from all warmth. He continued to offer love. His heart opened, and his chest expanded. Again, he described the feeling to Michael.

"You are well-loved, Kevin, and the universe is supporting you. Feel what that is like. Feel that love growing, like a ball of light, glowing, spreading warmth to every part of your body. See it expanding beyond your body and including all of your surroundings. You are more than a body."

A soft electrical charge energized and comforted him. Held in the spell of the present, he again lost track of time, forgot he was in a chair by the pool, but knew, without a doubt, that he was in his body. He swelled with confidence and self-love, and felt the smile on his face, the strength in his muscles, and the vibration in his nerves. His awareness expanded beyond his body. After a while the feelings peaked, and his positive emotion landed gently, evenly, and came to a place of calm.

Kevin's eyes flicked open. "Wow! That was quite a ride."

"Good. I have some practices I want you to do every day, and these will accelerate your progress. Take a few minutes and let me know when you're ready."

"I'm ready. Let me grab the laptop and get this down." Kevin reached for the computer, and opened it, his fingers poised and ready to type.

* * *

Kevin opened the diner the next morning. By 5:45 they were prepped and ready to greet the first customers who would arrive at 6:00 a.m. He sat at the counter with a cup of hot tea, and Jack sat next to him with coffee.

"Jack, I appreciate all that you do. You've been a great addition to the diner."

"What, am I leaving or something?" Jack set down his cup, and squinted at Kevin. "You getting rid of me?"

"Oh definitely not. I was just wondering what your plans are. Do you want to keep on doing this or what?"

Jack exhaled the breath he had been holding. "Well, I guess I haven't thought about it too much. I like it here. It's been four months, but I still feel grateful to have a job. I moved out of my mother's basement and got my own place."

"That must feel good. What I'm asking you is what are your plans for your career? Have you thought about culinary school?"

"Thought about it. I had some schooling in the navy. Why?"

"Because we're re-starting the Calico Grill, and I want you to come work in the kitchen."

Jack's eyes and mouth opened. "You want me to cook in a fancy restaurant?"

"I've known a few chefs and cooks over the past five years. You have a gift. It needs to be developed. You could enroll in culinary school, expand your skills. We'll pay for it."

Jack's face spread into a broad smile. "When do I start?"

* * *

Throughout the next month Kevin focused on feelings every day. He followed the steps that Michael had given him. The first was to instruct himself to stay open to feelings, to feel the love of the Source, or God, the One--he wasn't sure what he wanted to call

304

it. He settled on God, even though it brought up images of the angry Old Testament God, Bryce's God, who demanded sacrifice. He spent time dis-creating the negative charge he felt with the word *God*, feeling angry, disappointed, and suspicious. After several sessions it evoked a positive charge.

Secondly, Michael had taught him to use his will to love everyone and everything. He willed himself to radiate love from his heart to people and situations that came to mind, especially ones that irritated him. He also sent love to his negative identities when they showed up. This helped him to integrate the parts of himself that he had previously rejected.

Hourly he sent love to others and to himself. Often this created an inner ambience of love and confidence. Other times it evoked negativity, and he descended into his own personal hell filled with guilt, shame, anger, and resentment.

When negative emotion arose at work, he stepped into the office as quickly as he could and sent love to whatever part of himself that was the cause. Every afternoon by the pool he spent at least two hours in processing and meditation. As he confronted negative emotions and loved his identities, and as he spent time loving all that appeared negative, he had more access to positive emotion. One afternoon he finished his meditation and swam a few laps. He turned on the radio to float, listen, and enjoy the gentle warmth of a late October sunset.

> I can see clearly now the rain is gone
> I can see all obstacles in my way.
> Gone are the dark clouds that had me blind.
> It's gonna be a bright, bright, sun-shiney day.

Johnny Nash's song seemed like an anthem for this time in his life. The dark clouds of negative identities had blocked his joy, and the love that was inside of him. They had insulated him from God, and made him think that his painful experiences were real, and caused by others. They were just stories. He felt like an adult. Big. Accountable. Responsible. Less interested in drama and painful stories. A part of the greater whole. He still had much more to learn, and that thought excited him.

*　*　*

Kevin enjoyed contacting his former employees from the Calico Grill. Most of them wanted to come back. He invited them and his investors to a poolside meeting at Michael and Sarah's on a Monday evening in early November.

He found Ronnie and Jenny at a table. "Thanks."

"Thanks for what?" Jenny grinned.

"For making this possible--for believing in me enough to invest in the restaurant."

"You're welcome. I'm happy to do it given I feel partly responsible for what happened." Jenny stood and embraced him. "This is redemption for me. It feels good, and I know you'll be successful."

"Thanks." Kevin noted a change in Ronnie. "You look different. I mean that in a good way."

Ronnie smiled. "You're welcome, also" She turned her face away, then returned as if compelling herself to make eye contact."

"All right. What's going on?" Kevin shifted his gaze between Ronnie and Jenny.

"She's in love." Jenny smiled.

Ronnie shot a narrow glance at her.

It was in her eyes. "You are definitely glowing."

"Well, I do have a new man in my life. I wasn't going to bring it up." Ronnie shot another look at Jenny.

Jenny laughed. "Kevin can handle it. He's over you."

Kevin nodded. "Ronnie, I'm happy for you!"

Ronnie rose and welcomed him into a hug. They held each other as two old friends. "Thank you. That means a lot to me." She wiped a tear from her eye. "I still feel bad for the way I ended it with you."

"Nothing to feel bad about." *I care more about her now than I did when we were together? I don't need anything, or want anything from her. I just care.*

Later that evening he thought about how far he had come, letting Ronnie go, being okay with intermittent communication with Rachel, and even able to smile when he thought about Bryce. Life was good, he decided. There were still financial challenges, problems to solve in restarting the Grill, no doubt some challenges that would arise in the coming days, and plenty of work to do, but life was good.

Each day he practiced sending love. It was a discipline that he embraced, and it served others and himself very well.

Chapter Thirty-Four

It was almost sunrise when he stepped on to the trail and hiked into the canyon. It was a Sunday morning in early May. The air was cool, but the exertion warmed him. It had been his practice to meditate and process for two hours every morning by the pool since the beginning of the year, but today, Pima Canyon called to him. He found his spot and faced eastward waiting for first light.

Since the opening in December, Kevin had spent most of his time at the Calico Grill. It had quickly became a popular place to dine. His debts had decreased considerably with his increased income and by continuing to live simply at the poolhouse.

Soon the brilliant sun flashed over the top of the mountain, blinding him for a few moments. He closed his eyes and felt the rays on his face. The warmth slowly edged down his chest. Kevin focused on the self and imagined the rays as unconditional love bathing him. At first, thoughts of the restaurant rudely interrupted his meditation. This had been his experience every day--his desire to connect with Spirit vying with his mind and its multitude of thoughts, stories, and concerns.

He offered a silent prayer of *Thanks*. After a few dozen attempts, he finally arrived at being completely in feelings, focusing on love. Every rock and plant, and every molecule of air became the presence of God. Each breath inhaled love and each sensation-- the breeze on his skin, the sun's rays on his face, and the sand and pebbles beneath his feet--each a way that Spirit touched him. He lived and moved and expressed his being within God--within love.

Usually this practice triggered waves of joy in him, but sometimes it brought up fear and hurt. Either way it was effective.

The fear and hurt were welcomed as experiences, and the negative energy flowed and then dissipated. After spending almost a year with Michael and Sarah, and eight months of practicing at least two hours every day, he had learned to feel--to love his negative identities, and to accept responsibility for his self-created illusions of pain and need. The love and the connection were real.

It came to him that things had gone very well, but life on earth was dualistic. There was joy and there was sorrow. Gain and loss. Love and fear. He couldn't be in the dream and not experience duality. He scanned his feelings for any negative emotion.

He thought about Rachel, and longed for companionship. When the sadness flowed through him he remembered the last time he saw her in South Bend. He again felt the love and connection and envisioned her presence. Her voice from their phone call the previous night was embedded like a gem in his heart.

Having traveled the full range from loneliness to feeling well-loved in a few moments, he was complete. He was happy in knowing that love was alive within him. Even in sadness or loneliness he could return to happiness. He merely had to accept the sadness, to become it, love it, and let it flow.

Life in the dream was a movie. *Happily ever after is a photograph. You can't live in a photograph. But, Michael and Sarah? Don't they live happily ever after? But, they're awake within the dream. Whatever happens, they embrace it. Michael says that it's all illusion, and that happiness is completely an inside job.*

In that his happiness wasn't related to what others said or did, he didn't hope to live in a photograph, a still life of life--success and joy frozen in a frame. There would always be polarity. *Why am I thinking these thoughts?* He sensed dark clouds in the distance. He looked up at the sky. There were no real clouds in sight.

All the things that could go wrong flashed in his mind, and he plotted and planned how to manage each scenario. As drama assailed his mind and stirred up concern, he was aware of tension and anxiety in his gut. *Enough! Something has happened, but it's not any of these fantasies. Thy will be done. Whatever happens, happens. It's none of my business.* He welcomed life and told himself that everything occurred for a reason. He would find a way to accept and embrace it, whatever it was.

He arrived at the poolhouse before noon to find Michael and Sarah waiting in the usual spot. "Kevin, please sit with us." Michael waved him to the table.

Kevin felt the old fear. *This is it!* He breathed deeply, and gave his attention to his dear friends.

Sarah held his gaze. "Your mother called this morning, Kevin." She paused as if reading his face. "Your dad had a heart attack, and he's in the hospital. She wants you to come home. I'm sorry."

Kevin felt a blow across his chest. He forced himself to breathe.

"You should go, Kevin." Michael stood and placed his hand on his shoulder. "I'll call Chip, and he can run things at the restaurant. I'll check on them for you."

Michael and Sarah both nodded. Sarah gently embraced him as he sat, staring straight ahead.

Concern for his mother churned inside, but he noticed less concern for his father. His intuition spoke. *He's moving on. No worries.* "I don't think my dad is going to recover from this."

His friends were silent, but he appreciated their strength. He accepted their offer to drive him to the airport and rushed into the poolhouse to pack. In the back seat he reserved the next flight to Detroit with his cell phone. In eight hours he would be in Michigan, and in ten he would be at the hospital. He called his mother and each of his daughters as he waited for his departure. They asked him to hurry.

Kevin arrived at Metro Airport at 10:30 p.m. and called his mother again. His father had passed away a few hours ago. He held back on the automatic: *Are you all right, Mom?* Because he knew she wasn't. He simply asked: "Is someone with you, Mom?"

Bryce and Brenda were with her. "I'm sorry, Mom. I'll be there when I can." As he drove along the expressway his father's death seemed surreal. Just two months ago his parents had come to Tucson. When his father saw people lined up to get into the restaurant he teared up. He told Kevin he was so proud of him, and that he knew Kevin could do it.

Both Jim and Madeline loved the poolhouse. His father said it made sense to live simply and pay his debts. His dad smiled more that weekend than any time in his memory. Kevin carved that smile into his consciousness like a lover cutting initials into a tree. That was the image of his dad he would carry in his heart. The memory brought tears, and Kevin stopped at an exit to cry for his father.

Over the next few days the family was close. A few hundred people came to Jim's funeral. Kevin hadn't realized his father's effect on the community. He remembered his dad with gratitude. The entrepreneur's ring was his reminder. He twisted it on his finger.

Two days after the funeral, Kevin woke up to a gray morning. The mist seemed to suffocate the house and him within it, until he realized he wasn't breathing. He faced where the sun would have been, and inhaled deeply, raising his arms and circling them downward to his sides. The grief of his mother and brother weighed on him.

He had accepted his father's death and come to a sort of peace about it. Was it because he had experienced so much loss a year ago? Was it because his mother and Bryce were much closer to his dad? Bryce had always been the good son. He wondered how the good son would fare without Dad. He suspected his brother had never really been a fit for the business--that his real interests and talents had been stifled by his need for paternal approval.

Kevin stepped lightly through the house, while his mother slept. She'd been awake most of the night, unable to adjust to sleeping alone for the first time in fifty-five years. In the kitchen, tears welled up, as he remembered the last time they had breakfast around the counter. His mother would be eating alone from now on. Setting the kettle on the burner, he wandered around the dining area. The sliding door, which had been locked last night, was unlocked.

The whistling kettle caught his attention, and he turned off the flames. Earl Grey accompanied him outside to solve the mystery. He moved the sliding door slowly, quietly, and stepped onto the deck. Bryce was sitting, face in his hands, unmoving, his white shirt reflecting light as if from an unseen source. His head and hands appeared gray, like the fog. Kevin slid the door shut. Bryce turned toward him, blank-faced, and returned to the cradle of his hands.

Kevin sat at an angle to his brother. The haze lifted a few feet, and the clouds promised to let the sun appear soon. Only the green grass was visible at this point, as thin wisps of vapor arose from the lawn, seemingly holding the murky mist in place, like strings attached to a giant smoky balloon. They sat for several minutes in the silence, and were soon interrupted by the *Whoot whoot whoot, pewww pewww pewww* of a pair of cardinals. He peered at Bryce, and noticed a small amount of color slowly emerging on his skin.

"I can't go to work." Bryce shook his head. "I know they're waiting for me, but I can't do it without Dad." Bryce stared at the deck, his voice barely piercing the haze. "He was the heart and soul of the business. It's empty without him. Nothing. I can't think of a reason to go in today."

Kevin waited a few moments. "Go for the staff. You're the closest thing to Dad they know. They need you."

His brother lifted his head, made eye contact and turned up his voice. "I don't have Dad's charisma."

Kevin matched his tone. "Just show up. Ask people how they're doing. Reassure them."

"How can I? I don't know if I want to keep the business running. Maybe we should sell it, and I'll find something else to do." Bryce straightened up and stared into the fog.

"If that's what you need, do it. I'm sure Mom will agree. Besides, the sale will provide plenty of money for her. Today, the staff needs you. Like it or not, you're the new leader."

"I know that Dad wanted you to be the boss." Bryce returned to studying the deck floor.

"Doesn't matter. I wasn't qualified. You know I was never interested in working there. Besides, my knowledge of the business would fit in a Dixie Cup. Yours, on the other hand, would need an Olympic swimming pool."

Bryce turned his head toward Kevin and almost smiled. "Dad used to say that you took the easy way, becoming a teacher, and getting a regular paycheck. He said that working in a business was always a risk. We had to earn our money every month, even when the economy was bad."

"Yeah, well Dad never set foot in a classroom with twenty-five seventeen-year-olds. Talk about risk!" Kevin took the tea bag out of the cup and set it on a napkin. It bled dark liquid, and the paper absorbed it.

"For years I listened to him tell me how he wished you were more like me. You know, working in a *real* business. When you started the restaurant, he thought *you* were cool. Next thing I know, he's saying I should be more like you." Bryce rubbed his bald head with one hand.

"That must've made you angry."

"Yeah, it did. I was angry at you."

"Why?"

"The fact that you had his approval and didn't seem to care, pissed me off." Bryce glared at him. "I had a great relationship with Dad, and you ruined it."

"Maybe our father only had room in his heart for one son at a time." Kevin sipped his tea.

"Maybe I should have been mad at him, but it was easier to be mad at you. You being a heathen and out of state, and me seeing Dad every day, it was better to be mad at you."

Kevin ignored the *heathen* comment. "It was never my intent to replace you as the favored son. Are you still ticked at me for that?"

"I guess not, but I still disapprove of your lifestyle and your lack of belief."

Kevin lost control of his lips as words trooped out, armed and ready. "Lifestyle? I work sixty hours a week, live simply, and haven't had sex in a year. I pray every day. I'm practically a monk!" Kevin shook his head.

"You don't believe Jesus died for your sins." Bryce clenched his fists, and ripped the morning air with his tone. "You're not saved."

"So you think God is just like our dad?"

Bryce scrunched his eyebrows. "What are you talking about?"

"You said that you were Dad's golden child because you were living the life he wanted for you. Next, he loved me best because I started a business."

Bryce shrugged, a puzzled look fixed on his face.

"You think God loves you because you believe the way he wants, and that he'll make me suffer because I don't. Sounds like Dad to me. Sounds worse than Dad. I don't think Dad would've condemned either of us to eternal damnation."

"You don't understand."

"Don't I? You believe I'm going to Hell if I don't accept Jesus as my savior, right?"

Bryce nodded tentatively.

"Do you think over five billion people on this planet are going to Hell, because they aren't Christians like you?"

Bryce narrowed his gaze. "I'm sure God will give everyone a chance to accept his son."

"Look Bryce. Believe whatever you want. We're brothers. We've let both God and Dad come between us. Dad was imperfect, and I accept that. It may be that my earthly father was capable of disapproving of either of us, but I don't think God does that. God isn't a person who has emotions and preferences."

"But, the Bible says--"

"Let me finish before you quote Bible at me." Kevin's arms tensed as he pushed downward on his knees. "It's fine that you follow Jesus in your way." His volume increased with each sentence. "I'll follow my own path. That's the best we can do. Accept each other as we are, and care about each other as brothers."

Bryce looked at him, eyes wide. "The Bible says that anyone who repents of their sins, and believes that Jesus died and rose from the dead, and gives their life to Jesus will be born again and saved from Hell. 'For God so loved the world that he gave his one and only Son, that whoever believes in him shall not perish but have eternal life.' That's what I believe."

Kevin clamped his lips together, squeezing them into a straight line. He spoke softly. "I thought the message of Jesus was love. Love God. Love your neighbor."

Bryce folded his arms across his chest. "It is. We've sinned against God, and he loves us so much that he sent his son to pay the ransom for our sins. With Jesus, I'm forgiven." He unfolded his arms, and chopped downward with his hands. "That's God's love."

Kevin stopped himself from rolling his eyes. "To be honest, that makes no sense to me. The message I get from the Bible is that you practice what Jesus said and did, like loving, forgiving, not judging, putting God first, and prayer."

"Those things are important but not enough without belief in Jesus as your savior."

Kevin took a deep breath. "I admire your dedication, Bryce. You believe in the phrase, *Thy will be done,* don't you?"

"Of course. It's from the Lord's Prayer."

"I can choose to follow my ego, or do what God desires for me. So, if I'm following my purpose, doing what feels intuitively right-- that's God's will. Can we agree on that?" He felt satisfied with his response and smiled slightly.

Bryce leaned in toward Kevin. "But, God's will is that you be changed in Christ, and that the Kingdom of Heaven be restored on earth. You have to accept Jesus as your savior to be a part of that. The thoughts in your mind can be foolishness without Jesus and the Bible to guide you."

"According to you."

"No, according to the Bible."

"According to your interpretation of the Bible based on someone else's translation. You look for God's will in a book. Clarity about God comes from experience, not from studying a book. Books can point you in the right direction, but you're the one who has to take responsibility and walk the path."

Bryce shook his head from side to side. "There is no book as important as the Bible. It's God's book. I can't believe you're so against it!"

"I'm not against it. I just don't worship it. So let's agree to disagree. Okay?" Kevin held his hand out to Bryce.

"I heard you, but you're wrong. The Bible shows you how to be saved, and you're not saved." He stared at Kevin's hand for a several seconds, then grasped it quickly and let go.

He's so arrogant. Just doesn't get it. Oh, but you do? Kevin slapped his own face in his mind. *Damn it! It's not about religion or who's right or wrong. You've been fighting Bryce since you were kids. Same old fight, different battlefield. Can you see him? He hurts! Misses his dad! Wants to be good. Wants to be your hero. He's not the enemy.* Kevin softened his perception. *I want to see Bryce as he truly is. It's not my job to convince him of anything. My only role is to love him, appreciate him.* It seemed that Bryce changed in that moment. He felt Bryce's disappointment, his grief, his fear, his need to be loved. The feeling passed quickly, but he held on to the thought, knowing it was true.

"I need to be alone." Bryce bowed his head, his nose pressed against his folded hands.

He's not a thing you can change. He's an unfolding process. He's growing up, too. Be helpful, or be silent!

Bryce turned his head. "You have something else to say, or you just gonna sit there and stare at me?"

"Bryce. If I can help you with the business or anything, please ask. I'm sure that between you and God, you'll know what to do."

Bryce eyed his brother like a cat watching a dog walk by.

"I mean that. Pray for wisdom--that you'll make good decisions. You have my support." Kevin searched for his brother in Bryce's eyes. For a fleeting moment, he saw him.

"I appreciate that." Bryce returned to his folded hands.

Kevin noticed the rose bushes were now visible, green sprouts dotting the branches and stems. He scanned the yard, noticing how it had changed in the past few minutes. Floating well above the ground, the fog created a ceiling, blocking the sun. The path at the back of the yard opened between the tree trunks, inviting him to enter the woods. He returned his attention to his brother. "I've only had a few sips of my tea, and it's still hot. You want it?"

Bryce opened his eyes and shrugged. "Uh, okay."

Kevin placed the warm mug in his brother's hands. He rested his hand on Bryce's shoulder, and kept it there for a few seconds. "I'll see you later." He stepped off the deck and walked across the green carpet of grass.

Among the trees, the air was steeped in a brew of scents--old and new leaves, humus, spring blossoms--life and death, feeding each other. A garter snake slithered away at the snap of a twig.

I've worked hard the past several months, and I feel alive. Rebuilding the restaurant, rehiring employees, staying on top of the financials, praying and meditating. I've learned, and I'm done making up for past sins. I'm forty-eight, and I'm finally becoming a human adult. He entered a clearing and noticed a patch of trilliums. A shaft of sunlight slipped through the remaining mist, shimmering in the air as it spotlighted the white flowers.

He squatted and admired the trios of petals. As a boy, his mother told him never to pick trilliums. Picking the flower prevented it from blooming the next year. He gently touched the petals with his fingers, grateful for the warm memory of walks in the woods with Mom. Standing, he looked up into a bright sunbeam, letting it play upon his face, his senses alert to every nuance within and around him. These past several months had taught him to feel and to listen. A deer stood frozen by a beech tree, thirty feet away, and the distant tak-tak tapping of a woodpecker echoed in the trees. He again studied the flower.

Trilliums have no choice but to be flowers, to live and to be beautiful--to risk the elements, vulnerable to the possibility that some ignorant human may steal their magnificence. By tomorrow or the next day the petals will die; yet, the plant will bloom again next year. *The difference is I have a choice, whether to grow up, or not. I can choose to live and to feel, to forgive and to be accountable--to be a real adult--or spend my life in fear, holding back, defending my image. Seems I'm already on the way. No turning back, is there?*

318

* * *

"I can stay longer if you need me, Mom." Kevin spooned granola into his mouth.

"No, Honey. I'll be okay. I've got Bryce and Brenda here, and friends. Having you around would be nice, but either way, I still miss your da..." Madeline covered her face with her hands as her body shook. "Seems like I'm always crying." Her words were muffled by her fingers.

Kevin reached for her and held her. "Sorry, Mom. I wish I could do something."

"You already have. You came home when I asked. Now I'm just waiting for your dad." Madeline gently pushed off Kevin and carried her bowl to the sink.

"What do you mean?" Kevin followed his mother and rinsed his bowl.

"We had a deal. Whoever dies first is supposed to leave a sign for the other. I know I'll feel better when I see the sign." Madeline placed the bowls in the dishwasher and closed the door.

"Like what kind of sign?" Kevin leaned against the counter facing her.

She shrugged a little. "I have no idea. I'll know it when I see it. Even without the sign, I'm sure Dad's in Heaven. He's with God."

"What do you think Heaven's like?"

She took his damp hand and scrutinized it as if the answer were somewhere between his fingers. She grabbed a dish towel and dabbed it dry. "I don't know. No body, so no physical suffering I would guess. Meeting up with old friends and family, and everything is forgiven. Lots of love." She lifted her face and fixed her eyes on her son. "Do you believe in Heaven?"

Kevin studied his mother's face. "Well, I think Heaven is more a state of mind than a place." He paused and breathed, searching for the right words. "So, *whatever* happens when we die, it depends on our state of mind. Dad was more loving these past several months than I've ever seen him, so I guess he's in a place of love."

His mother smiled. "Thank you." She held him tightly.

He held her and gently stroked her back with his newly dried hand. "You'll be okay, Mom. I'm sure, that if it's possible, Dad will let you know. He'd *want* you to know."

She spoke into his chest. "He would. Your Dad wasn't perfect, and neither was I, but we always loved each other. I hope that you can find someone to love like that."

"I know you and Dad loved each other, and you were a great example." Kevin held his next words, then let them loose. "Also, it bothered me that he was rude to you sometimes."

"Really? Maybe to others, but not to me." She pressed her face against his shirt like someone does when they are getting comfortable in their pillow. "I don't remember any rudeness, but tell me about a time when he was sweet to me."

Kevin searched his thoughts for a scene. *She just wants to think about the good times.* "I recall when Dad gave you a surprise birthday party. I was in middle school then. He told me he'd forgotten your birthday the year before, but you never mentioned it. Dad was determined to make up for it. So he had all your favorite foods catered, invited about a hundred people and even hired a band. The next day he took you away for the weekend."

"I remember. That was wonderful! Talk about heaven! That time was heaven-on-earth for me. Your father knew how to capture my heart."

"Where did you go that weekend? You two were so secretive."

"The secret was part of the fun. We never told anyone, so it could just be ours. We flew to Paris. He took me to the *Musee d'Orsay*. He knew that I'd always wanted to see a Van Gogh painting up close. I saw several. They were so beautiful." The room became silent except for the sound of her breathing next to his heart. She sighed. "We had a good marriage."

"Yeah, you did. I must've missed that lesson."

His mother grasped his shoulders and stepped back, leaving a damp spot on his shirt. "All you can do is love, Kevin. It's a risk. You never know what the other person will do."

"Thanks." He kissed her on the forehead. "You're a great mom, and I love you."

As if on cue, tears rolled down her cheeks. "Now Honey, you've got me in tears again."

"It's okay, Mom. Just wipe them on my shirt." He pulled her close.

She laughed.

Chapter Thirty-Five

"*Lectio Divina*." Michael grinned at both men.

"What's that?" Kevin knew it was Latin.

"It's exactly what I'm talking about." Jeff nodded. "It means *Divine Reading*. It's a practice that was named in the sixth century by Saint Benedict, and it's the process I use to read the Bible."

Kevin shifted his look between the two men. Jeff had called yesterday from Phoenix and asked to visit. Memorial weekend had been especially busy at the Grill, and Kevin welcomed the opportunity to take a break and sit down with good friends. *Culture clash! The Christian path and the way of a semi-Hopi spiritual teacher--only it isn't a collision. It's a collusion! They agree on almost everything.*

"Tell us how it works." Michael leaned in and lightly placed a hand on Jeff's shoulder.

Jeff leaned in, elbows on the table, hands splayed, ready to accentuate his words. "The Bible isn't meant to be a roadmap. It's a compass. You can't take it literally, thinking every word is law. It's not a dead document carved in stone. It's the *living* word of God."

"How's it alive?" Kevin sipped on a glass of cold lemonade and set it on the table. The mid-afternoon sun threw handfuls of light, blue topaz across the surface of the pool. The reflection hurt his eyes, and he put on his sunglasses. A large rainbow table umbrella provided relief for the three men from the hot rays.

"There are four steps: First, you read a passage. Second, you meditate on it. Third, you pray, asking for guidance from the Holy Spirit, or God, or Jesus. Lastly, you sit with it and contemplate what it means for you. In this way it's alive and provides the seeker with realtime guidance for wherever you are in life."

"Did you teach this method back in Michigan?" Kevin ran his finger around Kwahu's head.

"Yes. In my sermons and my classes on the Bible. Some people understood it."

Kevin looked at Michael. "What do you think?"

"I like it. The Bible is a tool. There are many paths to God and many tools. Whatever leads you back to God is good."

Kevin turned to Jeff. "I don't mean to put you on the spot, but can you give an example of how it works?"

"Uh, yeah." He reached into a black leather book bag leaning against his chair, and pulled out a small Bible. "Here, Kevin. Pick out a verse for us."

Kevin leaned forward and flipped through the pages, not sure what he was looking for. He opened to a page and read aloud. "'Jesus said, Father, forgive them, for they know not what they do. And they cast lots dividing up his clothing among them.'"

"Thank you." Jeff reached for the book, closed it, and set it on the table. "That's Luke 23, Verse 32. Jesus was on the cross and prayed to forgive those who crucified him."

"Thanks for the review." Kevin sat back in his chair. "So now we meditate?"

"Yes. Get comfortable and focus on the passage. Ask God, or Holy Spirit, or Jesus, or whatever your version of divinity is to help you understand. Stay out of your thinking mind. In other words, don't analyze it. Let it come to you. Approach God empty-handed, assuming you don't know what it means. Sit with it, and then we'll talk about what we learned. Okay?" Jeff looked at Michael.

Michael nodded and closed his eyes.

Kevin concentrated his attention on feeling, letting his thinking go. All three men sat quietly. He could feel their presence as much as he could feel the heat. Several times he caught his mind wandering and brought his awareness back to the topic. Finally, after a dozen attempts to quiet his mind, blocks of thought flowed into his awareness--not logical word-building-upon word thoughts, but complete ideas.

"Let's see what you came up with." Jeff folded his hands in his lap. "Tell us what came to you, Kevin."

Kevin looked upward into the umbrella as he visualized what just happened in his mind. "Jesus forgave everyone, whether they asked for it or not. He loved them perfectly. I think of all the times I felt like I was being crucified and then felt justified in blaming others. It's kind of like the ultimate example of love.

"Puts things in perspective for me. I get this feeling of being on the cross looking at all of these people who wanted him dead, and, that to him, they must have been like small children misbehaving. Somehow he was above all that and didn't take it personally. I think I would have taken it personally."

Jeff nodded. "Thanks, Kevin. You're a great student. I think you could get really good at this."

Kevin smiled. "Well, I've had a great teacher here." He gestured toward Michael. "He's taught me a lot about being still and listening to my feelings for guidance."

"How about you, Michael. What does this mean for you?"

"This is a dream, and Jesus woke up."

Jeff sat up straight, and looked upward as if envisioning a question. "Woke up from what?"

Michael locked onto Jeff's eyes. "The dream. The illusion of individuality."

"Oh. I'm not sure about dreams or illusions." He squeezed his thighs with his hands. "Feels real to me."

"When you dreamed last night, did that feel real?"

Jeff stared straight ahead for a few seconds before he spoke. "It did. I dreamed I was back in Michigan, and that I stood in front of the altar at my church and saw only a few people in the seats. I felt like I had failed as a minister and that God, like my congregation, had abandoned me. Still carrying some of that trauma, I guess."

"Then you woke up. You discovered that what you had experienced wasn't true."

"Yeah. It was just a dream."

"So is life as you know it. It's no more real than your dream."

"I can't believe that." Jeff shook his head. "Life is very real to me. If it wasn't, what would be the point of being here?"

"That's a good question. Who am I? Why am I here? What do I want to come of it? It's all an illusion but also a giant amusement park where you get to play your games and one day find your way back to God." Michael sat still as he often did, his arms resting in his lap, his body, a favorite old suit he loved to wear.

Jeff rubbed his thighs, and his eyes darted between Michael, Kevin and empty space. "I don't buy it. I know I'm real."

"It's okay." Michael smiled broadly. "I'm not selling anything. You asked what I learned, and I told you. Here's the second part. When they cast lots for Jesus' garment, it was symbolic. People took his words, like they took his clothes, and divided them among themselves. They each walked away with a different meaning, and very few, maybe no one at that time, understood what he meant. Everyone had a piece of the truth, but no one had the whole thing. That's still true today."

Jeff inhaled and let his breath out slowly. "Interesting. Thanks. What I get from this verse is that God always forgives. God is love, and all we need to do is ask, to join with him in prayer. We forgive so we can be more like God, more loving. The more we can be like God, like Jesus, the happier we'll be. The Kingdom of Heaven is within, and we find it through love and forgiveness."

Michael nodded as if giving his approval for Jeff's words.

Kevin shifted in his chair to get comfortable. "I have a question for you, Jeff. Do you forgive Bryce?"

A smile spread across Jeff's face. "If it weren't for Bryce, I wouldn't be here. I'm living with Nate, and I just accepted a ministerial position with a church that welcomes me as I am. Life is good! I should thank Bryce, but I think my gratitude would be seen as gloating. So I thank him silently. To answer your question, there's nothing to forgive.

"There was a benefit for Bryce and Brenda's marriage. She was hurt when she found out about Nate. She was convinced I was condemned to Hell if I didn't repent. When I didn't agree with her, she was distraught. That was an opportunity for Bryce to offer her solace, which he did. It brought them back together."

"I'm glad you're doing well. Bryce and Brenda, too. Big difference from when I saw you last September. Although, your intent to forgive was very strong back then."

"It's the hero's journey, Kevin. The dragons I needed to fight weren't Bryce or the church board. They were in me. I wasn't living authentically, and Bryce's actions forced me to face that."

Michael nodded. "All expressions are perfect. You may see Bryce as annoying, or as a jerk, and he perfectly plays that role. He has played it well, for *both* of you. By taking your mind off changing him, he has helped you to change yourselves."

Jeff nodded. "I think you're right. The Jesus story is nothing without Judas and the Pharisees. Judas played his role perfectly, and that allowed Jesus to give his lesson on forgiveness."

"My business partner, Al, killed himself and left me with a bankrupt business. As a result, you came into my life." Kevin gestured toward Michael.

Michael sat motionless, then spoke with authority. "When you can see life as unfolding perfectly you become nonresistant to it. Like swimming in a stream, you go with the flow of life. Resist it and you're swimming against the current, and your pain and suffering increase."

"I like what you say, Michael, but I still think I'm real." Jeff laughed.

Kevin studied his two friends. *Am I real or not? I don't know. All I have to go on is that I'm conscious, and I have a point of view. Maybe this is a dream, but then, who's the dreamer?*

Michael and Jeff continued talking, and Kevin made note of the differences and similarities between their world-views. The main difference was that Jeff saw this physical life as very real, and Michael saw it as an illusion. Kevin was unsure. He wondered what the main similarity would be. "I have a question."

Both men turned toward him.

"What would you say is the main similarity between you two?"

Jeff faced Michael. "That's easy."

Michael tilted his head slightly, inviting Jeff to explain.

"Kevin, when you and I talked back in Michigan, we discussed the importance of listening to the Inner Voice, however you define it. The similarity here is that and more. It's not just about listening, but completely following the will of God. *Thy will be done.* That means allowing God to live and work through you." He shifted his eyes between Kevin and Michael.

Michael picked up the thread. "Kevin, you have strengthened both your will and your ability to love. The danger of having a stronger will is that you'll give in to the temptation to misuse power. Align your power with the One. Whether you call that God or Holy Spirit or Atman, doesn't matter. There is only one power, one light, one Source. You are here to use your gifts to be helpful by allowing the One Power to express through you at all times."

Kevin studied his two friends with gratitude. "I guess that's my next step--to consciously turn over my life to the One and to serve as best I can."

Chapter Thirty-Six

It was May, and a year had passed since the conversation with Jeff in the yard. Kevin continued to immerse himself in both his spiritual practice and the restaurant, and both efforts bore fruit. He led a disciplined life and felt pleased with himself. Whenever there were conflicts he practiced both dis-creation and integration. To those techniques he added the conscious act of aligning his will with that of the One.

Whenever a decision needed to be made, he opened his mind to guidance and the intention to allow Spirit to work through him. The next step was to trust that all was well. Often he would go through brief periods of longing to be with Rachel. The feelings were always bittersweet. The love was sweet, and the distance seemed bitter. At the same time, he felt no inner counsel to visit her. He trusted that the relationship would unfold perfectly.

On this day in May he was content--happy and grateful to be alive. He had taken the day off to help Sarah. A colorful canopy shaded them from the sun as they prepared the yard for Michael's eighty-ninth birthday party. He thought back to two years ago when his life fell apart, and he had nothing. *Less than nothing, considering how deep in debt I was. But, I've reached a milestone. I'm officially debt-free.*

Sarah sang to herself as she waltzed between tables laying out the settings. Kevin admired her latest creation, a mosaic tabletop of the Hopi Morning Singers. There were two, because in the legends, they appeared in pairs to sing from the rooftops and awaken the people of the village. Each wore a white headdress, red and white robe, and a turquoise mask. Kevin ran his finger over the tiles. The iron hinges on the gate groaned, interrupted his daydream, and echoed through the yard.

"Looks like a party. Hope I'm invited."

Sarah and Kevin looked toward the voice as she closed the gate. Kevin's heart quickened, and he let out a sigh. He could not control the smile that had taken over his face, but his speech was clear. "It's good to see you."

"It's good to see you, too. I probably should've called, but then I wouldn't have seen that glorious expression of surprise and delight I just witnessed on your face. Thanks for that."

"You're welcome. It's been a long time."

She approached, and Kevin embraced her. He noticed that Sarah had resumed placing napkins and silverware on tables. She was grinning.

"Sarah, I'd like for you to meet a friend of mine." Kevin gestured for her to join them.

Sarah walked over and stood before the newcomer, beaming, and then embraced her. "I'm so happy to finally meet you, Rachel."

Chapter Thirty-Seven

"It was a good party." Rachel sat on the edge of the pool, her feet dangling in the water. "I love Michael and Sarah."

A silent three-quarter moon watched over the yard, and a silvery glow streaked across the pool, slightly illuminating them. Kevin sat next to her, their shoulders touching. "So do I. Michael is a great mentor, and Sara teaches me to be joyful."

"When I looked around the yard, at yours and the Santos' friends, I saw joy. Usually I see pain and conflict in people, and I have to remind myself they are children of God--that somewhere beneath all that fear is perfection. I didn't have to do that here. These people are happy."

"Did you meet Ronnie and Jenny?"

"Yes. Jenny's happy. She's had a great deal of pain and guilt with her husband and feeling responsible for you and the restaurant. She's come through it. Sarah has been her mentor, and it's really helped."

"I'm glad for that. Jenny is like a sister to me."

"That's what she said. I think Jenny and I are going to be friends. I really like her."

"And Ronnie?"

"Before I came here, I did some research on the Sonoran Desert. Do you know what a dust devil is?"

Kevin laughed. "Yeah, I do."

"That's Ronnie. High energy, pulling people and money into her vortex, consuming everything in her path, fast moving. But, like every whirling mass, there's a place of calm at the center. She's beginning to expand that. Even *she* admits that most of her spiritual pursuits were really about creating social and material wealth. Now her focus is changing."

"You're good."

"I know." Rachel grinned and turned her head to face him. "I had a long talk with Sarah, and she told me things about you."

"Like what?"

"That you're an incredible man--not afraid to face his demons. She also said you're very talented at running a restaurant." Rachel played with her hair while her eyes connected with his.

Kevin beamed. "I know. As for the demons, I *am* afraid, often, but I face them anyway."

"Me, too. All the way out here I had this voice saying, 'He won't want you there;' and 'You're not ready for a relationship.' I came anyway."

"I'm grateful you didn't listen to your doubts. You said you'd come one day soon, and I told you I was waiting for you--now here you are. I hope you plan to stay."

"If you're ready for me." She turned, and her eyes met his.

"Your timing is perfect." Kevin returned her gaze.

She pursed her lips and nodded.

"What made you choose this time to come?"

"I missed you. When I saw you last time, I said I didn't miss you. There were times this past year-and-a-half when I wanted to talk, to be held, to be seen, and I thought of you. It came to a point when phone calls weren't enough. That's why I'm here. You *see* me."

Kevin reached for her hand and squeezed it, then entwined his fingers in hers. "I'm glad you came, and I *do* want you here. Yes, I *see* you, and I love what I see."

She smiled. "Tell me what you see."

He placed his hand on her cheek, and caressed her skin with his fingers. Her eyes were moist and warm. "You're beautiful. When you arrived earlier today, you took my breath away. You're brilliant and powerful, and I feel the joy in you. You being here feels so right it almost scares me."

"Almost?"

"Yeah, like, can it really be this good? But, it is, and it's not all you. If this were a few years ago, I'd be finding a way to blow it. Now, I know who I am, and I know what I want."

"You mean that about being beautiful and powerful?" She stroked his arm with the knuckles of her other hand.

"Yes." He let go of her hand and held her face in both of his. "You are beautiful to the core. Outside of my two friends here, I have never met anyone who radiates as much love as you do."

"You should know that I still get cranky at times. I will try to control you sometimes. Can you handle that?" The corners of her mouth turned up, and her eyes twinkled.

"We'll see, the next time you get cranky or controlling." He wrapped his arms around her and pulled her into him, resting his cheek upon the softness of her thick black hair. "Tell me what's been going on." He let go of her and gave her space.

Rachel withdrew her legs from the water and sat cross-legged, facing him. "I wrapped up with each of my clients. I'm licensed in Georgia, but not in Arizona. Have to look into that. I still think about Ben's passing--how he departed willingly and joyfully. I struggled awhile, considering my individuality to be an illusion."

"Do you still struggle?"

"Not so much. What about you?"

"I've fought against it in my mind. Lately I've come to accept it. Michael says he's not real, and he's the happiest guy I know. He says I shouldn't worry about it. I should experience life, question all beliefs, and go into deeper states of meditation and connection. He says if I do that, I'll discover the truth. So that's what I do."

"What do you mean by questioning all beliefs?"

"Anything we assume to be true probably isn't. If we can empty our minds, we can see. For example, you said that I see you. It's not because I figured you out--added up the facts and came to a conclusion, or made judgments and then convinced myself they were true. I allowed my Higher Self, or God, or whatever you want to call it, to be the perceiver. I opened myself to the possibilities of you."

"Makes sense. I was trying to figure everything out in terms of my direction, and then I stopped. Instead I asked myself what's most important." Rachel nodded.

Kevin lifted his legs from the water and brought his knees up under his chin and turned to face her. "What's important?"

"Love."

"But, what do you mean by love?"

She grinned.

"Why are you smiling?"

"You are *so* good. I mean, you listen. I just had a flashback to when we met in Las Vegas. I was hard on you, but look at you."

"So look at me, sitting here with an incredible woman who shines so brightly. We've both grown. Tell me about love."

"It's what I just saw on your face. It's the reflection I saw of myself in your eyes. You see perfection in me. You don't judge me. Just pure unconditional regard."

Kevin nodded and smiled.

"That's how I see you, too. Perfect!" Rachel moved forward on to her knees and kissed him on the forehead, her hands resting on his shoulders. "You've made quite a journey from Vegas to here."

"I fought the dragons, found a treasure, and now I win the princess?"

"Yes. And I get the prince." She reached her arms around him. They held each other while a pair of black-tailed gnat catchers flitted about the nearby bushes calling *ch ch ch ch* to each other.

Rachel kissed him near his ear. "I feel like a swim. You in?"

"Sure." He started for the poolhouse. "I'll get my suit."

Rachel grabbed his wrist. "Who needs a suit?" She scanned the yard. "Not a soul in sight." She let go, unbuttoned her blouse and tossed it aside, and quickly slid out of the rest of her clothes. Within seconds she slipped into the water and swam toward the other end.

Kevin hastily danced out of his clothes, placed his hand on the edge, and vaulted into the pool. Standing in water just above his waist, he watched her swim back toward him, each stroke smooth and effortless.

She stood before him, wet, naked and gorgeous. She grinned. "Swim with me."

They swam across the surface, and he tried to match her speed. After several laps she stopped. "Wow! Reminds me of high school!"

Kevin was breathing hard. "You're fast!"

"Second place in the Hundred in the league meet."

They were standing in the deep end, and the water was up to her neck. She reached for him and drew him close, opening her lips slightly, and closing her eyes. Their lips met, softly at first, the pressure gently increasing. One kiss led to another.

Rachel placed her hands on his chest and gazed into his eyes. "I love you." She kissed him above his heart, and lowered the tone of her voice. "Mmm. It's feels like you're getting excited. Maybe we should go inside." She laughed lightly, a glint in her eyes. Her face darkened. "I'm blushing! Like it's the first time."

Kevin enjoyed a moment of nervous anticipation. "It *is* a first for us, and I *am* excited. But, no hurry. I'd rather wait. Focus on you." He ran his fingers down her back. "I want to take my time." His hands moved to caress her face; his fingers smoothly skimmed down to her collarbone, then with his thumbs, lightly traced around her nipples beneath the surface of the water.

Rachel shivered. "That's not because I'm cold!" She pulled him close and kissed him, this time hard.

He pushed back gently and spoke softly. "Let's go inside."

*　*　*

As always, Kevin awakened at 6:00 a.m. It was time for meditation, contemplation, and prayer. Rachel slept on her side, facing him, and the soft rhythm of her breathing soothed his ears. He wanted to touch her, but held back, letting her sleep a little longer. Besides, as tired as he was with only a few hours sleep, his inner alarm clock urged him outside.

He quietly opened his dresser drawer and grabbed a pair of loose-fitting shorts and a tee shirt. As he turned, his clothes brushed the surface of the dresser and knocked something on the carpet. He reached down and grasped a circular object. *What's this?* He stared at it in the half-light, holding it close to his eyes. *It's birth control!* He remembered her mentioning the pill last night. Seeing it and touching the container, he exhaled. *No worries.* He set it down and quietly opened the door.

Naked, he jumped into the pool and swam two lengths. *Now I feel awake and alert.* He quickly toweled off and slipped into his clothes. The morning temperatures were in the mid-seventies, and the Arizona sky was its usual deep blue--not a cloud in sight. The sun was peeking through the branches of the Aleppo tree, and the black-tailed gnat catchers had continued their conversation from the night before.

Kevin entered the labyrinth to focus his attention. He spotted a zebratail lizard and slowly squatted down. It darted across his path and was quickly swallowed by a pile of rocks, its curved, black-striped tail slurped in before Kevin could reach it.

Kevin wound around the pathway until he arrived at the center next to the trunk of the Jerusalem tree, and there he paid homage to the day with deep breathing and his usual morning reaching and stretching. Retracing his steps, he exited the labyrinth and sat in a padded chair beneath the Palo Verde. Setting aside his thoughts, he focused on feelings. Joy and gratitude arose, and he let himself feel the full impact of those emotions. As details of the night before entered his mind, he intentionally redirected himself toward feeling.

He called forth the love at the essence of his being and consented to bathing himself in it. Letting go of all inhibition, he pushed it as far as he could--love, joy, gratitude, confidence in life. When he felt he had reached the limits, he propelled himself further. Within a few minutes doubt crept into his mind, turning him sour with the message: *You don't deserve this! What gives you the right to be this happy?*

Nonresistant to the intruder, he allowed it to play itself out, both observing it and experiencing it, then turning it over to his Higher Self. He then imagined love pouring forth from his heart toward the doubt, and it dissipated. Gradually he returned to love and joy. Continuing to breathe deeply and focus his attention, he entered the silence. When thoughts arose, he let them float by, like clouds on a windy day. He spent the next hour in this manner, as he had done every day for the past eighteen months.

When he opened his eyes the sun had risen above the trees, nearly blinding him with light reflected from the pool. He felt someone next to him, turned, and saw Rachel in the other chair, dressed in white, her damp hair fanned across a towel around her shoulders. Her eyes were closed, and he watched her in silence.

"I feel you watching me." She opened her eyes and beamed at him. "This yard is beautiful in the morning."

"How long have you been out here?"

"Almost half an hour. You've come a long way on the meditation. I hope you'll share your secrets with me."

"I will." He stretched his arms upward and yawned. "I need a nap before I go to work today. Suddenly, I feel very tired."

"Two or three hours sleep is probably not enough. Thanks for a beautiful evening, and night." She smiled with her whole face.

"You're welcome."

"So where did you learn to be such an amazing lover? I mean, it was like you knew exactly everything to do to please me. I felt completely safe and well-loved." She twirled a shock of black hair around her finger.

"I looked it up on Google."

She opened her mouth and stared. "Are you putting me on?"

"No. I read an article about delayed gratification, and how it enhances the experience. I got the idea online, but I learned it last night with you."

"You're a fast learner, and I'm pleasantly sore today." She stretched her arms and legs outward, flashed a frown, and quickly replaced it with a smile. Now, all I want to do is give you what you gave to me last night. So how about I tuck you in for your nap?" She raised her brows, her eyes sparkling.

Kevin vibrated with anticipation, and he nodded his head.

"Don't worry about delayed gratification." Rachel stood up and offered her hand.

Kevin reached for it, and she led him into the poolhouse.

Chapter Thirty-Eight

He opened his eyes--disoriented. A few seconds later the gap in his mind flooded with memories of the preceding night and morning. The clock next to the bed read 10:30 a.m. *No wonder I feel so weird. I'm never in bed at this time!*

Kevin quickly showered and dressed. He noticed the note laying on the table.

> *Good morning, Sweet Man .*
> *Sarah and Jenny are showing me around*
> *Tucson. I'll see you later. Call me when*
> *you have a chance.*
> *Love, Rachel*

"My life has completely changed in twenty-four hours!" Kevin spoke out loud as he closed the poolhouse door.

"Talking to yourself?" Michael shook his head in mock reproach. "Anything you want to share?" He sat on the other side of the pool at Kwahu's table, sipping a glass of water.

Kevin looked at the time on his cell phone. "Give me a minute." He called the restaurant to check in and quickly decided they could manage without him awhile longer.

He sat down with Michael, arranging his chair to catch the shade of the umbrella. "Did you work this morning?"

"From 4:00 a.m. until a few minutes ago. I need to rest. I meant to keep my birthday a secret, but now my body knows it's eighty-nine and says it wants a nap. I was just about to enjoy the wonderful Mexican tradition of the siesta. Tell me how you're doing."

"I was just saying how much life has changed in the past day."

"Seems like you have everything you wanted--good finances, work you enjoy, health, and now, a great woman to love."

"I'm not complaining. Now that I have it all, I'm not sure what to do with it."

"You mean you're not sure what to do with Rachel?"

"I know what to do with her. I don't know how it will play out."

Michael laughed. "Do what you've been doing for the past two years. Embrace the uncertainty. Love the moment and all that it brings to you."

"I know you're right. My mind wants to plan everything. It's been over two years since I've been in a relationship like this."

Michael shook his head. "I don't think you've ever been in a relationship like this. That girl is unbridled joy in the moment. She trusts her instincts and acts without hesitation."

"Sounds like you know her."

"I see her. Fasten your seat belt, and get ready for the ride of your life. It should be fun." Michael laughed, this time louder.

Kevin peered at him. "Do you know something you're not telling me?"

Michael leaned in and studied Kevin's face. "I don't *know* anything, but I sense some things I'm not telling you." Michael settled back in his chair, fingers tented over his lap. "That'd be like telling you the end of a movie and ruining it."

Kevin eyed Michael. "Now I'm starting to worry."

"You can choose to be with her or not. Either choice sets a story in motion. You don't get to control the story, only how well you play in it. Do you want the story to be a shared tale of the two of you, or do you want to go it alone?"

"What do you mean? I'm the creator for my life, aren't I?"

Michael smiled. "Life is the river, and you're on the raft. You've become very good at navigating the rapids and riding the current-- but you don't get to control the river. Can I give you one small piece of advice?"

"Sure."

"Make it a holy relationship. See all that is perfect and right in her, and do everything you can to draw those qualities out. Help her build on her strengths. Forget about deficiencies. Where she struggles; be helpful; be loving; be accepting. Let her do the same for you. If you think she needs to change, first think how you can change to be helpful. It's like that old story about Gandhi."

"What's that?"

"A woman brought her son to Gandhi and asked for help. She told him that the boy was always eating sweets and wouldn't change his habits. She was concerned for his health. Gandhi told her to come back in a week. Disappointed, she left. When they met again, the woman asked him why he made them wait a week. Gandhi said, 'A week ago *I* was eating sugar. Now, I'm ready to help you.'"

Kevin smiled. "Kind of like that verse in the Bible that says before you try to remove the speck from your brother's eye, you should first remove the beam from your own eye, that you may see more clearly."

Michael nodded, closed his eyes, and within seconds, he was sound asleep.

Kevin watched him sleep for a few minutes and thought back to his recent choices. *There's no turning back now. I'm in.* He took a deep breath. *The roller coaster has already left the starting point.* He remembered seeing the musical, *Wicked*, a few years ago and his favorite song from the show, *Defying Gravity.*

> Something has changed within me
> Something is not the same
> I'm through with playing by the rules
> Of someone else's game
> Too late for second-guessing
> Too late to go back to sleep
> It's time to trust my instincts
> Close my eyes and leap!

* * *

The poolhouse was small for two. It was a Saturday morning, and Kevin had finished his two-hour meditation. Rachel met him at the door.

"Good morning. No meditation today?" Kevin hugged her.

"I was there awhile, probably an hour. That's good for me. Hey, could you go in a little later today?"

"Why?"

"I was hoping we could go shopping and get a few things for this place. I need to make it mine, too."

"Sure. Go ahead. I trust you. Just don't make it all pink." He kissed her brow and slid past into the room, headed toward the shower.

"Wait! The point was I wanted us to go together." She stood there, hands on hips, face serious.

He felt her gravitational pull, but remembered he promised to be at the restaurant early. He noticed it was already nine. "I have to go to work. I'm supposed to be there in half an hour. I'm sure you can handle this. Why don't you call Jenny or get Sarah? I'm sorry."

She turned and walked toward the bed. "Well, I guess you have your priorities."

"I do. I'm not work-centered, or Rachel-centered, or even Kevin-centered. I do whatever is most important in the moment."

She whipped around. "I get it." Her volume rose. "Work is important, but where's the balance? You're been gone for more than twelve hours per day for the last four days. I didn't come out here to be by myself. I came here to be with you. I can be alone in Atlanta. And make sure you get these damn clothes off the floor before you go. I'm not your maid."

Kevin stared at her, unmoving.

She shook her head and closed her eyes tightly. "I'm fine. Just get ready for work." She gestured toward the bathroom.

He spun on one leg and marched to the bath. He showered, dressed quickly, and picked up his clothes from the floor.

Outside she was reading a newspaper at a table. He attempted to kiss her good-bye.

She ducked away. "No. I'm not in a kissing mood."

"Okay. I'll see you tonight." He studied her face. "Look. You need to get out of here. It's been over a week. Shop. Look for a job. Go for a hike. Do something." He paused. "I'll look at shortening my work hours."

"Yeah. Go. I'll figure out my day."

Kevin focused on the restaurant, but Rachel sat in the back of his mind. *Guess the honeymoon is over. This is real life.*

He arrived home around 10:00 p.m. and saw her sitting on the edge of the pool, legs dangling in the water. "How are you?"

She looked up. "Sit with me."

He removed his shirt and trousers and sat beside her in his boxers.

"Sorry I was so cranky this morning. You were right. I need to get out. Monday I start looking for work. I have a few strong leads."

He massaged her back. "We can shop tomorrow if you want."

"No need. I bought stuff today. It's looks more like a home now. Hanging around all day in someone else's place wasn't good." She stared into the water, curling her hair with her forefinger. "About this morning.--you work too much. Do you really have to be there for every meal six days a week?"

"No. I don't want to take my eye off the ball--like last time."

"You mean because of Ronnie?"

"Yeah."

"So, our relationship is like the one you had with Ronnie?"

"No, not the relationship. It's me. I'm afraid I'll get distracted."

"You're distracted all right. First few days I saw you a lot. Did everything fall apart when you spent time with me then? Could your assistants *not* handle it?"

"No. It was fine."

"So?"

"I've been overcompensating. This isn't like it was with Ronnie. I haven't lost my focus at work, and I don't want to take you for granted." He looked at her, then admitted. "I'm struggling here."

"I don't want you to give up your work for me, and I don't want you with me every minute. If you have to be at work, fine. I understand. This relationship needs to be a priority. You agree?"

"Yes. Tomorrow's Sunday. I'm going in to make sure everything's okay, and I want you to join me for dinner. After that we can do whatever you want. Okay?"

"Only if I can have your dad's barbecue chicken, specially made by Jack."

Kevin put his arm around her. "It's a deal. So we're good now?"

"Yeah. I still want you to keep your clothes picked up." A smile broke through the clouds of her face.

* * *

They decided they would move in the fall. Rachel found a practice where she could begin seeing clients and work toward her license as a Psychologist in Arizona. It was early July, and most of late spring and early summer had felt like a vacation by the pool. Kevin began to feel restless.

"What do you think it means?" Rachel asked him as they held hands and walked through Colonial Solana toward Reid Park.

"I don't know if it's me or the weather, but it feels like big changes are coming."

She looked at him, her green eyes dancing. "If I'm getting onto a roller coaster, I want to ride it with you." She reached for his shoulder, stopping their walk, stood on her toes, and kissed him.

He thought of roller coasters, the slow climb to the top, then speeding downward. Tucson had been a roller coaster. His years in Michigan had been flat. Moments of basketball and classroom excitement were fenced in by routine. "I was boring back in Michigan." Kevin raised his brows and glanced at Rachel.

She plunked her hands on his shoulders. "And now you're not. Let it go. I haven't been bored for one second since I've been here."

He studied her face. "Me, neither. When I first met you, I thought I could get lost in these beautiful eyes of yours."

"And now?" She pulled on his arm and they continued walking.

"I find myself in your eyes. I see God in you--perfection. I love you. I could never be bored with you." They crossed the arroyo. It was dry, and Kevin thought it was begging for water.

"Only if you forget."

"Forget what?"

"What you just said. You'll only be bored if you forget to look, or if you look, but don't see. I don't think people fall out of love. They just forget who they are." She stopped him again, on the edge of the neighborhood, under a velvet mesquite tree and faced him. "Don't forget, Kevin." Her eyes prayed, commanded, entreated in one vast moment.

Kevin paused, knowing his response was more than an answer to a request. It was a commitment. "I won't."

Rachel closed her eyes and nodded slowly. "I believe you." Her eyelids fluttered and opened as she grasped a small branch and petted a few leaves with her thumb. "This tree smells like rain." She bent down and picked up a fallen yellow flower. "I like this tree."

"What makes you like it."

"It has the deepest roots of all the trees in this neighborhood, and you can make flour from the seeds. Also, it's medicinal. The roots, bark and leaves have antacid, antibiotic, and many other properties. Animals eat from this tree, too. It's amazing."

"How do you know all this stuff?"

She laughed. "I learned it the same way you learned how to be a great lover--Google. When you were over-working that week I studied the local plants. Let's walk." She grasped his arm, ushering him out of the neighborhood.

They strolled on the trail alongside Country Club Road. It was hotter by the road, and Kevin thought about returning home. "You okay? It's over a hundred degrees, not the best time for a walk."

"I'm good. We have water, and there's a few shady spots in the park. Cloud cover is helping us, I think."

"You've adjusted to the climate."

"It was both hot and humid in Georgia. This is no big deal." She uncapped her water.

Kevin watched her tilt her head back and drink in one graceful, fluid movement.

She turned to him, lowering her water bottle, opened her mouth, and burped.

He screwed his face and shook his head.

Rachel laughed. "I want you to see me as perfect, but not too perfect. Okay?"

"Okay."

"You're my man, not my puppy dog." She searched his face.

"I won't apologize for admiring you, and don't worry--I'm very aware that you're human."

"What's that supposed to mean?"

"I've seen you when your coffee isn't hot. You're a beast!"

She grinned. "Gotta have hot coffee. Almost-hot is an insult to coffee drinkers everywhere."

"That and clothes on the floor, dirty dishes in the sink, and cupboard doors left open."

"I'm an orderly person." She turned and grasped his collar on both sides, straightening it. "There. That's better. Good thing is you're only slightly sloppy and nearly neat. You can be trained." She pulled him downward and kissed his cheek, then wove her arm through his as they continued their walk.

It was late afternoon when they found their way to a playground and sat on a couple of swings. "Now *I'm* feeling restless. Look!" She pointed to the Southeast. A bank of clouds tumbled toward them. They watched as towers of rain burst from beneath the black and gray billows, and a few droplets pelted them.

"We'd better find shelter. I forgot to tell you. It's monsoon season. This is the first one." He grabbed her hand and pulled.

"Oh. I know what a monsoon is."

"Of course you do, but have you been in the middle of one?"

She shook her head while they were running.

"I have." He grabbed her hand and, pushed by the wind, they dashed toward the restroom, a tan, brick building about a hundred feet away. The sky exploded above as the rain caught them, and a big wet hand smacked them across their backs. They stumbled, but kept their balance, as Kevin lunged for the door.

"Wait. I don't want to go in. We'll miss it. We're already wet."

Kevin hesitated. "Okay. Let's stand against the wall." He swaddled her shoulders with his arm, and they squinted into the storm. Wind and rain pounded their bodies as a pool of water gathered around their feet. Lightning slashed the heavens, followed by detonations of thunder roaring in their ears.

She yelled: "I love storms." She grinned, her hair blown wild and drenched, and then stared wide-eyed in rapture into the tempest.

Thousands of droplets battered them, but Kevin challenged the tumult before him--then closing his eyes, sought the inner place of calm. It was too loud to think. He focused his attention on feeling the thrill of the storm, sensing his link to Rachel, and a deep love for the moment. Thoughts drained from his mind as he raised his eyelids and merged with the woman, the wall, the wind and the water. He was not his body or his collection of memories and identities, but something well beyond that. He became the monsoon, the ground beneath the storm, and the woman beside him. They were all things and no thing. In that ineffable moment, they became lucid, awake in the dream, but not of it.

The moment dissolved into ordinary reality as they could no longer withstand the impact of the elements. Kevin sidled along the wall toward the entrance and pulled Rachel along with him. They slipped inside, and closed the door. It was cool and dark, and they shivered as his eyes adjusted. The rain continued to thrash the building, and the battering echoed throughout the room.

They embraced, not only to create warmth, but to reclaim their moment of union. He thought of nothing to say as they stood silently mirroring each other's wonder. Soon, the clamor died.

They emerged from the building, and sloshed through the moat left by the monsoon. Dark clouds raced northward trailed by a mass of gray, and the western sky metamorphosed into blue. The sun manifested itself, still well above the horizon. Rachel tapped his chest, then pointed to the East. "Look! It's beautiful!"

A double rainbow arched across the sky. They followed it home.

Chapter Thirty-Nine

They arrived at the poolhouse where Kevin made salads. Rachel toweled down the chairs, and poured some wine. They sat with the Hopi Morning Singers.

Rachel probed the dinner with her fork. "Chopped romaine, bleu cheese, dried cranberries, walnuts. Great! This is what I need."

Kevin managed to get each ingredient into one pile and forked them into his mouth. The flavors and textures triggered his taste buds. He finished his bite and breathed deeply. "I've been through a few monsoons, but nothing like that one. I think I, no *we*, caught a glimpse of what it means to wake up."

Rachel nodded and smiled. "Better than an orgasm, wasn't it?"

Kevin laughed. "It was better than anything I've ever experienced."

She grinned. "Me too." Rachel dug around in her salad. "Funny how we fight to hang on to our separateness, when oneness feels so free."

"I don't think many of us experience oneness, so we don't know it's free."

"True."

The clinking of forks on bowls replaced words for a few minutes.

Kevin glanced over at Kwahu's table, remembering a conversation. He pointed. "Michael and I were sitting over there two years ago, and I told him I wanted what he and Sarah had. He said there was nothing except me that could prevent it."

Rachel looked up. "And?"

"We have it."

She smiled; her eyes shimmered. "I know."

"And something else. This idea about being in a dream. I get it. The storm taught me."

She nodded. "It's the same for me. I was inside you, and you were in me, and we were both in the wind and the rain. All my lines were blurred. It felt heavenly!"

"Good job of explaining the unexplainable." He speared the air with his fork as if he were impaling her words, and then ate them with his food. He chewed on both, digesting her story first. "How can we remember it? Let's remind each other about Reid Park-- often."

Her eyes held him. "And not forget what we are." She placed her elbows on the table and rested her chin on her folded hands. "How much daylight do we have?"

"About three hours. Why?"

"Can we go to Pima Canyon?"

Kevin did the math in his head. "If we leave right now. I don't think there'll be another storm."

"We'll keep our eyes on the skies this time." Rachel grabbed the plates and hurried to the poolhouse.

They gathered water and footwear and drove to the canyon, avoiding roads that might still be flooded. When they arrived, Kevin looked at his cell. "Okay. If we walk at a good pace we can be to my spot in forty-five minutes, have ten minutes there, and then forty back. It'll be almost dark by the time we're back here.

"Those hiking boots look good on you." Rachel folded her arms as she studied his feet.

"Thanks for the gift. They feel good. About time I gave up the old tennis shoes."

They hiked in silence, single file up and into the canyon. The sun had regained control of the sky, and the warmth reassured them. When the trail widened, Kevin waited for her to catch up. Their hands drifted together, and they again, found their voices.

Rachel smooshed his hand. "I've been thinking. Most couples spend so much time talking about their individual pasts, but we haven't done that. I mean, when we first met we shared a little of our histories, but not since."

"Is that good or not good!" He held her hand firmly as they edged sideways up a set of natural steps.

"It's good. I want to live in the here and now. As far as I'm concerned, the past doesn't exist. But, I haven't told you anything about my childhood. Sometime soon you'll meet my parents, and I'll meet yours. It might be helpful to know some background. So, ask me anything tonight, but after that I don't want to go there."

"We're almost to my spot." Kevin couldn't think of anything he wanted to know. "How about this: Give me a one paragraph summary of your family and growing up--and I'll do the same."

"Okay, one paragraph each." Rachel pointed. "Is it over there?"

"Yes." Two hawks circled above, wings spread, gliding easily around the canyon. Kevin wondered if they remembered the past. "Look." He pointed for Rachel.

"Beautiful! What a day this is!" She stopped to observe. Transfixed for a few minutes, they watched the hawks work the air currents with subtle twitches of their wingtip feathers.

"Okay, Smart One. What kind of hawk is that?"

She squinted at the birds. "Harris Hawks."

Kevin shrugged. "You are amazing!"

"Sometimes Harris Hawks practice polyandry. That is, the female has two mates, and both of them help to raise the babies." She grinned.

"Don't get any ideas." Kevin frowned. The hawks soared up and out of the ravine.

"Let's go." She grabbed his arm and moved forward.

"Are you ready?" Kevin asked.

"When we get to your spot."

Adrenaline coursed through him when the clearing that had fostered so many realizations came into view. It was now a place to share with Rachel. "*Our* spot. You've been here a few times now."

"Thanks."

They arrived, and stood among the remnants of Michael's medicine wheel. Rachel clasped his hands and faced him. She angled her eyes upward to the right, searching the past.

"My mom and dad met in Korea. He was an American soldier, and she was a local girl who fell for his green eyes and charm. 'She looked like an angel.' He told me. They came to the States and were married. His family wasn't too excited about him marrying a Korean girl, but she won them over. For twenty years they tried unsuccessfully to have a baby, and then they gave up. Seven years later I was born. I was their little miracle. School was difficult, with churlish girls and immature boys. Middle school--awkward and painful--high school a little better. People always told me how beautiful I was, but that seemed to make other girls envious. Most boys were intimidated, but the stronger ones competed for my attention. There were plenty of boyfriends, but nothing satisfying. I found comfort in books and learning, swimming, and in the solitude of my room at home. College was better. I made some real friendships, and I had a wonderful boyfriend in my senior year. He went off to Afghanistan and was killed in the war."

"I'm sorry." Kevin brushed his hand across her back.

"Thanks. It was a long time ago, and that was a long paragraph."

"It was perfect. I can't wait to meet your parents."

"I know they'll like you." Rachel squeezed his hands. "Now for your story."

Kevin pressed his tale into a paragraph and related childhood years of being ignored or disapproved of by his father, loved by his mom, existing in Bryce's shadow, college days, and starting a family with Dana. It seemed he talked about someone else.

Rachel pulled him close so their foreheads touched. "And now, we are grown-ups!"

They remained connected through their hands, their eyes in a slow dance, while the world glimmered and faded, destined toward darkness. Kevin pulled back, in slow motion, not wanting to end the moment. "We should go."

"I know. I was hoping to recapture what we found in the storm--that elusive oneness."

Kevin placed his hand over her heart. "It's here." Then he touched his own chest. "And here. We'll always have it."

She kissed his chest, and his heart remembered, for a second.

Darkness nearly overtook them as they scuttled over the trail. They talked on the way home and then by the pool, not about the past, but about their lives today. Later, they moved inside, and Rachel sat on the bed. "What do you see as your purpose?"

Kevin studied his hands, wondering how he touched people. He picked up a lighter and lit two candles on the desk. "I provide a space for people to see each other. That's what sharing food does. People talk, and laugh, sometimes cry, and we offer them a sumptuous repast and great service. They leave feeling nourished."

A soft glow of light flickered upon Rachel's face. The right side was her strong side, the left, softer. He felt loved by both sides. "Also, I help whoever needs help. Like Jack. He's a sous chef now, but really, he's got more natural talent than our executive chef. I'm helping him to live his purpose."

"He told me that you and Michael changed his life. I think you're succeeding." Rachel patted the bed. "Sit with me."

Kevin sat on the flowered, lavender duvet that she had added to their small home. He felt her fingers run up and down his back. He turned to her. "How do you see your purpose?"

She leaned back, supported herself on her elbows, and gazed at the ceiling. "Transformation. That's why I love therapy. I help my clients change, and they change me. But, we don't become something different. We become what we are--children of God, expressions of the Divine, channels for love. I lead people through the labyrinth to find their way home, and that includes you and me. I help the prodigals return to their Source. They learn to stop wasting time and energy in silly and painful games."

"No more silly games for you?"

"I answered that question the day we met." She sat up, and the two sides of her face united in one purpose. He found himself gently, slowly kissing both sides, brushing her eyes with his lips, tracing her cheeks with his fingertips, burying his nose in her thick black hair, then gently pressing his lips on her neck, aware that his affection was physical but intending to caress her soul.

She turned--their noses and foreheads met again. "I feel your love. It's in the way you kiss me. Not out of need. Each touch from your lips, your fingers, the way you look at me--it's all a blessing."

A pleasant chill ran down Kevin's spine, and he felt energy swelling inside. "I'm a monsoon. I'm bursting with love for you."

She laughed. "Sounds like the perfect storm to me. I want you inside me, Sweet Man--like we were at the park, inside each other-- only softer and warmer instead of stormy and soggy."

They slipped under the duvet and wove their bodies together. Lightning flashed through the window, and the rumble of thunder rattled the panes. They became still, listening, until the room lit up again and shook as the heavens roared. The rain pelted the roof; torrents of water splashed into the pool, and the man and the woman plunged into their love.

Chapter Forty

July and August passed. One Saturday morning Kevin sat in the lounger across from Michael, under the Palo Verde tree. He finished a call on his cell.

"You look worried." Michael folded his hands across his butterfly belt buckle.

Kevin spoke louder than normal. "Are you ready for this?"

"Whatever it is, yes." Michael kept his tone even.

"That was my mom. She's coming here. This weekend! To meet Rachel. She invited my daughters, and Bryce and Brenda. They sold the business, and she wants to celebrate. Bryce says he'll stay in Phoenix. He's still remembers the last time he was here. Mom says they aren't flying into Phoenix, and they already bought the tickets."

"That's it?"

"Rachel and I decided to get married."

"Wonderful! When?"

"Late October. We want you and Sarah to stand up with us, here by the pool. Will you?"

"Of course. Autumn is coming and change is in the air."

"I wasn't expecting my whole family, at least not until the wedding. I just informed my mom about it. She's thrilled. They'll just be here a few days. Then we'll get back to normal."

"I don't think so. As I remember, you gave up normal some time ago. In a month or two you'll be moving, and in November, Sarah and I are going away."

"For how long?"

"Indefinitely."

Kevin stared at Michael, unbelieving. "Where?"

"Peru."

"Why?"

"To visit friends and to get away from you."

Michael's words jabbed Kevin in the stomach.

Kevin found his voice. "Is it something I did?"

"Yes. You grew up. You learned. You don't need me, so it's time for us to move on. For now, our work together is complete."

Kevin cleared his throat to cover the emotion that welled up inside. He swallowed. "You saved my life. You and Sarah. This place." He gestured toward the poolhouse and pool.

"I didn't save your life. You did. I gave you information."

"And a beautiful place to live, and a job, and a new restaurant, and your friendship, and great spiritual training."

"I told you long ago that giving is an honor."

"Thanks--for being my friend, my teacher. For giving so much."

"You're welcome. Now you'll teach."

"Who?"

"Whoever shows up. Jack, for one. They'll find you. In the meantime, you have plenty to keep you busy this fall."

Kevin thought about the coming changes and sorted them in his mind. "I can handle this."

"I don't doubt that, but your plate isn't full yet. Look there."

Sarah and Rachel walked slowly. Rachel talked, waving her arms, and Sarah seemed to be calming her. As they approached, he noticed that Rachel was in tears. They stopped, facing the men, both women suddenly silent.

"What's going on?" *Is she hurt?* "Are you okay?" Kevin leaned forward, elbows pushing on the armrests, and studied her face.

Sarah turned to Rachel. "Just tell him, Honey. It'll be all right."

Rachel nodded and wiped the tears from her cheeks. "I'm late."

Kevin studied her reddened face. "Late for what?"

She fell into his lap and wrapped her arms around his neck. Crying again, she grasped his face and stared into his eyes. "I did a test, and it came out positive. I'm pregnant!"

Kevin closed his eyes and felt them roll back in his head; his throat locked up; and he struggled to maintain control, to set aside the explosion of emotion inside. *I'm almost fifty for God's sake!* He opened his eyes, and resumed breathing. "Are you crying because you're happy, or not happy?"

"I don't know. I'm shocked." Rachel raised her voice. "I'm on the pill! This wasn't supposed to happen!" She touched her forehead on his and spoke softly. "How do you feel about this?"

How can I think at a time like this? Give me the right words, please. He waited a few more seconds before speaking. Glancing sideways, he noticed Michael and Sarah, holding hands, walking toward the house. "I don't think the universe cares what *we* think should happen. I agree with what you said awhile back--if you're going to ride the roller coaster, you want to ride it together. The universe is our amusement park, as Michael often tells me." He felt a shift, and he was transported to a place of calm. "So, let's enjoy the ride!"

Rachel nodded and kissed him. "I love you, Kevin." She beamed at him. "It was the night of the storm."

He searched her eyes and found his image looking back. "Looks like we're going to have our own little miracle."

She nodded again, smiling.

Kevin reached around and pulled her into an embrace. "I love you." A grin inched across his face. "Wait'll I tell you what's happening this weekend!"

"What?"

He pictured his family meeting Rachel, and then Bryce's reaction to the little miracle, and he shook with laughter.

Epilogue

Kevin opened his eyes to the bright morning sun and his last day at the poolhouse. Michael sat next to him, eyes closed. Rachel had left for work, and he planned to move the last of their things.

Michael stretched his arms out and smiled. "Today is a good day. You're leaving for your new home and your new life. Sarah and I depart for Peru in a few hours."

"It's been quite an adventure living with you." Kevin sighed.

"There is nothing more gratifying for a teacher than to see one's student learn. Thank you. I enjoyed being with your family."

"When they visited in September, I didn't tell you this, but we were all sitting by the pool when my daughter, Jessica, asked Bryce what he thought about me getting married and being a father again.

"Bryce opened his mouth, but then looked around the circle. Rachel, my mom, Sarah, Jessica, Melissa, and Brenda all stared at him, and waited for his answer."

"What did he say?" Michael grinned.

"He said he was glad I was finally settling down, and he hoped all would be well with a new baby. Then he quickly added that we might want to consider having the baby baptized."

"So, who changed, you or your brother?"

"Both. I'm at peace with him. He was even respectful to Jeff."

Michael nodded. "Jeff did well. It was a beautiful wedding."

"Yes, he did, and I need to get going. Any final words?"

"You have achieved what you asked for, Kevin. Don't get comfortable. Go further. Love more. You've only begun." Michael rose from his chair, and they embraced.

In silence, Kevin watched his mentor walk away.

Acknowledgments

No one writes and publishes a book by him or herself. Many thanks to my editor, Bill Koons, for his comprehensive work and encouragement. I am grateful to Richard Lassin for additional editing. Thank you to members of my writers' group: Matt Bliton, Bill Koons, Jonathan Stars, and Jim Rauschert, all fine writers themselves.

A number of people assisted in the production of this book. My thanks to Mike Limauro and Eric Bowers for contributing to the actual writing of this book with stories, and for their help in producing the book. Thank you to Pat Tessmer, to Marty and Joyce Lovse, and to the Life Enrichment Center for their support in the production of this book.

I would like to thank Thomas Powell for his mentoring. It is upon his system of Psycanics that many of the methods for growth and change used by Michael and Kevin are based. You may find more information on Thomas' work at http://psycanics.org .

The term: "Human Adulthood" is a term used by Jed McKenna, in his enlightenment trilogy, although this book is not in any way a representation of his teachings.

Thank you to Karel Moonen, a skilled Tucson photographer, who provided the photo used on the cover of this book. Thanks to Melanie Diedrich for her cover design.

Thank you to many friends and colleagues who offered support to me in the writing and publishing of this book. I am blessed because of you. Lastly, thanks to all of my readers. You make this work complete.

Music References

The following songs are represented with mention of titles and/or a few of the lyrics. No musicians or songwriters were harmed in the writing of this book.

Margaritaville, by Jimmy Buffet, ABC, 1977.
Stairway to Heaven, by Led Zeppelin, Atlantic, 1971, Lyrics by Robert Plant.
Old Time Rock and Roll, by Bob Seger, Capitol. 1979, Written by George Jackson.
We Gotta Get Outta This Place, by Eric Burden and the Animals, MGM, 1965, Lyrics by Barry Mann and Cynthia Weil.
Bring Me To Life, by Evanescence, Wind-up, 2003, Lyrics by Amy Lee.
You Can't Always Get What You Want, by The Rolling Stones, London, 1969, Written by Mick Jagger and Keith Richards.
Life in the Fast Lane, by The Eagles, Asylum, 1977, Written by Joe Walsh, Don Henley, and Glenn Frey.
Are You Lonesome Tonight? by Elvis Presley, RCA Victor, 1960
Beautiful Loser, by Bob Seger, Capitol, 1975.
We Will Rock You, by Queen, EMI Elektra, 1977, Written by Brian May
Heart of Gold, by Neil Young, Reprise, 1971.
Losing My Religion, by REM, Warner Bros., 1991, written by Michael Stipe.
Girl On Fire, by Alicia Keys, RCA, 2012.
I Can See Clearly Now, by Johnny Nash, Epic, 1972.
Defying Gravity, Idina Menzel and Kristin Chenowith, Decca Broadway, 2003. Written by Stephen Schwartz.

Notes on the Author and the Book

For more information on Human Adulthood: A Spiritual Romance, or other books, go to http://humanadulthood.com or to http://noblaming.com.

The techniques illustrated in this book are based on real methods developed by Thomas Powell. To learn more about Mr. Powell's work (Psycanics) and to purchase his books, go to http://psycanics.org.

This is the first novel by William Frank Diedrich and his fifth book. His non-fiction books are:

The Road Home: The Journey Beyond The Spiritual Quick Fix
This is an autobiographical work written in a dialogue format about the author's spiritual and psychological growth.

30 Days to Prosperity: A Workbook for Well-Being
This workbook leads the reader through a process to attain greater prosperity.

Beyond Blaming: Unleashing Power and Passion in People and Organizations
This book teaches personal responsibility through principles and stories for both professional and personal life.

Adults at Work: How Individuals and Organizations Can Grow Up
This book explains the process for achieving true adulthood along with specific emotional and spiritual intelligence techniques. Stories of real-life adult role models are presented.

William Frank Diedrich, M.A. (Counseling) offers personal and executive coaching via Skype or in person. Go to:
http://humanadulthood.com for details. Or write Bill@noblaming.com

www.ingramcontent.com/pod-product-compliance
Lightning Source LLC
Chambersburg PA
CBHW051228260626
47162CB00002B/321